"I have never had such a conversation with a man before," she said frankly.

"I suppose if I'd had brothers—I might have talked so with them."

"Lass, I *don't* want to be your brother." He spoke with feeling but also with those twinkling eyes.

"I don't think I have seen you laugh before," she said, rather stunned.

"Ah, lassie," he said, reaching for her and pulling her closer, "I have not often felt like laughing these past few years, but I think that I may laugh more easily now," he said. "Look at me."

Obediently, she shifted her gaze to meet his.

"Raise your chin just a wee bit."

When she did, he touched her lips lightly with his and reached to untie the white ribbon lacing of her bodice . . .

"A fine piece of historical romance fiction."
—TheBookBinge.com

"A great start to a trilogy that brings historical Scotland to life." —NikkiBrandyBerry.wordpress.com

"Written with great details...The end was wonderful."
—MyBookAddictionReviews.com

HIGHLAND LOVER

"4½ stars! The last of the Scottish Knights trilogy is Scott's reward to her fans. The exquisite, yet subtle portrayal of her characters, coupled with their budding romance, hastens the reader's emotional involvement with the novel. Excellent melding of historical events and people into the sensuous love story greatly enhances an excellent read."
—*RT Book Reviews*

"With multiple dangers, intrigues to unravel, daring rescues, and a growing attraction between Jake and Alyson, *Highland Lover* offers hours of enjoyment."
—RomRevtoday.com

"A rollicking tale...will grab your attention from the very beginning...Ms. Scott's unique storytelling ability brings history to life right before your eyes...Adventure on the high seas, passion, treachery, pirates, danger, visions, suspense, history, humor, and romance run rampant in this exciting, swashbuckling tale. If you are looking for a great Scottish romance, look no further than Amanda Scott!" —RomanceJunkiesReviews.com

"The latest Scottish Knights romance is a wonderful early fifteenth century swashbuckling adventure. As always with an Amanda Scott historical, real events are critical elements in the exciting storyline. With a superb twist to add to the fun, readers will appreciate this super saga."
—GenreGoRoundReviews.blogspot.com

HIGHLAND HERO

"4½ stars! Scott's story is a tautly written, fast-paced tale of political intrigue and treachery that's beautifully interwoven with history. Strong characters with deep emotions and a high degree of sensuality make this a story to relish."
—*RT Book Reviews*

"[A] well-written and a really enjoyable read. It's one of my favorite types of historical—it's set in medieval times and interwoven with actual historical figures. Without a doubt, Amanda Scott knows her history...If you enjoy a rich historical romance set in the Highlands, this is a book to savor." —NightOwlRomance.com

"[A] gifted author...a fast-paced, passion-filled historical romance that kept me so engrossed I stayed up all night to finish it. The settings are so realistic that the story is brought to life right before your eyes..."
—RomanceJunkiesReview.com

HIGHLAND MASTER

"Scott, known and respected for her Scottish tales, has once again written a gripping romance that seamlessly interweaves history, a complex plot, and strong characters with deep emotions and a high degree of sensuality." —*RT Reviews*

"Ms. Scott is a master of the Scottish romance. Her heroes are strong men with an admirable honor code. Her heroines are strong-willed...This was an entertaining romance with enjoyable characters. Recommended."
—FreshFiction.com

"Deliciously sexy...a rare treat of a read...*Highland Master* is an entertaining adventure for lovers of historical romance."
—RomanceJunkies.com

"Hot...There's plenty of action and adventure...Amanda Scott has an excellent command of the history of medieval Scotland—she knows her clan battles and border wars, and she's not afraid to use detail to add realism to her story."
—All About Romance

TEMPTED BY A WARRIOR

"4½ stars! Top Pick! Scott demonstrates her incredible skills by crafting an exciting story replete with adventure and realistic, passionate characters who reach out and grab you...Historical romance doesn't get much better than this!"
—*RT Book Reviews*

"Captivates the reader from the first page...Another brilliant story filled with romance and intrigue that will leave readers thrilled until the very end."
—SingleTitles.com

SEDUCED BY A ROGUE

"4½ stars! Top Pick! Tautly written...passionate...Scott's wonderful book is steeped in Scottish Border history and populated by characters who jump off the pages and grab your attention...Captivating!"
—*RT Book Reviews*

The Warrior's Bride

Other Books by Amanda Scott

AMANDA SCOTT

The Warrior's Bride

FOREVER

NEW YORK   BOSTON

This book is a work of fiction. Names, characters, places, and incidents are the product of the author's imagination or are used fictitiously. Any resemblance to actual events, locales, or persons, living or dead, is coincidental.

Copyright © 2014 by Lynne Scott-Drennan
Excerpt from *Moonlight Raider* copyright © 2014 by Lynne Scott-Drennan
Excerpt from *The Laird's Choice* copyright © 2012 by Lynne Scott-Drennan

Forever
Hachette Book Group
237 Park Avenue
New York, NY 10017

www.HachetteBookGroup.com

Printed in the United States of America

First Edition: February 2014
10 9 8 7 6 5 4 3 2 1

Forever is an imprint of Grand Central Publishing.
The Forever name and logo are trademarks of Hachette Book Group, Inc.

The publisher is not responsible for websites (or their content) that are not owned by the publisher.

Donald R. MacRae
December 13, 1932–July 19, 2013
I miss you, Donal Sean

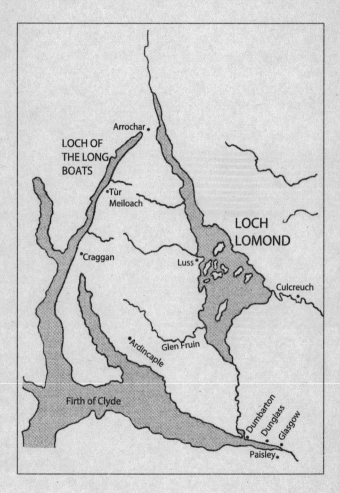

LOCH OF THE LONG BOATS

Arrochar

Tùr Meiloach

LOCH LOMOND

Craggan

Luss

Culcreuch

Ardincaple

Glen Fruin

Firth of Clyde

Dumbarton
Dunglass
Glasgow

Paisley

Author's Note

For readers' convenience, the author offers the following guide:

Clachan = village

Coracle = an ancient small boat, its wicker frame covered by hide or leather

Fain = eager, eagerly, glad

Forbye = besides, in addition, furthermore

Garron = small Highland horse, very strong, agile enough for the landscape

"In ward" = under arrest and confined

Lachina = Lock EEN a

Lassock = young girl

Plaid (great kilt) = Pronounced "Played," an all-purpose garment from length of wool kilted up with a belt. Excess length flung over the wearer's shoulder.

Scáthach = SHAW hawk

Tarbet = isthmus, an arm of land connecting two bodies of water

Tùr Meiloach = Toor MIL ock

The Warrior's Bride

Prologue

Damn your impudence! Are ye daft? What the *devil* did ye think ye could accomplish wi' such foolishness? D'ye never *think*?"

Facing his irate father, dark-haired, dark-eyed Dougal MacPharlain sought in vain for a prudent answer to the question. If his scheme had succeeded, Pharlain would be praising him now. But since he had failed... again...

"Well?" The powerfully-built Pharlain took a threatening step forward, and Dougal winced despite having sworn to himself that he would defend his actions. He was tall, agile, and strong himself but had never successfully challenged his father. Also, his body was a mass of bruises already from the previous night, when Andrew Dubh MacFarlan's men had savagely beaten him.

"Answer me, damn ye!" Pharlain snapped.

"The charters," Dougal said hastily. "I'd expected to get Andrew's charters. God kens, the woman promised to bring them when she agreed to meet with me."

"Aye, sure, she did," Pharlain said, his tone more

sardonic and scathing than ever. "Ye speak o' the lady Aubrey MacFarlan, aye? Andrew Dubh's *wife*?"

"I tell ye, sir, she promised! Forbye, she did meet with me."

"Aye, but Andrew's men captured ye, so 'twas nobbut a trap. I note, too, that ye failed tae tell me he sent ye home in your tunic, looking as if ye'd been mauled by rogues. What happened tae the rest o' your clothes and your weapons?"

Dougal kept silent. If Pharlain knew that much, he also knew that Andrew had ordered him escorted home that way, *with the laird's compliments.*

"Ye'll keep away from Andrew and Tùr Meiloach, or ye'll answer tae me," Pharlain snapped. "I ken fine that ye hoped tae marry one o' his daughters, and I'll grant ye, 'twas a good notion, that. Such a union could well reunite the two factions of our clan. But now Andrew's got only the one daughter left. And, thanks tae your previous ineptness, he'll likely see the lass dead afore he'll give her tae ye."

"Perhaps, but as long as he has his royal charters to show the King at Inverness, we stand to lose Arrochar. And if we do—"

"Ye'll let me worry about Inverness," Pharlain interjected curtly. "Aye, and Arrochar, too. I dinna tell ye everything, and this place is my concern, not yours."

"I should think the future of Arrochar is my affair, too," Dougal said. "After all, I am your sole heir."

"An ye should live so long, aye," Pharlain retorted. "Now, get out o' me sight, for I canna stand tae look at ye. If I see your face again today, I'll have ye flogged."

Dougal fled, but resentment filled every cell of his

body, aimed not only at his father for his rebukes but also at Andrew Dubh and the Fates in equal measure.

Nevertheless, by the time he reached the courtyard and could breathe the fresh air, he had his temper in hand again. He reminded himself that the Fates, and Andrew, had let him survive the previous night's beating.

Moreover, Pharlain had acknowledged two plain facts: that Dougal's notion of marrying one of the MacFarlan sisters to unite their long-divided clan was a good one *and* that Andrew still had one unwed daughter.

To be sure, that daughter had declared to anyone who would listen that she would *never* marry any man. However, that declaration merely told Dougal that he could bide and plan with more care this time.

Winter was coming, but spring would follow. And when he had a plan...

Chapter 1 —————————

The boy stood perfectly still as he scanned the high granite cliffs to the east and the barren rocky slopes below them for sign of the deer he had been stalking since dawn. Standing as he was at the edge of the woods, he knew that his dust-brown tunic and cap blended with the woodland foliage, making him invisible to man or beast above, had there been any to see him.

He saw no movement on the slope, only five or six hawks circling above.

His quarry had vanished without making a sound.

Bow in hand, his quiverful of arrows slung over one still thin shoulder, the boy reminded himself to be patient. The deer *had* come this way.

Behind him, stretching westward to the Loch of the Long Boats, lay his master the laird's land of Tùr Meiloach and the tower of that name where the laird's family lived. The name meant a wee tower guarded by giants, but the boy did not think the tower wee at all. It was five stories tall and large enough to need two stairways. However, if real giants did guard it, perhaps *they* considered it wee.

Not that he had ever seen any giants, for he had not. But the lady Muriella MacFarlan told stories about them, and if she said they were real, it must be so. Forbye, others told similar tales about Tùr Meiloach's land—many, many such tales. Even the laird said that the land was sacred and protected its own.

A distant, barely discernible rattle of stones drew the boy's attention upward to his left, northeastward, to movement in a scree-filled declivity there. It was not his deer scrambling up the slope, though. Deer did not dress themselves in pink kirtles.

"What the deevil be that pawky lass up tae now?" he muttered, echoing a frequent question of his favorite person at Tùr Meiloach.

Sir Magnus Galbraith-MacFarlan, husband to Lady Muriella's eldest sister, the lady Andrena, enjoyed the godlike traits of immense size—nearly large enough to qualify as one of Tùr Meiloach's guardian giants—a heroic repute for wondrous deeds, and the equally godlike habit of swift retribution to ill-doers, large or small. Sir Mag was a warrior exactly like the boy hoped to be, if his shoulders ever widened and grew muscles and he grew a bit taller . . . well, more than a bit, then.

"She has nae good cause tae be there," he told himself. "What's more, the laird tellt her she were never tae venture near yon pass. I heard him m'self."

He was about to leave the shelter of the woods and follow her when his peripheral vision caught more movement above but southward, to his right. A man, a stranger, stepped briefly into sight from behind a boulder and vanished behind another one the size of a small cottage. Despite the loose scree the lad could see up there, the man made no sound. Nor did the gray, wolflike dog that followed him.

Alarmed now, because strangers were rarities on Tùr Meiloach land—most offlanders respecting tales they had heard of its ground opening to swallow whole armies and such—the boy hesitated where he stood. He had seen strange things occur himself, but the land held no terrors for him. He belonged there.

Looking northward again, toward the lady Muriella—for the figure in pink was certainly she—the boy stiffened, his alarm surging to fear. Another figure had appeared above her and was slinking from boulder to boulder down toward her.

Although she seemed unaware of both men, it occurred to the boy that she might have slipped out to meet one or the other of them. Some lassies did do that sort of thing now and now, he knew.

He dismissed the thought, though, because even he knew that Lady Muriella had small use for men. She cared only for her storytelling and assured anyone who would listen that she would one day be a seanachie, charged with passing the tales of Scotland's history and folklore on to future generations. Most of the seanachies he had seen were men, but her ladyship said she would be one, and he believed her.

The man above her was much closer to her now than the one to the south. Moreover, the chap above her was behaving in a way that suggested he had even less business showing himself on that part of the ridge than her ladyship did.

Frowning, eyeing the man with distrust while making his way toward the two, the boy realized that the man's voluminous plaid was familiar. So, too, were his long, dark hair and the arrogant way he straightened and stood, feet spread, his hands on his hips, watching her ladyship, as if he dared her to look up and see him.

All of these traits were familiar to the boy.

"That be the wicked Dougal," he murmured, walking faster. He took only a few steps, however, before he realized the futility of haste. Her ladyship was too far away for him to do aught if Dougal meant mischief to her, as likely he did, since he had threatened *and* created mischief for the laird's family several times in the past.

Thinking fast, the boy put two fingers to his mouth and gave a piercing whistle. When she looked back and he could be sure that she saw him, he shifted the strung bow to his forearm, cupped his mouth with both hands, and shouted, "Lady Murie…the laird…wants ye! He says… come…straightaway!"

She hesitated, and the man above her stepped out of sight again.

Looking southward, the boy saw that the stranger stood in plain sight, looking right at him. He was a big chap, not as big as Sir Mag, to be sure, but big enough to make the boy wonder again if he was friend or foe. He wore no plaid, just leather breeks, boots, and a leather jack over a tan shirt. He carried a bow and had a sword in its sling across his back, so he might be a warrior, or posing as one. The boy was a bit of a cynic about such things. He had seen much in his thirteen years.

Looking back toward Lady Muriella, he saw that she looked displeased, but at least she was scrambling down the slope toward him.

The man above her was still there, too. But Dougal—if

it was indeed he—was moving upward, back toward the pass, and the hawks were circling lower as if to urge him on his way. So that was all right.

Striding to meet her ladyship, the boy saw as they drew closer together that he had underestimated the extent of her displeasure.

He hastily tugged off his knitted cap, freeing his unruly red curls.

"What are you doing up here, Pluff?" Lady Muriella demanded as soon as she was near enough to do so without shouting. "You should be minding the dogs and helping MacNur with the beasts."

"I did me chores earlier, m'lady. I saw deer tracks again and thought I'd fetch home some venison. Did ye no see the man above ye in yon rocks?"

"I suspected that someone was up there, because of the hawks. Who was it?"

"In troth, there be two o' them the noo," Pluff said. "One o' them were just yonder," he added, pointing to where he had last seen the stranger. "But the one above ye, 'less I be mistook, were that villain Dougal MacPharlain."

"How would you know Dougal MacPharlain?" she asked.

"I seen him last year when he come here wi' all his impertinence tae beg for the lady Lina's hand on the same day she married Sir Ian," Pluff said. "I'd seen Dougal afore then, too, now and now," he added glibly, seeing no point in saying more and hoping that she would not ask him to explain.

"Well, Dougal MacPharlain has no right to be on our side of the pass," she said. "And so I would have told him had he dared to accost me."

Pluff opened his mouth to remind her that Dougal was

unlikely to heed such a warning but remembered in time that it was not his place to do any such thing.

She said, "Why does the laird want me, Pluff? Do you know?"

Much as he would have liked to make up a story to tell her, he knew that if he did, he would soon find himself in the suds. So, bracing himself, he said, "I only said that tae turn ye away from that Dougal. He's a gey wicked man, is Dougal."

"He may be, aye, but I can take care of myself," her ladyship said roundly. "And if my father does *not* want me, I have things I want to do."

"Ye'll no be a-going back tae that pass, will ye?" Pluff demanded daringly.

That his words irked her was obvious to one of Pluff's experience, but before she could voice her annoyance, a deep male voice behind them startled them both by saying firmly, "She will not."

~⁓

Muriella whirled to face the man who had spoken and stopped with her mouth agape when she saw him in the forest shadows. He was tall, broad-shouldered, and looked as darkly tanned as if he had spent his life outdoors.

She could see that his hair was thick, shoulder length, wavy, and the soft color of walnut shells. His features were barely discernible under the shadowy trees, but there was something familiar about him even so.

Frowning, she said, "I know you, do I not?"

"We have met, aye," he replied evenly.

Her memory was excellent. Most people thought it was infallible, because she never forgot what anyone told her. But it was weaker when it came to faces. Although she could accurately draw from memory those that interested her and people she knew well, she did not remember every person she had seen or met.

His voice—liquid smooth, deeply vibrant, and musical to the ear—plucked a memory chord.

As if he knew she was studying him, he stepped into the sunlight, where his hair turned from light brown to golden brown with sunny highlights.

However, when he stepped closer, his eyes drew her attention, because in the stronger light, she saw that they were the soft green of forest ferns where sunlight touched them. They were set deep beneath dark brown, slightly arched eyebrows, and their lids boasted long, thick, dark lashes. They were, in fact, extraordinary enough to fill the gap in her memory.

Her first impulse was to tell him that she remembered exactly who he was. But, when she realized from his silence that he did not mean to identify himself, although courtesy demanded that he do so, a second, more mischievous impulse stirred to see what he would do if she prodded him.

Accordingly, she said lightly, "I do not know why you should think you have the right to make decisions for me when you stand uninvited on my father's land. Men have died for trespassing so."

"My business here is none of yours, lass. I spoke only to prevent you from making the grave mistake of confronting Dougal MacPharlain. Not," he added dryly, "that MacPharlain lingered after he saw me."

"He saw you?"

"Aye, sure, for I showed myself whilst you descended

to speak to this lad. Not until I saw that he was departing did I come down here."

"I doubt that Dougal took fright merely from seeing another man on that hillside," she said, cocking her head to watch for his reaction to that statement.

He revealed no reaction but held her gaze as he said, "Mayhap he did not. Still, I'd wager he was merely indulging his curiosity in Tùr Meiloach and would have ventured no further down that slope had your presence not enticed him to do so." Gently, he added, "Do you often engage strangers in conversation, lass?"

"I would remind you that you inflicted *your* presence upon us," she said. "Sakes, you spoke to us first! *I* did not invite this conversation."

The green eyes narrowed, and Muriella was just congratulating herself on getting a rise out of him when Pluff said, "What did ye do wi' your dog, sir?"

The fascinating green eyes held hers for a moment longer before the man turned to him and said, "She stands yonder, lad. Would you like to meet her?"

"Aye, sure, if she's friendly."

"She is whatever I tell her to be," the man said, giving a snap of his fingers.

To Muriella's astonishment, an animal that looked more like a wolf than a dog emerged from the shrubbery and loped gracefully to stand before the man.

"Coo," Pluff said in a near sigh. "Are ye sure she's just a dog, sir?"

"I'm sure," the man said. "I cannot speak so surely of her ancestors, though."

"What d'ye call her?"

"Scáthach."

Impressed but skeptical, Muriella raised an eyebrow and said, "You named a dog descended from wolves after the most famous of the Celtic warrior queens?"

His lips twitched as if he were suppressing a smile. "I'd forgotten that you are the one interested in history and fairy tales."

"The *one*?" Muriella fought down the flash of irritation. He made her sound like some oddity of nature.

Robert MacAulay easily conquered his amusement. The lady Muriella had matured in the year since he had last seen her and had become more beautiful than ever, even with her fine flaxen hair in untidy loose plaits and her pink skirt and red underskirt kilted up to reveal shapely but mud-spattered lower legs and bare feet.

When he'd seen her earlier, he had not recognized her and had followed her only because he thought it reckless for any young lass to wander alone on such notoriously unpredictable terrain. As small and slender as she was, he had thought from the distance that she might be a child. Looking at her now, he wanted to ask why she was not wearing a cloak and boots on such a chilly morning.

In truth, though, she would one day make some man an enviable wife. If he'd had any inclination to assume such a burden, he might be interested himself, although he suspected that she would present a rare challenge for anyone who tried to domesticate her. That was, however, no business of his.

The only thing that concerned him was that she was either unaware of the danger she had courted or dangerously indifferent to it.

Speaking as evenly as he had from the start, he said, "I seem to have offended you. That was not my intent. People often speak of the MacFarlan sisters, and when they mention *you*, they talk of your flawless memory and your love of folklore and tales of Scotland's heroes. In fact, since you have such a fine memory, I suspect that you remember me perfectly well, do you not?"

"If you know who I am, then you should behave more courteously," she replied, raising her chin.

Glancing at the too-interested boy, Rob said quietly, "If you would like to throw a stick for Scáthach, lad, she will be happy to accept your friendship. She has not had much exercise yet today, so you would be doing me a good turn, as well."

"Aye, sure," the boy replied, grinning. Unstringing his bow, he rested it against a tree, quickly found a suitable stick, and heaved it away from the trees.

Scáthach chased it eagerly up the slope, tossed it high, caught it, and then turned back. When the boy dashed off to meet her and throw the stick again, Rob said to her ladyship, "You do know that you were in danger up there, do you not?"

"If you know who I am, why do you not address me properly?"

"Because you are not behaving much like a lady," he retorted.

Flushing scarlet, she gave him a look that he was sure she hoped would wither him where he stood. Her expressive, thickly-lashed, sky-blue eyes flashed sparks, and her kissable pink lips parted as if she meant to give him a piece of her mind. Wisely, she shut her mouth again without saying a word.

Then, when he remained silent, having no reason to say more than he had, she drew a deep breath and said, "You have not changed one whit since last year."

"So you do remember me."

"Aye, sure. You are Master Robert MacAulay of Ardincaple. You came here with my good-brother Ian. I did not think you were rude then, though, just a bit dull."

"But now you think me rude. Why?"

She rolled her eyes as if his rudeness should be self-evident.

He glanced toward the lad again, saw that his attention was wholly on the dog, and returned his own to the undeniably tempting but perilously saucy and naïve Lady Muriella. "Are you going to answer my question, lass? If you expect me to read your mind when you roll your eyes like that, you will soon learn that I dislike guessing games. If you want me to know what you think, you must tell me."

"I think that I do not want to talk to you anymore. In troth, since no one invited you here, I think you should go home."

"What makes you think no one invited me?"

~

Try though she did, Muriella could get no more than that out of the man. When she asked him if her father *had* invited him or even knew that he was on Tùr Meiloach land, Robert MacAulay said, "You will have to ask Andrew Dubh."

Irritated, and with her curiosity now aflame, she said, "If you will not talk to me, I see no reason to talk to you. You may therefore go where you will, but you should know that I mean to tell my father that you are trespassing on our land."

"You should tell him," MacAulay said. "Be sure that you also tell him where you were going and that Dougal MacPharlain was likewise on his land."

Tossing her head, she said, "I have no cause to say that Dougal was here. I did not see him."

"The boy did, though, and so did I," MacAulay said. "You would be wiser, I think, to tell your father about Dougal before one of us does. For now, I will see you safely back to Tùr Meiloach, since you refuse to promise to return on your own."

"Would you believe me if I did promise?" she asked, raising both eyebrows.

"Should I?"

Muriella hesitated. Something about Master Robert MacAulay suggested that lying to him outright might be a mistake.

Meeting his gaze, she saw to her consternation that a knowing twinkle lurked in the green depths of his eyes.

Her temper bristled. "I expect that even if I did promise, you would follow me to be sure I do go home."

"I expect I would," he admitted. "I do not know you well enough to trust that you keep your promises." With that, he gave a low whistle, and Scàthach dropped the stick she was carrying and loped to his side.

Pluff followed more slowly. "Be we a-going back then?" he asked.

"We are," MacAulay said. He waited only until the boy had collected his bow and quiver before gesturing for Muriella to lead the way.

Tempted though she was to press him for more information, she suspected that such pressure would be futile, so she strode silently on ahead.

When they reached the tower gate, and a guard opened it, MacAulay showed no inclination to enter the yard but nodded for Muriella to do so.

"Do you not mean to come in with us, then?" she asked.

"I have no reason at this hour to impose my presence on Andrew Dubh. But do not disappoint me, lass. Tell him that Dougal was on his land."

Giving him a slight smile in response, and relieved when he did not insist again that she tell her father where *she* had been, Muriella passed through the gateway with dignity. When Pluff followed, she said firmly to him, "You go and ask MacNur if he has tasks for you. I will talk with my lord father alone."

"Aye, sure," Pluff said, turning to wave good-bye to MacAulay and Scáthach.

Deciding to see her father straightaway, since MacAulay had left her little choice, Muriella went in search of Andrew and found him at the high table in the great hall, talking with his steward, Malcolm Wylie.

In his fiftieth year, Andrew Dubh MacFarlan was still a fit warrior with only specks of gray in his dark hair. More gray showed in his bushy eyebrows, but the dark blue eyes beneath them shifted alertly at his youngest daughter's approach.

Making her curtsy, she said, "May I speak with you, sir?"

Andrew smiled. "Aye, sure, lassie, whenever ye like."

Muriella glanced at Malcolm, who was of an age with her father but grayer and more heavily built.

Nodding to show that he had received her unspoken message, the steward rose, saying, "I must speak wi' that young gillie, laird, but I'll be within hail."

Nodding, Andrew gestured to the stool that Malcolm had vacated, saying, "Sit down and tell me what's troubling ye, lass."

Obeying, she said, "I met Master Robert MacAulay near the northeast slope, sir. Did you know that he was wandering about there?"

"D'ye think I dinna ken who comes onto my land, Murie-lass?"

"Usually you do, aye," she said. "But sometimes people do succeed in trespassing despite your precautions. I should tell you that MacAulay and our Pluff both said they saw Dougal MacPharlain on our side of the north pass."

Pleased with the way she had phrased that information, she was nonetheless relieved when Andrew said only, "One of the lads told me he'd seen Dougal there a few days ago. Doubtless that young lout seeks to know if we're awake or asleep. If Rob MacAulay saw him there, he'll likely tell me more about that anon."

Disconcerted by that news, she said, "Are you going to meet with him, then? Why is he here?"

"Because when our Mag told me that Rob had been seeking solitude to think, we decided that, whilst Mag and Andrena be away, Rob might look after the cottage they've built for themselves on the east slope."

Muriella knew that the cottage, which stood a mile or so from the north pass, was temporarily unoccupied, because Andrena and Mag had gone to Dumbarton to show their wee Molly off to Lina and Sir Ian. Afterward, they would go on to visit Mag's two older sisters and their husbands in Ayrshire. His younger sister, Murie's good friend Lizzie Galbraith, would be coming soon to Tùr Meiloach to visit.

Thoughts of her sisters, their husbands, and Lizzie stirred yet another notion in her agile mind. "You are not thinking of arranging a marriage between me and Robert MacAulay like the ones you arranged for Dree and Lina, are you, sir?"

"Ye needna fret, lassie," Andrew replied. "I offered just such a union to the man whilst he was here last summer with Ian. He turned me down flat."

Indignantly, Muriella exclaimed, "He did *what*! But why? What can he possibly think is wrong with *me*?"

Scáthach pushed her rough-coated head into Rob's palm as they strode along together, so he gave her a fond pat. Having come over the southern pass late the day before, just as he had the previous year with Ian, he had found Mag's cottage easily by following a narrow, undulating path along the timberline.

Earlier that morning, he had followed the timberline trail on from the cottage northward. Now, he wanted to see the river that formed Andrew's north boundary, separating Tùr Meiloach from Arrochar. His intent was to follow that river down to the cliffs where it plunged nearly a hundred feet to the Loch of the Long Boats. Then, he would meet with Andrew shortly before midday, as they had planned.

While he walked, Rob's thoughts drifted from the beautiful but perilously headstrong lady Muriella to the upcoming meeting with Andrew.

He needed the older man's advice. However, before they talked, Rob wanted to gain a clearer picture of Andrew's situation, and this was the first time he had had both the leisure and an opportunity to explore Tùr Meiloach.

He knew that Clan Farlan had split into two factions near the time that the King of Scots, then but a laddie, had set sail for the safety of France and ended up a captive in England instead. Many Scottish estates had changed hands during the two decades of his captivity, either through machinations of his uncle, the first Duke of Albany, or because other powerful lords had usurped them from weaker ones.

Albany, as Guardian of the Realm, had continued to rule Scotland in his older brother's stead, and then his nephew's, until his own death six years ago. He had rewarded his friends with land and punished his enemies by taking theirs away.

Men said that his grace's father, Robert III, had died of grief when the capture of his younger son, now James I, had followed by mere months the death of his heir. Many believed that Albany had arranged both events so that he could go on ruling the country and not have to contend with a regency for a boy king.

Since Jamie's return to Scotland two years ago, most of the House of Albany had died. Only Albany's good-daughter, the duchess Isabella, her youngest son, James Mòr Stewart, and a few daughters still lived. The duchess resided on an island in nearby Loch Lomond.

James Mòr, after seizing the castle and burgh of Dumbarton last year and then losing them, either had fled the country or was in hiding.

The King, in his thirtieth year, had returned to a law-less country. Not, Rob reminded himself with a half-smile, that the Scots were ever particularly law-abiding. But Jamie wanted to institute a rule of law similar to England's, with Parliament issuing laws that would prevail throughout the land. Most men, whether they supported the endeavor or not, believed that the King would fail.

His nobles were too powerful to curtail so easily.

Moreover, whether he succeeded or not, nobles would still need to protect their property from those who coveted it. That had been the way of things since the dawn of time, and one young king's resolve to make everyone law-abiding was unlikely, in Rob's opinion, to alter the reality of Scottish life.

Thanks to Ardincaple's strategic location on the Gare Loch and the peninsula separating it from the Loch of the Long Boats, the estate was one that many powerful men coveted. Lord MacAulay controlled the unions of those two lochs with the Firth of Clyde, just as his ancestors had.

For a century, lairds of Ardincaple had allowed vessels to pass freely in and out of the lochs. Now others wanted to charge fees, large ones, for passage.

Campbell of Lorne, a powerful lord in the Isles with influence in Argyll, sought to extend that influence to the firth. A kinsman of his by marriage, Pharlain of Arrochar, had broached that very plan to Lord MacAulay nearly a month ago.

When MacAulay refused to participate in a plan that exempted the Campbells and Pharlain of Arrochar from all fees, Pharlain warned him that if he would not do it, Pharlain and Campbell would simply seize Ardincaple. If the laird did agree to the fees, they would graciously share *some* of the profits with him.

Chapter 2 _____

Andrew smiled at Muriella's outburst and said, "There's nowt amiss with ye, lassie. 'Tis plainly with the man himself, but if ye want to ken why he refused me offer, ye'll have to ask him. I can tell ye only that he said I'd done him great honor but that he'd no inflict himself so on *any* woman."

"Inflict!" she exclaimed. "What can he have meant by that?"

Eyes dancing, Andrew said, "Ye'll have to ask MacAulay that, too. But what difference can it make? Ye've nae wish to marry at all, or so ye've oft told me."

"I *don't* want to marry," she said. "Certes, I would not marry any man who would always be telling me what to do and what to think, the way most men do."

The twinkle vanished. Andrew said, "Is that what ye think I do?"

"Sometimes," she said. Then, seeing him frown, she added, "You can be more reasonable than either Mag or Ian is, sir, *or* the Laird of Galbraith. Galbraith treats Lizzie and me exactly the same way, although I'm years older than she is."

"Not so many years older as that," Andrew said evenly. "Nor do ye always act your age, lass."

Realizing that she had overstepped, Muriella hastily apologized. "I should not have spoken so about Galbraith, sir," she added. "But Robert MacAulay irked me, and I fear that my irritation with him has addled my senses. Smiling wistfully, she said, "Prithee, will you forgive me?"

"I will, aye," Andrew replied with a reassuring smile. Seconds later, a remnant of the frown stirred his brow again. "Was MacAulay rude to ye?"

Recognizing treacherous ground, she said lightly, "I doubt that you will think so. He insisted on escorting me all the way to our gate, as if I could not find my way through our own woods."

"Ye're right," Andrew said. "I'll no hold that against him. Ye may think that ye're as skilled in our woods as your sisters be, lass, but ye lack their ability to sense approaching danger, as well as Andrena's keener sense of her surroundings."

"But I have the same abilities that they have," Muriella protested.

"Ye may share their ability to sense more than most do about what others are thinking or feeling, and ye may share some of Andrena's woodland skills," Andrew acknowledged. "But ye do nowt to hone your skills, lass. Nor have ye shown Lina's ability, let alone Andrena's or your mam's, to sense danger."

"But—"

"Nay, lassie, ye're in the wrong now," he went on sternly. "Whatever abilities ye may have, ye're more apt to lose yourself in your imaginings than to heed your surroundings closely enough for safety."

Much as she'd have liked to deny it, she knew better than to argue with him. He was a kind and loving father, but his temper was uncertain, so arguing with him was unwise. Besides, Lina and Dree had said similar things to her about practicing and improving her gifts, and she did lose herself in her thoughts when she walked.

With a rueful grimace, she met his gaze and said, "You are right, sir. Sithee, new stories often come to me whilst I'm walking. But I'll try to pay more heed."

"A good notion," he said. "Now, take yourself off, for I've things to do afore MacAulay comes. He has summat he wants to discuss, and I mean to invite him to eat with us." The twinkle returned. "Ye can ask him then what's wrong with ye."

Rising, she made her curtsy, resisting the impulse to tell him she would die rather than ask Robert MacAulay any such question.

She was certain she would *not* like his answer.

⁓

Having followed the wildly churning, swiftly flowing river until it plunged over the cliff to the loch below, Rob stood gazing at the part of Arrochar that touched the river on its other side. He had seen the river on Andrew's south boundary from the pass over which he'd walked into Tùr Meiloach. Andrew's well-armed guards had stopped him three times then to demand his business.

He wondered how MacPharlain had avoided guards in the north pass.

Rob had ridden from Ardincaple by way of west Lomondside, leaving his horse with folks at a wee clachan opposite Inch Galbraith, the island on which the Laird of Galbraith lived with his youngest daughter. Having experienced the steep, boulder-strewn path over the pass the year before with a party of Sir Ian Colquhoun's, Rob had decided this time to spare his mount and walk in.

Both rivers, north and south, were too swift and dangerous for swimming, and the precipitous, granite ridge between Loch Lomond and Tùr Meiloach that connected them was impassable, except through a treacherous pass at each end.

How Andrew Dubh MacFarlan had protected his family and remaining estate for so long had puzzled Rob at first. But standing where he was now reminded him that sheer cliffs rising from the Loch of the Long Boats' eastern edge limited access from its water. Not far from where he stood, he could see Andrew's wharf, looking more like a castle drawbridge than a proper wharf, because it was vertical now, hugging the cliff wall. For a friendly visitor, if Andrew agreed, his men would lower the wharf to float on the water. In truth, therefore, it was more raft than bridge, or so Rob had heard. He had never docked a boat there himself.

Noting the sun's position high in the cloudy sky, he realized that if he wanted to talk to Andrew before the midday meal, he would have to step along. Accordingly, he set off up the footpath and soon came to the one that led back to the tower. Minutes later, he saw it ahead, looming above its surrounding wall. Men on the inner walkway peered down at him.

At the gate, the guard admitted him and Scáthach without question. As Rob stepped into the yard, he heard a shout from above and turned to see a grinning Pluff waving at him from the walkway. Scrambling down a nearby ladder, the boy said, "I'll take ye in, sir. I ken fine where ye'll find the laird."

Glancing at the guard and receiving a nod, Rob said, "Lead the way, lad."

"Send him out again whilst ye talk wi' Himself, sir,"

the guard called down. "Else his ears will be a-burning tae hear all ye say."

"I doubt that he'd hearken to Andrew Dubh's privy talks," Rob replied. Then, catching Pluff's eye, he added gently, "I ken fine that he'll know better than to hearken to mine."

Pluff's eyes widened and he shook his head fiercely. "I'd niver," he told Rob. "I'm no a dafty!"

"I never thought you were, lad. Shall we go in?"

Murie stood near the wall in the chamber where her father kept important documents and tended to affairs of his estate. To her left stood the shelves holding his accounts and other documents. Behind her stood the large table and a two-elbow chair where he worked or spoke with men who had erred or had made their way to Tùr Meiloach and wanted to swear fealty to him.

He also, from time to time, scolded a daughter there, and she knew that she would be in for just such a scolding if he caught her now. The reason she had entered his sanctum was that it shared a wall with the great hall below. In front of her, at eye level if she stood as she did now, on tiptoe, was the laird's squint overlooking the hall. She could see Andrew at the dais table.

Her sister Lina had once caught her in his private chamber and had roundly condemned such behavior. But if Lina had spoken of that incident, even to Andrena, Murie knew naught of it, and she was sure that Dree, had she known, would have scolded, too. In any event, both of her sisters were at Dumbarton, so it was Murie's secret now, and as long as she could see Andrew below, she was safe.

Just then, Pluff appeared in the main entryway, looking puffed up enough in his own esteem to tell her that she had not been wasting her time. The boy entered, and MacAulay strode in behind him.

"I've brung ye Master Robert MacAulay, laird," Pluff said loudly enough for anyone up or down the stairway, let alone in the great hall, to have heard him.

"I thank ye, Pluff," Andrew said. "Ye can help the lads set up the trestles, if ye will. As for ye, lad," he added, looking at MacAulay, "I'll take ye up to me own wee chamber, where we can talk without the din they'll create whilst they set up the tables here for the midday meal. Ye'll dine with us, aye?"

MacAulay nodded, and Muriella, warned that her time was short, turned abruptly from the squint and hurried toward the door.

It opened just before she reached it, to reveal her mother.

"What are you doing here?" Lady Aubrey MacFarlan asked with a frown.

"I...I wanted to see..." Murie paused, swallowing hard. She would have to tell her mother the truth—a portion of it, at least.

"You wanted to see what?" Lady Aubrey's tone had hardened ominously.

Hastily, Murie said, "Father said that Robert MacAulay of Ardincaple was coming to talk with him and perhaps to take the midday meal with us. I remembered Father's squint in here, and...Mam, he told me that Robert MacAulay...that he—Father, that is—offered me to MacAulay last summer when he was here with Ian. I just wanted to see...that is, to hear—"

"You have *no* reason to come into this chamber without your father's permission, Muriella," Lady Aubrey interjected sternly. "To have come in here to spy on him and his guest is a breach of good manners far beyond..." She drew a breath. "What *can* you have been thinking?"

"I was just so curious..." Belatedly realizing that to offer as her excuse the curiosity that both parents had often condemned as her besetting sin would not aid her, Murie fell silent. Although she could often beguile her father, such tactics had no good effect on her mother.

A tremor stirred when the image of her father, coming up the stairs with Robert MacAulay, filled her mind's eye. If they entered to find her there, with her mother thoroughly scolding her...

Leaving Scáthach to enjoy the warmth of the fire, Rob followed Andrew Dubh up the twisting stone stairway, wondering again if the lady Muriella had reported Dougal's trespassing. Andrew had not mentioned it below and was understandably silent as they went upstairs. Most people avoided all but trivial topics on such stairs. The well up which they twisted carried voices too easily.

As it was, Rob heard lighter, quicker steps than theirs above them. He saw no one, though, and heard no voice.

At the next landing, Andrew opened the door on his right and led the way into the chamber where Rob had talked briefly with him the year before. It was similar to one that Lord MacAulay used to deal with Ardincaple's affairs.

Andrew's chamber was smaller, containing a wide table with a two-elbow, red-cushioned chair behind it, shelves of rolled documents and account books, and sev-

eral back-stools. In the far left corner, beneath a narrow
window so deep in the thick wall that the shutter latched
back beside it must rarely be needed, stood a large basket containing a number of rolled documents—charts or
maps, Rob suspected.

Gesturing broadly, Andrew said, "Pull up a back-stool
and sit down, lad. Mag told me ye wanted advice about
summat, and ye're welcome to aught I can tell ye. In troth,
though, I've scarcely set foot off Tùr Meiloach land since
I arrived twenty years ago, so I canna think what I might
say that could aid ye."

Waiting politely until Andrew sat in the chair before
seating himself, Rob said, "You do know more than anyone else does about one man, my lord."

"Ye must have questions about Pharlain, then."

"Aye, and if you know Campbell of Lorne, I'd welcome
any information about him, as well. I believe that your
lady wife has Campbell kinsmen."

"She's cousin to Campbell of Argyll, aye," Andrew
said. "He lives just across the loch. But Campbell of
Lorne lives much farther away, on the Firth of Lorne. I
ken little about him," he added, rubbing his bristly chin.

Noting the gesture, Rob suspected that his host was
thinking about what and how much to say to him and
decided to let the man think.

Andrew straightened in his chair at last, grimaced, and
said, "I'd not trust any Campbell save Argyll, and then
only with family affairs. From all I've gleaned of Argyll
over the years, though, he isna fond of Lorne. Sithee,
Lorne has oft behaved falsely. Some say he has committed murder more than once, but Argyll does nowt to tame
him. What the devil are *ye* doing here?" he exclaimed

when a small, long-haired, orange-and-white cat leaped onto the table between them.

"It came out from behind that basket of charts yonder," Rob said, feeling a rare touch of amusement stir. "It must have been sleeping there."

The cat glanced at him as Andrew reached for it. Easily eluding his hand, it leaped to Rob's knee and regarded him speculatively through golden eyes. Except for a snowy white mustache, chest, and four white-booted paws, the cat was orange.

"Just shove him to the floor," Andrew said. "He shouldna be in here. My lady must have stepped in to tidy up and failed to notice that he'd slipped in, too."

"He won't trouble me," Rob said, stroking silky fur. "What's his name?"

"Ansuz," Andrew said with a grimace. "A daft name for a cat."

"He's named for a runic god that controls the fates of men," Rob said.

"Dinna tell me ye believe in the runes," Andrew said.

"Nay," Rob admitted. "But I know the tales. I suspect that his name means this laddie belongs to the lady Muriella."

"Ye'd be wrong then," Andrew said with a smile. "He belongs to her sister Lachina, who, as ye ken, married Sir Ian and lives at Dumbarton. Due to the size and noise of that place, they decided Ansuz would be happier here, and he seems content enough. I've never seen him take so quick to a stranger, though."

"Animals usually like me," Rob said. "But you were saying...about Campbell of Lorne..."

"Only that I dinna ken the man. I can tell ye that nary

a Campbell supports Jamie Stewart's desire to impose his laws on the country. Like the Lord of the Isles, the Campbells and many other Highlanders who answer to him think they needna answer to the King of Scots. To such men, the Lord of the Isles is equal to or greater than the King. And the Lord of the Isles lives too near for them to defy him."

"What about Pharlain, sir? I ken fine that he opposes James and supported the House of Albany. Does he likewise support the Lord of the Isles?"

"As to how supportive he is or has been, I cannot say," Andrew said. "Pharlain usually seeks only to learn who supports *him*."

"He did take an army as far as Doune to support Albany last year when he and his cohorts tried to seize the throne from Jamie," Rob reminded him.

"During his second Parliament, aye," Andrew said. "But Pharlain returned to Arrochar when the fighting started and brought most of his people with him."

"His son, Dougal, supported James Mòr Stewart when he seized the royal castle and burgh of Dumbarton," Rob said.

"I recall that ye ken much of Dougal and Dumbarton, aye," Andrew replied with a reminiscent air. "To my mind, Dougal is the villainous spit of his father, and the sooner both be underground, the happier I'll be. Aye, but just listen to me," he added with a rueful smile. "I had Dougal by the heels last year and let him go, hoping that Pharlain would take note of such mercy and imitate it. If he has, though, I've heard nowt of it." He paused for a beat, eyeing Rob from beneath his shaggy eyebrows. Then he said, "I did hear that ye'd seen Dougal on my land."

So the lass had reported it. "I'm glad the lady Muriella told you, sir."

"Why would she not?"

Cursing his clumsiness, Rob said truthfully, "I did not mean to imply any doubt of her ladyship, only my relief that you heard about Dougal so quickly."

"My lads keep close watch on the passes," Andrew said, regarding Rob with rather more shrewdness than Rob thought necessary. "Unless they come with an army, I'd liefer see what intruders get up to than stop them afore they reveal their intent, especially when one ventures alone onto my land. Often, such intrusions bring men fleeing Arrochar who seek to join me."

"I doubt you suspect Dougal of such intent, sir."

"True," Andrew agreed. "What I suspect is that he'll be testing some of the tales he's heard about Tùr Meiloach. He did manage to trespass unseen twice last year, so I increased my watchers to make sure that won't happen again."

"How would he test tales of whole armies disappearing here?" Rob asked mildly. "Or of rockslides that bury trespassers or fiercer than normal birds or beasts that tear them to shreds?"

Andrew smiled. "I see that ye've heard some of the tales, too. I suspect from your tone that ye've as little belief in them as Dougal says he does."

"Dougal is a member of Clan Farlan," Rob reminded him. "Doubtless, he believes he is as safe as any other member of the clan on its lands."

"Tùr Meiloach protects only true MacFarlans," Andrew said, more sharply than he had previously spoken. "Those would include only MacFarlans who follow their true chief, not those who support the murderous usurper. And so our Lina told Dougal last year. She warned him straight out that Tùr Meiloach would betray him. But ye didna answer me, lad. D'ye believe in such things as clan sanctuaries?"

"If you tell me that the tales are true, sir, I will not offend you by refusing to believe you," Rob said diplomatically. "I will admit, though, that I have more belief in things that my own experience proves to be true. So far, I have walked safely here."

"Aye, sure, because ye're here as my guest," Andrew said. "But my lass told me that she met ye this morning near the northeast slope. Be that where ye saw Dougal, or did ye see him yestereve when ye came in through the south pass?"

Uncertain whether Andrew had deduced the route he must have taken or meant to show him how closely he guarded his passes, Rob said, "I saw him this morning on the northeast slope, sir."

"And ye met our Muriella somewhere nearby?"

"I met her ladyship with the lad Pluff near the timberline," Rob said, taking care not to emphasize the word "met."

He might have spared himself the effort, though, because with a gimlet gaze, Andrew said, "Just where was she when ye first clapped eyes on her, then?"

⌣

Although Muriella was grateful that the open door of her father's chamber had let Lady Aubrey hear the men's footsteps on the stairs below, she doubted that the brief interlude between that moment and their hasty flight from Andrew's chamber to the next landing would aid her.

Entering the bedchamber that Murie had once shared with her two sisters, Lady Aubrey shut the door. "We will continue our talk here," she said. "I expect your father means to talk with Robert MacAulay in his privy chamber."

"Aye, Mam, I did hear him say so," Muriella said quietly.

"You ought not to have heard one word of their conversation," Lady Aubrey said austerely. "In troth, Muriella, your behavior shames me. I thought I had taught you better manners."

The last two statements stirred Murie's sense of guilt more strongly than anything her mother had said in Andrew's chamber. "Mam, I am the one at fault, not you," she said. "Sometimes, my curiosity to know what is happening grows so strong that I don't seem able to control it. When that happens, I just don't think."

"Then, you must learn to think first," Lady Aubrey said flatly.

"What are you going to do?"

"I ought to forbid you to dine with us, but our guest might wonder at your absence. Faith, I do not even know why he sought to speak with your father. After all, it is possible that—"

When she broke off, the look on her face told Murie exactly what she was thinking. She said quickly, "Robert MacAulay did *not* come here to offer for my hand, Mam. Of that I am certain."

"How can you be? Mayhap he's changed his mind since last year."

Recalling the twinkle in her father's eyes when he had said she could ask MacAulay what was wrong with her, when he dined with them, Murie had a dreadful feeling that her mother might be right. Although common sense told her otherwise, because she had seen only irritation in

Robert MacAulay's attitude toward her earlier, the uncertainty persisted.

In truth, the man *had* behaved as if he had a right to tell her what to do.

~~~

The silence in Andrew's chamber lengthened uncomfortably for Rob, who had no desire to answer the older man's blunt question about where, exactly, he had first seen Muriella that morning. On Rob's knee, Ansuz purred contentedly, making him wonder what the little cat would think of Scáthach.

"Speak, lad. Where was she?"

Rob met Andrew's gaze and said, "With respect, sir, I'd liefer discuss Pharlain or Dougal. I ken fine, though, that before we do, you will want to know the cause of my interest." Perceiving an arrested look in the older man's eyes, he added, "My father thinks that Ardincaple may be at risk. He fears that Pharlain and Campbell of Lorne—mayhap *all* the Campbells—want to seize control of the area."

"Control? What manner of control does he fear?"

"He believes they want to seize the castle and demand fees for passage into and out of the Gare Loch and the Loch of the Long Boats," Rob said flatly.

"Sakes, did one of them say so?"

"Pharlain told him that with so many boats coming and going, we should charge fees for all save our own. He added that if Father refused to do that and share the profits, he and Lorne would see to collecting such fees themselves."

"Let me see if I understand ye," Andrew said. "I ken fine

that MacAulays control both sides of the Gare Loch, and Campbells control the west shore of the Loch of the Long Boats from the firth to the loch's head, where their land meets Arrochar. So, either they'll charge everyone else who enters either loch or the only people they will charge, if MacAulay agrees, would be boats entering the Loch of the Long Boats to come *here* or go back and forth to Colquhoun's Craggan. Do they truly want to anger Colquhoun? Recall that Ian Colquhoun is Governor of Dumbarton, a royal stronghold. Sakes, his grace the King is their good friend."

"The Colquhouns are my friends and yours, too," Rob said. "My father, as you ken fine, is a man who likes peace above all, as does Colquhoun. Pharlain and evidently Campbell of Lorne believe they can persuade such men to submit to their will. Pharlain told my father that Colquhoun spends most of his time at Dunglass now that Ian is nearby at Dumbarton. He said that since they keep only a small staff and a few guards at Craggan Tower, they would not be troubled by such fees."

Muriella was still considering the dreaded possibility that MacAulay might have changed his mind and come to see if Andrew's offer remained good, when Lady Aubrey spoke again.

"I do not know what punishment you deserve, Muriella," she said. "But I do know that you must change out of that filthy kirtle and wash your face and hands before you go down to dine. Tibby will be here soon, so I will leave you to wait for her. Be sure to have her comb your hair and arrange it in a more becoming style."

"Aye, Mam. I'm sorry I disappointed you."

"Then take more care in future, my love," Lady Aubrey said gently. "I'll meet you downstairs."

Murie watched her go and then turned to the washstand and poured cold water from the ewer into the basin. It seemed to her that she found herself in the briars more often now that both Lina and Dree were away. Was her own behavior so much worse than before, or did her parents just notice it more than they had when they'd had three daughters at home?

She had not yet decided which it was when Tibby came in to help her dress.

The maidservant, plump and cheerful, flung up her hands. "What ha' ye done tae that sorry pink kirtle, m'lady? It looks as if ye rolled doon a mud hill in it."

"I'll wear my yellow one with the white lacing, Tib," Murie said. "Mam wants you to tidy my hair, too, if you will."

"I should think I will," Tibby said. "Were there a windstorm outside that we didna hear inside?"

Knowing it was useless to scold Tibby for speaking disrespectfully, since Tibby had known her from her infancy and would heed strictures only from the laird, his lady, or Tibby's own mother, Annie Wylie, Murie said, "Just comb out my plaits, Tib, and put my hair in a net. We will have a visitor at the high table."

"Aye, sure, Master Robert MacAulay of Ardincaple. I took a wee peek at the man afore he and the laird left the hall. He were here last year, too, aye?"

"I don't want to talk about him. I just want to change my dress."

"Och, aye, then," Tibby said with a knowing grin.

Muriella clamped her teeth together and began to

scrub her face. Even Tibby did not believe in her decision never to marry.

~

"It may be true that an imposition of fees willna trouble the Colquhouns," Andrew said. "But I'd wager they would take exception to Pharlain or the Campbells seizing control of yon peninsula. In troth, if Campbell of Lorne is involved, I begin to suspect the fine hand of the Lord of the Isles in this mischief, because it is to Alexander of the Isles, not to Jamie, that all Campbells submit."

The cat, Ansuz, still purring, pushed its head into Rob's palm, and he stroked it idly as he considered Andrew's suspicion. At last, he said, "I tend to agree, sir. However, my father has enjoyed peaceful relations with Argyll and rejects any suggestion that he might be party to such a conspiracy."

"Aye, he would," Andrew said thoughtfully. "'Tis a pity, but—"

He broke off at a light double-rap on the door, then said, "That means our dinner be ready to serve, lad. Ye'll want to refresh yourself afore we join the ladies, so I'll take ye across the landing to me bedchamber, where ye can use the basin and aught else ye might need. First, though," he said as he stood. "I'm thinking that my lass went where she should no have gone this morning. If I be wrong..."

Rob sighed. "You are not wrong, sir. I should have told you straightaway."

"Aye, well, I just want to see that the wee baggage keeps safe," Andrew said.

Chapter 3 —————————

Muriella was taking her place beside her mother at the high table when Andrew stepped through the archway from the privy stairs at the northeast corner of the great hall, just beyond the ladies' end of the dais.

Robert MacAulay followed Andrew, and to her surprise, Ansuz padded at MacAulay's heels. Glancing at Scáthach, who lay on the sprawling hearth near the crackling fire, Murie saw the big dog rise to its feet and begin to approach.

Ansuz stopped to glower at it, but the dog continued undaunted, so the little cat arched high with its fur on end and hissed.

Scáthach cocked her head and looked at Robert MacAulay, as if seeking his advice. Looking from one animal to the other, MacAulay made a small gesture, and Scáthach moved warily around the cat and lay down near the archway.

"Ansuz rarely comes into the hall," Lady Aubrey observed mildly. "He spends most of his time in the solar."

"That fool cat stays upstairs because it dislikes dogs, and there are nearly always some here," Andrew said. "He must have taken a strong liking to ye, Rob."

"But not to Scáthach," Murie said, noting that although the little cat had relaxed, it stayed right where it was and eyed the dog with disapproval.

Lady Aubrey said to MacAulay, "Is that your dog's name, sir?"

"Aye, my lady," he said as Andrew motioned him to the place at his right.

Lady Aubrey's eyes twinkled. Glancing at Murie, she said, "Then I suspect you have an interest in Highland folklore."

"Perhaps someone else named the dog," Murie said lightly.

Whether MacAulay might have risen to the lure, she'd never know, because Andrew held up a hand, silencing everyone before he said the grace before meat.

Afterward, gesturing for all to sit, he took his seat and said to Lady Aubrey, "As ye see, my lady, I've invited the lad to dine with us. I told ye he'd be staying in Mag's cottage, and I ken fine that ye'll recall him from Lina and Ian's wedding."

"I do, aye," Lady Aubrey said, smiling across him at their guest. "I hope your parents are well, sir. It has been some time since last I saw them."

"They are both in excellent health and spirits, my lady," he said. "My mother commanded me to extend her greetings and affection to you."

Murie kept her eyes on her trencher, trying to ignore the effect that MacAulay's presence was having on her.

When he was not annoyed with a person, he certainly had a pleasant voice, calming and melodious. She would have liked to hear him recite poetry or tell a story. Since he knew about the female warriors, he might know some of the other great tales of Scottish folklore and heroics. But it was more than just his voice that stirred her senses. She would be wiser to ignore him.

Andrew's carver had finished his carving, and the gillie Peter Wylie held the platter of sliced meat for Andrew to make his selection. After he had put two juicy-looking slices on Lady Aubrey's trencher and chosen several for himself, Peter moved to serve their guest and then, at last, came to Muriella.

As she selected her usual two slices, she heard Andrew say abruptly to Lady Aubrey, "Your daughter has been exploring farther from home than I would wish, madam. That displeases me."

Murie froze with a slice of meat dangling from the point of her knife. Over the platter, her gaze met Peter's, but the gillie displayed his usual stolid expression.

Whether he was aware that MacAulay must have betrayed her to Andrew or not, she knew that Peter was unlikely to sympathize with her.

Recalling then that Pluff had also known where she'd gone, she looked at the boy, seated beside burly MacNur, whom he aided with the animals inside the wall.

Pluff was interested only in his dinner, though, and experience reminded her that he did not carry tales to Andrew or to MacNur about anything she did.

The traitor had to have been MacAulay. She would like to have seen how he reacted to Andrew's words. But to see him at all she would have to lean forward and look past both of her parents. She decided it would be wiser to pretend she was unaffected by her father's comments and could easily explain herself.

"I have learned that this morning she went near the

northeast pass," Andrew went on. He chewed as he talked, but Murie understood him perfectly and sensed her mother's stiffening annoyance beside her just as easily.

The first question was which one of them would scold her? Then, how soon afterward would she be able to murder Robert MacAulay?

~

Rob also heard Andrew's comments to his lady. He might have been happier had the older man held his tongue at least until the meal was over, but what Andrew Dubh chose to do in his own house with his own family, or when he chose to do it, was no concern of Rob's.

He therefore kept his attention on his food. It was plain fare but cooked and roasted well. Although it lacked some of the variety that attended meals at Ardincaple or the royal strongholds with which he was familiar, Rob had a practical nature and was a good trencherman wherever he ate. Food supplied the energy a warrior needed to do his job properly. Therefore, one ate whatever one's servers or hosts offered and did so without complaint.

Rob also habitually studied his surroundings, so he looked up now and then to scan Andrew's people at the trestles in the lower hall. He did so then, caught a glimpse of Lady Muriella's beautiful profile, and knew in a blink that she was angry. He had no doubt that he was the focus of her anger and wondered if she would tell him so. From what he had seen of her so far, he decided she would not hesitate to tell him exactly what she thought, little good though it would do her.

He returned his attention to his food only to note minutes later that gillies were putting up a privacy screen.

"I want to talk with my lassie for a minute or two afore we talk, lad," Andrew said quietly to him then.

"Then, doubtless, you will excuse me, sir," Rob said, reaching for the cloth provided to clean off his eating knife.

"Nay, nay, lad," Andrew said. "Finish your meal and pay me nae heed. Sithee, I needna say much. We'll take our leave together when ye're done."

Much as Rob would have liked to insist, he still needed advice from the man and did not want to offend him. So he turned back to his meal.

No sooner had he done so than Andrew dismissed the gillies and said sternly to his daughter, "Ye've disobeyed me, Muriella, as I think ye ken fine. Ye should have told me where ye'd been *and* that ye'd seen Dougal MacPharlain for yourself."

"But I didn't!"

"Whisst now," Andrew said. "I'll hear nae backchat. Forbye, ye should ken fine that any argle-bargle will gain ye nobbut grief. Ye've gone your limit this time, lass, by wandering dangerously near that pass, and I mean to put a stop to such behavior. Ye'll bide inside our gates now for a fortnight."

Rob heard Lady Muriella gasp and decided that such a punishment had likely not come her way before. She well-deserved it, though, and he felt not an ounce of pity for her.

Glancing at her, he saw that words of protest hovered on her tongue.

She looked at her mother, saw that no help would come from her, and then caught her lower lip in her teeth as if to lock the perilous words inside.

Andrew evidently saw the same things. He said grimly, "Ye're wise to hold your tongue, lass. I ken fine how much ye love your wanderings, so it should take only a few days of such confinement to bring ye to your senses."

Rob growled under his breath, thinking that Andrew had yielded to her ladyship's distress. Still, it was no business of his.

"Thank you, sir," Muriella said on a note of profound relief.

"Dinna be thanking me yet. Ye'll take Peter Wylie with ye wherever ye go. I mean to give him strict instructions regarding your boundaries, too. Ye'll go nae farther than Peter allows. Nor will ye plague him to give ye more freedom," he added sternly. "If ye do, it will go much worse for ye. D'ye hear me, lass?"

"Aye, but to put a gillie in charge of me, even Peter! To shame me so..." Tears welled in her eyes, and one trickled down a smooth, now pale cheek.

"'Tis harsh punishment, I'll grant ye," Andrew said. "I expect I could do summat a wee bit more palatable. *If* ye agree...and," he added when her tears ceased as if she had turned a tap and a tiny smile touched her lips, "...if *he* does."

Her eyes widened. "Peter?"

"Nay, nay," Andrew said. "I was thinking of Rob MacAulay here." He turned to Rob with a guileless smile. "Since ye'll likely bide with us here at Tùr Meiloach for several days more, until we sort out what ye mean to do, I've nae doot ye'll agree to escort the lass now and now, will ye no? Sithee, ye've shown that ye can persuade her to mind what ye say, so she'll give ye nae trouble at all."

Rob's jaw dropped, and he stared aghast at his host.

Muriella's outrage ebbed when she saw the stricken look on MacAulay's face, but it flooded back when he recovered enough to say evenly, "I am wholly at your service whilst I remain here, my lord."

"Good o' ye! My lass will stay in the solar this afternoon and contemplate her sins whilst we continue our own discussion. I'm hoping ye'll sup with us, and mayhap, if she behaves herself, ye'll take her out for a wee stroll after supper. Ye've shown interest in the landscape here, and I'd have ye see as much as ye like. If ye take her with ye, she can answer any questions ye may have."

Seething with anger but aware of her mother sitting stiffly beside her and uncertain whether Lady Aubrey's anger matched hers or Andrew's, Murie kept quiet. Since her father had practically made her punishment public knowledge, protest would be useless anyway. It was possible that no one at the trestle tables in the lower hall had heard all that he had said. Still, in sending the gillies away as he had, he might as well have announced that his intent was to scold her.

The worst thing, though, was that Robert MacAulay had carried tales of her to her father. Her first inclination when Andrew had said that MacAulay could escort her was to ignore the so-called easing of her punishment and stay inside, but walking with Peter was too humiliating to contemplate, and she knew that Andrew had meant it to be. He was truly angry with her.

As always, though, her wily father had put his goals first. His primary aim was the same as it had been the year before, to marry her to MacAulay and thereby gain a third well-connected warrior as a good-son to help him win back the estates that his cousin Pharlain had usurped from him when Andrena was a newborn babe.

She would go for that stroll with MacAulay, Murie decided. If she could not charm him into being sorry for rejecting her father's offer the year before, she could at least tell him exactly what she thought of him for carrying tales to Andrew.

~

Rob felt as if Andrew had drawn him into a maelstrom, and he could think of no civil way to swim out of it. For his host to involve him in what should have been a private matter of parental discipline was unconscionable, but Rob had heard enough about Andrew Dubh MacFarlan and seen enough of the man to know that Andrew's conscience rarely interceded when he wanted something.

Rob's position was such that he'd have liked to excuse himself, not only from the high table but also from Tùr Meiloach. Nevertheless, having requested Andrew's advice, he could hardly leave before learning what the man could tell him, at least about Pharlain. In truth, Rob admitted—if only to himself—he would welcome almost any plan that the crafty Andrew helped him devise.

Rob's own nature was forthright. However, his two best friends had warned him separately that trying to talk sense into Pharlain over something as lucrative as he and Campbell of Lorne believed collecting passage fees at Ardincaple would be, would prove futile at best.

"Get yourself up to the ladies' solar now, Muriella, and dinna show your face below stairs again until I send someone to fetch ye, unless ye would suffer my strongest displeasure," Andrew said then, diverting Rob from his reverie.

He stood when Andrew did but did not watch her lady-ship's departure. As the two men ascended the stairs after her, Rob was tempted to point out to his host that including him in her punishment was no treat for him.

He held his tongue, though, and soon realized that courtesy was not what stopped the words on his tongue. Nor had the concern that someone, even the lady herself, might overhear him if he raised such a subject in the stairwell. The fact was that his irritation was gone, replaced by intriguing conjectures of how her ladyship might react when next they met.

That thought struck him as illogical. His first reaction had been the realistic one or should have been, because it had been reasonable. He should be anticipating nothing save the sort of trouble that Andrew had assured him the lass would not create. Sakes, since Ian and Mag had warned him that talking to Pharlain without learning how to protect himself against the man would be sheer lunacy, what would they say to this?

"Sit ye doon, lad," Andrew said as they entered his chamber and he stepped around the table to his chair. "I've had some notions since we talked afore. Nowt that I'd recommend from the outset, mind ye, but some that do warrant discussion."

Rob nodded, took the back-stool again, and warned himself not to let his mind wander from the subject at hand. He had a feeling that if it did, his host would notice. And, rather than being offended, Andrew would be delighted.

⁓

Muriella went obediently to the ladies' solar and felt no surprise when her mother failed to join her there. Not only would Lady Aubrey doubtless believe that Murie deserved solitude, but rarely did she spend any afternoon in the solar.

She was more likely to visit people or make her presence felt in the tower, supervising the turning out of a chamber to clean it or another such wifely task.

Murie took her customary seat with her back to the southeast-facing window, unshuttered now to let in the light and the crisp spring air. Preparing her leader, she attached it to her spindle. Then, with her left hand, she plucked a handful of lamb's wool from the large basket beside her, overlapped it with her leader, and began gently turning her wheel with her right hand.

Soon she was working with her usual rhythm and letting her imagination soar far from the solar into a flight of fancy. Robert MacAulay somehow became the central figure, a foolish one who suffered well-deserved trials and tribulations.

The door opening after what seemed to be only minutes startled her so that she nearly snapped her thread.

Seeing Tibby in the doorway, Muriella stopped the wheel.

"What is it, Tib? You nearly startled me witless."

"The laird said ye should put on your cloak and take your walk now," Tibby said, her tone carefully neutral. Nevertheless, Murie easily sensed the maidservant's curiosity straining for satisfaction.

Refusing to reveal more information than Tibby had doubtless gleaned since the midday meal, Murie said lightly, "I have not missed supper, have I?"

"Nay, nay, though Himself did say ye might wonder," Tibby admitted. "It be so cloudy that he feared it might begin tae rain, and he kent fine that ye'd no want tae miss your walk. Forbye, he said that they had nowt more tae discuss today."

"Thank you," Muriella said absently, her thoughts speeding ahead to all that she still had to say to MacAulay. The imaginary punishments she had inflicted on him had eased her fury, but she could not allow him to imagine that Andrew expected him to control her every movement.

"Ye'll no be going out in that yellow kirtle without a cloak, m'lady," Tibby said. "Ye should put on a cap, too. We'll fetch them from your bedchamber."

Muriella went meekly, deciding to save her arguments for MacAulay.

Ten minutes later, she found him patiently waiting by the fireplace in the great hall with Scáthach.

Greeting MacAulay with a nod and the dog with a friendly pat on the head, she led the way silently to the stairs, outside, and across the yard to the postern gate.

Pluff dashed to open it for them, earning himself thanks from MacAulay.

Passing through the gateway, Murie hurried across the clearing and into the woods. When they were amid the trees, beyond view from the wall, she continued to stride ahead of him but said bluntly, "This is *all* your fault."

"Is that so?"

The note of amusement in his voice swept her fury back again. She whirled to face him, determined to tell him exactly what she thought of him.

⌒

Seeing the color flood her ladyship's cheeks, Rob waited to hear what she would say next, although he might have guessed. She did not disappoint him.

"It *is* your fault," she insisted. "Did you not tell my father that I had gone too near the pass? Had you not done that—"

"Even if I did, how does that make your *father's* reaction my fault?"

She rolled her eyes. "Faith, but you try to turn a simple fact into a puzzle. Had you *not* told him, he would have *had* no reaction."

"What happened was a natural consequence of your own actions," he replied calmly. "I warned you to tell Andrew before I, or Pluff, or anyone else did."

"But why carry tales to my father at all? That was a vile thing to do. Pluff would *not* have done it."

Still maddeningly calm, he said, "I did not carry that tale, lass. You did what you did. Then you told your father only that Pluff and I had said we'd seen Dougal. Because apparently you did not describe any of your own actions, Andrew asked me some pointed, quite logical questions. Would you have had me lie to him?"

He could tell from her expression that that was exactly what she had hoped. But when she looked angrily into his eyes and he continued to gaze steadily back at her, she expelled a frustrated breath and said, "I suppose you would not do that."

"You are right; I *could* not. I don't hold with lying in any event, and I came to Tùr Meiloach a-purpose to seek his advice. A fine turn I'd have served him, had I given him a lie in place of the honest information he requested."

With a thoughtful frown, she looked searchingly at him. "He asked *you* where I had gone walking? That seems most unusual for him."

"He was more specific than that," Rob said. "He asked

me where you were when I first saw you. Sithee, you evidently told him that we'd met near the northeast slope. You also told him that Pluff and I had both seen Dougal. Do you not think your father is canny enough to draw his own conclusions after that?"

She grimaced and turned away, heading toward the cliffs that overlooked the Loch of the Long Boats.

Andrew had said nowt to him about setting boundaries for her. Moreover, no matter how angry she was with them both, Rob doubted that she would fling herself into the icy water far below, so he followed without comment.

Scáthach glanced at him. Then, Rob having given no other command, she loped past her ladyship and began to range back and forth ahead of them.

Lady Muriella's silence continued until they emerged from the woods near the clifftops. Then she turned, gave him a rueful smile, and said, "You do know that my father has done this because he still hopes you will agree to marry me."

"There is *no* danger of that," he said, taken aback by her candor.

Her fading smile turned sadly winsome, "I know," she said. "But he hopes you will, even so."

Discerning the likely implication of her phrasing with a sense of shock, and only after she had repeated the word "hopes," he eyed her more warily. "Do you mean to say Andrew told you that he had suggested such a union to me?"

"Aye, sure," she said with a shrug. "He offered me to you last year when you were here with Sir Ian, did he not?"

Rob hesitated, wondering how much more she knew about the day her sister Lachina had married Sir Ian Colquhoun.

Murie hoped she had put MacAulay on the defensive for once. If she had not, perhaps she had at least diverted his thoughts from what he called the consequences of her actions. His silence was encouraging.

Pressing further, she said sweetly, "You did say you don't lie, did you not?"

"I was not tempted to lie to you, my lady," he said, meeting her gaze with apparent ease. "I just wondered how Andrew came to tell you about that day. Did he tell you about it then or more recently?"

Uncertain if the truth would aid her or not, she caught her lower lip between her teeth and tried to think. He was harder for her to read than most men were.

"When did he tell you, lass?"

Sensing no annoyance in him, only determination, Murie shrugged again and said, "If you must know, he told me this morning. He also said that you informed him last year that you would not *inflict* yourself on any woman. Why is that?"

"If I were wooing you, I might be obliged to explain. But I am not wooing you, nor will I, Andrew's hopes notwithstanding. Do you mean to stand talking, or would you liefer walk farther? Your father invited me to sup with him, so I'm in no hurry. However, I did not think to ask him what time your people serve supper."

"We have an hour before we need return," she said.

"Are you so certain of the time?"

"Aye, sure. Should I not be?"

"You did not even glance toward the sun, although with those clouds in the west, one cannot be sure of its exact location."

"I don't need the sun to tell me what time it is," she said with a smile. "I just know. Lina always knows, too. We were born that way."

He made no comment on that statement, making her hope he would accept that she spoke the truth. He would test her again, though, because people did that whenever she or Lina displayed their gifts for knowing the time and the tides.

"I have heard that the MacFarlan sisters have some unusual gifts," he said. "Ian swears that your sister Andrena knows what men are thinking and that Lina can even foretell the future. I should perhaps tell you that I don't believe in such abilities."

"That is your right, sir, but I should perhaps tell *you* that they are real."

"I do know that some people have a strong sense of time," he went on as if she had not spoken. "Such people usually explain their ability by noting things that aid them, such as changing light or animal behavior. In troth, most people know by the extent of their own hunger that a mealtime is drawing near."

"I expect that is all it is, then," she said, although she knew it was not. To return him to the more interesting subject of his objection to marriage, she said wistfully, "Is it just that you think you would make any woman a dreadful husband or is it something wrong with me in particular?"

The flash of anger she sensed in him surprised her. She had seen nothing in his expression that she could describe as warning that such fury might ignite.

⁓

As surprised by the strength of his anger as he could see that her ladyship was, Rob quickly controlled it. He was not angry with her but with himself for making her think that he believed she had something wrong with her.

However, he also suspected that she was seeking change to a topic that might be more comfortable for her. Accordingly, he said, "I am not ready yet to marry, lass. That is all. I don't intend to discuss my past with you or to bandy words on such subjects. You have two good-brothers who are warriors. I think you would agree with me that any man whose liege lord may summon him to battle at any moment is unlikely to make you a satisfactory husband."

"Aye, well," she said, looking thoughtful, "I would not have married Ian or Mag. They are both too bossy to suit me. Come to that, I have yet to meet a man who is *not* domineering. Men are all much too apt to debate one's decisions."

"I can easily believe that the men in your life object to some of yours," he said. "Having witnessed the result of one of them, I think you'd do better to consider the wisdom of your decisions before blaming Mag, Ian, or your father for objecting to them. These cliffs provide a fine view," he added. "I saw that from your north river boundary this morning. But, from here, one sees nearly the full length of the loch."

"The clouds are thinning, so the view will soon be better, and we'll see a splendid sunset. But you are just trying to change the subject, are you not?"

"Nay, I thought *you* were."

She shot him a wry smile. "I was," she said. "I do not want to talk more about consequences."

"Something tells me you don't even like to think about consequences."

"I don't."

"You should not only think about what they might be but also learn from them when they occur," he said. "Experience comes more from consequences than from anything else. It is not only foolish but foolhardy to ignore them."

"But, see you, I know what I want to do, so I dislike things—and men—that get in my way."

"And now I am in your way," he said, nodding.

"*Now* you are trying to make me feel guilty," she said, raising an eyebrow. "I do not dislike you. In troth, I am grateful that my father's hope for our future stirred him to ask you to come with me. That saved me from days of confinement in my bedchamber or the ladies' solar."

"If that is all that Andrew had in store for you, you have reason to be even more grateful that I did not accept his offer of a marriage to you," Rob said with more feeling than he had intended.

"Why?"

"Because if you *were* my wife and did aught as dangerous as what you did this morning, you would be feeling much less cheerful now and less able to sit."

Chapter 4————————————

Muriella felt a strange thrill shoot low through her midsection in reaction to MacAulay's threat, but she recovered quickly. "If that is how you think," she said, raising her chin, "then *I* think you are gey wise not to inflict yourself on a wife."

As the words flew from her tongue, she wondered how he would react. Despite her strong friendship with her good-brothers, Ian and Mag, she was sure that if she dared speak so saucily to either one, he would seek swift retribution.

Again, MacAulay surprised her. He met her gaze as easily as he had before and without anger, incipient or otherwise.

"You may think what you like about me or aught else," he said. "Everyone has that right. You might also recall what I said about consequences, though. Not everyone is as charitable as I am about tolerating other people's beliefs."

She eyed him uncertainly. "You don't care what I think about you?"

"I did not say that. I said you have the right to think as you like."

"Then what did you mean about consequences?"

To her annoyance, his lips twitched as if she had amused him again. He did not smile, though, and she realized that she had not yet seen an actual smile from him. Not that that mattered, she told herself. It mattered more that, despite his apparent success at suppressing his smiles, he *did* seem to be laughing at her.

Before she could tell him what she thought of such impudence, he said amiably, "Are you now more willing to discuss such consequences?"

"I just want to know what you meant."

"I thought I had made myself clear," he said, his casual tone making her wish again that she could read his true feelings. "Apparently I did not," he added, "so I'll try again. Surely, you know people—especially men—who would react differently than I did to what you said to me just now and the manner in which you said it."

"Aye, sure, I do," she agreed, wondering if this irritatingly unpredictable man realized that she had been thinking of Mag and Ian, and if he might tell them about this conversation. She sincerely hoped that he would not.

He was watching her as if he knew exactly what she was thinking and was giving her time to sort her thoughts. Then he said, "Since you do know such men, you must also know that there are many others who would also react badly."

"But I can always tell if I'm making someone angry," she said. "I would not speak so to—"

"Don't be a dafty," he interjected, his tone still calm despite the command. "I can tell when I make someone angry, too—especially people I know well. That does *not* mean that I would expect to know what a stranger is thinking. Few men wear their emotions plainly enough for others to see."

"But I can—"

"*No* one can always know what someone else is thinking or how that person is reacting, or what he might do next," he said, his tone still gallingly reasonable.

"Well, I can," she retorted, feeling her temper rise and fighting to control it.

Without any change of expression, he caught hold of both her shoulders hard and pulled her close to him, looking down into her eyes as he did and lowering his face close enough to hers for her to feel his breath like a warm breeze on her lips.

"*Can* you, lass?" he asked, the tension in his voice plain for anyone to hear now, the look on his face indecipherable. "Then tell me what I'm about to do."

She could scarcely breathe, let alone answer his question. Her anger had fled. Her heart thumped hard and fast in her chest.

Easily reading her astonishment and trepidation, Rob let the moment lengthen, hoping he had frightened her a little. If he had shown her something of what men were capable of, he was doing her a favor. As he held her, he realized that his grip was hard enough to bruise her soft flesh and eased it a little.

Her lips softened then. Her limpid gaze seemed to melt under his.

Abruptly, without a second thought, he released her and looked away. What had he been thinking to have touched her in such a possessive way? Had he forgotten so easily that Andrew Dubh had entrusted her safety to him?

Had the lass's beauty and innocence bewitched him?

Forcing himself to meet her gaze again, he was on the brink of apologizing when he saw the shock on her face and realized that he might have accomplished his goal after all.

"You see?" he said then. "You did not know."

Her right hand came up in a flash of anger with the full weight of her slender but so-curvaceous body behind it.

He caught her wrist easily and held it.

The villain was bruising her again. "Let go of me," she said angrily.

"Certainly, just as soon as I know you won't try that again."

"I warrant it would be useless if I did."

"It would, but there might be other consequences, as well, lass. Sithee, I want you to understand the importance of consequences. It seems likely that you have suffered few useful ones in your short life."

"I am eighteen," she said. "I cannot be much younger than you are."

"I am four-and-twenty," he said.

"That is *much* older, to be sure," she agreed dryly. "But even being such a graybeard does *not* give you the right to issue orders to me."

"Your father did give me that right, though," he reminded her. "Not that I am issuing orders. I am just pointing out that the consequences of striking a man much larger than you are might be worse for you than for him."

"A chivalrous man would let an irate lady strike him, knowing that he deserved such a *consequence* for angering her. He would then apologize."

"You may believe that," MacAulay said. "However, in this matter, your belief conflicts with mine."

"Still, I am entitled to mine, am I not?"

"You are, but I should tell you that although I'll apologize when I know I'm in the wrong, I don't believe I did aught that should have angered you."

"But—"

Interrupting without hesitation, he added, "You should be grateful to know the danger of striking someone so much larger and stronger than you—even someone as aged and decrepit as you pretend to believe I am. Sakes, if having a truth proven to you makes you irate instead of grateful, you have much to learn."

"*You're* the one who made such a point about being old," she retorted.

~

Oddly irritated that she would think six years the chasm of a millennium, Rob nevertheless brushed his irritation aside to say honestly, "I meant only that, from what I have seen, you have lived a sheltered, even isolated life here at Tùr Meiloach. Your parents love you dearly, and I'd wager that your older sisters do, too. Therefore, I surmise that such consequences as you may have suffered have been too lenient to teach you due caution."

"You are right to say that my parents love me," she said, drawing herself up stiffly and apparently ignoring the rest of what he had said. "In fact, I think that when I tell my father how mistaken he was to place his trust in you, you will suffer some dire consequences of your own."

"Do you?" he said, mildly amused again. "What will you tell him?"

"I shall tell him what you just did, that's what."

"I thought you disapproved of talebearers."

"He is my father. He would want to know."

"Know what?"

She glared at him. "I told you. What you did to me."

"But what did I do, my lady?"

Hesitating only briefly, she said on a note of near triumph, "You grabbed me. I'll wager you left bruises on both of my shoulders to prove it, too."

"That would certainly make Andrew Dubh angry enough to demand to know why I had behaved so roughly," Rob said, nodding. "What would you have me say in reply to such a demand?"

Her eyes widened, then grew thoughtful again. She remained silent.

While she thought, Rob gestured gently toward the forest path that had brought them to the cliffs. "I think we should start back, don't you?" he said.

Glancing toward the horizon, where the only sign of a setting sun was a dull orange glow behind low, still dark clouds, she shrugged and turned toward the path.

He walked beside her, but she kept her head down, apparently watching the pathway ahead, so he kept his counsel but glanced at Scáthach.

The lean, shaggy, gray dog was trotting through shrubbery a short distance away, more interested in what might lie within that shrubbery than in aught else. Such behavior being proof that no intruder had entered the woods, Rob looked again at his beautiful companion.

She was thoughtfully chewing a fingernail, or what was left of one.

Noting that the other fingers of that hand had suffered

similar fates, his own fingers itched to remove that one from her mouth. He resisted the temptation. The *last* thing he wanted was to involve himself with the saucy lass in any way.

———

Muriella was lost in a fantasy, wherein tiny devils flew at, poked, and pinched the arrogant brute beside her. The man deserved even worse punishment.

However, when a contrary voice from one of her imaginary devils demanded to know why she disliked their victim so, she could think of no answer.

In truth, she did not dislike him. She disliked the fact that he seemed determined to dislike her. He had said he did not, but to have rejected her as quickly and completely as he had, he must have believed or at least heard something about her that caused him to do so, so absolutely. *That* was only logical.

Remembering that he had used the word himself, she felt rather pleased to think that even he would have to agree that her reasoning was logical.

His hand on her arm, although gentle this time, startled her into stopping.

Looking up at him, she said, "Why did you do that?"

With a nod, he indicated the low branch ahead of her. Another step and she would have walked into it headfirst.

"Do you not walk here often?" he asked solemnly.

Knowing exactly what he would say if she admitted that she did, and not wanting to hear it, she shook her head and said, "Not very often."

"Then you should watch where you are going, should you not?"

An admonitory note in his voice made her think she would be wiser not to look at him. She said lightly, "You are right. I was thinking about a story."

"And are now telling me one, I think."

Stiffening, gritting her teeth, she knew nevertheless that she would be foolish to lie again. Looking at him from under her lashes, she smiled ruefully and said, "I *was* lost in my imagination, sir. But I did mislead you about how often I walk here."

"You lied to me, in fact," he said. "Don't do it again, lass."

His demeanor and tone remained as calmly unrevealing as ever. But a shiver shot through Muriella's body, spreading its chill from her core to every other cell.

Something deep within her sensed that she had just stirred a devil deep inside him and was warning her that she did *not* want it to come fully awake.

⌐

Her face had paled, and Rob decided that, for once, he had made his position clear to her. He hoped she would not lie to him again but thought that the hope was likely misplaced. Not only had she lied by omission in not telling Andrew where she had been when she reported Dougal's trespassing, but if she had lied once, she would lie again.

She seemed to live in a world that belied reality and to have created much of that world for herself. That she might have done such a thing was both maddening and strangely intriguing. But, for the moment, she was taking his words to heart.

They reached the tower a short time later, and the smell of roasting meat reassured him that she had been right about suppertime.

She thanked him politely when they met her maidservant on the stairs. After watching her disappear upward with the wench, he went in search of Andrew and found him in his privy chamber, ready for his supper.

"My lady went down to confer with Annie Wylie about summat or other," Andrew said. "So ye can come into me bedchamber and ready yourself to sup with us. Did ye enjoy your walk?"

"We walked out to the cliffs," Rob said as they crossed the landing. "The clouds in the west have thickened, so I think we'll soon have more rain."

"Aye, and if it does rain, ye'll no want to be seeking Pharlain out until it passes. Looking like a drowned man when ye reach Arrochar will do ye nae good, but we'll talk more later about how ye'll want to approach him."

"I'd prefer to talk more tomorrow if that will suit you, sir. I'm both willing and grateful to sup with you, but I'd liefer not impose myself longer than that, because we'll have no moon tonight. Moreover, I want to ponder the things we discussed earlier, and I'll sleep better at Mag's cottage than I will here."

"He did tell me ye're fond of your solitude."

"Sometimes aye, sometimes nay," Rob admitted.

"Ye've said nowt yet about your walk with our Muriella."

Rob met the older man's gaze and said quietly, "I have not changed my mind, sir. You would do well to accept that."

"Sakes, I dinna ken what ye be nattering about," Andrew said. "I've done nowt save ask how ye enjoyed your walk on the cliffs."

Perhaps, Rob told himself with a sigh, her ladyship had come by her vivid imagination naturally.

Grateful for the two cressets that Tibby had lit in her bedchamber, Muriella resisted the urge to ask the maid-servant to fetch a more becoming kirtle for her than the yellow one she wore. Her discomfort after MacAulay warned her not to lie to him again had passed, but her thoughts had returned to him nevertheless. Talking with him had stimulated her in a way that she had not experienced with anyone else.

The truth was that she enjoyed talking with him when he did not contradict her or talk about things she did not want to discuss. Even on those subjects, though, she felt a kind of eagerness, even excitement, when they talked.

One moment she wanted to kill him, the next to say something outrageous to see how he would react.

He was, in fact, an intriguing man, if only because she could not tell from one minute to the next what he might do or say. When he had grabbed her...

It would be wiser not to think about that.

"Ye must make haste, m'lady," Tibby said. "Your mam isna so pleased with ye that ye'll want tae vex her again by going late tae the table."

Wishing again that Tibby were a newcomer and not someone who had known her forever, but aware that she was right, Murie pushed her thoughts aside. Then, after attending quickly to her ablutions, she hurried down to supper.

MacAulay wasn't at the table yet, but Lady Aubrey was.

Murie went to her and said sincerely, "I know I was wrong this morning, Mam. I hope you are not too displeased with me."

Giving her a steady, rather speculative look, Lady Aubrey said quietly, "You must take care, my love, not to give your family or friends reason to distrust you. Sithee, when you lose someone's trust, it is gey difficult to win it back again."

Murie's throat closed with an ache that brought tears to her eyes. Her mother had said much the same thing to her before. This time, though, for some reason, it struck her with greater impact.

Noise from the privy stair diverted Lady Aubrey's attention.

Andrew and MacAulay had arrived.

In the usual ritual that accompanied the serving, Murie had little time to think. Her mother introduced topics of conversation, and she responded, but her attention drifted more than once to the two men seated beyond Lady Aubrey.

Andrew and MacAulay were chatting too quietly to hear what they said, but she judged it unlikely that MacAulay had said aught about their conversation on the clifftop to her father. If he had, she would sense Andrew's disapproval.

"Art ready for us to excuse ourselves, Muriella?" Lady Aubrey asked.

"Aye, Mam," Murie said, despite a sudden reluctance to go. MacAulay would return to the cottage when he finished eating, and she was curious to know when he would come back. She could hardly ask, though, without sounding as if she were interested in the man, which of course she was not.

As they passed Andrew's wee chamber, she wished she might slip inside and use the squint again to see if MacAulay was already preparing to depart.

"You will retire early tonight, Muriella," Lady Aubrey said when they reached the next landing. "Your father has asked me to see that you keep to the solar or your bed-chamber until Friday morning, except for such times—if any more occur—when Robert MacAulay agrees to walk with you."

It was only Monday, so three more whole days and nights! "Mam, you must know that Father hopes MacAulay will change his mind and offer for me."

"If that is so, it is your father's business to discuss it with you, not mine."

"But, Mam—"

"Goodnight, Muriella."

Stifling a sigh, Murie turned toward her door, only to turn back again and hug Lady Aubrey. "I'm sorry, Mam. I seem to make one mistake after another."

"Doubtless, you miss your sisters, love. Andrena will soon return, and Lina will come here to stay with you both whilst your father and I journey to Inverness for his grace's Parliament there. That won't be too long now."

Bidding her goodnight again, Murie entered her bed-chamber to find that Tibby had put out a fresh shift for her to wear in the morning. Wondering how she might spend the time until she was tired enough to sleep, she did what she usually did when she was bored and let her imagination roam free.

Deciding to lose herself in folk tales and not think a single thought about Robert MacAulay, she went to bed and tried to imagine what her sisters might be doing. The only thing she sensed about them was that each was safe and in good health. Whatever her father might think about her abilities, the instinct that warned her if either

Lina or Dree met trouble or danger was as keen as ever it had been.

～

Rob took his leave of Andrew as soon as he could politely do so. With Scáthach at his heels, he collected his sword, bow, and quiver and strode out to the postern gate, where he found young Pluff standing guard.

"So you are also the keeper of the gate, are you," Rob said lightly.

"Aye, sure, when naebody else wants tae stand here. I dinna mind. It be good practice for when I grow big enough tae be a warrior. They stand guard, too, aye?"

"They do, indeed," Rob said, tousling the boy's wild curls.

"When be ye a-coming back then?" Pluff asked as he lifted the latch.

"Oh, tomorrow or the next day. It may rain tonight, and if it does, I'd liefer stay close by the cottage fire."

"Mayhap I'll visit ye, then, if ye'll let me," Pluff said. "I've a mind tae learn more about being a warrior, and MacNur said I might ask ye aboot it."

"You may if MacNur or the laird says you may," Rob said. "But I'll wager you've asked Sir Ian and Sir Magnus most of the questions you want to ask me."

"I have, aye," Pluff admitted. "But men I've asked give different answers tae me questions, so I learn summat from each one I ask. Also, even Sir Ian said ye ken more aboot fighting hand-tae-hand than he or Sir Mag. He said ye're gey strong, too, and that ye might teach me how tae grow stronger."

"You have a keen mind in that fiery head of yours, lad.

You come and talk to me whenever you like. But mind you get permission first."

"I will, aye," Pluff assured him. Then, patting Scáthach's head, the boy opened the postern gate and shut it again when Rob and Scáthach were outside it.

Rob made haste, because the air was heavy with rain, ready to begin at any minute. He had left a fire banked in the cottage, so it would take little to stir it to life, but it would be wise to get there before he got soaked.

~

She was flying through the air, her favorite blue-green kirtle billowing around her legs and her hooded, fur-lined cloak draped over her shoulders. She was doing naught to make herself fly, but she had only to think about going in a certain direction to do so. In truth, she had found a quite magical place, yet she had no memory of coming here.

In the distance ahead a man appeared, flying toward her. Although he was as far from her as Dree's cottage was from the tower gate, his golden-brown hair and vivid green eyes were clearly visible.

So, where was Scáthach if Robert MacAulay was with her in this strange world where people could fly as easily as birds? More easily, come to that, since she didn't have to flap wings here to fly and, apparently, neither did MacAulay.

Without any sense of time passing, he was right in front of her, catching hold of her as he had before but kissing her this time. Strangely, she wanted him to keep doing it. His lips felt warm and his breath tasted of smoke and whisky.

He vanished, and the taste in her mouth changed to something bitterly sour. To her horror and dismay, Dougal MacPharlain had taken his place.

She tried to shove Dougal away, but she couldn't. He was flying off with her! With every shove, he went faster and faster until they were flying at breakneck speed. Suddenly, they plunged downward, then deeper and deeper into that strange, unnatural world.

More abruptly than Dougal's appearance came a flashing sense of light between them. Just as she recognized MacAulay and saw him grab Dougal, MacAulay flung him into the clouds and caught her instead. She struggled both to thank him and to free herself, but no words would come. She tried harder . . .

. . . and heard herself say clearly, "I *could* have flung him away *myself*."

Blinking rapidly, trying to reorient herself, Muriella realized that she was sitting up in her own bed. Familiar gray dawn light spilled through a crack in one of the window shutters. She could hear wind and pelting rain outside.

Wondering what MacAulay might have to say about such a strange dream, she wondered, too, if she would dare to tell him about it. Deciding that she would, she hoped he would brave the rain and return to the tower soon so that she could.

The rain continued all day Tuesday, and although any number of their own people sought shelter inside the castle and great hall, Robert MacAulay did not.

Wednesday and Thursday passed in much the same way, although the rain did stop for a time Thursday afternoon, and Andrew went outside. When Muriella learned at supper than he had visited MacAulay at the cottage, the surge of envy and irritation she felt astonished her. She nearly asked Andrew why he had not taken her with him but fortunately recalled before she did that he would hear such a question in a much different way than she would mean it.

He would certainly decide that she was attracted to MacAulay.

That the three days of confinement Andrew had ordered had ended cheered her. When the fact dawned on her that her parents would have forbidden her to venture out in such rain, punishment or none, she felt even better.

She was thoroughly tired of the rain, so when she awoke Friday morning to blessed silence and then heard birds begin to sing, she arose, dressed in her warm pink kirtle, and pulled on her rawhide boots without waiting for Tibby.

Noting that what she could see of the sky was clear, Murie hurried down to the dais to break her fast, hoping to find Andrew in the hall. However, he had gone out and her mother had eaten and gone to the kitchen to confer with the cook.

With a sigh, Murie helped herself to cold sliced beef and a manchet roll and began to eat, wondering if anyone else even remembered that her days of confinement were over.

She was finishing her meal when Lady Aubrey entered and said, "I'm glad that you are up, my love. Doubtless you intend to finish spinning the yarn you mean to give Annie Wylie, but first I have some other chores for you."

"Aye, sure, Mam," Murie said, that being the only acceptable response.

Rushing through her chores with her usual efficiency, she thought briefly of looking for Andrew again, to ask if she might now walk outside the wall. If he refused, she would ask him if MacAulay meant to visit that day.

Knowing that Andrew was likely still busy and that he would surely ask if she had tasks left to do before permitting anything else, she went to the ladies' solar and finished spinning the last bobbin of yarn for Annie Wylie. Tucking the four balls she already had for her into a cloth sack with the fifth one, Murie went down to the hall, found it empty, and continued downstairs to the postern door.

Her fur-lined, hooded cloak hung on a hook by the door.

Glancing at the cloak, she nearly passed it by but took the precaution of looking outside first. The sky that had looked wonderfully clear earlier had acquired a host of scattered clouds in the meantime. The air was ice cold.

Setting the sack with Annie's yarn on the floor, Murie donned her cloak, left the sack of yarn where it was, and hurried out to seek her father. Seeing Pluff at his favorite post near the postern gate, she asked him if he had seen Andrew.

"Aye, sure, he went out a whiles back, m'lady," the boy said, turning toward the gate. "I think he were a-heading tae Sir Mag's cottage tae visit MacAulay, but he'll no ha' got far yet. If ye follow yon path, likely ye'll fine him gey quick."

Lifting the latch, Pluff opened the gate for her.

Chapter 5 ———————————

For some time, Rob had been pleasantly sitting with his back against a warm granite slab a half-mile southeast of Mag's cottage, idly watching a flock of drifting clouds in the cerulean sky overhead, while Scáthach dozed at his feet.

The clouds were gathering slowly, as if collie angels nipped at their heels, herding them eastward. Rob watched two clouds in particular as they drifted nearer and nearer to each other, kissed, and separated. They drifted close again, then apart and close once more, as if yearning to become lovers but uncertain of the risk.

The smaller cloud, to his right, drifted farther away toward another wee one. When it did, the larger one darkened, as if angry, holding its lover at fault.

Rob grinned at the odd flight his imagination had taken. He had not thought in such a way since he was a laddie seeking animal shapes in the clouds. Nor had he thought of clouds as lovers then, potential or otherwise.

He wondered what impulse had taken his imagination in such a direction.

The splatter of raindrops caught him unaware. The sky overhead was blue, the dispersion of smaller clouds still looking carefree and innocent, although the billowing one that chased them had darkened more despite the late-morning sun.

"I think we're about to get wet, Scáthach," he murmured drowsily.

The dog perked its ears but did not move another muscle. Its muzzle rested on its forepaws. Its tail stayed still. Scáthach knew Rob's every tone and nearly every habit. Such a sleepy murmur rarely resulted in movement, let alone haste.

The single dark-gray cumulus mass seemed to slow, although the once-lazy, albeit chilly breeze from the northwest was picking up energy and the raindrops came closer together. The sky above him grew darker. Tilting his head, he saw that more clouds were drifting westward from beyond the ridge, evidently having gathered on the other side and now moving to meet the oncoming storm.

Distant, ominous rumbles from the west and steadying rain urged him to return to the cottage. He sighed, collected his wits, and got to his feet.

Scáthach opened her eyes and lifted one gray eyebrow. Then with a sigh that echoed her master's, she rose, shook herself, and awaited his command.

The first chilly drops of rain caught Murie as she passed through a clearing in the forest, making her glad that she had worn her boots and the warm, hooded cloak. Soon, she heard thunder, but the canopy overhead kept most of the rain off her. That would not be the case when she returned, though. By then the forest, still damp from the previous days of rain, would be drip-drip-dripping all over her.

She had seen no sign of her father, but she was enjoying

herself too much to think about that. He had likely taken another path, something she had realized when she had not caught up with him quickly. But she had reveled in her freedom and was in no hurry to turn back. She would be soaked before she got home, though.

Walking faster, she decided that if she could reach the Wylies' cottage before the rain grew too heavy; she could stay with Annie until it stopped. Then she could follow the river path, which dried faster, back to the tower. At this time of year, storms usually began wearing themselves out after an hour or two, although it was possible that the rain might continue through the night as it had on Tuesday.

The thought of Annie reminded her of the yarn, still in its sack near the postern door. Having had no reason to carry it while she looked for Andrew in the yard, she had forgotten about it when Pluff opened the gate for her.

"Just as well, too," she murmured. "It would only have got wet."

She could hear rain spattering on leaves high above her. The forest canopy was dense, a mixture of beech, pine, birch, and lesser trees. The evergreens were more useful now than the others, though, because the beeches—which were the tallest trees—and the birches had only just begun sprouting new leaves.

Her mother would doubtless say that she ought to turn back, but it was Murie's first outing in days, and she yearned to talk with someone besides Tibby and the other women in the tower. Yarn or none, she wanted to see Annie.

Her mother had been right in suggesting that she missed Lina and Dree more now than ever before, Murie decided. They had done nearly everything together until—

Her skin prickled as if every hair on it had risen and

gone stiff. The woods that had darkened just moments before lit up, and a deafening crack of thunder sounded so nearby and so loud that instinctively she wrapped her arms protectively around her head and folded low to the ground. It was as if the thunderclap had erupted from the nearest tree for the sole purpose of scaring her witless.

Its first reverberations were beginning when she heard other nearby cracks and crashes, as if limbs, branches, or even whole trees had fallen. Drawing breath, she straightened, but pounding rain drowned out every other sound.

It was useless now to think of going to Annie's. If she did not drown before she got there, Annie would scold her when she arrived for not having had the sense to turn back as soon as she saw clouds gathering or heard muttering thunder.

It was a pity that Andrena and Mag were gone and had let...

That random thought ended with a mischievous grin. "What would he do, do you think?" she asked the ambient air. Delight surged through her. She had been bored for days. But now, adventure beckoned.

Surely, if her father had gone that way, she would have seen him by now. Likely he had agreed to meet MacAulay elsewhere.

"If so, the cottage might be empty," she murmured.

Then, smiling again, she decided that would be good, too. She wanted to know more about Robert MacAulay, and if he *was* there, he could no more refuse to let her in than Annie would. And in any event, she would at least see if he was keeping Dree's cottage tidy or had created the chaos that so often accompanied the men of Tùr Meiloach when they slept on pallets in the great hall.

Without further ado, she altered her course, glad that Dree's cottage was closer than Annie's. Both were in the forest, but Dree's was nearer the timberline.

Lengthening her stride with increasing eagerness, Murie soon spied the cottage in a small clearing ahead. Her skin tingled again at the thought that MacAulay might be there, and she wondered if Scáthach would bark to warn him.

No sound but rain, two more cracks of thunder, and their rolling echoes greeted her approach. Hurrying to the door, she lifted the latch and entered, deciding that if he was there and unhappy to see her, she could say she had been in such a hurry to get out of the rain that she had forgotten he was staying there.

Remembering his warning about lying, she felt a distinct chill before she saw with relief that the main room was empty, and shut the door. The cottage's slate roof barely muted the drumming rain.

She saw at once that the dusky interior was as tidy as usual. Unlike most cottages on the estate, Mag's boasted not only a slate roof instead of thatch, but a front room with a hooded hearth *and* a proper chimney.

The wee kitchen beyond possessed a small stone oven built into the fireplace wall. A loft occupied the area directly above Muriella, which one could reach by means of the sturdy ladder that angled upward near the wall to her right. In the curtained corner beyond that ladder stood Mag and Andrena's bed.

With her back to the door, Murie faced the fireplace. The floor of the loft above provided a lowered ceiling for two-thirds of the front room, so it was warm. The open door to the kitchen was beside a small settle just left of the fireplace.

"Is anyone here?" she called out loudly enough for anyone in the cottage to hear her. No one replied.

Inspection proved that the front room was indeed tidy, the bed in the corner neatly made. The cauldron hanging from a pothook over glowing, half-banked coals on the hearth had mutton-scented steam puffing from under its iron lid.

That sight gave Murie pause. Surely, even in a cottage with a slate roof and a deep stone hearth, MacAulay would not have left live coals to burn untended for long. Looking into the kitchen, she saw nothing to interest her. Perhaps the loft...

Casting her cloak onto the wooden settle by the hearth, she went to the ladder, kilted her skirts up high enough to keep them out of her way, gripped the ladder's rails, and put her right foot on the bottom rung only to hesitate when she heard a slight rattle of stones outside.

Keeping an eye on the door, she listened intently but heard only wind, rain, and grumbling thunder, distant again. Deciding that a pine cone or branch must have fallen but keeping a wary eye on the door, she climbed until she could see into the loft. Faint gray light through the small loft window revealed only Wee Molly's cradle, a bundle or two that likely contained some of Mag's and Andrena's things, and a pallet like those that her father's men slept on in the tower's great hall.

"What the devil are you doing up there?"

Startled, instantly recognizing his voice, Murie froze.

He had certainly not come through the front door, but perhaps he always used the other one. In any event, although he had spoken evenly, she discerned a note in his voice that warned her to tread carefully.

He did not seem angry, though, only surprised.

Drawing breath, reminding herself to take care as she descended the ladder so she would not make a fool of herself with a misstep or fall, she glanced over a shoulder just long enough to see him filling the kitchen doorway.

Scáthach stood before him, her gray head cocked, eyeing Murie curiously.

MacAulay revealed no curiosity, but he had begun to look irritated.

Murie did not look at him again until she reached the bottommost rung. Pausing there, still reluctant to face him, she turned just enough to see that he had pressed his lips together, reminding her that she had not answered his question.

"I got caught in that downpour," she said hastily, striving to sound normal. Her voice squeaked, though, and she knew that the cause was the green, stonelike glint in his eyes when his gaze collided with hers.

She swallowed. Whatever his mood was, he was not happy to see her. Unable to think, let alone to take that last step to the floor or speak, she moved her right hand to her mouth and nervously nibbled a fingernail.

Rob stared at her, wondering just how foolhardy she was. To have come into the cottage when she must have known that a man she scarcely knew and had no reason whatsoever to trust was staying there alone—

His body's sudden stirring stopped that thought in midflight. With her damp plaits loosened, her pink skirt rucked up as high as it was, and one finger in her mouth, she resembled an untidy child. But the softly rounded breasts under her bodice, and her splendidly shaped knees and calves, proved that she was *not* a child.

Nevertheless, the uncertain way she eyed him now made him want to reassure her, even comfort her, instead of telling her bluntly what he thought of her behavior. So perhaps he was the one who was mad. A suspicion stirred that she was accustomed to disarming even truly angry men in just this sort of way.

His body stirred again at that thought, so sharply that he was glad he was able to hold her gaze and keep it focused on his *face*.

He said, "Why are you out alone in this storm and so far from the tower?"

With a slight shrug and still looking into his eyes, she said, "I was going to visit Annie Wylie. She is married to Malcolm, our steward."

"I do recall that," he said. "Their daughter, Tibby, is your maid, is she not?"

"She is, aye, and their Peter is one of our gillies."

"Then why is Peter not with you? Did your father not say that he should be?"

"I did not see either of them," she said, stepping down at last and turning fully to face him. "Moreover, when I asked Pluff where Father was, he said he might have come here to visit you again. Then Pluff opened the gate, so here I am."

He was glad that she stayed by the ladder, because she had evidently forgotten that she had kilted her skirt almost two inches above those splendid knees. They were barer now than any he had seen in six months.

"You should not be here," he said flatly.

She shrugged again but with a tiny, mischievous smile.

"Where else could I have found shelter so quickly?" she asked, lowering her eyelids with demureness he did not believe. "You surely won't send me back out into this dreadful storm."

Feeling stirrings of real anger that she might be truly so naïve about a matter that could create real trouble for her—perhaps even for him—Rob kept silent long enough to be sure he would say nothing more than he had good cause to say.

"Do you *fear* my being here?" she asked, looking away while she flicked something from her skirt. "You need not, you know. I can see that you are taking good care of the cottage. And I would not tell Dree or Mag even if you were not."

"It is good to know that you can keep *some* things to yourself," he said dryly.

She gave him a sour look, raised her chin, and said, "You might at least offer something to warm me. Your man seems to have left soup or a stew in that pot, and I confess that I neglected to eat enough to sustain me before I came outside."

"Then you must be hungry," he said, exerting himself to keep his eyes off the bare skin between her rucked-up skirt and the tops of the muddy rawhide boots that covered ankles and feet likely to be just as shapely as what he could see.

"However," he said firmly, "you are wrong about who left the food to cook. Mag did ask someone named Calum Beg to look in on me and see to aught I might require, but I can look after myself. I put the pot on at dawn, before I went out, but the meat was fresh yesterday and will not be ready yet to eat."

"It should be cooked enough in an hour or so, though, should it not?"

"It might be, but you will not be here," he said firmly. Much as he might enjoy the pleasures her body would offer a man, honor forbade such activities with young noblewomen to whom one was not married. Come to that, whether the lady Muriella knew what she was doing or not, she was doubtless still a maiden.

Looking at him from under her lashes in what she must have thought was a winsome or mischievous manner, she said, "But I cannot go anywhere else, Master Robert MacAulay, not until this rain stops."

"You are wrong about that," he said, measuring his words and holding her gaze again. "You are going home."

Before Murie could overcome the stunning effect that his stern gaze was having on her, let alone contradict him, he added, "You had to see how early those clouds appeared this morning. You must also have smelled rain in the air again. Therefore, to have come out at all was foolish. To come this far, by yourself, means only that you will reap the results of such behavior. The consequences—"

"But you are *creating* the consequences!" she exclaimed, her anger igniting. "If you were at all chivalrous, you would *protect* me from them."

"Sakes, lass, I am trying to protect you. You must know you have no business being alone here with me, or I with you."

"But if you cared about my safety—"

"Don't interrupt me again," he said curtly.

And rudely interrupted her *to do so!*

She would have liked to tell him just what she thought of such rudeness, because it was certainly more disrespectful for a gentleman to interrupt a lady than the other way around. However, the look he was giving her warned her that he might reveal even greater rudeness if she pushed him too far.

⁓

Easily reading her reaction and determined not to let her fire up his temper to match hers, Rob continued calmly to explain that she should not trust any man she barely knew. When she started to interrupt him again, he gave her another look that silenced her before she could, and caused her to put that finger in her mouth again.

"Don't do that," he said.

Snatching the hand away and holding it at her waist with the other one, as if she had heard such commands before, she scowled and said, "You cannot mean to send me back out into that horrid storm. I'll drown!"

"You won't drown. The rain has eased, and the thunder has moved on, so no lightning bolt will strike you, either. You know as well as I do that you cannot stay here. Only think what Mag would say to you—and to me, come to that—if he learned that you had done so. You have already stayed too long."

"But I don't *want* to go. I'll be soaked through!"

"Which is, I'm afraid, exactly what you deserve," he retorted, picking up her cloak from where it lay on the nearby settle. "You will dry off quickly when you get home, so I doubt you'll catch as much as a cold from the experience."

Striding to the front door, he pulled it open before he could change his mind and held her cloak for her until she unkilted her skirts and came close enough for him to drape it over her shoulders. Then, still stern and commanding, he gestured for her to be on her way and waited implacably until, with one more furious look at him and her chin in the air, she stepped outside.

He watched until she moved out from under the eaves into the downpour.

~

Muttering under her breath, Muriella stalked out of the cottage, certain that if she did not obey him, MacAulay would pick her up and throw her out. The moment she left the shelter of the jutting eaves, however, the rain enveloped her. She could barely see her way across the clearing, but snatching up her skirts, she ran.

How she wished she could command Scáthach to bite the beastly man!

That thought brought an unladylike snort. The dog had lain quietly by the hearth and watched sleepily with its head on its forepaws while they talked.

Glancing back as she raced across the open space to the trees, Murie saw that the door had shut behind her.

He had not even been polite enough to shout farewell.

"Putting me out of my own sister's cottage, too," she muttered. "What sort of brute dares to order a lady outside into such a deluge?"

The last word made her smile, mocking herself. It was hardly a deluge now that she was amidst the trees again. Faith, it wasn't that much of a storm anymore. The lightning and thunder had moved on and were no longer a threat, although the rain was heavy enough in the open and the trees were dripping enough now to soak her to the skin long before she got home.

She would not return to the tower yet, she decided. She would go on to Annie's, which was closer and where she could dry out and get warm. Annie might scold. She surely would if she learned where Murie had been, and with whom. But Annie would see that she got warm, and Annie would have food to share.

~

Inside the cottage, Rob tried not to think about her ladyship, reminding himself again that actions always had consequences, and consequences formed the best pathways to better decisions. Better that she suffer a soaking than the cost she might have suffered had he been a different sort of man.

Warriors often took their pleasures where they found them, and the chivalry she mentioned had long since become scarce in the Highlands, if indeed, chivalry had ever held sway there. Jamie Stewart and his beloved queen, Joanna, might hope to encourage chivalry again, but, for more than two decades, Scotland had been a lawless, untamable country.

Rob knew he might easily have become like many other noble heirs, who grew up believing that when they inherited their father's lands, they could simply impose their will on their tenants as nobles in the past had done. His father had taught him otherwise, and Rob's own experiences as a warrior and leader of other warriors had taught him even more than Lord MacAulay had about some things.

Lady Muriella had seemed only naïve when she had put herself in Dougal MacPharlain's path. But today's behavior proved she had learned nowt from that experience.

Pluff would have done better to have kept the postern gate shut this morning, and he might have done her a greater favor that first day by just keeping silent.

Shaking that angry and admittedly stupid thought from his head, Rob thought instead of the way she had stomped outside before the driving rain had chased her across the clearing through its puddles. Even that image failed to cheer him.

What if something did happen to her? How would he feel then? How much of his anger arose from the fact that she had invaded his privacy as she had?

To Scáthach, he said soberly, "I suppose we cannot let her tramp home alone without making sure that she gets there safely, can we, lass? I'll just change from this wet tunic into my leathers and fetch my wool cap and an oilskin. Then we'll go after her. She need never even know that we are following her."

〜

Having turned onto the narrower, less traveled path to the Wylies' cottage, Muriella cursed MacAulay again under her breath. In truth, she would rather have shrieked her curse to the heavens, or wherever curses flew. But shrieking with one's head down, to avoid an unfortunate sluice of icy water into one's face from the overhanging trees, or worse, into one's hood or down one's neck, was nearly impossible and the feeble result not worth the effort.

Water had soaked through her rawhide boots, so her feet were wet and getting cold. Under her cloak, her clothing felt damp against her skin.

Thanks to the thick fur-lined wool of that cloak, and by tucking her hands into her armpits, she was warm enough otherwise. Nevertheless, Annie's cottage seemed farther from Dree's than it had ever seemed before.

"May the devil fly away with that horrid man," she muttered grimly.

With her head down, her hood limited the view ahead while she watched her footing on the narrow path. By glancing up now and then to mark her progress she also made sure that she did not inadvertently bump into any lurking low branch.

Her gaze had lingered on the wet pathway for some time when suddenly a pair of large black boots appeared right before her, their toes pointing her way.

She looked up into Dougal MacPharlain's smirking face.

"Ay-de-mi," he murmured. "How thoughtful of ye to meet me here, lass."

Rob loped across the clearing faster than her ladyship had, with Scáthach splashing at his heels. He slowed when he reached the trail to Andrew's tower but lengthened his stride. He hoped she had not got too far ahead but had no reason to hurry until it occurred to him that if she was still angry and getting well soaked, she would be walking faster than usual, perhaps even running.

Scáthach ranged ahead, moving here and there around trees and shrubbery as if she were finding interesting scents beneath the leaves and not following any particular scent. Surely, the lass would not have taken such a circuitous route. The path between Mag's cottage and the tower was plain to see.

They soon came to a place where Scáthach hesitated and glanced at Rob. He saw that a barely discernible fisherman's path forked away downhill and northward along a rushing but still narrow rill that rainwater was trying to turn into a burn.

"If you are saying that we might want to hurry back, lest we have to ford this thing later, I do see it," Rob said. "But I'll wager it won't get wider than a foot or two." He gestured for the dog to move on and stepped across the rill to follow.

Moments later, Scáthach paused to shake herself after passing under leafy, low-hanging, wet shrubbery, and Rob realized that anyone moving ahead of them would have struck the branches in passing. Muriella could not possibly be so far ahead that, in the time since her passage, the shrubs had loaded up again with water.

He called the dog to heel and made his way more carefully. Studying the path and shrubbery, he soon became certain that her ladyship had not passed that way.

"She must have gone to the Wylies'," he muttered.

A barely audible canine sound of inquiry drew his glance back to the dog.

Scáthach's head was up, her muzzle aimed northeastward. Just then, Rob heard a distant, unnatural sound but one clearly audible over the rain still pelting the canopy above. It sounded like a bird's cry, but—

The sound came more loudly, shockingly recognizable as a woman's scream.

Signaling Scáthach to lead the way, Rob set off running toward the sound.

⌒

Muriella fought Dougal fiercely, but her strength was no match for his. When she screamed, he clapped a hand across her mouth. She bit him.

He snatched his hand away long enough for her to scream again but clapped it back so hard that she tasted blood and feared he might have loosened her teeth.

Holding her tightly against him, he put his mouth to her ear and said grimly, "I will make you sorry that you did that, lass. If you do it again, I'll knock you senseless and carry you the rest of the way." Taking what looked like a rag from somewhere under his plaid, as well as a slender rope, he ordered her to open her mouth, stuffed the rag in willy-nilly, and tied the rope across it to keep it in.

She wanted to tell him that she could barely breathe. Faith, she wanted to kill him! But she could do neither, so she fought to calm herself and to think.

Her first thought was that MacAulay would say she had come by her just desserts again because she had not obeyed his order to go straight home. Tears sprang to her eyes at the thought of home. What would Dougal do to her?

As if in answer to that question, he released her, saying, "Move along, lass. I'll carry ye if I have to, because ye canna weigh more than a bundle o' feathers. I'd liefer not do that, but I will if I must, and it'd be right painful for ye."

When she hesitated, he shoved her up the slope ahead of him toward the pass. She walked obediently until he pushed her again and ordered her to go faster. Stumbling on a loose rock, she cried out under the gag but let herself fall, hoping to slow him down, just in case anyone had heard her scream.

Chapter 6

Through the still-driving rain, Rob scanned the few portions he could see of the high, rocky slope beyond the woods. Several times he caught sight of movement between the trees, but he could not tell exactly what it was that he was seeing.

Nearing the edge of the woodland, he saw brief movement again, near the pass where he had spied Dougal days before. Fear surged through him at that memory, but he forced it back into the recesses of his mind. He would do no one any good by leaping to conclusions before he had gleaned a reliable fact or two.

When he emerged from the trees and Scáthach stepped ahead of him, he saw that despite the rain, fur on the scruff of her neck had bristled, making her tension clear to the man who had trained her. He murmured, "Doucely, lass, doucely."

Her perked ears twitched in response, but she kept close instead of ranging yards ahead, as usual. Although such behavior suggested that she anticipated danger, he knew she was likely only sensing and mimicking his state of mind.

Two figures came into view on the steep, boulder-strewn slope, two-thirds of the way to the pass. One, clearly female, walked just ahead of the other.

Recognizing Lady Muriella easily, Rob reached to be sure his sword was secure in its sheath, and the sheath secure on its baldric. He did not want to lose it while scrambling up the slope, although he knew that the other two were too near the pass for him to catch up with them before they reached it.

"Doucely, Scá," he said again as he increased his pace. He had nearly come out barefoot, as he had that morning, for he often walked so in sunshine or rain and had assumed that he would be following the lass on damp, spongy ground. At the last minute, finding his boots beside the oiled skins, he had decided to wear them.

Grateful for the decision now, since raw leather would grip wet, slick granite better than bare feet would, he moved as fast as the rugged terrain allowed.

The next time he looked up, he saw that Muriella had fallen.

Growling low in his throat at the sight, Rob murmured, "I shall owe Dougal something special for letting *that* happen."

Scáthach growled, too, and eyed Rob tensely.

Although he understood the dog's uneasiness, he said, "Nay, lass. I'd be glad to see you put an end to that villain. But he'd likely see you coming, and I fear he'd be too skillful with his dirk for your safety or hers. He could injure or kill you both before I could catch up with you, so we'll keep them in sight and seek a better chance to take him down."

Aware that he was just thinking aloud, Rob lengthened his stride, giving thanks for the oiled skin as well as the boots. Not only was the rain still pelting down, but if he had to follow them far, he'd be camping that night under oilskin.

Her ladyship was standing again. Mayhap she would have the sense to limp or do something else to slow them down.

As the thought occurred to him, he saw Dougal pick her up as if she weighed nowt and sling her over a shoulder.

Being picked up and flipped over onto Dougal's shoulder knocked the wind out of Murie but did not seem to affect Dougal at all. She tried to kick him, but the devilish man pinned her cloak-covered knees to his chest with one steely forearm. Then, using his other hand to steady himself as they went, he strode up the treacherous path with more speed than she thought could possibly be safe.

At least he had taken the awful gag from her mouth after she had fallen, so she could breathe more easily, and the rain was no longer stinging her face.

To think that I wanted *to see that wretched pass*, she reminded herself, trying not to watch the rocks slipping downward each time he took a step upward. When that thought ended, the image of Robert MacAulay filled her mind's eye, frowning as heavily as he had when she had lied to him. Her memory shifted abruptly to the truth, that he had not frowned at all then. His expression and demeanor had remained as stoic as usual. So why did she feel now as if he *had* frowned?

And why was she able to picture that frown so easily?

The answer was not far to seek. She had sensed anger in the man at the time. But, having focused on his face, expecting him to frown, she had ignored what she was sensing. She had simply allowed herself to feel relieved that he was calm.

To divert her thoughts from MacAulay, she raised her head from Dougal's back and observed the slope below. However, so strong was MacAulay in her mind that she imagined she saw him following them through the downpour. Boulders obstructed the phantomlike image then, making her certain she had imagined it.

Even so, and despite lacking strength enough to keep her head up for long with Dougal bouncing her as he picked a path amid wet bounders on wet granite, she raised it as soon as they moved into the open and she could see the slope again.

Seeing Scáthach trotting ahead of him told her that it really was MacAulay. Oh, why did he not order the fleet wolf-dog to kill Dougal?

The voice of common sense—one that, admittedly, she rarely heeded—suggested that Dougal might be wholly willing and able to kill the dog.

She continued to hope that MacAulay would catch up with them. Hard as it was to keep her head up enough to track his progress, she kept trying to do so until Dougal smacked her hard enough on the backside, even through two skirts and her cloak, to make her cry out.

"Stop wriggling," he snapped, "or I'll skelp ye good to *make* ye mind me."

"Do your worst," she retorted. "It won't help you, because someone is following us. When he catches you, *you* will be the one who is sorry."

To her shock, he chuckled, patted her backside again, and said, "Sakes, lass, d'ye think I've failed to plan for such?"

A chill swept through her. "What have you done?"

But Dougal just chuckled again, a fiendish sound if

ever she had heard one. Only then did she wonder why they had not met any of her father's watchers.

———

Rob saw that Dougal had reached the pass and disappeared amid the huge boulders there. But Rob, too, was making rapid progress and still had a good chance to catch them, especially since Dougal was carrying her ladyship.

The continuing rain was irritating, and the steepness of the slope took its toll on Rob, but the danger to Muriella and the plain fact that he bore at least some responsibility for her predicament spurred him on.

Reaching the crest of the slope, where its steepness eased at last, he could easily discern the way they had to have gone. Sheer, rocky walls and high cliffs flanked the uneven, boulder-strewn declivity that evidently served as the pass.

It looked as if someone had rolled boulders off those walls to block the way, though. Certainly no army could invade Tùr Meiloach by this route.

"Trail, Scáthach," he said. The dog's nose went down, up, then to ground again. Her ability unimpeded by the rain, she trotted confidently, following a mixed but unmistakable scent of humans that revealed the most common route to her.

As he followed, Rob's thoughts drifted back to Andrew's defenses and the guards who had stopped him at the south pass that first evening. In truth, both times he had taken that route to Tùr Meiloach, watchers had guarded it closely.

So where were Andrew's watchers today? He had seen

no one keeping guard and doubted that Andrew's men would dare use rain as an excuse for shirking their duty. Also, although Andrew had said that his watchers let lone intruders pass but watched them carefully, no one had stopped Dougal on Monday or today, despite his having had a screaming, doubtless struggling Lady Muriella in tow.

Frowning, Rob ignored a flow of images depicting what Dougal *might* do to her and considered instead what he might have *done* to Andrew's guards.

None of it eased his concern.

As he stopped, he spoke softly to halt Scáthach. Then, untying and doffing his oilskin, he shifted his baldric to draw his sword. Putting the baldric back where it belonged, he held the oilskin in place with his free hand and went on.

Making his way through the rubble-strewn pass with Scáthach moving confidently before him, he walked more rapidly than he would have on his own and soon was close enough to the east end of the pass to see the snowcapped peak of Ben Lomond looming into the sodden, gray northeastern sky.

The loch of that name soon came into sight below, its long, narrow northern tip all that he could see. The greater part, miles south of him, widened into an eventual five-mile expanse at its outflowing end. Without the rain, he knew he would likely see where the widening began. Mag had said the place lay twelve miles north of Inch Galbraith, his father's island seat in the wider part of the loch. A few miles north of where Rob stood lay Arrochar and its Tarbet, a narrow neck of land that was flat enough for men to drag their boats from Loch Lomond to the upper end of the Loch of the Long Boats and the other way around.

From Arrochar's Tarbet to the north end of Loch Lomond, Mag had said, was yet another seven miles. The loch's west shore from Galbraith's land northward was all MacFarlan land.

Pausing when the path began to slope downward toward the loch, Rob saw his quarry below but much farther down the path than he had anticipated.

Neither Lady Muriella nor Dougal was walking now. Evidently, Dougal had left a horse waiting, and not the usual small but surefooted Highland garron. Instead, the bay was large enough to carry them both with apparent ease.

Since Rob was as sure as he could be that her ladyship would not have mounted such a horse unaided, let alone with dispatch, he surmised that Dougal had put her on the horse, ordered her to sit astride, and then mounted behind her. They were moving rapidly down a track that, by comparison to the pass itself or the rough track on Andrew's side, looked rubble free. Realizing that he'd be unlikely to catch them before they reached Arrochar, Rob thought he might do better to—

Scáthach growled.

Whirling, casting the oilskin like a whip ahead of him as he did, Rob saw a longsword blade descending toward his head and—just beyond it—a flash of movement that he recognized as Scáthach leaping at something or someone.

⁓

"I wish you would not hold me so tightly," Muriella said. "I don't like it."

"Be quiet unless ye want me to gag ye again," Dougal said. "Had I known what a bletherer ye are, I'd ha' thought twice afore abducting ye."

"Then I wish you *had* known," she said with feeling. "If you want me to be quiet, then tell me what sort of traps you laid for my father's watchers and whoever is following us now. Whatever you contrived, I doubt it will succeed."

"Och, but it will," he said with the same awful confidence he had shown before. "Whoever followed us earlier is not following us now."

She knew that was true, because after he had put her on his horse, she had taken a look backward whenever the path curved. To her regret, she saw no one.

"You simply cannot see him in this rain," she said, striving to sound as confident as Dougal had. "I'll wager you don't know who he is, either."

"I don't care who he is. My lads will see to him."

So he had posted armed guards to shield his escape.

Somewhat daunted by that realization, she said nonetheless firmly, "You *should* care who it is. My goodbrothers say that Master Robert MacAulay is one of the finest warriors they know. And *you* must know that Sir Ian Colquhoun and Sir Magnus Mòr Galbraith-MacFarlan are two of the finest knights in all of Scotland."

"They *think* they are," he muttered.

She recalled then that he did know them both, and better than he might have liked. So she said sweetly and with a fervent hope that neither Mag nor Ian would ever hear what she had said, "I do not know about such things, for no female can. But, if I recall aright, *they* said MacAulay is a *much* finer warrior and *much* more skilled with a sword and a dirk than either one of them is."

He made a strange groaning sound in his throat.

"What was that you said?" she asked innocently. "I did not quite hear you."

"I said nowt. Now, hold your tongue."

If MacAulay *was* somehow still following them, Murie decided, she had to do whatever she could to divert Dougal's attention. Accordingly, she said, "Ian said that MacAulay once defeated six opponents all by himself."

"Blethers."

"I know, but Ian did say that," Murie said lightly. "In troth, I did not believe him at the time. But then Mag said that he had *seen* MacAulay take on four or five men, so I do think now that Ian's six might well be possible."

Dougal fell silent then, which was eminently satisfactory to her, especially if he was worrying about MacAulay.

He looked back up the hill behind them, though, and that would not do.

She tried another topic. "You do seem to like abducting young women, which I think is a most dishonorable trait in a man. In troth, though, you have not been a successful abductor, have you? I know of at least two who outwitted—"

"Devil take ye," he swore. "It were bad enough that ye made up that bletherish tale, calling me Donal Blackheart and reciting it at God kens how many *ceilidhs*. But, by God, I'll soon teach ye the wisdom to hold your tongue!"

Murie shut her eyes, wincing in horror of what she might have unleashed.

⁓

Focusing on the sword slashing down toward his head, Rob leaped sideways and, with one hand, brought his own sword up so fast and hard that it crashed against the other one and wrenched it from his opponent's grip. As it flew with a clatter into the rocks, Rob gripped his own sword's hilt with both hands and whipped the flat of its blade back hard against the side of his opponent's head.

The man lost his footing on the treacherous ground, fell, and cracked his head against a boulder.

Scáthach's man was also down and still, blood still oozing from a wound in his neck, the dirk he had wielded lying some distance away. The dog stood guard over him with every muscle and sense alert.

Scarcely had Rob noted these facts than, with a shout of fury, a third swordsman appeared from behind a boulder, accompanied by a fourth.

"Weapon!" Rob bellowed when he saw the fourth man move toward Scáthach. The dog was too agile and quick to let a swordsman hurt her, and she would now do all that she could to keep the villain occupied.

With the well-sharpened point of his own blade and without ceremony, Rob dispatched the nearest man and then whirled to confront the one still standing.

That chap, suddenly finding himself between the darting, growling dog and a highly skilled swordsman, turned tail from both and ran.

Catching him easily, Rob jerked him back and around.

The man flung down his sword and cried, "I yield, sir. Prithee, I yield!"

Since none of the four attackers had tried to aid Lady Muriella, Rob deduced that this one, like the others, was Dougal's minion.

A sweeping look at the three on the ground, unmoving, told Rob they were dead, and he felt no remorse. To attack a man from behind was a dishonorable act for any warrior. They had brought death on themselves.

"Prithee, sir," the live one cried. "We did nobbut what we was told tae do."

Keeping the man's right arm in an iron grip, Rob said, "You and these others take your orders from Dougal MacPharlain, aye?"

"Aye, sir. Though, we all of us answer tae Pharlain in the end."

"Did you see the lady with Dougal?"

"Aye, sure, though, in troth, sir, I…I ha' me doots she'd be a lady." The man was shaking, either from fear or from cold.

Rob did not care which it was. "Do you not know who she is?"

The man shrugged. "She were comely enough. So, 'tis likely, she be a lass Dougal wants. He takes his pleasures where he finds 'em, and we all ken fine that Pharlain keeps a spy or two at Tùr Meiloach. Mayhap she'd be one o' them."

"Was she not struggling to escape from Dougal?"

The man hesitated.

Hardening his tone, Rob said, "Was she not?"

Visibly swallowing, the other nodded. "Aye, but if a chappie values his hide, he doesna put hisself betwixt Dougal and his lassies—or nowt else, come tae that."

Rob's hands itched to smack the man. He held his fire, though, aware that the person he really wanted to punish was riding farther away by the minute.

Therefore, he said grimly, "That *lady* is Andrew Dubh MacFarlan's youngest daughter, the lady Muriella. Dougal abducted her by force. Since it is the second time he has taken one of Andrew's daughters, I mean to teach him better manners, but I will leave you to bury your friends if you can figure out how to do that."

"Aye, I'll bury 'em," the other said on a note of relief. "I'll dig wi' me dirk."

"You will not, for I mean to dispose of your weapons over the first cliff I come to," Rob said. "You can dig your friends' graves with your hands, or you can go back to Pharlain and Dougal and tell them where they lie, or..."

He paused, eyeing the man's ashen face thoughtfully.

"Prithee, m'lord, I canna tell Pharlain or Dougal we failed. They'd order me flogged for no being dead m'self. Sakes, I'd liefer niver go back there at all."

"Then I'll offer you one more choice," Rob said. "Go through yonder pass to Andrew Dubh's tower and tell him all that happened here. Then yield to him."

"But them what go to Tùr Meiloach do never be seen again," the man cried. "Rockslides claim them if bogs or vicious birds and beasts dinna get 'em first."

"But true MacFarlans are safe at Tùr Meiloach, because its land provides sanctuary for them," Rob said gently. "Men say that, too, do they not?"

"Aye, but I ha' long served Pharlain. Andrew Dubh would be more like tae hang me than gi' me sanctuary."

"I have heard that Andrew welcomes any MacFarlan who swears fealty to him. Sithee, though, I'm told he can tell if the swearing is heartfelt or not," Rob warned, seeing no reason to add the fact that he disbelieved that part himself.

"If I say it, I'll mean it," his erstwhile assailant said morosely. "In troth, I've nae choice. But likewise, I've nae wife nor bairn at Arrochar tae miss me. I'll go."

"Good, but tell me one more thing before you do. Were there not watchers up here—Andrew's watchers?"

The man tensed again but said, "Aye, there were, but

Dougal said tae render them harmless. So them lads ye just killed, they killed them all and said that, by Pharlain's reckoning, that were the only way they'd *stay* harmless."

"You had nowt to do with their deaths?"

"No tae say 'nowt,' sir," the man said wretchedly. "I watched tae be sure nae one else interfered."

"I'll not hold you responsible for that, but go quickly before I change my mind," Rob said. "Tell Andrew Dubh that I'll make sure Dougal and her ladyship are truly heading for Arrochar and will report back to him as quick as I can."

"They'll be going tae Arrochar, aye," the man said. "Dougal were a-cursing the rain when we got here. He'll be gey wroth with it by now."

Nodding but unwilling to trust the man completely, Rob followed him long enough to be sure he continued west through the pass. Then, calling Scáthach to heel, he made his way back as fast as he could to where the four had attacked him.

Returning his sword to its baldric and the sheath that protected its sharp end and tip, he collected the other men's weapons and hid them well off the path.

Being soaked through and no longer planning to spend the night out, he left his oiled skin where it lay, to retrieve later, and took a minute to slick his hair back from his forehead and retie it at his nape. Then, pulling his wet wool cap on again for added warmth, he set out, cautiously traversing the steep, wet slope of talus and scree beneath the precipitous ridge that extended northward from the pass.

Scáthach moved in his wake with graceful ease, either unaware that she was soaked to the skin and traversing a dangerous slope or indifferent to both facts.

The two riders below had reached the Lomondside

path. Rob had no fear that they might see him or Scáthach, although he could see them, because looking downward kept the rain from pelting his face as he watched them. Looking up through the downpour, as they would have to do to see him, would be much harder.

He let his thoughts dwell briefly on an image of the rain drowning Dougal if he looked up long enough, but focused on keeping them in sight. That the route Rob had chosen was a more dangerous one than theirs did not trouble him one whit.

Firmly gagged again and grateful that Dougal had done no worse, Murie tried to imagine how she could escape. For the first time in her life, though, her imagination failed to provide mental relief from the reality of her situation. She tried to focus on what she had heard described in folk tales or otherwise about people escaping from dreadful danger. Instead, images of Robert MacAulay failing to fight off dozens of attackers filled her mind's eye.

In every one of them, he fell quickly and lay where his attackers left him.

With tears welling in her eyes, she remembered her strange dream, when he had flung Dougal into the clouds, and wondered if that might mean she shared some of Lina's prophetic abilities. That hope soon died, though. If she shared the gift of prophecy, would not the images that had just come to her be the prophetic ones?

If they were not, how would she know the difference?

Considering that you were wanting to murder the man just hours ago, a mean voice in her head whispered...

What it might have whispered next, she did not know,

because she shut her ears to it in much the same way that earlier she had shut her eyes to Dougal's anger. She would not, must not, think of MacAulay being dead. Reminding herself that Mag and Ian *had* said that Rob was a fine warrior, albeit no finer than either of them, Murie let herself hope that MacAulay was at least skilled enough to fight off any man stupid enough to serve Dougal.

Not that she cared so much about Robert MacAulay, she told herself firmly. He *had* tried to follow her and must have had thoughts, at least, about rescuing her. For doing even that much, one was obliged to be grateful enough to pray that he was alive. Because, if he was dead, *no one* would know what had become of her.

Fortunately, her cloak and the heat of Dougal's body against her back and legs kept most of her warm, but she had been hungry for a long time now. The aroma of the steam emanating from MacAulay's cauldron had merely teased her senses before. Now she could hear and feel her stomach growling. She had missed her midday meal, and with the supper hour drawing nearer each minute...

"I ken fine that ye're hungry, lass," Dougal said as if he were hearing her thoughts, or her stomach. "My lads and I ate the food we brought with us at midday, so I've nowt to give ye, but we'll reach Arrochar by suppertime, and we'll be near enough to hear the bell ring even if we're a bit late."

She would have liked to say that she would eat no food he provided. But, since she could not talk, she made no reply. Her stomach rumbled again, though.

The rest of their ride was uneventful, and tedious. Although she kept hoping that someone would rescue her, no one did, but she realized that she *was* a little curious about Arrochar. After all, it had been her parents' home until her sister Andrena was born, and Murie had never clapped eyes on the place.

Darkness descended, and the rain continued, so at first all she saw were pinpricks of light that shimmered in the rain. She was soaked to the skin by then, her hair dripping even under her hood. But she kept warm enough until Dougal drew rein before a small stone outbuilding and dismounted.

"I'll help ye down, lass," he said. But she had already leaned forward, thrown her right leg over the horse's rump, and splashed to the ground.

Dougal caught her by an arm as if he feared she might try to run, but she was grateful, because she had trouble just standing. She felt tired and weak but retained spirit enough to tell herself that she was *not* afraid of Dougal.

Then he took her to the stone building, which was no more than a shed. Removing her gag, he pulled the door open to reveal the darkness within and shoved her inside.

Stumbling over her skirts on the uneven dirt floor, Murie nearly fell. The door slammed shut, and she heard a heavy bar fall into place on the other side.

"May God rot your black heart and soul and see you underground for this, Dougal MacPharlain," she muttered into the unknown, terrifying blackness. "If He does not, I swear that when I get out of here, I *will*."

Although cursing him did make her feel better for a moment, it was sheer bravado.

The one place a fertile imagination is a dreadful affliction is in a small, pitch-dark, doubtless spider-filled shed with its walls rapidly closing in on one.

Chapter 7 ——————

Tùr Meiloach

Rob met Andrew Dubh, a number of his men, and four Highland garrons halfway between the pass and the timberline. The rain had eased at last to a drizzle, but Rob was soaked and tired. Greeting Andrew with more relief than any other emotion, he said, "I found your fallen men, sir. They all lie to the right of the path where it begins to slope down, so I trust you've brought torches."

"Aye, well-wrapped ones, tinderboxes, as well." Andrew turned to the two men walking right behind him and said, "Take three or four others and the garrons. Ye'll bury our lads in our graveyard, o' course, after ye bury them others. If ye need more shovels or aught else, send someone, and I'll see ye get all ye need."

"Aye, laird," the two said in unison.

"Where is she, lad?" Andrew demanded as he turned and they started back down the slope toward the woods.

"Dougal has her, sir. I assume that his chap found the tower and told you what happened."

"Aye, he did, and swore fealty to me, withal. I told him I'd decide in the morning what to do with him, but likely I'll keep him. I canna blame the man for obeying Dougal's orders, as he says he did. Pharlain isna the right-ful chief of Clan Farlan, but he has acted as such for so long that even folks who support me but still live on the land he controls have nae choice but to obey him. Jamie's Inverness Parliament may change that, though."

"'*May*' change it?" Rob said, surprised. "I thought you were going to prove *your* rightful claim to Arrochar there."

"I thought so, too," Andrew said. "But to do that, I must be able to present my royal charters to his grace."

"Do you fear that someone might seize them on the way to Inverness?"

"Nay, for I'm canny enough to protect them from theft." With a grimace, Andrew added dourly, "In troth, I canna lay my hands on them just now."

"Sakes, sir, don't you know where they are?"

"I did until last summer when they vanished," Andrew said. "I dinna want to talk about that now, though. Tell me instead how the devil that contermacious lassie of mine contrived to get herself abducted by Dougal MacPharlain."

"She told me she had come looking for you, sir," Rob said.

"Our Pluff told me as much, aye. I expect she were hoping for permission to walk outside the wall after her confinement, and Pluff didna ken he should keep her in. Sithee, I hadna told him or the others to do so, because I'd liefer not humiliate her so. But how did ye come to know what happened to her?"

Without hesitation, Rob said, "I walked out with Scáthach this morning and stayed away until the rain began. When I returned to the cottage, I found that she had taken shelter inside."

Andrew snorted. "More likely, the curious lass took advantage of a few raindrops to see how ye were living in the cottage."

The image of her ladyship on the ladder, peering into the loft, leaped to Rob's mind. "I won't debate that," he said. "I told her she should not be there, and when she said I'd not dare send her back out in the rain, I said it was the natural consequence of her own actions and put her outside with orders to go home."

"Good on ye, then," Andrew said, nodding.

"I don't know about that, sir," Rob said, grimacing. "I was thinking about her reputation—and my own, come to that. The result, though, was that instead of returning to the tower, she went toward the Wylies' cottage and ran into Dougal."

"How d'ye ken that?"

Rob explained, adding, "I'm afraid I had put Dougal's trespassing out of my head, sir, believing that he would not do it again. But he did."

"Aye, that's plain."

"When I heard her ladyship scream, I ran toward the slope and saw them heading up toward the pass." Rob did not mention Muriella's fall or Dougal's manner of carrying her, but he did tell Andrew about the horse.

"Had he nae others with him save the men he'd left to guard his back?"

"None that I saw," Rob said cautiously.

Andrew nodded.

Rob said, "Dougal's man told me he was sure that Dougal would take her to Arrochar, but I followed high along the ridge and far enough to see that he was right before coming back here. I sent him to you because I knew you'd want to know about her ladyship and see to your dead. We must not leave Lady Muriella long at Arrochar, sir. Her reputation will be in shreds afterward now, in any event."

"Nay, nay," Andrew said. He added bluntly, "Likely, Dougal hopes to marry the lass, so he and Pharlain will take care to prevent any suspicion of rape."

Rob stared at him, wanting to ask why the devil he would voice such an evil prospect for his daughter. Fighting down that unexpected surge of fury, he reminded himself that Andrew was entitled to his opinions, even if they were daft. Then he said with forced calm, "I'm not sure that even Pharlain controls Dougal."

"Aye, 'tis true," Andrew said with a heavy sigh. "Dougal may be as self-willed as our Muriella is. Mayhap they deserve each other."

Rob glowered at him.

Andrew seemed not to notice.

Both men fell silent then, because Rob could not trust himself to speak respectfully and they had come to the woods. It was much darker under the canopy than in the open, but Rob had excellent night vision and assumed that his host did, too. It did take a moment, though, before he could see clearly ahead.

A short time later, Andrew glanced back at the men following them and then looked upward. "I dinna hear the rain on the leaves now," he said. "Likely, it has stopped, but ye'll sleep at the tower, lad. I want to hear all ye can tell me."

"I'll need dry clothes and food," Rob said. "I have both at the cottage, so with your permission, I'll head there now and meet you at the tower."

"Ye'll sleep at the tower," Andrew insisted. "We must plan what to do, aye?"

"Aye, sir," Rob said equably.

"Be ye sure ye can find your way to and fro in this darkness?"

"Without difficulty, sir. I have Scáthach, and her nose is keen."

"Aye, well, watch out for boggarts," Andrew said. "Ye ken fine that Tùr Meiloach boasts guardians of its own."

Rob resisted the sudden, strong urge to roll his eyes.

Arrochar House

Dougal faced his father in the spacious but simply appointed great hall of Arrochar House. Pharlain had ordered everyone else out when his son told him what he had done. The silence since then had lengthened until Dougal ached to break it. He knew better than to say more, though, until he could judge Pharlain's reaction.

So far, he had revealed none.

After clearing the hall, Pharlain had poured claret into his own mug from a jug on the high table but offered none to Dougal. Nor had he invited him to sit or to eat, although plenty of food remained on the table. The gillies had departed in haste before clearing it.

Pharlain was a large man with thinning salt-and-pepper hair that had once been as dark and thick as Andrew Dubh's. He had similar dark-blue eyes, too. Dougal thought the two men resembled each other in many other ways, more so than most cousins. Pharlain's build was heavier than Andrew's and he was grayer, but he had defeated Andrew before and Dougal was sure he would do so again.

"Why did ye take her?" Pharlain asked at last, his low-pitched voice and even tone still concealing his emotions.

"She walked right into me during the storm," Dougal said with a shrug. "We were but a short distance from the pass, so I carried her over it and put her on my horse. I've locked her in the old shed near the stables. I knew that I should tell you before I showed her to anyone else."

"Surely, other people saw her."

"Only two or three of our own who were in the yard. The rain kept everyone off the Lomondside path. And I put her in the shed without anyone seeing her face."

"What d'ye mean tae do with her?"

"I can think of more than one possibility, sir."

Pharlain gestured for him to continue.

"First, we might bargain with Andrew Dubh. Perhaps we might offer to exchange the lass for Tùr Meiloach."

"He wouldna agree tae that," Pharlain said. "Forbye, having brought her here under duress, as ye did, ye'll ha' destroyed her good name. Nae one else will marry her, and God kens that marrying off a third daughter be nae easy task tae begin. Now, wi' things in an uproar as they be wi' that devil's spawn, Jamie Stewart, on the throne… ay-de-mi!"

"Perhaps I should marry her myself," Dougal said. "We could make it look like a romance, an elopement, could we not?"

Pharlain frowned heavily enough to send a chill through his son. "Ha' ye lost your wits, ye dafty?" he demanded. "D'ye think anyone hereabouts will forget the tale she told about ye and the two lassies ye captured last year? Sakes, she called ye Wicked Blackheart, and many others gleefully bruited her tale from hither tae yon!"

Dougal winced. He had hoped that his father had never heard about the wretched poem that Lady Muriella had made up about him.

"She fancies herself a seanachie," he said. "But she never said my name."

"Wicked Blackheart betrayed his rightful chief. When he arrives in Hades, may he linger there in grief!" Pharlain ended with a near growl.

His recitation of the tale's last bit was too accurate for Dougal's comfort.

Pharlain said, "Not only do people ken fine that she meant ye, me lad, *and* agree that two wee lassocks outwitted ye, but they also believe ye ought never tae ha' kept your head after Andrew Dubh learned of it." Pausing for breath, he added, "Forbye, many be talking now o' the 'rightful' chief of our clan. *That* must stop."

"The easiest way to stop it, sir, is to keep the lady Muriella here," Dougal said. "I am willing to marry her, just as I would have married either of her sisters when you suggested that course. I still agree that such a marriage is the best way to unite the two factions of Clan Farlan with you as our chief and me as your heir."

"Ye may be right about that," Pharlain said, reaching for a second goblet and the jug. "Sakes, ye've taken her," he added, pouring wine into the second goblet. "So we must hope her abduction keeps Andrew's mind busy and out o' me other business till after the Inverness Parliament. Now, sit, lad. Ye must be hungry."

"Thank you, sir," Dougal said with relief. "I must

change out of these sodden clothes and see to one other small matter first. I'll not be long, though."

Pharlain nodded. "Aye, go then. Did ye no say ye had a horse with ye?" he added casually as Dougal turned away.

"I did, sir," Dougal said, pausing. "One of the lads is looking after it."

"I never thought otherwise. But when ye return, I'll want tae hear a wee bit more about yon horse."

           ⌒

Frightened, cold, wet, and furious, and hating the thick, cloying darkness of the small shed, Muriella was having all she could do to keep her wits about her and not shriek her fury and her fear for all to hear. She was too miserable to be brave.

Moreover, although she hoped she had persuaded Dougal that she did not fear him, the truth was that she did.

She feared his father even more.

Stories about Pharlain and how he had usurped her father's chiefdom and all of its estates except Tùr Meiloach had filled her life. She had heard how ruthless Pharlain was, how he had murdered all three of her brothers, not one of whom had been old enough yet to wield a sword, and how her father and mother had fled to protect the newborn Andrena. Faith, the lengths to which Andrew had gone to save Dree was a tale that seanachies likely told all over the Highlands and beyond.

Mag had told other tales of Pharlain's brutality, and Mag had experienced it firsthand. The thought that she, too, might experience it terrified her.

"Consequences," she muttered angrily to herself. "*He*

would say you deserve every bit of your terror, my lass."
She was not referring to Mag.

Tears sprang to her eyes again. What if MacAulay had
died trying to rescue her? She had reassured herself all
afternoon that he was too big, too strong, and too skillful a warrior to let Dougal's men defeat him. The truth,
though, was that she had not seen him again after Dougal
admitted having set a trap for him.

However, she reminded herself, if Dougal *had* left men
to guard the Loch Lomond side of the pass, to prevent
anyone from following him, those men had not caught up
with them or shown themselves, either.

How could they? her contrary inner voice demanded.
They were afoot, whilst you and Dougal rode.

That was true. Also, Dougal had ridden their laden
mount at a faster pace than safety should warrant in such
a sluicing rain. His men—and MacAulay, too—would
have had to run through that rain to catch up with them.

Thinking about the rain again made her realize that
she couldn't hear it anymore. The thatched roof of the
shed had muted it, to be sure. But it was silent now, so the
rain had eased to silent drizzle or had stopped.

Shivering, she wondered if Dougal meant for her to
die of the cold. Perhaps he wanted her to suffer from an
ague brought on by sitting in the darkness, soaked from
tip to toe. She began to curse him again but stopped when
she heard the bar that held the door shut from the outside
scrape upward. Someone was lifting it.

~

Rob and Scáthach managed to reach the cottage without
meeting a boggart, which did not surprise him, since he

didn't believe in boggarts or any other mythical beast. He fed Scáthach by ladling some of the warm meat and broth from the cauldron over the coals into a large bowl from the kitchen.

Then, starving and determined to assuage the worst of his own hunger straightaway, he cut open one of the manchet loaves that someone had left in a basket for him and stuffed meat inside it to eat on the way back to the tower.

The cauldron was still half full, so although he debated the wisdom of leaving it, he decided to do so. Adding a ladle of fresh water to the stew from a pail he kept in the kitchen, he stirred the embers beneath it to life, carefully added dried peat from its basket, and left the fire burning while he changed his clothes.

Without tugging off his boots, since doing so would take more time than it was worth, he doffed everything else, dried himself by the fire, and changed into a fresh tunic and his plaid. Before sleeping that night, he would give his boots to Andrew's man to dry and brush clean.

Then, banking the fire, Rob left enough open coals to keep the stew simmering. Scáthach had finished her meal, so he picked up his meat-filled roll, called her to heel, and set out for the tower.

Scáthach's noticeable interest in Rob's food made him wonder if Andrew, had he been present, might suggest that boggarts liked meat rolls.

The shed door opened, and a pathway of golden light spilled inside from torches burning in the yard. A woman stepped into the shed, carrying a lighted candle in one hand and a large bundle cradled in her other arm. As soon as the door shut solidly behind her, Murie heard the bar thud back into place.

Stiffly she got to her feet, saying, "I hope that bundle contains dry clothes."

Nodding, the woman moved past her to a shelf that Murie had not known was there, dripped tallow onto the board, and held the candle upright until it stood by itself. Then, turning to Murie, she made a sweeping if indecipherable gesture.

"I don't understand you," Muriella said. "Talk to me."

The woman shook her head fiercely and glanced toward the door. Putting a finger to her lips, she looked around in brief bewilderment and then set her bundle down on a rickety-looking stool near the shelf wall. Turning again to face Murie, she dramatically took off the shawl she wore and reached toward Murie's cloak.

"You want my cloak? It is the only thing keeping me warm!"

The woman nodded as fiercely as before.

With a sigh but realizing that she would have to take her wet clothes all off there in the freezing shed, Murie said, "Aye, then." Removing the cloak and unlacing her bodice, she said, "Have you got food in that bundle, too?"

Looking rueful, the woman shook her head. With her shawl in place again, she unwrapped her bundle, revealing a rough towel, a simple linen shift, and the ragged wool cloth that had contained them. Setting those items on the stool, she shook out the remaining one, a baggy-looking lavender kirtle similar to some that Lady Aubrey had kept from her girlhood.

Murie stripped the rest of her sodden clothing off as quickly as she could.

With a small, hopeful smile, the woman handed her the towel.

"Won't you tell me your name?" Murie asked as she rubbed herself hard with the towel, hoping to ease some of the numbness she felt from sitting hunched on the dirt floor. Her feet prickled painfully, but she could barely feel her legs.

"Please," she said. "Talk to me."

The woman shook her head again but less fiercely. Glancing at the door again, she looked at Murie and silently mouthed, *"I dare not."*

Murie nodded. She would not ask the one person at Arrochar who had been kind to do aught that might endanger her.

The towel helped restore her circulation, but as she dried herself, it occurred to her that her numbness was yet another consequence of her actions—or lack of any. She had not moved from where she first sat down, fearing that if she did, she might touch something ugsome or disturb some heavy implement stored in the shed and bring it down on top of her. Not to mention that she might touch a spider or something else that could bite her.

The silent woman handed her the shift, and as Murie hastily donned it, she tried to imagine defending her reasons for sitting still so long to MacAulay. Easily picturing a scornful response, she nearly smiled. He had not struck her as a man who would sympathize about repulsive sensations, clumsiness, or even spiders.

The oddest result, though, was that she could just as easily imagine talking about such topics with him. Despite his frank disapproval of her behavior, he had somehow made her feel as if she could safely discuss anything with him... *If*, the voice in her head added, *you can tolerate hearing unsavory truths in return.*

Her silent companion, holding out the lavender kirtle for her to step into, cocked her head inquisitively. Murie realized only as she helped pull the garment into place that imagining MacAulay's reaction had put a smile on her face.

"'Tis naught," she said to the woman, while pulling the kirtle's bodice laces tight and tying them. "I was just trying to imagine how I'd explain what happened to me to someone who will think it was all my own fault."

The woman shook her head but pressed her lips together, doubtless to keep herself from speaking. Then, putting a finger to her lips as if to silence Murie, too, she handed her the ragged-looking cloth that had contained the rest of the bundle. It proved to be a worn but nonetheless warm-looking gray wool cape.

Whispering her thanks, Murie added, "Did you think to bring a comb or a brush? My hair is still wet, despite being always under my hood."

The woman began to reach through a fitchet in her skirt, mayhap to a pocket tied round her waist, but she snatched the hand out at the scraping of the bar going up again outside. Gathering up Muriella's clothing with an apologetic look, the woman turned toward the door as it opened.

"I'll hold them things for ye," a masculine voice outside growled at her. "Ye're tae tak' the wench's supper in tae her the noo. Master Duncan said ye can leave the candle but ye're tae fetch it oot again as soon as she's had her sup."

The woman nodded, handed him the bundle, and

returned with a small bowl on a wooden tray. Looking around the small space, she shook her head, clicked her tongue in annoyance, and set the tray on the rickety stool. Then, with a look at the still-open door, she nodded at Muriella and left.

The door shut again, and the bar thumped into place.

With a sigh, Murie examined her supper.

The steam rising from a bowl of some sort of soup or stew lacked the enticing aroma that MacAulay's cauldron had emitted.

Irritated, she grumbled, "Stop thinking about that man! He cannot help you now, even if he wanted to. And he would *much* more likely say you are suffering no more than you deserve. You will just have to look after yourself, my lass."

She would eat first. Then, before they took the candle away, she would see if the horrible shed contained anything she might use as a weapon.

⌒

Andrew greeted Rob in the hall and drew him to the high table, where the privacy screens were already in place.

"My lady has retired," Andrew said. "The lads who sleep in the lower hall will be drifting in anon, but they'll murmur amongst themselves and pay us nae heed. I've reflected on what ye've told me so far, lad, and I'm thinking now that Pharlain will no let anyone harm my lass."

"I doubt he deserves such trust," Rob said, taking the place that Andrew indicated at what was normally the ladies' end of the table, near the fireplace.

Andrew drew a stool around to the opposite side and sat facing him with his back to the lower hall. "We'll keep warmer here and we can look at each other," he said. "Ye're right to distrust Pharlain—Dougal, too. I dinna trust either man as far as I can piss. Even so, neither be likely to hurt or kill our Muriella. Pharlain's own followers would rebel against hurting a lassie. Even so..."

When he paused, Rob said firmly, "We must fetch her back as soon as we can. Even if they do her no physical harm, keeping her captive is unconscionable. The gossip that is bound to come of it will destroy her good name."

"Aye, 'tis true," Andrew said, nodding. "So what d'ye think I should do?"

Rob eyed him with concern, for it went against most of what he knew about the man to hear him ask anyone else for advice. Conversely, Ian and Mag had both told him that Andrew wanted good-sons to help him regain his chiefdom and also that he had once or twice deigned to hear their suggestions.

Perhaps their excellent advice had made him more amenable.

"In troth, sir, I hope you will let me help," Rob said. "As I said earlier, I bear some responsibility for her ladyship's predicament. I did turn her out of the cottage, after all, and she was certainly·safer there than she is at Arrochar."

"Ye can help, aye," Andrew said. "Sithee, it occurred to me that your own wee problem—that is, your da's fear that Pharlain and the Campbell may be after seizing Ardincaple—might give us a way to approach Pharlain. He'd be more likely to agree to meet a lad who seeks to discuss summat *other* than Muriella's release."

A gillie hurried in with a platter of succulent-looking roast beef, another with rolls and some chicken in a sauce. Rob began eagerly to pile food on his trencher.

When the gillies had gone, he looked up to meet Andrew's expectant, twinkling gaze. "What exactly do you have in mind, sir?"

Andrew grinned. "Why, just what we've discussed afore now, lad. Ye'll send a message to the man, saying ye hope to discuss matters of possible business betwixt Arrochar and Ardincaple. 'Course, after he agrees, we'll take a different tack than ye might have afore. Ye'll begin with Ardincaple, but then ye'll seek to learn if he means to give Muriella back to us or keep her for his damnable son."

Rob nearly choked on the meat he was swallowing but managed—he hoped—to conceal his dismay by concentrating fully on getting it down safely.

Arrochar Hall

"Ye took longer than I'd expected," Pharlain said bluntly when Dougal returned to the hall dais warmly clothed and impatient for his supper.

Wondering if he would ever hear his father express actual approval of something he had done, Dougal signed to a hovering gillie to fetch him some food. He could not recall ever hearing praise without caveats about how his father would have done it or how *he* could have done it better, faster, or to greater advantage.

Taking his usual seat next to Pharlain, Dougal said, "I wanted to see that the lass got food and dry clothes. I've locked her in the shed, so she'll keep dry. But it's as dark as the devil's den, so 'tis likely she'll be more compliant tomorrow."

"She is disobedient?"

"She is angry," Dougal said. "She'll mind *me* well enough, though. Why did you ask me about the horse?" he added.

"Claret?" Pharlain asked, reaching for the jug.

"Aye, thanks."

Handing him the jug, Pharlain said, "Tell me the rest o' your tale. But, first, did ye both ride the horse?"

Dougal told him exactly what he had done and why.

When he finished, Pharlain said, "Aye, good. If ye mean it about marrying the lass, I'm thinking now that I've heard summat of a way tae do that without raising a dust amongst her lot or our own."

Dougal raised his eyebrows. "How? Her father won't approve such a wedding no matter how much good it would do her or the clan in the end. As for our lot, they'll do as they're bid, just as they always do."

"None o' that will matter if I'm right in my thinking. It's been long since I heard the tale, though. I must send for my mother's cousin in the morning."

"What cousin?"

"Fingal Morrison. He's a Brehon justice, which means he kens more than most men do about Celtic law."

"But what do you think he can do?"

"I'll say nae more until I ken what's what," Pharlain said. "If I'm wrong, it will come tae nowt. I'm thinking, though, that it be time I held me laird's court."

"Would you *force* her to marry me?"

"If necessary, aye." Pharlain smiled grimly. Then he added, "If I'm right, though, mayhap we can do the thing legally and without any fuss."

*Chapter 8*_____

Having found nothing remotely resembling a weapon but likewise finding no implement that might fall on her, or spider webs, Muriella paced back and forth the short distance from the door to the candle shelf. She was trying to think.

Usually, when she walked, she fell easily into reverie. Much as she needed to think now, though, she could not seem to do so. Her quick ears caught too many sounds beyond the walls. Each one interrupted her concentration.

She had begun to hope her captors would leave the candle, and was trying to estimate how long it might last, when she heard the bar outside going up again.

Turning toward the door, she felt deep relief when the silent woman entered again, but a man followed her. At first Murie thought it was Dougal, but the man was shorter, with a less muscular build.

"Be quick," he said to someone behind him.

A second, younger man stepped past him, carrying over one shoulder what looked to Murie's experienced eye like a rolled-up pallet. She welcomed the sight and welcomed even more the blanket she saw when the man laid the pallet out.

She had had distressing visions of having to sleep on the dirt floor.

As it was, she had no pillow, and both pallet and blanket were thin. Tempted to demand better quality or a second blanket, she resisted. To grouse without first having some idea of how her captors might react would be foolhardy.

Common sense told her that the men were following Dougal's orders and would be unlikely to defy them. So, she held her tongue.

The woman moved to the shelf and unstuck the candle. As she turned back toward Murie, she allowed herself a slight nod.

Turning with her as she passed, Murie said clearly, "Thank you, all of you. I am grateful for the food and clothing you brought me, and for the bed."

None of the three spoke.

In the glow of the woman's candle, Murie saw her casually put her free hand behind her back. The men, outside the doorway now and waiting for her, could not see her wiggle her fingers at Murie as if to say, "You're welcome, aye."

Then the door shut behind her and blackness filled the shed again. With a sigh, Murie felt her way to the pallet.

⁓

With the snoring of men on pallets in the lower hall as background noise, Rob and Andrew talked over mugs of whisky. As soon as Rob had finished eating, the older man produced a jug of the potent stuff and filled mugs for each of them.

"You know, sir," Rob said quietly, "rescuing her may take some time."

"Aye, it might, but dinna forget we must be in Inverness by mid-May. That journey will take time, too, lad. We need to leave by the end of the month."

"We may have to forgo Inverness," Rob said. "With

respect, sir, if you cannot find your charters, I'm surprised that you still want to go. Not only is the journey long but Pharlain controls the pass into the northwestern Highlands."

"Sakes, that doesna trouble me," Andrew said. "As for the charter, our Lina cast her runes when she and Ian last visited us. She saw nae sign of disaster, so me charters will show themselves in good time."

"Forgive me," Rob said, striving to conceal his disbelief. "If you hid them and they disappeared from that hiding place, how do you expect them to reappear?"

"Tùr Meiloach protects its own," Andrew said placidly. "I ken fine that ye've heard that afore, lad, and dinna believe it. Not long ago, unbeknownst to me, the charters were in grave danger. That is, certain people did fear as much."

"You refer to the events of last summer, aye?"

"I do, and so ye do ken summat about Tùr Meiloach and how the land protects true MacFarlans. Nowt be more vital to the safety of our clan than that the King confirm the royal charters granting me the rights to Arrochar and its estates."

"I know that Dougal captured the lady Lina and held her captive at Dumbarton Castle. Did he hope to exchange her for the charters?"

"That was one of the lad's daft hopes, aye. He also sought to marry her."

"I remember that, too," Rob said with a nod.

"Dougal is a fool," Andrew said with a growl. "In any event, I wouldna give him Lina. And that, I suspect, is why he's taken our Muriella."

"Even so, it is gey unlikely that he stole those charters himself."

"I tell ye, lad, the charters are here," Andrew said,

shaking his head. "Dougal never set foot in this tower, nor will he. The land of Tùr Meiloach will reject him if he does aught more to endanger any of us. As spawn of the devil that killed my three young sons, Dougal doesna count as one of us, himself. Neither he nor Pharlain will lay a hand on me charters, whatever else they may do."

"Then how do you explain Dougal's twice laying hands on your daughters?"

"They cast themselves into his path, both of them," Andrew said. "Our Lina did so through nae fault of her own, but she survived, aye? Ye'll see, the charters will show themselves in time for me to present them to his grace."

"Because Lady Lina cast her runes?" Rob said, allowing a strong note of doubt to enter his voice. Briefly, he worried that it might offend his host, but the twinkle returned to Andrew's eyes, which was even more unsettling to his guest.

Andrew paused with his whisky mug halfway to his lips and eyed Rob over its rim. "Ye dinna believe in the runes, then."

"No more than I believe in wee folk, fairies, or boggarts," Rob said.

"Yet ye call yourself a Highlander, aye?"

"I do, and an Islesman, as well, as I think you ken fine."

"'Tis a pity then that ye didna sail here in one o' your galleys," Andrew said.

"My father would agree with you," Rob admitted. "In troth," he added, meeting Andrew's gaze, "I wanted to see more of Tùr Meiloach."

"So ye have summat in common with Dougal then. Likely he slipped in to explore and test Tùr Meiloach's powers, but the land kens fine that he can do little harm by himself. I'll wager he caught sight of my lads beyond the pass the first time he ventured here and sent his men ahead to kill them today."

"In fairness, I should tell you that the one I sent to you said that Dougal had ordered them to render your men harmless," Rob said. "He might have expected his men simply to tie yours up."

"Then he should have said so," Andrew retorted. "More whisky?"

"Not tonight, sir. I've been up since dawn. Moreover, I'm thinking you'll want to talk more tomorrow about how we should apply to parley with Pharlain. For the nonce, your whisky or simple exhaustion has befogged my mind. So, if you will excuse me and tell me where to find a bed, I would seek it."

"Aye, sure, I'll have one of me lads show ye. Ye've been sleeping in Mag's bed at the cottage, so ye might as well have his here, too. Will ye need aught more than the bed, water for washing, and a night jar?"

Denying any further necessity, Rob bade him good-night and, with a snap of his fingers, summoned the ever-alert Scáthach from her place by the fire.

As they followed a gillie up the twisting stairs to a quiet, spacious chamber under the ramparts, Rob thought about the long talk he had had with his host.

He could not help thinking that, often, when Andrew said one thing, he was thinking something else. Perhaps, on the morrow, after a good night's sleep and with a fresh mind to guide him, Rob could figure out what the man was up to.

⁓

To Murie's surprise, she not only fell asleep almost the moment she drew the blanket up and put her head down, she slept the night through. When she awoke, she saw that although the stone walls of the shed were solid, a few cracks here and there let in tiny bits of the gray dawn light.

Although she had arrived in darkness and quickly lost her bearings, she needed only her reliable instinct to know it was the dawn sky rather than an overcast one. She also knew that the tide was on the turn and the rain had stopped.

The air in the shed was icy. Knowing she would stay warmer between blanket and pallet than if she got up, she stayed where she was until she heard noises outside. Certain that they meant her breakfast was coming, she scrambled upright, rolled up the pallet and blanket, and shifted them out of the way.

After the usual ritual of the bar going up and the guard opening the door, the silent woman entered with a tray and set it on the stool.

"Good morning," Murie said, moving out of her way.

"She won't answer ye."

Whirling to see Dougal filling the doorway, Murie said, "Why won't she?"

"Because I told her I'll have her flogged if she says one word to ye."

"I've heard tales about the brutality at Arrochar," she said scornfully. "But I had not heard that you treat the women as badly as you treat the men."

"Watch your tone, lass. Remember, ye've *become* one of our women."

"I am no such thing!" she snapped. "You will gain naught by holding me, Dougal MacPharlain. Good sakes, you would earn scorn from all other Highlanders if you were to treat me the way you threaten to treat that poor woman."

"Ye seem gey sure of yourself, lass. If ye'll recall,

Arrochar did not protect your family in times past, nor did Tùr Meiloach protect ye yesterday."

She could not deny those words, for they were true. But she would not let him see how much they distressed her.

Instead, she said, "Tùr Meiloach has its ways, and I do not know them all. It was folly yestermorn for me to let my thoughts go a-wandering. Even so, what happened was not my fault, Dougal MacPharlain. It was yours. Our land and our beasts know *that* as well as you and I do," she added, looking him in the eye.

Even in the dim light of the shed's interior, she could see that his face paled. So, despite his successful forays onto their land—if one counted as successful his having abducted her without being buried in a landslide or drowned in a bog—he did clearly still have reservations about his safety there. She would do all she could to increase his uneasiness, too.

Accordingly, she said, "You have put me at risk now, and the spirits of Tùr Meiloach will remember that. Sithee, I ken fine that my sister Lina warned you that the land *will* reject you. You would be wise to remember that and let me go home."

"We'll see about that," Dougal said in his usual superior way. He was still pale. "By my troth," he added, "I mean ye nae harm, lass. I just want tae marry ye."

"Well, I don't want to marry you," she retorted. "Moreover, you cannot *make* me marry you. By law, no one in Scotland can force a woman to marry if she refuses to do so. And, by my troth, I will cry 'Nae' as loudly as ever I can."

"Lassie, ye ken nowt of laws if ye think that, for they are nobbut compliant beasts to the men who interpret them. Sithee, my father will hold his laird's court to decide your fate. Mayhap he will agree with ye, and mayhap he will not."

Muriella felt her stomach clench. A gasp from the hitherto silent woman, as she returned to the doorway, made it clench tighter.

Her own face, she feared, was probably whiter now than Dougal's had been.

In Pharlain's own laird's court at Arrochar, far from Jamie Stewart and his hope of instituting one set of laws throughout Scotland, Pharlain would have the power to decide her fate in any way he chose.

He would also be able to *enforce* that decision by any means he chose.

~

"I'm thinking ye'll want a galley," Andrew said to Rob, as the two walked together in the still-damp woods later that morning. Watching Scáthach range through the shrubbery in search of a snack or a chase, Andrew added, "Ye'll look more impressive than if ye walk in alone. I'll send some of me lads with ye."

"I thank you, sir, but nay," Rob said. "I planned to go alone, and I think I can count on my name to get me in. Pharlain's desire to partner with us and collect fees from all who enter the lochs from the firth should win me a meeting with him."

"Ye'll be taking a greater risk than ye need, though," Andrew said. "What would keep Pharlain from taking ye prisoner if ye're on your own?"

"I hope he'd have better sense than to cast such a gauntlet at my sire," Rob said. "The MacAulay may be a man of peace, but he *is* my father."

"He is, aye, lad. And a chief's son should travel with a proper tail, if only to remind that lout Pharlain that your da is a baron *and* chief of his clan, as well as being Laird of Ardincaple."

"The number of men that the King's rules allow me in my tail would be of little use in a fight," Rob said. "I'm neither knight, lord, bishop, abbot, nor earl."

"'Tis true, but ye're nae dafty, either," Andrew said, affecting an air of quiet patience that Rob knew went wholly against the older man's character. "Forbye, ye *are* a gentleman, entitled to take six armed men wherever ye go."

"I do know that," Rob said, suppressing a sigh.

"Take what ye're allowed, then. Sakes, lad, think what happens when Pharlain hears that your father won't partner with him, or when he learns that your true reason for meeting him is to win our lass's freedom."

"In either event, six men would do me no good against Pharlain's hundred or more," Rob said. "Nor would an earl's allowance of a full score be much better, come to that, not on Pharlain's home estate."

"Then we must think harder," Andrew replied. "Meantime, we'll send someone to Craggan Tower to borrow a Colquhoun galley. That will take less time than sending a running gillie all the way to Ardincaple."

To that suggestion Rob agreed. He knew the Laird of Colquhoun's people would willingly lend one galley, or more, to either Andrew or himself.

"There, ye see," Andrew said, grinning. "Ye *can* be reasonable."

"With respect, sir, when you talk like that, I begin to wonder if you recall that we are discussing how to rescue your daughter from her captivity."

"And when ye talk like that, laddie, *I* begin to wonder if ye've formed a softness in your heart for our lassie," Andrew said, giving him a shrewd look.

"Then let me set your mind at rest," Rob said, keeping his temper with unexpected difficulty. "I don't mean to marry any woman for years yet. Even if I did, you must be as aware as I am that my parents expect me to marry someone rather more..." Recognizing dangerous ground, Rob fought to gather his wits and added, "...rather older."

Andrew snorted. "Older, is it? And here was me thinking that your lady mother has set her mind on the Duchess of Albany's youngest daughter for ye. How old would that lassie be, d'ye think?"

Ever honest, Rob said, "Fifteen, sir, but I have no intention of marrying her, and so I have told my mother. You are right in that she wants me to marry a lass from a higher-ranking family than ours, but I have never sought such a marriage. Nor do I want any young woman who has to be forced to marry me."

"Aye, well I'd no force any lass of mine to wed a man she doesna want," Andrew said. Then he asked curiously, "What *do* ye want then?"

"To choose my own way as much as I can, considering the responsibilities I will likely inherit," Rob said. "At present, I would continue to serve his grace the King as a warrior. But I do recognize my duty to my lord father, as well. That is why I did agree to talk with Pharlain."

"But ye came to me first," Andrew reminded him.

"Aye," Rob said. "I knew almost nowt about Pharlain and little of Dougal, although I did hear much about *him* from Ian and Mag. My father insists that I need only have a quiet, reasonable talk with Pharlain. Father believes that if I simply point out the wisdom of keeping the lochs open to all vessels that want to enter or leave them, Pharlain will understand that the fees he and Campbell want are a bad idea. I thought you might believe, as I do, that such a course would be futile."

"Aye, then ye were right to come to me," Andrew said, nodding. "I doubt there be anyone in Scotland who kens as much about me cousin Parlan MacFarlan, for all that he chooses to name himself now after our great ancestor, Pharlain. As Parlan, he were a sly lad, who thought better of himself than anyone else did, including *his* father. He's gey sly now, too, and greedy withal. So, whatever he might say, dinna trust the man. He's right daft about Arrochar and least trustworthy when he gives ye his 'solemn promise.' Those were the words he said to me the day afore he attacked us at Arrochar."

"Is that why you were able to get away? Because you understood that he meant the opposite thing and distrusted his solemn word?"

To Rob's surprise, the twinkle lit Andrew's eyes again. He said, "That were no the main reason. But I willna lie to ye, and ye'd no believe the truth, so I willna weary ye with it. 'Tis enough that my lass and I did flee. Sithee, I had a bolt hole, as any man of such wisdom as m'self would. So we scooped up our newborn lassie, Andrena, and fled here to Tùr Meiloach."

"How did you get over that pass before they caught you?"

"Aye, well, ye must ask our Muriella that question when ye find her. She kens the tale as well as anyone does."

Rob eyed him shrewdly. "I have heard some absurd versions of that tale, I believe," he said. "Surely, you will not insist that *they* are true."

"I'll insist nowt," Andrew said with another mischievous grin. "'Tis such tales that have kept us safe since then. Now, with only a short time left afore I can present me charters to his grace, we must retrieve Muriella as fast as we can. This afternoon, we'll devise a tactful and enticing message for ye to send to Pharlain."

Accepting the change of subject, Rob wondered if Andrew would be patient enough to await the results of such a message. He wondered, too, if a quick retrieval of any sort could be possible.

The rest of the day passed slowly for Muriella, whose patience was straining if not nearing its end. She had racked her brain for ideas of how to escape, but not one plausible method occurred to her.

The silent woman had brought food again at midday but had not left the candle. Murie could see well enough in the faint light through the cracks to reveal that the food was plain and held little appeal. Nevertheless, she ate, if only because she had nothing else to do. The guard took away her tray afterward, and she did not see the woman again until darkness had fallen.

She brought a candle then and set it again in its own tallow on the shelf. Then, taking the tray from the guard, she carried it to the stool.

As she turned to leave, Murie had an inspiration. "Don't go," she pleaded. "'Tis cold in here at night, and that blanket is too thin for warmth. If I am not to be sick, I must have another blanket and my own warm cloak. It must be dry by now."

The woman shook her head.

"Do you think Dougal or Pharlain will let me have just one more blanket?"

The woman shrugged.

"Come away now, woman," the guard said firmly. "Ye shouldna even listen tae her 'less ye want tae find yourself in the suds."

"Prithee, *ask* Dougal," Murie urged. "Just ask if I may have another blanket."

Hesitating briefly, the woman nodded.

"And a bath?" Muriella added hastily. "A hot bath?"

The woman looked at her.

"Mae, come out o' there *now*," the guard snapped.

Without another word, the woman left, and the guard slammed the door shut and barred it.

But Murie had the candle, and now she knew the woman's name.

Moreover, if they did let her bring a tub and hot water, they might let her stay in the shed while Murie bathed. If so, even if Mae remained silent, Murie could at least talk quietly to her and perhaps persuade her to help her escape.

At Tùr Meiloach Sunday morning, Rob ached for the peacefulness and solitude of the cottage so he could think. He had spent the previous afternoon and evening with Andrew, discussing possible tactics to employ when meeting with Pharlain. But none of Andrew's notions seemed either tactful or plausible to Rob.

The message they had finally composed to send Pharlain had taken only a few minutes before supper. When Rob asked *how* they would send it, Andrew said he would have to think about that. Then, at supper, he made more outrageous suggestions, none of which were actions or arguments that Rob could approve.

Declaring exhaustion at last, he excused himself to sleep, only to waken the next day and find Andrew eager to talk more while they broke their fast.

Hoping to change the subject, if only briefly enough to let him finish his meal, Rob said, "How soon should we expect that galley to arrive from Craggan, sir? And where will they dock it when it comes?"

"They'll have a towboat," Andrew said. "The lads who come ashore will use that and send a lad back with it. Others will stay on the galley and anchor offshore."

Rob chewed the food in his mouth and swallowed before saying, "They will not want to sit idle for days, sir. Nor do I. The sooner I can talk to Pharlain, the better I shall like it. We must get my request to him at once."

"Aye, sure, lad, I'm that road m'self," Andrew said. "But he willna listen to explanations or agree to suggestions from you or your da. He'll want his own way. Ye said yourself that that's why ye've come to me."

"It is, aye, but I cannot see myself doing or saying aught that you suggest."

"Then I'll cudgel me brain more," Andrew said. He glanced around, but the gillie who had served them was helping others take down the breakfast trestles in the lower hall. Speaking quietly, Andrew said, "Meantime, I've a question for ye."

Smearing butter on a crust, Rob said, "What is it?"

"Ye told me last summer that ye'd not inflict yourself on *any* female. At the time, I thought ye might have said that because ye believed a warrior would make a devilish husband. Thinking it over, though, I did wonder if ye'd already inflicted yourself on some other lass. Did ye?"

Rob met his gaze, wondering what he could say. Anything other than the truth would likely cause trouble later, so drawing breath, he said, "I did nowt by choice, sir. You revealed earlier that you know about my mother's hopes for me. What you may not know is that she and my lord father arranged to betroth me to a young woman of good family. I was reluctant then to assume the burden of a wife, because I was in the midst of my training and still yearned for action."

"Your father couldna back out of whatever offer or agreement he'd made, though," Andrew said. "What happened, then?"

Bluntly, Rob said, "The lass jumped from her tower window to her death."

⁓

When Mae entered the shed with Murie's breakfast tray, the guard stood in the doorway as he had before while she carried it to the stool.

Despite his presence, Murie said, "Did you ask about a bath and blankets?"

Mae gave only a curt nod in passing and vanished out the door.

As the guard shut it, he leered at Muriella and said cheerfully, "Sakes, lassie, *I'll* bring ye a bath if ye want. I'll even scrub your lovely back."

⁓

"Bless my soul!" Andrew exclaimed in response to Rob's candid statement of how his first "betrothal" had ended.

"You should be blessing *my* soul," Rob said ruefully. "Her parents damned it to hell, because they blame me, and only me, for her death. Her mother told mine that I'd frightened the poor lassie so much that..." He paused to stifle the rest of that thought. Then, when Andrew remained silent, he added, "By my troth, sir, I did nowt that should have terrified her so. We'd met only twice and were never alone."

"Did you never learn aught more than that?"

"My mother did say that it was likely my size and strength that gave her such a fright. She believes that I could have wooed her less clumsily. Even now, she plagues me to treat women with greater chivalry." He grimaced. "I'll admit that I do tend to speak my mind rather than mouthing pretty phrases meant to flatter. I doubt that such stuff would have helped then, though. Her ladyship barely spoke to me when I did address her. She *was* small and slender, however—much like the lady Muriella in stature. And, in troth, she did comment once on my size, saying that I was overlarge for a husband. Perhaps my lady mother recalled that, too."

"So now ye see yourself as an affliction to the lassies. I ken little of those feelings, lad, having never suffered such. But I'd say ye're condemning yourself unfairly. We men will never understand women. I ha' me doots that God Hisself understands them or that He intended for us to do so. Another fact of wicked Nature is that we're drawn to women nonetheless," he added with a knowing grin.

Rob ignored both the grin and Andrew's apparent ability to understand the intentions of the Almighty. Instead, he said, "Have you thought of any *sensible* way that we can quickly arrange for me to talk with Pharlain?"

"Aye, sure... *if* ye should happen to have a MacAulay banner amongst the things ye brought with ye."

"I do," Rob said. "I carry one with me always."

"I thought ye might," Andrew said with a grin.

Chapter 9 _____

Worried now about her safety from Dougal's guards, Murie paced the area inside the shed, trying to think how she might escape. The only possible weapon she had so far was the candle that Mae had left behind two nights before.

But what good was a candle, other than for light, in a shed built of stone?

Imagining herself attacking the lecherous guard with it, Murie could easily envision the man erupting in flames if she could set him alight. But doing so was a remote prospect at best, even if she could bring herself to do it.

Like Dougal and many other men she had seen on her arrival, the guard was much larger than she was. And a candle was dangerous only when its flame was lit.

Glancing up, she considered the thatched roof, but it still dripped in places. Even where it did not drip she could assume that the thatch was damp throughout.

The light, rickety stool was useless. The door opened outward, so she could not hide behind it and hope to surprise anyone.

Perhaps if she pretended to faint or be sick—

The scrape of the bar on the door stopped that thought

dead, and Murie quickly moved behind the stool. She could hit the guard with it if he expressed more notions of helping her bathe. The stool would break, but it might deter him even so.

Daylight poured in when the door opened. Two men stood outside, holding a tub between them large enough for bathing. Behind them stood Dougal.

Just beyond him, in a clearing, she saw other men attending to their duties. Catching a glimpse of thick red curls, she thought of Pluff.

That cheeky lad would doubtless be as irate with her as her father would, but she'd welcome even Pluff's scolding if she could just get safely home again.

She watched the men carry the tub in and set it down.

Dougal said, "I hope ye'll show proper gratitude for this kindness by mending your attitude toward me, lass. These men will bring hot water, so ye can take your bath. Afterward, they'll take the tub away."

"I won't bathe unless you send the woman to me again," Murie said firmly.

"Ye'll do as I bid."

"Nay, I won't, for I dare not trust your guards any more than I trust you."

He frowned heavily. "What d'ye mean by that?"

"When that woman left this morning, the guard with her offered to bring me a tub himself *and* to scrub my lovely back," she replied angrily. "If you think I will undress, let alone dare to bathe, with such men as guards and no one to protect me from *them*, you are even wickeder than I depicted you in my tale."

"I'll fetch her then," Dougal said curtly. "Ye willna be

troubled by such ill manners again, m'lady. Ye may also have as many extra blankets as ye want. Ye should have requested them straightaway."

Stunned to realize that his anger was not for her but for what the guard had said to her, Murie nevertheless felt a distinct chill.

By the time Mae arrived, carrying a fresh towel, a washrag, and two more blankets, the two men who had carried in the tub had also filled it with hot water. One of them also brought a large ewer of cold water, saying that she might need to lower the water's temperature. Steam rose from the tub in welcome clouds.

Somewhat to her consternation, Dougal had returned with Mae. "I'll be right outside until ye've had your bath," he said. "Ye'll have nowt to worry ye."

Although Murie thanked him politely, she greeted the news with less gratitude than he might have expected. She was grateful, but his presence so nearby would prevent Mae from speaking to her.

As soon as the door had shut with the men all outside, though, Murie said quietly, "Thank you, Mae."

Nodding but without any expression to indicate her feelings, Mae deftly helped Murie take off the lavender kirtle and the shift.

"I wish I could wash my hair," Murie said as she dipped a foot in the water. "It would not dry in here, though, and I doubt Dougal would let me dry it outside."

Mae shook her head, looking distressed.

"Are you saying, 'No, he won't' or that I should not talk?" Murie asked her.

To her surprise, Mae rolled her eyes.

"He won't allow it," Murie said flatly, realizing that

Mae could not answer two questions at once, certainly not without talking.

Mae shook her head and gestured authoritatively into the tub.

Resigned, Muriella stepped in, sank down, and accepted a bar of soap from her. "Are you so afraid of him that you dare not even whisper to me?" she asked.

With a nod, Mae put a finger to her lips.

Understanding, Murie whispered, "You are afraid that if I keep talking, he may think that we are both talking. In troth, Mae, if we both whisper, I doubt that even he would be able hear us."

Mae shook her head and mouthed, "Too dangerous."

Muriella sighed.

For a time, she concentrated on getting warm to her bones and clean. But silence was no friend when conversation beckoned. The older woman's silence soon made Murie want to shake her. That thought brought a sense of shame when her imagination instantly summoned up an image of Dougal flogging Mae. He might do it if he even suspected they had talked. Faith, she thought, he might even flog *her*.

Murie assured herself that the second possibility was irrelevant, that no matter what he might do to either of them, she had to know one thing.

She whispered even more quietly, "Does my father know I'm here?"

Mae shrugged, her expression rueful.

"He will be gey worried," Murie said. "My lady mother, too."

Mae nodded again. Then, to Murie's surprise, she looked thoughtful.

"What?" Murie demanded, barely remembering to whisper.

Mae shook her head and moved the two folded blankets from the stool to the rolled-up pallet. Then, shaking out the towel, she held it up invitingly.

With a sigh, Murie stood and let Mae wrap the towel around her.

While she did, Murie murmured, "I do wish you could talk, Mae, but even though you can't, I'm glad you are here. That guard this morning scared me."

Mae grimaced and looked as if she might speak, after all, or mouth words as she had. A brisk rap at the door ended both possibilities.

Dougal opened it a crack and said impatiently, "Are ye no done yet? I've more important matters to see to."

Murie called back, "I'm just getting out. Prithee, be so kind as to let me have a wee bit more time."

"Aye, lass, but I've no got all day."

Mae handed her the shift and when she had it on, held the kirtle for her to step into. Since its bodice laced in front, Mae then turned to fold the towel and take the washrag from the side of the tub where Murie had draped it. Then, with a quick glance at Murie, now safely dressed, Mae rapped on the door.

Dougal opened it and held it open for her, shifting his gaze to Murie.

Hearing a scream outside as Mae hurried away, Murie expected him to leave at once. Instead, he held her gaze.

"Why do you look at me like that?" she demanded when the scream came again. "Do you hear so many screams here that you pay them no heed?"

"I ken fine what causes those screams," he said. "I told

ye, that guard will never be uncivil to ye again. Mae will bring ye your dinner anon."

~~~~

Andrew's running gillies were speedy, so the Colquhoun galley arrived just before sundown Monday evening. Rob walked down with Andrew to meet it.

"Is it safe to send them straight on to Arrochar?" Rob asked.

"Aye, and 'tis the wisest thing, too," Andrew said. "Sithee, Pharlain posts men along Arrochar's cliffs. Since they'll tell him that a galley put in here, 'tis best if that same galley continues to Arrochar with your message, under your banner, then vanishes in the ensuing darkness. Pharlain will then think only that it also carried a message for me. Afterward, Colquhoun's lads can put into a cove a mile south of here, where nae one will see them except me own people."

Rob nodded. "Be sure that whoever delivers the message is unknown to Pharlain. He must know some of Colquhoun's men, I should think."

"Aye, we'll make sure. He doesna ken all of mine, though," Andrew added as they approached the now-floating wharf, where the towboat had docked. "Nor could his lads on the cliffs be sure o' recognizing any of mine at the distance."

Greeting the captain of Colquhoun's galley, he explained their plan and sent him on to deliver their message. Then he and Rob turned back toward the tower.

Halfway up the path, they heard a shout and saw Pluff hurrying toward them.

"What is it, lad?" Rob asked when the boy halted before them.

"Lady Murie be a prisoner at Arrochar, laird!"

"I ken that fine," Andrew replied. "How did ye come by that news?"

"Never mind that yet, sir," Rob interjected, realizing that the boy had more to say. "What else do you know, lad? Have they hurt her?"

Pluff turned to him gratefully but shot a wary look at Andrew before he said, "She be safe enough for the nonce, sir. But Mae did say—"

"Mae!" Andrew exclaimed. "D'ye mean to tell us ye've been visiting Mae and Annabel MacNur again?"

"Aye, sir," Pluff said. "But only 'cause I heard that Lady Murie had...that Dougal MacPharlain had taken her. I kent fine that if he took her home wi' him, Mae would ken where he'd put her. I thought ye'd want—"

"Never mind what you thought," Rob interjected. "What did Mae say?"

"That Dougal means to marry Lady Murie, even though *she* tellt him she wouldna do it. Dougal's da means tae hold a laird's court and *make* her marry him."

"Behear the lad," Andrew said, shaking his head. "D'ye no recall what I said I'd do to ye an ye sneaked over to Arrochar again?"

"Aye, sir, that ye'd leather me good. But Lady Murie—"

"Mae and Annabel MacNur?" Rob said. "Are they kin to *your* MacNur, sir?"

"They be his wife and daughter, aye," Andrew said. "When he fled Arrochar years ago, Mae was afraid to come with him. But I'm more concerned about a lad who risks his hide to satisfy his curiosity. I'm thinking the time has come to put an end to that." Looking at Rob but plainly meaning the words for Pluff, he added, "I saved

him from a hiding the first time I learned of such doings.
But this time—"

Hastily, Rob said, "It might be wiser to make use of
the lad's courage, sir. If he is wiling to return, he can ask
Mae to tell the lady Muriella—"

"Nay!" Pluff exclaimed. "Mae canna tell our Lady
Murie nowt, or Dougal will flog Mae. Forbye, he tellt her
that if she decided it were worth a flogging tae help Lady
Murie, she should ken that Dougal will flog Lady Murie,
too, and make Mae watch. Ye canna ask her tae say nowt
tae nae one!"

Putting a hand on the boy's shoulder, Andrew said in
a gentler tone, "We willna put Mae at risk, laddie. But ye
must no go back there. I mean that now."

"Aye, laird, I kent fine that ye meant it afore. But, see
you, at Arrochar nae one pays me heed, 'cause they've
seen me afore. Come tae that, they think I'm nobbut a
bairn *and* that me kith and kin live Lomondside."

Rob looked more closely at Pluff. "How old are you,
lad?"

"I'm nigh fourteen," the boy replied.

To Andrew, Rob said, "I guessed he was younger,
myself, sir."

"His age, nae matter what it be, wouldna keep Dougal
or Pharlain from hanging him," Andrew said, giving Pluff
another stern look. "I'm grateful to ye for the news ye've
brought us, lad. But I did give ye my word, did I no?"

"I ken that fine, laird," Pluff said, meeting his stern gaze
without fear. "But ye will get our Lady Murie back, aye?"

Rob said, "Do you know when Pharlain means to hold
his court, Pluff?"

"Mae said only 'anon.' He's waiting for a kinsman he

sent for Friday after Dougal took Lady Murie. As soon as he arrives, though, Mae thinks it will be then."

"Where will he hold his laird's court?" Rob asked Andrew. "Has he a hall large enough? I've never been to Arrochar."

"The hall be a good size, but he'll no hold his laird's court there. Ye must ken as well as I do that such events must be public."

"I do, aye, because my father holds his courts quarterly," Rob said. "But if the law ordains how large the area must be, I've heard nowt about that."

"It must be large enough and accessible enough for all who want to attend," Andrew said. "Pharlain holds his on the Tarbet." Turning to Pluff, he said, "Ye go inside now, lad, and wait for me in my privy chamber."

"Aye, laird," Pluff said.

"He shows little distress over the leathering he faces," Rob observed as the boy strode ahead of them to the postern gate.

"He's a good lad, is Pluff," Andrew said. "I admire his courage, but I do *not* want him going to Arrochar."

"How old is Annabel MacNur?" Rob asked.

Andrew chuckled. "Two or three years older than what the lad is. But he would no be the first lad to admire an older woman."

"So what do we do now?"

"We wait, lad, until we learn if, when, and where Pharlain will receive ye. 'Tis possible he'll agree tae meet with ye straightaway."

Rob nodded. It was possible, he thought. But if Pharlain hoped to exert pressure on Lord MacAulay to force his compliance, he would more likely claim that he had to hold his laird's court before he could turn his mind to aught else.

~

Murie had eaten little of her midday meal, finding it hard even to think of food after hearing the guard's screams of pain. Knowing that he had brought the flogging on himself—for a flogging it must have been to draw such screams—did not absolve her from her own responsibility, she knew. Had she not complained to Dougal, the guard would not have suffered so.

Had you not told Dougal, that lout would have tormented you more or done worse, her internal mentor argued. *Your father would have flogged him, too.*

Mae had come in then to take the food away, giving Murie a worried look as she did.

"I wasn't hungry," Murie muttered. But that had been hours ago, and although she had not been hungry then, she was ravenous now.

When she realized she had started to nibble a fingernail, she thought better of it and put both hands behind her back.

As she did, a mental image formed of MacAulay standing in Mag's kitchen doorway, scowling and curtly ordering her not to bite her nails. She wondered what his story was. Everybody had one, and their stories all became part of history. Not all were told and retold. But MacAulay was a man who might do much in the world.

She knew almost nothing about him, and she realized with an unfamiliar pang that she wanted to know more. What had brought him to Tùr Meiloach, to her father? Perhaps if she tried to imagine his reasons, she could imagine a tale about him to pass the time. She did not need to know the truth. She could make up a good story about him simply by giving her characters fictitious names.

Smiling as she considered MacAulay's likely scowl in reaction to that manner of entertaining herself, she recalled the night she had first recited her tale about Dougal for her family's—and MacAulay's—entertainment.

He had scowled then, too. So had Ian, come to that, the minute he heard himself named Sir Goodheart. As for Mag, he had made his disapproval of her tale-spinning known to her long before then, in no uncertain terms. She knew what they had all thought of her spinning tales about Dougal.

With a sigh, she tried to shove such depressing thoughts out of her head. That tale had been true, which was *all* that mattered.

Closing her eyes, she leaned back against her rolled-up pallet and tried to imagine MacAulay soundly beating Dougal in a heroic swordfight. Just as she was seeing Dougal's head fly into the clouds, the way Dougal himself had in her dream, a clatter at the door startled her upright.

The door opened, and Dougal filled the doorway again. "What's this I hear about ye refusing to eat, lass?"

Unwilling to talk to him from the floor, Murie scrambled to her feet, saying, "I couldn't eat with the image in my head of that man being flogged to death."

"Sakes, he's no dead," Dougal said. "I thought ye'd be pleased that I'd taught him to behave more respectfully."

"I loathed what he did," she admitted. "My father would have punished him, too. But I would not have been able to eat then, either. My imagination portrays such things so clearly in my mind that it makes me too sick to eat."

"I ken fine that ye've a wild imagination," he said grimly. "But we'll no fratch about that now. I'll tell Mae tae bring your supper early, and I dinna want to hear again that ye've refused to eat."

She hoped he would leave now that he had said what he'd come to say. But he stood there, looking down at her from his superior height, making her wish she could stretch taller to glare back at him. She squared her shoulders.

When he continued to gaze at her, she said, "Is that all you came to say?"

He frowned. "Ye should address me as 'sir.'"

"Perhaps when you address *me* properly, I will," she replied.

"Aye, I'll call ye 'my lady' when ye *be* my lady," he retorted.

She was silent, wishing he had not just stirred another vision of MacAulay.

"Ye'll need to mend your ways if ye want to go to Inverness with us to see the King," Dougal added sternly.

"What make you think I'd want to do that?"

"Because ye'll be my wife then, and Jamie is bringing his Joanna. She'll bring some of her ladies, and his grace wants his nobles to bring theirs, too."

"I ken fine that he is meeting with the Highland chiefs next month," she said. "But your father has no charters to present to prove his claim to Arrochar. So why should you or he be going to Inverness?"

Dougal shrugged. "'Tis simple, lass. We mean to make it plain that we'll no have Jamie's new notions imposed on us. The reason Highland chiefs opposed him afore is that our Celtic laws be gey older than any daft English ones."

"Our sense of freedom also derives from those Celtic

laws," Murie said. "I have not heard anyone say that his grace opposes them or wants to change them. He just wants the laws to be the same for everyone throughout Scotland. Then people will know what they are wherever they go, and that everyone has to obey them."

"Aye, well, we'll see," Dougal said. "Meantime, my father expects his cousin here soon and has sent word out that he'll hold his laird's court on Friday."

Murie felt a chill all the way to her bones. It was only Monday, but much as she wanted her ordeal to be over, she did not want Friday to come.

Rob returned to the cottage that night with Scáthach, meaning to sleep late Tuesday morning. Instead, he wakened abruptly at his usual time from a nightmare in which Dougal MacPharlain danced on the grave of the lady Muriella. As he did, he cried out to her father and Rob, "See what you've made me do!"

Shaking his head to banish the lingering image, he saw Scáthach leap to her feet, from peaceful sleep to full alertness.

"Easy, lass," Rob murmured. "'Tis nobbut Andrew's boggarts playing 'wile-me, beguile-me' with my dreams."

As he spoke, he thought of tales he had heard of the Mac-Farlan sisters' so-called powers. He also recalled Andrew's confidence that Lina's reading of her runes meant that he would find his charters. Ian and Mag had said little on the subject, but Mag had warned him not to discount anything he heard or saw at Tùr Meiloach. And Rob had heard that the lady Aubrey possessed the gift of foresight.

"Blethers," he muttered to himself, only to recall

Andrew's reluctance to tell him exactly how he had managed to flee Arrochar the day Pharlain and his men had attacked and seized the place.

Ian had insisted that the lady Andrena knew what men were thinking and could nearly always tell if someone was lying, to her or to anyone else.

"Of course, people also say Andrena can communicate with the birds and beasts," Rob muttered. When Scáthach's ears twitched, he added, "We know that has to be blethers, don't we, lass? Unless, of course, *you* know otherwise."

The dog lay down again and rested her head on her forepaws. Eyes open, she fixed her gaze on Rob and kept silent.

"I thought so," he said. Grinning at his own fancy, he got up, dressed, and broke his fast. Then, slinging his sword across his back, he set out for the north pass with Scáthach at his heels.

Moving silently and using boulders for cover long before he reached the usual route to the pass, he managed easily to surprise one of Andrew's guards.

The man had his back to Rob and was watching the narrow path up to the pass. When Rob kicked a stone, the man—a youngster by the look of him—leaped to his feet and whirled with his dirk in his hand.

Rob's weapons remained sheathed.

"I am Robert MacAulay of Ardincaple," he said calmly.

"Sakes, ye should ha' spoken up long afore now," the lad said. "I might ha' killed ye!"

"Nay, you would not," Rob said. "However, I might easily have killed you. A good watchman does not stay in one place, as you were. He moves about quietly, under cover, and keeps his eyes open. What is your name?"

The lad's eyes widened, but he said, "Ulf, sir. Means wolf, me da' said," he added, looking warily at Scáthach as if she might take exception to his name.

Rob's lips twitched. He could not imagine anyone less wolflike than the youngster before him. Although taller and broader than Pluff, Ulf looked no more than fourteen or fifteen. He had sandy hair, pale blue eyes, and skin as smooth as a lassie's. His chin was firm, though, and he carried himself well.

"You need to take more care, Ulf," Rob said. "Your comrades who died were likely caught off guard just as I caught you today. The men who caught them were enemies. How many are guarding this pass with you now?"

"Four, sir," the lad said, sheathing his dirk. "We ken fine what Pharlain be up tae, though. He's got half a dozen men down below the ridge on his side, and they be showing themselves regular. He be more worried about us seeking tae invade Arrochar, Calum Beg says, than t'other way round."

"Were you here yesterday?" Rob asked.

"Aye, sure, and Sunday, too."

"Did you see Pluff up here yesterday?"

Ulf hesitated, but his wary expression was answer enough for Rob.

"Was he coming or going when you saw him?"

The lad swallowed, then caught his lower lip between his teeth.

"I see," Rob said. "You saw him leave and return then, aye?"

With a grimace, Ulf said, "Ye're as scary as the lady Dree, sir, if ye can see intae a man's head like that. I did see Pluff, just as ye say. He slipped over yon pass yester-morn and hied hisself back just afore sundown."

"Does he do that often?"

"No to say 'often,'" Ulf said. "By me troth, sir, I'd no seen him go through yon pass for months now, 'til yestermorn."

Thanking him, Rob made his way to the other guards. Two of them behaved in ways that told him they were experienced, the fourth less so but warier than Ulf.

Not one saw him before he spoke, but he had not expected them to.

He took supper that evening with Andrew, as he had the evening before. No word had come from Arrochar.

Sleeping again at the cottage, he spent Wednesday there, and roasted a rabbit in the fireplace for his supper. As he cleared up, heavy rapping thudded on the door.

Before he could shout his visitor in, the door opened and Pluff said, "Good, ye're here. The boat from Arro-char came, and the laird says ye're tae make haste!"

Feeling the same urge for haste that Pluff did, Rob quickly banked the fire. Scáthach was on her feet, danc-ing with the same impatience as the boy's.

When they reached the great hall, Andrew beckoned them to the dais.

"Ye'll be disappointed to learn that Pharlain has an obli-gation on Friday that prevents his seeing ye afore Satur-day or mayhap Monday. He's disappointed that MacAulay didna take the trouble to come himself, but he'll see ye."

"An obligation on Friday," Rob said. "That would be the laird's court."

"Aye, sure. But Saturday, even Monday, be none so far off."

"However, a laird's court *is* a public event."

Andrew's eyes twinkled with mischief. "Aye, it is then, withal."

~

Friday morning, Muriella awoke before dawn in pitch darkness. She had not slept well, but she could not trouble her head about that. She needed to think.

Accordingly, she arose and rolled up her pallet for perhaps the last time, whatever her fate might be. Donning the baggy lavender kirtle, she began to pace her usual route, because she thought best while she walked.

She paced for a long time, trying not to think about MacAulay or her failure to escape. Dougal's watchfulness having provided insufficient time to persuade Mae to help her, Murie had given up trying.

Mae's visits were brief, anyway, and always overseen by a guard or Dougal himself. When Murie requested another bath, suggesting that it would be suitable for her to take one before the laird's court, Dougal refused.

"Ye can take all the baths ye want, lass, as soon as we're wed."

Much as she wanted to assure him that she would *never* marry him, she had not. She decided that it would be better to let him believe he had cowed her into obedience than to risk doing or saying something that increased his vigilance.

There would, after all, be many others at a laird's court. Of course, most people came to watch the punishments, but most of them would also be members of Clan Farlan. If she could find an opportunity to appeal to them—

Noises that usually preceded Mae's entrance diverted Murie from her reverie. When Mae entered, she carried a bundle like the one she had carried the first day. One difference was especially welcome, though. Whatever Mae carried in that bundle she had wrapped in Murie's own warm cloak.

"Bless you, Mae," Murie said sincerely. "Did you bring my pink kirtle, too?"

"Dress and feed her, Mae," Dougal said from the doorway. "Pharlain's court begins in an hour, and she must be ready. I'll come for her myself."

True to his word, he returned an hour later, but he was not alone. Two muscular guards accompanied him.

Murie was standing by Mae when he entered, wearing the pink kirtle she had worn the day he had captured her. She held her cloak draped over one arm.

"Give me that cloak, lass," Dougal said. "They'll bind your wrists behind ye, for that be my father's rule. I came with them to reassure ye that their sole task be to keep ye safe until sentence be passed on ye."

"Sentence? What sentence?" Murie demanded angrily. "I am not the one who committed a crime, Dougal MacPharlain. You are!"

"Aye, but ye did, lass. Ye'll see."

Moments later, her wrists firmly bound behind her, she stood rigid while Dougal draped her cloak over her shoulders. He went ahead, striding quickly. The two guards flanked her and followed him, taking her to meet her fate.

Chapter 10————————————

When Rob's borrowed galley landed that morning at Arrochar's wharf, near the head of the Loch of the Long Boats, he identified himself to the man who seemed to act as wharf master there.

"I've come a few days early," he added. "But Pharlain is expecting me."

"Aye, well, the laird be gey busy t'day, sir," the wharf master said, gesturing toward a line of people moving eastward on the Tarbet. "Dunamany more than usual ha' come for his laird's court and tae see his cousin, the Brehon, for theirselves."

"A Brehon justice? Why would Pharlain want such a man here?"

The other man shrugged. "Likely, he just invited his cousin tae watch. The man be a kinsman on his mam's Morrison side."

The reply failed to answer Rob's question. Cousin or none, it seemed odd that Pharlain would want someone as well-versed in Celtic law as any Brehon would be to witness his corrupt view of justice.

However, the MacAulays also had Morrison cousins,

so perhaps the news would prove less ominous than it seemed.

Despite the "many" the wharf master said had come, Rob could see only those few ahead of him, following the wide dirt track up a slight rise.

Boats had beached nearby, and more had anchored offshore. But the wharf master said naught to Rob's captain about moving his galley away from the wharf.

Most of the audience, of course, would be Clan Farlan men from Pharlain's lands who would not need boats to reach the Tarbet. Moreover, if the court was starting, Rob knew he should not delay.

He thanked the wharf master politely and assured him that he didn't expect Pharlain to extend him any ceremony. "I'll leave my crew here, though," he added.

"Aye, sir, as ye like."

Having seen that Colquhoun's captain knew *his* business, Rob headed out at once on the track toward Loch Lomond. The rise ahead, although low enough not to impede boats dragged along the track, blocked his view of what lay beyond it.

A gurgling burn flowed down toward him on its way to join the Loch of the Long Boats. The track was wide enough to accommodate boats, large and small, that men had, for years if not centuries, dragged from one loch to the other.

It occurred to him that Andrew Dubh likely missed the fees he had charged such men to access the Tarbet and for aid they might need to drag their boats across it. That was surely a lucrative business, because no other way existed for boats carrying goods or men to access Loch Lomond from the sea.

Steep slopes north and south of the Tarbet flanked it and the burn, creating the Tarbet's deep, vee-shaped, nearly flat-bottomed vale. Reaching the top of the rise, Rob saw the laird's court spread before him. The steep slopes eased away from each other there, creating an arena suitable for any such event.

Runoff from surrounding slopes fed another burn hurrying to Loch Lomond, a bit of which he could see now in the distance ahead, where sunlight sparkled on its water.

Below him, on the north side of a clearing around which the crowd had gathered, was a makeshift dais with a rectangular table sitting on it. A pair of two-elbow chairs occupied one side of the table, a single stool the other. Two men stood beside the chairs. One wore a faded red-and-blue great plaid and a red cap with eagle feathers sprouting from it, the other a black robe and cap.

Men, women, and children lined the slopes. A number of people had paused on the path ahead of Rob to seek out any places that remained to sit and watch.

Rob did not see Lady Muriella anywhere.

The glare of the midmorning sun was so strong after days in darkness that it hurt Murie's eyes. So, keeping her head down, she watched where she put her feet as Dougal's two burly minions urged her along the path from the shed and up a hill.

"Where are we going?" she asked gruffly.

"Master Dougal tellt ye," one said. "Tae the laird's court on yon Tarbet."

"Does Pharlain not hold his court at Arrochar Hall?"

"Not today," the spokesman said. "Master Dougal said

the laird wants folks tae see how kind he's been tae ye. So, he's asked a Brehon justice tae sit in, tae be sure ye be treated fairly."

"A Brehon! Good sakes, I thought they held sway only in the Isles."

"They sit wherever Celtic laws prevail, throughout the Isles, the Highlands, and elsewhere, even Galloway." The voice was Dougal's.

Startled to hear him speak, just as his minions drew her to a halt, Murie looked up, wincing at the brightness. Dougal stood right in front of her, so she shifted position slightly to put him between her and the sun.

"Brehon power is strong everywhere," he added, looking smug. "Moreover, a Brehon's word is law, lass. Not even the King can overrule a Brehon's decision."

Slightly cheered to learn that neither Pharlain nor Dougal was likely to have it all his own way in whatever happened, Murie nearly said so. Before she could, Dougal added, "Justice Morrison is the cousin I told you about. He comes from my maternal grandmother's family. Come now," he added. "We'll go this way."

Muriella grimaced. So much for fairness.

When they topped the rise, a din of voices greeted them.

Dougal stepped aside, and Muriella gasped at the sight of what seemed to be hundreds of people in the clearing before them and along the slopes that flanked it.

⁓

Rob saw two burly clansmen on the northeast slope forcing a pathway through the crowd to the dais. Two others followed, flanking a young woman.

Easily recognizing the lass as Lady Muriella, Rob watched stoically while her two guards urged her onto the dais. She looked pale, even stunned, as they held her, standing, beside the stool of judgment, facing the crowd.

Her awe was understandable. The throng spread before her was immense, especially if she had never witnessed a Brehon court before. Such courts, like other public events in the Highlands or Isles, were open to anyone who wanted to witness them. That hard and fast rule was what had given Rob the opportunity to attend despite Pharlain's instructions to wait until it was more convenient for *him*.

Doubtless, Muriella's study of clan lore and Scottish history must have taught her a few facts about the Brehons and the trials over which they presided. The ancient Celtic laws were, after all, the oldest codified laws known.

The only clear space now was a path about fifteen feet wide that guards kept open around the dais. Elsewhere, the slopes and flats teemed with humanity.

Rob found a place with a good view for himself. Although members of Clan Farlan took precedence, seated or standing, no one tried to oust him from his place. Nor would any man who tried succeed in doing so. He and Scáthach were guests of Clan Farlan's so-called chief, albeit unbeknownst to the man himself.

Scáthach sat beside him, alert and attentive. She would remain so unless Rob commanded her to do otherwise, or until something or someone threatened him.

It occurred to him that at Jamie's Parliament in Inverness, Andrew's charters or none, Pharlain might still lose his place as chief of Clan Farlan. He had, after all, done nowt to endear himself to the King and much to infuriate him. For the nonce, though, Pharlain's word would be law unless the Brehon overruled him.

That last thought gave Rob pause. Pharlain had to have good reason to summon a Brehon, because he could legally have rendered any judgment himself. Heaven knew he had done so many times since usurping Clan Farlan's chiefdom.

Recalling that Dougal had initiated the most recent villainy, Rob wondered if Pharlain feared that if he ruled in favor of Dougal, their own people might deem the trial unfair. It was also possible, since the Brehon was a kinsman, that Pharlain had corrupted him. He might, without dirtying his own hands, simply expect the Brehon to render the judgment that Pharlain desired.

To be sure, the Brehons were supposedly incorruptible. But men were men and some of them more easily corrupted than others.

Rob could see that the justice and Pharlain were of like height and age, but their similarity seemed to end there. The Brehon's demeanor seemed more youthful than his cousin's and calmer. His skin was whisky-dark. The hair bristling below his cap's rim was a shoulder-length mass of tight, snow-white curls. His shoulders were narrower than Pharlain's and his body so reed-slender that it barely stirred his robe when he moved. Had Rob believed in wee folk, he'd have said that the Brehon resembled a querulous elf, albeit much taller.

Pharlain's men-at-arms continued to keep the crowd back from the dais. Despite their swords and dirks, none would touch a weapon in the Brehon's presence unless he ordered it. Failure to obey that rule could mean hanging.

"What be they a-doing now?" muttered a youthful voice right behind Rob.

That voice was only too familiar. Looking back to find Pluff eyeing him warily, Rob said, "What the *devil* are you doing here?"

"This be summat that anyone can watch, aye?" Pluff replied innocently.

"It is. Nevertheless, you should still be smarting from your last visit and certainly have no business here now."

"I do so," Pluff replied stoutly. "That be our Lady Murie yonder, and these villains mean tae do her a mischief or summat worse, so I—"

"You will be silent if you want to stay," Rob told him sternly.

"Aye, sure, but they be a-going tae begin straightaway now, aye?"

Since it was clear that the word "silent" was foreign to the lad, Rob said, "Even so, I'll have time enough before they do to teach you to mind what I say. Do you want to test that likelihood?"

Pluff shook his head.

Frowning now, Rob held the boy's gaze.

"Nae, sir," Pluff said then. "But dinna send me away. I want tae see."

"Then keep your tongue firmly behind your teeth no matter what happens. What if Pharlain should hear you? What if he sees you? How would you like that?"

The boy opened his mouth and shut it again.

"Do you want to say something?" Rob asked softly.

Pluff nodded.

"Very well, but keep your voice down. What is it?"

"Pharlain *has* seen me now and now," Pluff confided in a near whisper. "He pays me nae mind."

Rob frowned, recalling young Ulf's report that Monday had been the first time he had seen Pluff at the pass in months. "How often of late?" he asked the boy.

"Only t'other day, but I was used tae come here last year tae visit Euan MacNur's Mae and her Annabel now and now, just tae see how they was a-getting on. Like I said t'other day afore the laird skelped me."

"Did MacNur *send* you to visit them?"

Shrugging, Pluff said, "Nay, I were just curious about Arrochar, 'cause the laird said Pharlain might ha' set some'un tae spy on us at Tùr Meiloach. I thought folks might talk tae me. They did, too, but I didna hear nowt about any spies. Sithee, they think I be an orphan a-looking after m'self. One o' the women tellt me who Mae and Annabel belonged tae. MacNur were that gruff without 'em, too, I tell ye!"

"Then Andrew Dubh found out, aye?"

"Aye, 'cause MacNur caught me and were a-going tae leather me even after I tellt him that Pharlain were a-goin' tae attack Tùr Meiloach. MacNur didna believe me, so he took me tae the laird. When I told the laird and Sir Mag what I'd heard, the laird said he'd save his judgment till he learned the truth. Then, if I'd lied, he'd take leather tae me hisself. But I hadna lied, so he didna—not then."

"What will he think of your being here today?" Rob asked.

Sending Rob a guileless look from under his carroty eyebrows, Pluff said, "I'll tell 'im I were with ye at a Brehon court. Lady Murie did say that anyone can watch the Brehons without fear. That be the law, she said."

"So it is," Rob said. "But you listen to me now, my lad. You *will* keep quiet throughout, or *I* will make you smart. Do you understand me?"

"Aye, sure," Pluff said, nodding vigorously. "I just want tae see how she'll get herself home again is all."

Rob wished that he could share Pluff's confidence in her ladyship. To say that she had flung herself into the briars with a vengeance was to understate the matter gravely. Pharlain looked far too confident for anyone to think otherwise.

Muriella, too, had seen Pharlain, for she was sure that the bearded man on the dais, wearing chief's feathers, must be he. Surely, no one else would stand in the central place on an Arrochar dais. Having heard his name often since her birth, she had been curious to see him. Now that she had, she found him unimpressive.

He had been the villain all her life. Now, she realized that she had envisioned him as the devil, horns and all. Sadly, he was just a much lesser form of her father. Admittedly, Pharlain had tied his hair back more neatly than Andrew ever did, perhaps in honor of the occasion. But he did not look chiefly, and Andrew did.

Dougal and his father both boasted Andrew's broad MacFarlan shoulders. Doubtless they were both skilled swordsmen, too.

Her bound wrists were making her hands numb.

Trying to clear her mind of such extraneous thoughts so that it might be more useful to her, she felt disoriented, as if she had been in that dark shed for weeks. Time had crawled there, to be sure. Even so, her own reliable awareness of its passing told her she had been at Arrochar for just three days and four nights.

The sun still seemed overly bright, but her eyes were adjusting.

She scanned the sea of onlookers, seeking a familiar face. Despite the multitude—or, more likely, because of it—she saw no one she knew.

"The accused will face her judges."

She had no idea who had spoken, but she was sure "the accused" was herself.

The two men who had escorted her to the dais turned her to face the two still standing behind the table, and then stepped away.

The Brehon stood at Pharlain's right. She noticed that another minion stood near the dais edge at his left.

The justice and Pharlain glanced at each other and then sat in their chairs.

Shifting her attention back to the justice, Murie tried to get some sense of him. He seemed calm and relaxed. She could discern no more than that.

Then the same voice, now obviously coming from the minion at Pharlain's left, declared in stentorian tones, "The accused will state her name, her clan, and the chief of her clan."

Addressing a point between Pharlain and the Brehon, Muriella said with forced calm, "I am Muriella MacFarlan, third daughter of Andrew Dubh MacFarlan and the lady Aubrey Comyn. The rightful chief of my clan is my father, who does not bind people's hands in *his* court until they have been found guilty."

"Nor do I," the Brehon said evenly. "Untie her hands at once."

The guard at her right hurriedly obeyed.

"Do you know why you are here, Lady Muriella?" the Brehon went on.

Looking directly at him as she rubbed feeling back into her hands, she replied, "Because Dougal MacPharlain captured me on my father's land and carried me here on his horse, wholly against my will."

The blue eyes under the bristly white eyebrows never wavered from her.

"You stand accused of abduction," he said gravely.

"I *did* no such thing, however. I was seeking shelter from the storm when Dougal MacPharlain snatched me up and brought me here by force."

"You may answer the charge against you in due time," the Brehon said. "We will hear both sides of that tale before I render judgment. But do you understand that my judgment will be the final word in this matter, your ladyship?"

"I *know* what happened to me," she retorted, feeling as if he had ignored all she had said. With a sweeping gesture that encompassed half the crowd and forced one guard beside her to step hastily back, she added vehemently, "I do not even *understand* why all of *this* is necessary."

Grimly, before the Brehon could reply, Pharlain said, "You will understand soon enough, lass. For now, you will hold your tongue and let this trial proceed."

The Brehon said, "You must sit on the stool so that we and all the onlookers can see you, Lady Muriella. We will first hear your accuser, Dougal MacPharlain."

She nearly protested, but the Brehon's utter serenity stopped her. Then, as she turned, frantic movement drew her attention to a familiar-looking redheaded lad on the west hillside, waving his hands high. As she digested the fact that Pluff had managed to insinuate himself into the crowd, she saw that he was not alone.

MacAulay stood beside him with Scáthach. Despite the distance between them and the dais, MacAulay's scowl was as recognizable as Pluff's excited grin.

Her lips parted. Aware that she was gaping, she pressed them together and obediently took her place on the stool of judgment.

Doubtless, Master Robert MacAulay thought her predicament well-earned, a consequence of her own actions. However, she would not let him see her fear, any more than she would reveal it to the villainous Pharlain or his lying son.

It was bad enough that the Brehon who would judge her wanted to hear Dougal's lies first. Her declaration that Dougal had abducted her did not seem to have penetrated the Brehon's skull to stir a single sensible thought inside.

~

Rob forced his clenched fists to relax, knowing that he'd do better to pretend he cared not a whit about what happened on the dais. Pharlain could not legally expel him for simply watching, but if the Brehon was a close cousin, the two of them and Dougal had likely contrived some nefarious plan of which Muriella knew nowt.

"If that be a judge and this be a trial, why do they force her ladyship tae sit there in front of this scaff and raff?" Pluff asked in quiet, albeit grim, disapproval.

Rob looked at him. The boy was a distraction, but he *had* remembered to keep his voice down. "I don't know exactly what they hope to achieve, lad," he replied honestly. "Your Lady Murie has told them truthfully what happened, but they seem to expect Dougal's version of the events to make things clearer."

"Dougal's wicked clean through," Pluff said flatly. "He willna tell the truth."

"Well, we're about to hear what he says," Rob said. "There he comes now."

Muriella watched Dougal stride across the open space in front of the dais and step onto it as if he owned it. Come to that, she reminded herself as he faced his father and the Brehon, he did expect to inherit Arrochar and even Tùr Meiloach if he could persuade her father to cede their estate to him.

Andrew would never agree to that, though.

"Do you swear before all of us gathered here to speak the truth and only the truth, Dougal MacPharlain?" the Brehon asked him plainly enough for all to hear.

"I do, aye," Dougal replied firmly, nodding. He did not look at Muriella.

Murie watched him, forcing herself to forget her concerns and focus on what he said and how he acted. From where he stood, he looked northward, and the way he stared straight ahead of him as he spoke drew her attention. He was lying, of course. No wonder he did not want to look at her or at the judge, but…

Just then, she saw his eyes flick toward his father.

The Brehon said, "You and your father claim that you are the injured party, Dougal MacPharlain. Explain why you both believe that to be so when her ladyship so firmly denies it."

"I can tell you only that she begged me to take her with me," Dougal said glibly. "I feared that someone had mistreated her, because she was crying when I found her. She cried out in despair several times afterward, too."

"Do you mean to say that she cozened you into escorting her?"

"I believed I was right to bring her to the safety of Arrochar, aye."

Murie heard a note of reservation in his tone and immediately fixed on it. Could that be a twinge of guilt? Could Dougal possibly feel guilty about lying?

The Brehon said mildly, "Her ladyship mentioned a horse, I believe."

"Aye, my lord justice," Dougal said, nodding again.

"Do you recall who rode in front?"

"Why . . . why, she did."

The note was there again, and he swallowed visibly, and hard. Then he looked at the judge. Guilt! Still just a twinge, but there it was. She sensed it, however briefly, as clearly as if his guilt had colored him bright orange.

If, as Lina had suggested, she could do aught to increase that guilt . . .

The Brehon exchanged a look with Pharlain, and a silent message seemed to pass between the two. When Pharlain nodded, the justice leaned back in his chair and regarded Muriella sternly enough to make her tremble.

"I need ask you only one question, your ladyship, and you must answer it truthfully. The answer is either aye or nay, nothing more than that. Did you ride in front of Dougal MacPharlain on that horse?"

"I did, aye, but—"

"No buts, my lady. You have affirmed his testimony, and you have agreed that an abduction took place. By Celtic law, you, not he, are the abductor…or, in this case," he added with a wry little smile, "the abductress."

"But that's daft!" Murie cried. "I did no such—"

"You will be silent," the Brehon ordered. When she reluctantly obeyed but sat stiffly glowering at him, he added, "It is my judgment that, according to our ancient laws, you did abduct Dougal MacPharlain. However, the sentence I pass may be tempered by what the current Chief of Clan Farlan deems to be fair."

A familiar, deep voice called out, "Is it not a matter of fairness under ancient Celtic law for a Brehon to ask if anyone present witnessed the crime or has other personal knowledge of it? And should he not do so *before* rendering judgment?"

With profound relief, Murie saw that MacAulay had moved much closer. His redheaded and gray-furred shadows stood right behind him. Crossing his muscular arms over his broad chest, he eyed the Brehon and Pharlain with equal disdain.

Pluff struck a similar pose. Scáthach, too, seemed to await the ruling.

Pharlain glanced at the Brehon, who nodded without looking at him.

"Step forward, sir, and declare your name," the justice said. "If you witnessed this abduction, we must certainly hear your testimony. We will do so before rendering final judgment and passing sentence on her ladyship."

Heart pounding, Murie watched as people in front of MacAulay parted to let him through. Scáthach took a few steps to follow, but when her master put out a hand, fingers spread, she sat back on her haunches and glanced at Pluff.

The two of them watched as MacAulay strode to the dais.

~

Rob stopped at the foot of the dais, stated his name, and then drew a deep breath. He had had no trouble interpreting the Brehon's words to mean that he had already made his decision and did not expect to change it.

He remained silent, eyeing Rob solemnly.

Dougal now stood beside his father. Both of them were watching Rob, and neither displayed any concern about what he might say.

While everyone waited for the Brehon to speak, Rob wondered at himself.

But the lass had the right of it. The law *was* daft if it declared her the abductress when the facts as she had described them should have proven otherwise—or at least led to further questions. There might be good reason for the law's having survived as it had, but any fool could see—

"Robert MacAulay," the Brehon said at last, "do you swear by your honor and before God that you did witness this abduction?"

"Aye, a significant portion of it. I heard things, too, before I saw them."

"Describe what you saw and heard."

"I was in the woods and heard her ladyship scream at MacPharlain to let her go," Rob said. "I followed them over the pass. Then I saw that he had put her on his horse and they were riding down the Lomondside slope."

"Stop there, and tell me this," the Brehon said. "Who rode in front?"

"He had put her ladyship up before him so that he could hold her there."

"She rode in front then, with MacPharlain holding on behind."

"Not holding on," Rob retorted, reminding himself at the same time to keep his suddenly unstable temper under rigid control. "It was perfectly plain to me," he added, "that Dougal, *not* her ladyship, controlled that horse."

"The law does not speak of control but is a gey simple law, withal," the Brehon said. "The person riding in front is ruled the abductor, the one clinging on behind, the abducted. Our judgment is therefore also simple. Under the law, Lady Muriella abducted Dougal MacPharlain and must face the consequences of her act. The consequences may be dire if she expected to gain by her crime."

He paused then, as if expecting someone to declare that she had. No one did.

"However," he added, "Pharlain tells me that to unify the two factions of Clan Farlan and protect the reputations of the parties involved in this abduction, his son is willing to marry her ladyship. I urge her to agree, because if she refuses that generous offer, I will allow Pharlain to order her penalty. How say you, Lady Muriella? Will you agree to marry Dougal MacPharlain?"

⁓

Muriella's whirling thoughts refused to compose themselves. Surely she was having a horrible nightmare. The law was senseless if a man could abduct a woman, swear to tell the truth, lie through his teeth, and have a notable Brehon justice decide that *she* had abducted *the man*.

She was about to shout her thoughts at them all when her sister Lina's voice echoed through her head, reminding her that recriminations rarely succeed, that one is wiser simply to act on the facts as they stand. Memories of bards' tales that Murie knew swiftly coupled with a related memory from Lina's wedding day.

All of these thoughts sped through her mind in less than a blink.

Drawing a breath and avoiding MacAulay's fierce scowl, she said with careful dignity, "I fear that I cannot consent to such a marriage. Dougal was gey mistaken if he thought I wanted him to snatch me from my home. But you have rendered that fact insignificant now. As to Robert MacAulay's testimony, I believe that, by law, this court ought not to have let him speak against me."

Tilting his head slightly, the Brehon said, "I do not know why you should say such a thing, my lady. MacAulay testified only to what he saw and heard. He did not even contradict aught that you or Dougal MacPharlain said."

"What he *heard* was me screaming at that villain to put me down and leave me be. For Dougal to carry me off my father's land by force was a crime under anyone's law, sir. But I do understand that you have declared that fact irrelevant, too. Even so, I doubt that anyone here believes that *I* abducted Dougal. He is not only a foot taller than I am but twice my weight. Nor can anyone possibly believe that I abducted him on his *own* horse. But I will say no more about that, either."

She paused, knowing by the familiar, expectant silence

that had fallen on her audience that everyone was listening intently now to her every word. Clinging to the sense that she was merely telling a tale at a *ceilidh*, she said casually, "What must be relevant, though, is that by *all* the laws of Scotland and those of the Holy Kirk, I cannot, for any reason whatsoever, marry Dougal MacPharlain."

"You are mistaken," the Brehon said sternly. "If you mean to suggest that your father will disapprove, I fear that his disapproval is also irrelevant."

"Is it irrelevant that I already *have* a husband, my lord justice?" Murie asked with demure dignity.

"*That* is a lie," Pharlain snapped.

Dougal remained silent, looking from one speaker to the next.

"If true, that would certainly be relevant," the Brehon said, frowning. "But if you *are* married, my lady, where... or, more pertinently, *who* is your husband?"

"Why, he is right there," she said, pointing. "My lord father offered me to him a year ago. My husband is Master Robert MacAulay of Ardincaple."

Chapter 11 ———————

The crowd gasped in near unison, and some wag cried out, "I warrant MacAulay will ha' more tae say tae his lady *and* tae our Dougal then, aye?"

Muriella, Rob noted, wisely kept her gaze fixed on the Brehon.

Rob wanted to throttle her, not only for her declaration but for daring to fling an outright lie in the face of a Brehon justice. That was surely a hanging offense if anyone should gainsay her, as others besides Dougal likely would.

"What say you to that declaration, sir?" the Brehon demanded.

Realizing that the man addressed him, Rob returned his steady look. "Honor forbids me to contradict her ladyship, my lord justice."

"Nevertheless, Master Robert MacAulay, *you* must tell the truth."

"Her ladyship spoke the truth from the outset," Rob said. "That you and these others chose to play lairds-of-all with Celtic law does not alter that fact."

"Then why did you not object to the charge of abduction immediately instead of supporting what Dougal MacPharlain had said?"

"Pray, forgive my ignorance, sir. I assumed that justice would prevail, giving me no cause to mortify her ladyship further than these proceedings already have."

"You would mock the ancient laws of this land?"

"I had no such intent," Rob replied, fighting for calm. "I saw what happened, though. And, to my mind, for a man of justice to declare the truth irrelevant and decide that her ladyship abducted MacPharlain when that is plainly absurd... Sithee, my lord, I expected the truth and my honest testimony to be sufficient."

"You should show more respect for Highland law, sir. Good reason lies behind even this one." Rob noted that the Brehon did not reveal that reason. Instead, he added hastily, "We do not cast aside our laws for seeming strange. Forbye, I think you must agree that, however your lady came to be riding foremost on that horse, the event itself came about due to her own careless actions."

"I do agree with that," Rob said grimly, shooting Muriella a look that ought to have frozen the marrow in her bones.

"I should hang them both," Pharlain snapped. "If MacAulay is indeed her husband, then by God, he is as guilty as she is. His wife is *his* responsibility."

"He is indeed responsible for her actions," the Brehon said mildly. "But only if he knew that she intended to abduct your son, sir." Looking at Dougal, he asked sternly, "Do you believe that MacAulay did know and was a party to the act?"

Rob saw Muriella stiffen and gaze fiercely at Dougal. Her demeanor, every fiber of her body, seemed to be straining to speak to him.

Don't you dare say it, you villain! Heed your guilt. Murie concentrated hard. She had no idea if her thoughts were having any effect, but at least Dougal had not immediately declared that Rob was party to this outrageous, *wickedly* made-up crime.

Dougal hesitated until people in the audience began to grumble, but at last, he shook his head. Then, without inflection, he said, "One might more accurately call it all an unhappy misunderstanding."

"Aye, then, you leave me nae choice." Turning to Pharlain, the Brehon said clearly enough to reach most ears, "We can proceed with the case against her ladyship if you insist, my lord. However, you should be aware that Robert MacAulay would then be within *his* legal rights to charge your son with wife-stealing. You should also be aware that the ancient laws make it impossible to blame a wife for allowing herself to be stolen. Moreover, the penalties for wife-stealing are far more severe than any common penalty for simple abduction."

Pharlain's expression gave nothing away. When he eyed MacAulay for a long moment, perhaps measuring his steel, Murie's fears flooded back.

Surely Pharlain would not try to pursue such a self-defeating course. She wanted the business finished before it occurred to anyone to ask more probing questions of MacAulay or of her.

At last, with a dismissive gesture, Pharlain said, "Release her to his custody. We can only hope that she has learned a lesson from this."

The Brehon said gravely, "I hereby order her ladyship released to your custody, Robert MacAulay. I will add this, though, sir. Your wife deserves stern chastisement for the carelessness that resulted in taking up the time of this laird's court—and *my* time, as well. What say you to that?"

"I can only agree, my lord."

"Then we can trust you to see to that matter?"

"I give you my word," MacAulay said flatly.

Muriella, meeting his flintlike gaze, shuddered and wondered if, possibly, she might have been safer with Dougal.

Rob's words echoed in his ears, and he wondered what sort of chastisement, exactly, the justice expected him to mete out to her ladyship.

He would not, however, ask him that question.

Recalling that he was supposed to discuss potential fees at Ardincaple with Pharlain, he gave him an appraising look and decided that no words, however diplomatic, would gain the assurances his father desired. Not, he told himself sagely, that Pharlain had ever been likely to agree to aught that did not accord with his own wish, and the Campbell's, to impose control over Ardincaple. Rob's own opinion was that forthright confrontation would accomplish more than any parlay.

Shifting his gaze back to the Brehon, he moved closer to Muriella and said, "Do I understand that I may now take her ladyship home?"

"You may." Raising his voice, the Brehon added, "And all here should know that you must both be allowed to depart in safety. Have you transport nearby?"

"It lies at Arrochar's wharf on the Loch of the Long Boats," Rob replied.

"Then I advise you to take your lady and go. I shall

stay, since Pharlain has other grievances to hear. But the truce ends with my departure, as you know."

That took care of that, Rob thought. Muriella still had not looked at him, so he touched her nearer shoulder and said, "Come, lass."

Obeying silently, she waited only until they had passed beyond the crowd before she said lightly, "Do you not think it was clever of me to recall how Lina and Ian married and other tales I had heard about declarations of marriage?"

Knowing that she would dislike his answer to that question, Rob kept silent. He would not let her linger much longer in her fantasy, though.

⁓

Disturbed by Rob's silence but undaunted, Murie went on blithely, "I confess that it was horrid being locked up in that dark shed. Faith, I would have done almost anything to escape, so I am gey relieved to be safe at last."

"Safe from all but the chastisement I promised the Brehon I would deliver," MacAulay muttered in a near growl.

Dismayed, she exclaimed, "But you cannot mean to punish me! Sakes, you *cannot*, for you have no righ—"

The last word ended in a hastily stifled screech when he gripped her arm hard enough to leave bruises and spun her to face him.

"As to my rights or lack of them, my *lady*, you would do well to hold your tongue until we are well away from here," he muttered. "Not only would you liefer no one else overhear such a denial after your declaration—under oath, I might remind you—that I am your husband. But the fact is that now I have *every* right to put you across my knee, right here where everyone can still see us, and flail you with my hand or any implement I choose until you scream to heaven for mercy."

"You don't! You wouldn't!"

"Thanks to your so-clever declaration back there, no one would deny me that *privilege*," he snapped. "After what the Brehon said, they'll more likely applaud."

"Mayhap they would. But the truth is that you are *not* my husband. I told them you were only to make them let me go. You *know* I never meant it."

"Under every marriage law of Scotland, your declaration was legal when I failed to contradict it," he said more calmly. "You must know that as well as I do."

"Then I will *un*declare it as soon as we are away from here," she retorted. "If you don't contradict me then either, you can go about your business free and clear forever. You have made it plain enough that you *don't* want me for your wife."

Rob sighed. Heaven knew she was right about that. He had recalled only when she had mentioned it with her declaration that she was aware of Andrew's offer and *his* rejection of it. Not that either of those things made any difference now.

"It is not that simple to end it, Muriella," he said, striving for patience. "All I meant is that when you declared us married before witnesses and received no contradiction from me, you created a marriage as legal as any in the land."

"But that's—"

"The law," he interjected flatly, urging her along the path. "The only way we can annul it is with the Kirk's permission. I won't embarrass you by putting such a request to any clergyman. Nor, I think, do you want to embarrass yourself so."

She paled but did not deny that statement.

"Whatever possessed you to do it?" he demanded. "Nay, though, do not try to tell me now. Hold your tongue until we are safely aboard the galley. Where the devil is— Oh, there you are," he added when Pluff ran up beside him. "You have Scáthach, too. Good lad, but don't you say a word until we're on that ship, either."

"I think I should tell ye," Pluff said, meeting Rob's frustrated gaze, "that these two wi' me must go home with us, too."

The still fuming Rob eyed the woman and young girl in servants' attire behind Pluff with near exasperation but nodded, easily guessing who they were.

~

Muriella's temper had flared at MacAulay's scolding. First a witless Brehon, she thought, now a witless and unwanted husband. But MacAulay was also still an unknown entity, so when Pluff spoke, she was fighting to curb her anger.

Having focused her attention so narrowly on trying to figure out what MacAulay was thinking and saying, she had been unaware that anyone followed them. Whirling when she heard Pluff speak, she beheld not only the boy and Scáthach but also Mae and a girl of fifteen or sixteen.

"Mae!" she exclaimed. "Oh, how glad I am to see you!"

"Aye, 'tis herself," Pluff said, clearly delighted that Murie was pleased. "And Mae's Annabel, too."

Turning to MacAulay, now eyeing them all with

unconcealed truculence, Murie said, "They must go with us. Oh, prithee, do not say that they cannot. Mae is the only one here who was kind to me, and Dougal swore to flog her if she said a word to me. She is terrified of him, sir. And one cannot wonder at that. Surely—"

To her surprise, he said, "They may come, aye." To Mae, he said, "I ken fine that you are Euan MacNur's wife and that Annabel is his daughter."

"Aye," Mae said in low-pitched, mellow tones. "I couldna stay, sir, and I dared not leave Annabel behind."

"Nor will I, mistress, but I suggest that since people on those slopes can still see all of us, we should go faster. Take longer strides rather than quicker ones, though. It will look less as if we are suddenly eager to make all speed. Our galley lies over this rise, and whilst I doubt that anyone will think much of two women and a lad walking behind us, we'd be wise to give them no cause for curiosity."

"I am glad you will come with us, Mae," Murie said. "You cannot know how much I've yearned to hear your voice. Are you truly MacNur's wife?"

"I am, m'lady. I'm sorry I couldna talk tae ye."

"Faith, you need not apologize. I'd have been terrified to talk to anyone if Dougal had threatened to flog me for it."

Mae bit her lip, and her gaze slid away.

"Good sakes!" Murie exclaimed. "Did he *make* such a threat?"

Nodding, Mae said, "I think he feared I might speak for your own sake, so he swore that if I did, before he whipped me, he'd whip ye and make me watch."

"Good sakes, when I think how hard I tried to persuade

you…" Tears sprang to Murie's eyes at the thought of what might have happened to them both if she had persuaded Mae to talk and Dougal had heard them.

A sound beside her, as if Scáthach had growled, drew her attention to MacAulay. His jaw was set, his lips pressed tight, and he stared straight ahead.

"Sir?" Murie said. "Is aught amiss?"

Without looking at her, he said, "Pluff, glance back and make sure that no one is following us yet."

"All's clear, sir."

"Right then, when we reach the top of the rise, I want you all to go—"

Breaking off with a frown, he said to Mae, "Will you likely know the men on guard at yonder wharf, mistress, and they you?"

"Aye, sir, they'll be Pharlain's men, and most do know me. But they willna ken her ladyship, and since she didna come wi' ye, they may object tae ye taking her away wi' ye. Ye might claim that the Brehon or Pharlain gave permission."

A chill shot up Murie's spine. Surely she had not finally made her escape only to have Pharlain's minions at the wharf prevent it.

Rob's thoughts were racing, too. His earlier plan of trying to persuade Pharlain to release Muriella had been a distant possibility. But he had not thought about taking her home *without* his agreement. Therefore, the possibility that he might have to fight their way clear had not dawned on him until now.

Even if it had occurred to him, before Pluff introduced himself and the other two females to their party, he would have assumed that he could handle anyone who objected to his taking Muriella with him on the galley.

Now he wanted to kick himself. A warrior, off the battlefield or on, ought to consider every possibility in any given situation, and he had failed to do so.

Striding faster, he reached the top of the rise and counted four guards near the wharf, including the chap he had talked with earlier. Just four.

The Colquhoun galley, although small, carried a captain, a helmsman, and sixteen oarsmen. And, since Sir Ian Colquhoun was now Governor of Dumbarton, all of the Colquhoun oarsmen carried arms.

Rob knew they would recognize him, even with his companions, and hoped they would also recognize that he might need assistance.

More confidently, he led the way and warned the others to keep close. For a wonder, her ladyship kept silent. He had expected questions, comments, even further debate. But perhaps she had understood from his demeanor that she would be unwise to press him further until they could talk privately.

~~~

Murie had been surprised to hear MacAulay tell the Brehon he had a galley at the wharf but had given it no more thought until he mentioned it to Mae.

Since Andrew did not keep a galley, and since she knew that MacAulay had walked from Ardincaple to Tùr Meiloach, she wondered whose boat it was.

One look at his grim expression had been enough to keep her from asking him, and now that she knew

Pharlain's men might object to Mae's leaving with Annabel, she could think only of their safety.

She was nearly certain she had influenced Dougal to admit that MacAulay had had naught to do with any abduction. Dree could do such things easily, but Murie thought her own efforts had been closer to what Lina called quiet persuasion. Whatever it was, she had felt something happen. The feeling had been similar to what she felt when she knew that a friend or kinsman was approaching or that one of her sisters was in trouble or sick.

Thinking of that latter gift, one that all three of them shared, she realized with a start that both Dree and Lina had likely worried about her. Perhaps, though, not as much as she and Dree had worried about Lina when Dougal captured her.

Lina's terror had been strong then. Murie doubted that hers had matched it, even in the horrid, dark shed that first night with imaginary spiders.

The nearer they got to the loch shore, the more closely she watched the sole galley at the wharf. Oddly, for an Isles galley at rest, its banner still flew from its mast. Andrena would have known it, but Murie did not.

MacAulay was scanning the area. When his sweeping gaze paused, she looked to see why.

A score or more of men were emerging from woodland to the north.

～

Rob, too, saw the men coming from the woods but did not pause in his stride. Two men from the galley were walking along the wharf toward the wharf master. One of them was Colquhoun's captain. Just then, he waved at the galley, and all but two of the oarsmen stood as if to disembark. Each one held his sword in hand.

Although Rob's right hand automatically went to the dirk sheathed at his left hip, he did not draw it but watched to see what would happen next.

He had eighteen men, nineteen if he counted himself, against perhaps two or three more on Pharlain's side. Good enough, he decided.

Pharlain's men had surely expected anyone who came that day to have come for the laird's court and therefore to honor the truce and be generally friendly. The men-at-arms from the woods should also know that they had small chance of defeating those they knew only as MacAulay men if it came to a fight. Galley oarsmen, in particular, were known to be fierce, unpredictable warriors.

However, Rob also knew that many of Pharlain's oarsmen were men Pharlain had captured and kept as slaves. The man was certainly not the only Highlander or Islesman to keep slaves, but men who did, did not arm them. Therefore, at such times as this, Pharlain had fewer fighting men to rely on.

Moreover, he still sat beside his Brehon justice, possibly condemning more captured men to slavery.

Confident now that he and his charges were safe, Rob led the way to the wharf. He felt undeniable relief but little surprise when no one challenged them.

Pharlain's wharf master looked uncertain, and some of his other men glowered at them, but none raised a weapon.

Running up beside Rob, Pluff asked, "Will they no try tae stop us then?"

Glancing at him, Rob saw that Muriella also looked anxious, as did Mae and Annabel. He said loudly enough for them all to hear, "They have better sense."

"Who'd ha' thought that o' Pharlain's lot?" Pluff said with a derisive snort.

"Don't let them hear you say such things," Rob replied. "We'll just board our ship as if we ken fine that they will allow it. I want to get out of here."

Colquhoun's captain strode to meet him, saying, "All's peaceful, sir."

"You handled it well," Rob said sincerely. "I trust that you invoked my lord father's name, though, and not Colquhoun's."

"I invoked none save your own, sir. I told Pharlain's wharf master ye'd likely arranged wi' Pharlain tae provide transport for others here. I expect I made it…um… plain tae him that we'd take unkindly tae interference."

"I see," Rob said dryly. "Then we will depart straightaway."

Escorting his charges along the wharf, where several Colquhoun men stood with swords drawn, they passed among them to the galley. Men aboard helped Lady Muriella and Mae, but Pluff, grinning now, jumped in by himself and extended a hand to the lass, Annabel.

The captain spoke to two of his men, who quickly untied the galley and boarded. The captain stepped aboard as it began to drift, and the helmsman ordered his oarsmen to push off and prepare to row. Seconds later, they were away.

Rob kept an eye sternward to be sure that no other boat followed them.

"Thank you, sir," Muriella murmured from right behind him.

He turned to meet her wary gaze.

In a voice that sounded gruff even to his own ears, he

replied, "I did nowt for which ye need be thankful, my lady."

⁓

Easily sensing the anger that had surged within him but unable to discern its cause, Murie licked suddenly dry lips, drew a steadying breath, and said frankly, "You are angry, sir. Is it because I thanked you or because I contrived it so that you had little choice but"—she glanced at the nearest men—"to rescue me?"

"My lady," he said more gently, "this is neither the time nor place to discuss my feelings. Forbye, I am not angry with you. I spoke only the truth. However, the less we say before these men about that laird's court the better I shall like it."

"Sir!" a man cried. "Yonder, another boat. Coming at speed, sir."

When MacAulay turned, Murie could see the oncoming galley for herself. Its oars churned spray high into the air so that it sparkled in the sunlight.

They watched until the boat was near enough for her to make out its banner. "That banner looks just like the one we're flying," she said.

"Almost, aye," MacAulay said. Then, to the captain and the lookout who had shouted, he called out, "It's friendly!"

"Aye, sir," the captain said. "I see now that it flies MacAulay's banner."

Trepidation stirred deep inside Muriella at hearing that news. "Mercy," she said, "is your lord father aboard it, then?"

"'Tis likely," MacAulay muttered, but she sensed only disquiet as he did.

Rob could not imagine why his father would have taken ship from Ardincaple all the way to Arrochar to find him. Lord MacAulay was not one who interfered with a man to whom he had entrusted a duty, least of all his son. Having known that Rob would stop at Tùr Meiloach, he would much more likely have stopped there for news of him. Had he done so, he'd have learned that Andrew expected Rob's return by sundown and would have awaited him there.

A tickle of fear stirred. Rob tried to ignore it, to tell himself that worry without cause was wasted energy. But as the other galley drew nearer, his fear increased. Had Lord MacAulay been aboard, he'd have shown himself when the galleys drew near enough for each to recognize the other's banner. MacAulay, of all people, would know that the only other one flying such a banner would be Rob.

Hearing the helmsman's command to "weigh enough," he watched the other galley's oars feather above the water while its momentum carried it nearer. He also saw that the oarsmen, helmsman, and captain were the only ones aboard.

The latter two men eyed the women on the Colquhoun galley curiously. Their oarsmen looked sternward as they rowed, so they hadn't seen them yet.

The captain's gaze shifted to Rob and back to Muriella. He frowned.

In near unison, the helmsmen on both galleys roared, "Hold water!"

Every oarsman dug his oar into the water. The two galleys eased closer, then alongside each other, and stopped side-by-side.

Rob had not shifted his gaze from his father's captain, a man he had known all his life but who seemed reluctant now to meet his gaze.

Instead, the captain looked from the bedraggled Lady Muriella to Mae and Annabel MacNur, then back to Muriella again.

At last, with visible effort, he met Rob's gaze. "I am glad tae find ye, sir," he said. "I bring news, but mayhap ye'll prefer tae hear it more privately."

"What is it, MacKell?" Rob demanded, unexpectedly irritated by the way the MacAulay oarsmen were now gaping at the lady beside him.

"Ye're tae come home, Master Rob," the captain said. "The laird..." He hesitated, the catch in his throat clearly audible. Then, rushing his words, he added, "The laird be a-dying m'lor—that is, sir."

Distantly, as if from somewhere far away, Rob heard Muriella gasp.

He frowned at MacKell and said, "He was dying when you left? Are you sure of that? Did he send you to fetch me?"

The older man grimaced, looked away, and then gathered himself. Looking directly at Rob, he said bluntly, "In troth, m'lord, Lord MacAulay died gey early yestermorn. The mistress said I must tell ye that he still lived. I did tell her it rubbed sore against me heart tae lie tae ye, 'cause his death means ye'd be our laird now. I said I'd likely muck it, but she said I must let her break the news tae ye."

Swallowing his fury and fighting to keep his grief at bay, knowing that the captain was not the right target for the fury and was suffering his own sorrow, Rob said with forced calm, "If my father is dead, MacKell, you have a new mistress now, although you do not see her at her best. This is the lady Muriella, youngest daughter of Andrew Dubh Mac-Farlan. She has become my lady wife."

MacKell gaped but recovered swiftly and managed a polite nod to Muriella.

She said quietly, "I am pleased to make your acquaintance, captain, despite the tragic news you bring. I hope we have time to stop at Tùr Meiloach," she added, looking up at Rob. "I need a bath, sir, and fresh clothing. Also, we must decide what is to be done about this coil that I have created for you."

"There is nowt to be done about that save explain matters to your father," Rob said. "In troth, it may be wiser for me to leave you with him, whilst I go to Ardincaple and see to matters there."

He saw relief in her eyes and could scarcely blame her, since she was likely more concerned about the Brehon's orders than about Lord MacAulay's death. Since he had given his word, though, he would have to think of a suitable punishment for her, one that the justice would approve.

However, the Brehon had not said that it had to take place straightaway.

For that matter, fretting about what it *might* be could serve as part of her punishment. Anticipation of forthcoming chastisement was often more worrisome than the event itself. In fact, as he recalled from boyhood experience, the punishment, when it did come, sometimes came as a relief.

Chapter 12 ——————

Murie felt a measure of relief to hear that MacAulay—faith but she would have to call him something else now—would likely leave her at Tùr Meiloach.

She was sure that Andrew would rather have her at home, under his eye, than see her traipsing off with a husband he had not expected her to acquire. Moreover, he would not have the same commitment to punishing her that her new husband had.

"It be an honor to make your acquaintance, m'lady," Captain MacKell said to her. Turning to MacAulay, he added, "I ken that ye willna take all these people tae Ardincaple, m'lord. But Lady MacAulay did insist that we make all speed, sir."

Murie sensed MacAulay's irritation at hearing that. It radiated from him.

"If my father is dead, MacKell, I see no reason to hurry," he said. "The weather has remained chilly enough for us to delay a day or two."

"It be nae place o' mine tae be telling ye what to do, m'lord," MacKell said diffidently. "Forbye, I do think I should tell that ye we dinna ken just how his lordship died. As ye ken fine, he were in good health, just fretting about this business wi' Campbell o' Lorne and Pharlain o' Arrochar. We did hope ye'd be bringing us good news from your talk wi' Pharlain."

Having no idea what MacKell was talking about, Murie glanced at MacAulay and saw a wry grimace touch his lips.

"What is it, sir?" she asked.

He gave her a rueful look. "My original purpose in visiting Arrochar was to persuade Pharlain that collecting a fee from every boat that enters or leaves the Loch of the Long Boats would be unwise."

"Good sakes, I should think so," she said. "That would anger everyone!"

"My father deemed it a matter of freedom for boats to come and go as they please. But the Campbells—Campbell of Lorne, at least—and Pharlain wanted him to charge fees for everyone except themselves and to share the profits with them."

"Well, if Pharlain wants that, I doubt that you could have changed his mind," she said. "He never changes it when he is set on something. In troth, sir, he rarely cares a whit for what anyone else says."

"My father had not yet said nae to them," he said musingly. "He said only that he would have to think about it." When she raised her eyebrows at the thought that immediately occurred to her, he turned to MacKell and said, "Did you mean to imply that his lordship died mysteriously?"

Muriella's thought having been the same, she watched MacKell closely.

He looked uncomfortable, as if he did not want to commit himself to an opinion. Then he said, "They found him in the woods near the Gare Loch shore just south o' the castle, m'lord. His head were stove in."

"How far was his lordship from the castle?"

"Nobbut a mile, mayhap a mile and a quarter. Ye'll ken the place, sir. There be a shingle beach near where the shoreline hooks out into the loch and gives shelter from the north winds. We beach galleys there now and now."

"I do know the place," he said. "'Tis gey rocky there. Might he have fallen?"

"There was rocks and boulders nearby, aye. But 'less he got up again after he hit one and wandered off, none was close enough to him for them what found him to think it had done him injury—only if a strong chap clouted him with one."

"Woodland abuts that beach east of the shingle and southward," MacAulay said. "The shingle is mostly underwater at high tide. A boat or someone hiding in the woods may have surprised him."

"Aye," MacKell agreed. "The laird were lying near the woods but not in them. We saw nae blood, Master Rob. I'd say some'un gave him a wicked clout."

Neither man seemed to note MacKell's slip.

MacAulay glanced thoughtfully northeastward, toward Arrochar.

Murie said, "It cannot have been Pharlain, sir. He was at home. That is, I think he was," she added. "In troth, I saw him only at his laird's court."

"Pharlain rarely bloodies his own fingers," he said.

That was true. She kept silent.

"We'll stop overnight at Tùr Meiloach, MacKell," he said then. "If we set out immediately for Ardincaple, it will be dark before we reach Craggan." To the Colquhoun captain, nearby, he added, "You'll stay at Tùr Meiloach, too. Andrew Dubh will insist on it, as doubtless ye ken fine."

"I do, my lord," the man replied. "We won't linger past dawn though, unless ye have further need of us."

"We'll see," MacAulay said. "If Pharlain sends boats out, we might be wiser to keep together until we reach Craggan. But we'll decide that in the morning."

"As ye wish, m'lord."

Murie turned away then, to talk to Mae and Annabel. The men had apparently finished their discussion, and she had much to think about before engaging MacAulay in further talk.

Rob watched her turn away, thinking how small and solemn she looked and wondering what sort of marriage they would have. Neither of them wanted it. If the truth were known, he suspected that Muriella wanted it less than he did.

Not only had she made it clear that she did not want to marry anyone; she also had what she considered good reason for her decision. Few women had served as keepers of clan history and folklore. Those who had done so possessed fine memories, just as men who served as seanachies had to have.

From what he had heard, Muriella's memory was nearly flawless.

Her understanding of what she recalled was, he thought, another matter. If that also had been flawless, she would have understood that an unchallenged declaration of marriage was legal *and binding* on both parties involved.

He could not alter that. Nor could she. His thoughts shifted to his father with a strong sense that someone had erred. Lord MacAulay could not be dead or *he* would feel more than the bleak emptiness he felt now, as if everything in him had shut down. He loved his father and did not want him to be dead. Nor did he want the burdens that would... that *had* descended on *him* if MacAulay had died.

He reminded himself that events were what they were, that he had no good reason to disbelieve MacKell. The man had served them loyally all his working life.

Swallowing hard, Rob stared blindly at the water. After a time, he began to see the way the sun made shining paths where the water rippled. So intently had he focused his attention that a gentle touch on his elbow startled him.

He turned abruptly to find Muriella looking anxiously at him.

"What is it, lass?"

"I was going to ask *you* that, sir. I can see that you are unhappy. Since you will not let me thank you, will you at least let me tell you how sorry I am that your father has died and apologize to you for flinging us into this muddle?"

"I did not mean for you to think I'd rejected your thanks," he said gruffly.

"Then what did you mean?"

"Only that I think it gey unlikely that you will remain thankful. I ken fine that I'm not the sort of chap that women seek to marry."

She stared at him, her lovely eyes wide. "Good sakes, why not? You are big and strong and heir to a barony. Even I know that, and I have never heard that such attributes rendered a man unfit to marry."

When he did not reply, her eyes grew even wider.

She said almost curtly, "Faith, sir, I should be smacked for saying that about the barony when you've only just learned that your lord father has died."

"No one will smack you, certainly not for that," he said. "I cannot seem to make *myself* accept it, so your words sounded perfectly sensible to me."

She met his gaze, and to his surprise, her eyes began to twinkle. "I cannot recall anyone ever before uttering those exact words to me," she said. "About sounding perfectly sensible, I mean."

A bubble of laughter began to rise in him, surprising him even more than her twinkle had. He swallowed the bubble but felt better and said honestly, "It sounded sensible to me, lass. You need not apologize for what happened, either. If you feel that you must, I'll willingly forgive you, and we need think no more about it."

"Then I think we may deal well together, sir...that is, if you have no objection to my becoming a seanachie."

The last trace of Rob's near-amusement vanished in a trice. "*That*," he said firmly, "is another matter."

"But—"

"Muriella, you seem to forget that by marrying me you have become a MacAulay. As my lady, you cannot become a Clan Farlan seanachie."

"But seanachies are seanachies, not just tale-spinners for their clans alone. And I will always be a MacFarlan, just as Mam is still a Comyn."

"And a Campbell," he reminded her. "I doubt that she will be expressing pride in her Campbell roots if that clan refuses to support his grace. Will she?"

Her eyes flashed furiously then, but she wisely held her tongue.

Murie wanted to stamp her foot and shout at him, but she did not. She had long since learned to curb her temper where her father and her good-brothers were concerned. And, after all, husbands had similar rights.

Recalling that a husband wielded more rights over his wife than a father wielded over married daughters, she wondered what demon had possessed her to say that she and Robert MacAulay would deal well together. Clearly, if he meant to deny her deepest wish, they would *not* get along at all.

Awareness stirred then of his connubial rights, and heat surged into her cheeks. Would Robert demand those rights straightaway? Surely not. But the more she thought about that, the more contrary her thoughts and feelings became.

She did not speak to him again until they reached the wharf at Tùr Meiloach. Then it was only to thank him politely when he assisted her onto its planks. Because the wharf sat on the water, it shifted with the weight of persons stepping onto it from boats, so she was grateful for his strong arm. But she still did not want to talk to him. Nor, she realized belatedly, did she want to talk to her parents until after MacAulay told them what had happened at Arrochar.

"I must have a bath," she reminded him as they started up the path to the tower. "I'll just go straight to my chamber—"

"Nay, madam wife," he said, putting a hand at the small of her back as if he did not trust her to keep her footing even on that familiar path. "Andrew may be a trifle displeased about what happened. Your mam, too. We'll tell them together."

"But I don't want to meet them in all my dirt! Surely—"

"Muriella," he said curtly, "what is *sure,* if you argue with my decisions, is that we will fratch. And when it comes to such things as this, you will lose." He paused, still eyeing her sternly. Then, in a calm voice, he said, "I'll do most of the talking, but we will talk with them together. Sakes, lass, they will both be more shocked by our marriage than by your appearance. But they will be glad to see you and cheered to hear that you'll stay here until I get things sorted at Ardincaple."

She believed him. However, the first hint that things would not go as he'd planned came ten minutes later when they entered the great hall. Not only were her mother and father awaiting them but also Murie's sisters and Mag, Mag's little sister, Lizzie, and their aunt, the dour, purse-mouthed lady Margaret Galbraith.

Murie gaped at them and felt unexpected relief to see her father hurrying across the hall, away from all the others, to meet them.

Hugging Murie tightly for a long moment, he eased his hold at last and said, "Come along in now, lass. Let everyone see ye. Did they harm ye?" Then, without giving her time to draw breath, he added, "How did ye win her free, Rob?"

"If we may, sir," Rob said, "we would prefer to discuss that privately with you and the lady Aubrey before we talk with the others."

"Then they did harm ye," Andrew said, peering into Murie's eyes.

"No, sir," she said, hugging him again and rubbing her

face against his broad chest as she had since early child-hood. "Dougal was horrid, but no one hurt me."

"So those villains have *some* good sense," Andrew said curtly. "But go to your mam now, Murie-lass. There can be nae need for ye—"

"Muriella and your lady should come with us, sir," Rob said firmly.

Eyeing her volatile sire warily, knowing he hated inter-ruptions, Murie held her breath. To her astonishment, she realized that she feared more that Andrew might roar at Rob than she worried about facing her parents.

Andrew looked at Rob and cocked his head. "Ye're gey sure o' yourself. I think Muriella would be happier to stay with her sisters and the others," he said. "You and I can better discuss what needs discussing without the women."

"Muriella will come with us, sir," Rob said. "I also think that Lady Aubrey should participate in the discussion."

"Ye do, do ye?"

"I do," Rob replied unflinchingly.

Looking from Rob to Muriella and back again, Andrew turned to a passing gillie and said, "Present me compliments to the lady Aubrey and ask her to join us in me wee chamber upstairs. Tell Sir Magnus and the others we'll return anon."

"Aye, laird," the gillie said and hurried to the dais.

"We'll take the main stairs," Andrew said, gesturing back the way they had come. Glancing at Rob, he added, "Unless ye object to that, too."

"No, sir," Rob replied.

He followed Muriella and her father up the spiral stairway. He was glad that Mag and Andrena had returned. But, since Lina was with them, Rob assumed that Ian had been unable to leave Dumbarton and hoped that his absence did not mean the Campbells were already stirring trouble along the Firth of Clyde or at Ardincaple.

They entered Andrew's chamber, and Lady Aubrey joined them as Andrew was about to close the door. Motioning for her to take one of the back-stools, he shut the door and moved to the chair behind the table, facing Rob and Muriella.

Watching him, Rob tried to gauge his mood.

"Now," Andrew said to him as they all sat. "What's amiss?"

"Nowt," Rob said. "You asked me how I'd won her ladyship's freedom. The truth is that she saved herself. Her method may displease you, though."

"I dinna care what she did if it brought her safe home to us."

"She will stay here for a short time, aye. Tell them, lass," he said to Muriella.

She gave him a beseeching look, but he turned to Andrew, wanting to see his face when she told him what she had done. Andrew's eyebrows shot upward, but Rob noted, too, that his eyes began to twinkle.

Lady Aubrey frowned at her daughter. "What have you done now, love?"

With a sigh of resignation, Muriella said, "By my troth, Mam, I did not mean to create trouble. I thought we could easily fix it."

After a silence, during which Rob continued to watch Andrew and Lady Aubrey simply wait for Muriella to say more, she said with another little sigh, "Pharlain wanted me to marry Dougal, and at the laird's court, the Brehon said that I must or I'd have to face whatever penalty Pharlain set for me. So I told them and…and a great many other people, that I could not marry Dougal because I was already married to…to him." Without looking away from her mother, she made a small gesture toward Rob.

"*What* were you thinking?" Lady Aubrey demanded. When Muriella flushed but kept silent, her mother began pelting her with questions, while Andrew grinned.

Then, abruptly, he said to his wife and daughter, "Whisst now, the pair o' ye. We'll hear all the details anon. For the nonce, I've heard just one thing with which I disagree. Rob, lad, although I understand your desire to be rid of the lass until ye get used to the notion, a wife belongs with her husband."

"Under any other circumstance, I would agree with you, sir," Rob said. "However, I expect you are unaware that…that my father died yesterday."

Andrew exclaimed, and Lady Aubrey expressed her sympathy with unexpected warmth, considering the news she had just had. Then Andrew seized control of the conversation again, saying, "'Tis but greater reason to take the lass with ye, lad. I'll wager ye've spared little thought for how your lady mother will react—"

"On the contrary, sir, I have given much thought to it, and I see no reason to expose the lady Muriella to—"

"Blethers," Andrew said. "Ye'd be wiser to take her along. Not only did she create the very marriage your mam will decry, but Murie has a knack for easing difficult situations." Looking at his daughter, he added, "All my lasses have that knack if they but exert themselves to use it. She'll be a grand help to ye in calming your mam after her tragic loss and deep disappointment."

"You do not know my mother well, sir, but even if—"

"Nae buts," Andrew retorted. "Would ye shame my lass by leaving her behind at such a time? Forbye, ye did as much as she did. If she declared herself married to ye, all ye had to do was deny it. 'Tis plain ye did nowt o' the sort."

Before Rob could think of a diplomatic reply to that, Andrew added, "I'll have me hands full here, just finding me charters and preparing to leave. We must depart in ten days to be sure of reaching Inverness by mid-May, so ye'll need to decide if ye'll be going, too, lad. I'd advise ye to, if only so ye can swear your fealty to his grace as soon as may be. Heaven kens when he'll get to these parts again."

That was something else that had not yet crossed Rob's mind. "Will I have to take my charters with me, sir?"

"Nay, nay," Andrew said. "I'm certain that MacAulay presented his to Jamie at Paisley Abbey when Colquhoun, Douglas, Scott, and others did. Ye should ask your mam, though. She'll know."

Rob nodded. Then, sensing Muriella's stiffness beside him, he glanced at her. She was regarding Andrew with an odd, quizzical look on her face.

"What is it, lass?" Rob asked quietly.

Starting, she looked up at him, then back at her father. "I was just thinking," she said slowly. "Father, how did our charters get to Tùr Meiloach in the first place? You cannot possibly have carried them with you the night that you and Mam fled."

"Never said I did," Andrew replied. "They were

already here, for I knew that I could trust Tùr Meiloach to keep them safe." He looked at his lady, who returned his gaze with her usual composure.

Muriella murmured, "I, too, trust Tùr Meiloach. They must still be here."

Seeing no point in commenting, Rob said to Andrew, "The lass wants a bath, sir. If you will give the orders, I'll see her to her chamber. I want a word with her."

"I dinna doubt that," Andrew said, grinning again. "I'll tell them to fetch your things from the cottage and take them up there, too."

~

Andrew's last few words made Murie feel utterly helpless. Of course, her husband would share her room. Her father would certainly not send him back to Mag's cottage. More likely, Mag, Andrena, and wee Molly would sleep there, leaving Lina and Lizzie to share Mag and Dree's room in the tower and the lady Margaret Galbraith to sleep in the room across the landing from Murie's.

With a sigh, she went upstairs ahead of Rob and entered her bedchamber. When he walked in behind her and shut the door, the room closed in on her more than it ever had before, even when she had shared it with both Dree and Lina.

"You do fill up a room, sir," she said, striving to sound as if his presence did not disturb her. "My father thinks you mean to scold me. I hope you won't."

He put both hands on her shoulders and looked into her eyes. "You have nowt to fear, lass. Not here, not tonight. I don't know how much you know about coupling or the duties of a wife to her husband, but..." He paused.

"I made Andrena tell me what happens on a wedding night after she married Mag," Murie said, knowing that he was seeking words to explain. "I'm not sure I understand it all, but Dree did say that coupling might be uncomfortable, even painful, the first time."

"You don't need to worry about it tonight, lass. I don't want you to be frightened or concerned about that."

"But if it's the usual thing, why should I be frightened? Forbye, they will ask me about it! Don't you want me? I mean, I know you don't want me for your wife. But if, as you say, we are bound together, do you mean that you don't want children?"

"Nowt of the sort," he said, almost fiercely and unconsciously echoing her father. "I just don't want to go too fast. I don't want to risk hurting you."

"You *don't* want me."

In reply, to her shock, his fingers tightened bruisingly on her shoulders and he pulled her close to him, saying, "You are dead wrong about *that*." One large, warm hand cupped her chin, raised it, and his lips came down firmly on hers.

His were warm, albeit hard at first, and the hand that cupped her chin moved to grip the back of her head instead, as if he thought she might pull away.

He need not have worried about that, though, because with the first touch of his lips on hers, melting warmth spread through every cell of her, and she could not have pulled away had she wanted to. Her body responded to his at once and in ways she had never known before or expected.

Sensations roared through her until she could scarcely tell if she was still standing. Realizing that her hands remained at her sides, just dangling there, she put both of them at his waist to steady herself.

The hand that still gripped her right shoulder shifted to her back.

Then his tongue touched her lips as if he wanted to taste her. And her tongue, evidently deciding on its own to taste his, quickly did so. Strangely, she did not feel at all daring. She simply felt as if she were free to do what she wanted to do.

⁓

Hearing her moan deep in her throat, Rob felt a hunger unlike any he had known for a woman before. He would have liked to scoop her into his arms and carry her to her bed. But men would soon bring her tub and hot water, her maid would come, *and* he had promised that he would not hurt or frighten her.

Her slender body felt soft and supple, and he hoped he had not bruised her shoulders. He had not meant to grab her so tightly, but he could not have borne to let her think he didn't want her. Sakes, he had wanted her since the day he'd found her in the cottage in the same pink kirtle she wore now, rucked up to her thighs.

And heaven knew he wanted her now, more than he had wanted any woman since the night he had first learned about coupling. Even so, he knew that his size and strength had frightened some experienced women and at least one maiden.

Her father had said that they were both responsible for their marriage. He was right about that, but Rob did not blame Muriella for her part in it. She had done what she thought she had to do, out of desperation. Nor would he blame himself for refusing to contradict her declaration. Not only would that have reflected on his personal sense of honor, it would also have condemned her to marry Dougal.

So he was reaping the consequences of his actions. Standing as he was now, with her in his arms, those consequences were having a strong effect on him, especially certain parts of him, one in particular.

She tasted sweet and a bit salty, which suited her. He did not want to stop kissing her, but he knew that if she stimulated him much more, he would have to fight hard later to keep his promise to her and to himself.

Regretfully, he ended the kiss and set her back on her heels.

"That was nice," she said. "If my father is having your things brought here, I expect that means you will be sleeping in my bed."

"Likely, it does," he agreed. "But as I told you, you have nowt to fear."

For a moment, she looked dismayed, but before he could ask her to explain, a rap at the door signaled the arrival of the men with her tub and hot water.

Rob opened the door for them and found himself face to face with a buxom young, rosy-cheeked lass in a simple blue kirtle and a white cap that covered her hair. Behind her came two gillies with Muriella's bathtub and hot water.

"I be Tibby, sir," the lass said. "The laird did tell me tae come up and help the lady Murie with her bath."

"Then I'll leave you to that," Rob said, and fled.

Chapter 13

Muriella stared at the doorway after Rob vanished, trying to make sense of the feelings that had filled her from the moment he'd put his hands on her.

"Mistress," Tibby said. "Your water be ready."

Startled, Murie realized that despite staring at the doorway, she had apparently failed to note the departure of the two gillies through it. Recovering her wits, she shut the door and said, "I'll wear the blue gown that Lady Lina made for me the last time she was here, Tibby."

"Aye, but first we'll have ye out o' this one," Tibby said. "Never tell me ye've had this pink kirtle on since I put ye in it m'self nigh a sennight ago."

Murie reassured her but added that she did not want to talk about her ordeal. "I just want to get clean and go downstairs to see everyone."

After hurrying through her bath and dressing, Murie returned to the hall to find her family awaiting her at the high table. Andrew stood at the central place, as usual. Her mother, sisters, Lady Margaret, and Lizzie stood to his left and Rob at his right. Their steward, Malcolm Wylie, was stepping down from the dais.

Murie stopped him. "Is Annie in the tower, Malcolm?" she asked.

"Nay, m'lady. She's awa' to our cottage. Did ye want her?"

"Not tonight, but do tell her I've returned safely. She must have worried."

"Aye, we all did, m'lady," he said with a warm smile. "Welcome home."

Thanking him, she stepped onto the dais and took her place beside Lina, who stood next to Dree. Their places had been customary for as long as Murie could remember, until Lina moved to Dumbarton. As guests, Lady Margaret stood next to their mother and fifteen-year-old Lizzie occupied the end place, at Murie's left.

Lizzie's simple white veil did little to conceal her long, thick mass of red-orange curls. Turning with a grin, she said quietly to Murie, "I heard you were captive at Arrochar, with the evil Dougal. Is he as handsome as ever?"

Murie grimaced. "I thought he was horrid. I'm just thankful to be home."

"And glad to be Rob MacAulay's lady, aye?" Lina murmured from Murie's right. "You should know that we stand in our usual places only by Mam's orders."

"Mercy, what do you mean?"

"Since Rob's father is gone, you must know that he is now Lord MacAulay. As his baroness, you now outrank Dree and me and are entitled to sit at Mam's left."

Uncertain of her feelings about that, although she felt a brief urge to tease Lina, Murie said only, "I'm glad Father told everyone what happened. I dreaded the thought of having to explain it to all of you by myself. It was bad enough that MacAu—that Rob made me tell Father and Mam what I did."

"I like Rob," Lina confided. "He has been a gey good friend to Ian and me, and to Mag and Dree, too. He will make you a good husband, I think. Although," she added with a chuckle, "if I recall aright, last year he said he did not mean to marry any woman until he had naught of greater interest to do."

"I did not think you or Dree and Mag would be here yet," Murie said to divert her from that topic. "I did not even *sense* that you had come home."

"We sensed your fears, of course, especially Monday night," Lina said. "I have never been so glad to see Mag or Dree as I was when they came to fetch me. Ian would have disliked sending me alone. Your own senses were likely fixed on more vital matters, but we do want to hear about all that happened at Arro—"

"Shhh," Murie whispered. "Father is going to say the grace."

When he finished and they had taken their seats, Andrena leaned forward to see Murie past Lina and said, "Imagine, I thought *my* wedding was unexpected!"

"How is Wee Molly?" Murie asked swiftly, knowing that the subject of their tiny daughter was one that never failed to divert either Dree or Mag.

It succeeded, as always, for Andrena was eager to share her daughter's latest accomplishments with them. But, after a time, Lina said, "You know, Murie, you'll have to tell us everything in time. Our curiosity is as great now as yours ever is."

"Perhaps later, when we retire with Mam to the solar."

But when the ladies Aubrey and Margaret stood to

signal that it was time for the ladies to leave the table, Rob also rose.

Since Murie had not seen or heard him excuse himself to Andrew, she suspected that the two had already discussed whatever Rob meant to do. She felt an unusual eagerness when he approached and extended a hand to her.

When she put her hand in his, he gave it a gentle tug as he said to Lady Aubrey, "Prithee, excuse Muriella, my lady. We have had a long day and will have another on the morrow when we take ship to Ardincaple."

Lady Aubrey consented with a smile, and Lady Margaret, Dree, Lina, and Lizzie all bade them goodnight in a chorus while Andrew silently beamed.

Although Murie felt self-conscious as she left the dais with Rob, her anticipation of what might lie ahead increased as they ascended the stairs. She tried to recall all that Dree had said about her wedding night. Some of the details had sounded odd then. Now, as she imagined Rob doing things to her that Mag had done with Dree, heat tingled through her body from its center outward.

When they reached her landing and Rob leaned past her to open the door, she realized with a start that if he'd spoken on the way up she had not heard him. With a less enticing jolt, she remembered the Brehon's order that he punish her, and Rob's agreeing—nay, giving the Brehon his word that he would. Surely, he would not...

Swallowing hard, she entered her bedchamber to find a half-dozen candles lit, the shutters closed, and the bed-clothes invitingly turned down.

Turning to Rob, she said, "Did my father say we should leave the table?"

"Aye, because he knows I want to get an early start

tomorrow," Rob said. "Also, he would like us to consummate our marriage tonight. But as I told you earlier, we can delay that for a short time at least."

She cocked her head. "But we will sleep in the same bed, aye?"

Even by candlelight, she saw his cheeks redden.

"I'm not sure I should sleep with you, lass," he said softly. "I do mean well, but you are gey enticing to me."

"If I am to be your wife," she said, relieved and warily delighted to hear him say again that she attracted him, "I want to be your wife in every way. Also, as I told you earlier, my sisters will ask me how it went, and they always know if I lie. So, if you are delaying because you fear I'll dislike it, then I reject your notion of consequences, sir. Consummation *is* one of the consequences of marriage, is it not? I begin to think that you are the one who fears it, but surely that cannot be so."

A twinkle lit his eyes, and her wariness fled.

Shaking his head, he patted the bed and said, "Sit, lass. I can think better and will likely explain my thoughts more clearly if we sit and do not touch each other."

"It makes me feel strange all over when you touch me," she said, climbing onto the high bed and sitting with her lower legs over the side. "Does it make you feel the same way if I touch you?"

"Not being female, I cannot tell you if it is the same," he replied, sitting beside her. "But if the strangeness you feel is pleasant, then it is similar."

"It is more than pleasant," she said. "When are you going to kiss me again?"

"Lassie, do you want to hear what I have to say to you or not?"

Cocking her head a little as she turned and drew her knees up so she could face him, she considered the question.

Unabashedly looking at her breasts, the tops of which rose plumply above her low-cut bodice, he said gruffly, "Sakes, lass, do not tempt me further."

"I want to know what you are thinking," she said as solemnly as she could, wondering how he could look so serious one moment and then surprise her with a twinkle in his eyes the next. "You did say that if you were wooing me, you would tell me why you had decided not to inflict yourself on any woman. Although you have not wooed me, Robert, we *are* married. So, will you tell me *now*?"

Rob had expected the question, albeit not at just that moment. He was reluctant to tell her, but he knew she had a right to know. Moreover, he knew she would not hide what she was thinking as he told her. Her animated face revealed her thoughts as clearly as if she said each one aloud.

Remembering his first impression of her—that she was childish—he nearly chuckled. She was not a child but a most enticing young woman. Nevertheless, she would require a firm hand, because she had gone her own way for too long.

That, though, was a subject for another time, and he owed her the plain truth now. So, drawing a breath, he said, "My parents tried to betroth me some years ago to the daughter of another nobleman."

"How old were you?" she asked. "Who is she? Might I know her?"

"One question at a time, if you please," he said. "Her

name is irrelevant, and I am sure you do not know her. Sithee, I was fourteen and just beginning serious training as a warrior. I had nowt in mind save that training. I had practiced archery, wrestling, and other such warrior's sports since early childhood. At fourteen, I had no interest in females or in the position I would one day inherit."

A spasm of pain shot through him when his father's image arose then in his mind. Rob swallowed carefully and was sure that he had concealed the emotion until she put her hand gently on his thigh. Although she did not speak, the compassion he felt from her was nearly his undoing.

Swallowing again, he said, "I met her only twice. Our parents thought that letting us get to know each other would lead naturally to the betrothal they sought. It didn't. She no sooner saw me, the first time we met, than she burst into tears."

"Mercy, why?"

"I don't know. I was tall for my age but still thin and gawky, hardly what any warrior would call large. But she said I was too big and strong, and she did not want a giant for a husband. She reacted the same way the next time we met."

"Sakes, how old was she?"

"Thirteen the first time, fourteen the next. Our parents did not expect us to marry straightaway, though. Our betrothal was to be two or three years long, and after we married, we were to live at Ardincaple. She had nowt to fear."

"She sounds plain daft to me," Muriella said with a spark in her eyes.

Her annoyance instantly eased his apprehension. "Does she?"

"Aye, but perhaps she was especially small."

"In size, she was much like you but not as nicely curved."

"Well, although you do fill up this room, you don't usually seem overlarge to me," she said. "Forbye, I have lived with Magnus Mòr, and *no one* looks large next to him. How did you end it?"

Looking toward the shuttered window, he drew another breath. Then, forcing himself to meet her quizzical gaze, he said, "I didn't. She hated and feared me so much that, to avoid a third meeting, she jumped from her window and died."

"Och, poor lassie!" Muriella exclaimed. "She does sound daft, though," she added a moment later. "And I still cannot see how it was your fault. More likely, it was something that someone else said or did, unless... Were you rude to her?"

Rob winced at that question. "I took good care to be polite," he said evenly.

"I see," Muriella said with a wry smile. "I take great care to be polite to Lady Margaret, too. But when she is rude to me..." She shrugged and the smile turned rueful. "Mam is forever telling me that I must have more consideration, but when a person, especially one older than oneself, says she believes in being forthright and then carps at one, one feels as if one ought to be able to speak plainly to *her*. But if I do, Lady Margaret takes offense. I expect your situation was different, though."

"Just a trifle," he said with a rueful smile that probably matched hers.

Murie wanted to hug him, but although he was her husband, she felt as if she would be taking a great liberty if she did. Otherwise, she felt at ease with him.

"I have never had such a conversation with a man before," she said frankly. "I suppose if I'd had brothers—from childhood, I mean, not good-brothers who are years older than I am—I might have talked so with them."

"Lass, I may not have come eagerly to this marriage, but I do know I *don't* want to be your brother." He spoke with feeling but also with those twinkling eyes.

"I believe you," she said. "Sometimes, when they are wroth with me, I think that neither Ian nor Mag wants to be my *good*-brother, even now."

"That is not what I meant, and I think you ken that fine. Moreover, I do not propose to spend all night talking. We both need to sleep. And before we do—"

"We should consummate our marriage," she interjected boldly. "I hope you know what to do, though, because although Dree did tell me things about her wedding night with Mag—"

"I don't want to hear about it," he said, laughing. "I do know what to do."

"I don't think I have seen you laugh before," she said, rather stunned.

"Ah, lassie," he said, reaching for her and pulling her closer, "I have not often felt like laughing these past few years, but I think that I may laugh more easily now. And that, madam wife, is a compliment."

"Is it?" She wrinkled her nose and looked up at the curtain rail, although she knew he was sincere. "It does not precisely *sound* like a compliment."

"Look at me," he said.

Obediently, she shifted her gaze to meet his.

"Raise your chin just a wee bit."

When she did, he touched her lips lightly with his and reached to untie the white ribbon lacing of her bodice. Soon, the bodice was open, and he was deftly untying the ribbons of her shift to bare her breasts.

Murie watched his face, wondering why such simple acts, acts she had done herself or that Tibby had done for her, had never sent sensations through her body like the ones that Rob's actions caused. Her breasts swelled, her nipples hardened, and whenever his fingers brushed bare flesh, she gasped at the pleasure of his touch.

He kissed her again. This time his kiss was firmer, far more possessive.

Curious now about the reactions he was stimulating in her and even more curious about what she might stimulate in him, she reached for the buckle of the wide leather belt he wore over his plaid.

"Art sure about this, lass?" he asked.

"Aye," she said, surprised when her voice sounded hoarse. "I don't know why you thought I'd be afraid. This is astonishingly pleasurable. Dree did say that some of it was a trifle unpleasant, but I don't find it so. Do you think I should?"

Rob felt a sudden, utterly unfamiliar sensation deep within him that was warming but not sexual. Again, he felt like smiling. This time, though, instinct stopped him. Her demeanor was earnest and innocent, making him realize that what he felt was an overwhelming desire to protect her and not shatter that innocence.

"I don't think it is unusual that you should be confused," he said. "We have only just begun. What Andrena meant is that a maiden's body takes some time to grow comfortable with coupling. Will you let me finish undressing you?"

"Only if you take your clothes off first," she said, smiling mischievously. "I shall feel much too vulnerable to be naked with you if you keep your clothes on."

"That," he said, "is a request I am happy to grant."

With that, he stood, undid his belt, and cast it and the sheathed dirk on it aside. Next went the plaid, although he took time to fold it and place it on a nearby stool. When he stripped off his tunic, he heard her gasp.

The sound sent a shiver through him. Realizing that she had likely never seen a rampant male before, he reached out a gentle hand to touch her shoulder.

She slipped nimbly away and to her feet, saying as she did, "You look odd, standing there in only your boots. I hope you won't keep them on in bed."

Looking down, he shook his head at himself. Usually, he took his boots off first, if he wore any. He loosened the right one's tie and removed the wee dirk he kept in a sheath sewn into its side. The weapon was large enough to fit his hand.

"Sakes!" she exclaimed. "Do you always carry an eating knife in your boot?"

"'Tis more than an eating knife," he said. "I usually take it with me if I wear boots, and I took it today in case Pharlain banned weapons at his court. I prefer to be armed in enemy land." He gestured at her gown. "What are you waiting for?"

Her smile turned impish. "Dree told me that Mag likes to peel her clothes off of her. I thought you—"

"I'd liefer see how a lady disrobes," he said, although the truth was he did not want to hear about Mag's choices. "I have never watched one do so before."

"Aye, then," she said. "Usually, Tibby helps me, but everything is loose and ties in front, so I can just pull it all down and step out." She proceeded to do so, and then straightened and looked expectantly at him. "Now what?"

His body stirred sharply at the sight she made, and without another thought, he scooped her into his arms and placed her gently on the bed, shoving the covers further down. "Scoot over, lass, and make room for me."

She watched, wide-eyed, as he got into bed, but when he took her in his arms and gently kissed her, she opened her mouth to him at once. Smiling against her lips, he proceeded with her first lesson.

~

He was so big that he took up most of the bed, and Murie wondered how she and Lina had shared that bed for years without sparing a thought for its size. Only after Dree married had they slept in separate beds.

Nevertheless, she loved the way Rob held her, and his kisses stirred her blood in ways it had never stirred before. His lightest touch excited her. His fingers drifted over her skin as if to test her responses as well as its smoothness. When his right hand cupped a breast and his thumb brushed lightly across its nipple, the sensations he stirred were enough to make her gasp. The hand did not linger but seemed to wander where it liked while he continued to kiss her.

Daringly, she touched him, too. With every one of her senses now alert, she tried to sense what he was feeling, to know if what he felt was anything like the feelings his lips and fingers ignited in her. When she brushed her thumb across one of his nipples, she thought he smiled against her lips, but he did not gasp until she stroked his belly and reached lower.

Then he murmured, "You are playing with fire now, lass. I'm nigh to taking you, as it is."

Instead of making her wary, as he had so clearly intended, his soft-spoken words ignited more feelings than ever, firing her curiosity as well as her sensuality. "Then take me," she murmured seductively. "I want to know what lies ahead."

With what sounded like a growl in his throat, almost worthy of Scáthach, he muttered something. Whether it was a prayer or a curse she couldn't quite tell. Then his hand moved to the fork of her legs and cupped its crux gently.

Slipping one finger inside her, then another, he moved them gently but firmly until she moaned. Then, just as gently, he eased them back again and began rubbing her there in a way that sent flames all through her.

Her own exploring hand also moved lower then. In her passion, she grabbed the first thing her hand came to that seemed to want grabbing.

Rob gasped then, and a moment later he rolled toward her. "You are gey eager for a maiden, lassie. At this speed, you will not be one much longer."

"I don't care," she said. "I want to know everything that married people can do."

He laughed low in his throat. "Since I have been married exactly as long as you have, I can hardly know all there is to know about what married people do. I do know a few things we can do in bed, though. Let's start with those."

Capturing her mouth again, he kissed her thoroughly and used his fingers to tease her nipples and stimulate her below until she felt as if her body would explode. Just as she thought it might, he stopped kissing her and moved to adjust his body to hers. Easing his cock to her opening, he slipped it slowly, gently inside.

No longer on the verge of exploding, her body contracted there as if to expel him, but curiosity overwhelmed every other feeling or thought. She held her breath, every fiber of her now focused on what was happening below.

"Breathe, lass," he murmured. "Try to relax. It will make things easier than if you stiffen up like a poker."

"I suppose you know all about it," she said, more grimly than she had intended. The thought that he had likely done this with other...

His chuckle stopped that half-formed thought. "I know only what I have heard about women's feelings at a time like this, *mo chridhe*. But I suspect that when a male my size invades the body of a female your size, a certain amount of readjustment becomes necessary. I'm being as gentle—"

A much stronger contraction below ended his words in another gasp. He was silent after that but pressed himself farther inside and began moving in and out, slowly and gently at first, until she felt a sharp pang and cried out. Then, instead of stopping, he moved faster and faster.

Murie had all she could do to endure then, let alone ponder what she was feeling. It was over soon afterward, and except for the fact that Rob seemed to have collapsed atop her, she was glad when it was.

"I hope I didn't hurt you too much, lassie," he murmured as he rolled off her and pulled her close to him.

"I won't die of it, but is that all, sir? Because next time I'd like to feel the good things a while longer."

His body seemed to shake then, or tremble.

"Robert? What is it?"

He rose up again onto his side and looked into her eyes. His were twinkling. "I'll see what I can do about those good things, lass, but you can call me Rob now. It is your right, and when people call me Robert, I fear that I have vexed them."

"Never mind that," she said. "What's wrong?"

"I was just trying not to laugh," he said. "There is much more that can happen between married people, but this is all that we will do tonight. We both need to sleep, and you will be sore tomorrow, as it is, so let's get cleaned up now."

He helped her first and then tucked her back into bed.

She watched while he attended to himself and opened the window shutters. He did not ask her what she thought about that, but she preferred them open herself, especially after her nights in the pitch-blackness of the shed. Rob climbed into bed then, and pulled her close, nestling her against him as if they were spoons.

When she awoke Saturday morning, she became aware of a dull ache inside her where his cock had been. It was not bad, though, and seeing the familiar gray dawn light pouring in through her window filled her with such delight to be home that she could not lie abed. Moreover, she had something important to do before Rob woke, lest he insist on departing for Ardincaple straightaway or, worse, forbid her to do it.

Taking care not to wake him, she slipped out of bed, quickly donned a fresh shift and her moss-green kirtle, and quietly left the room. Stopping just long enough to visit the garderobe, she hurried down to the postern door. Then, taking her cloak from its hook, she flung it over her shoulders and went outside.

As usual at such an early hour, Pluff was helping Mac-Nur and now perhaps Mae or Annabel feed the animals inside the wall. So, with a cheerful wave to the guard on the walkway, Murie opened the gate herself and slipped outside. There was no latch on that side, so she would have to shout for someone to open it again, and Rob would likely be up by then, looking for her. Even so, he had not forbidden her to go out, and if she was going to talk with Annie, she had to do so at once.

Hurrying along the still damp woodland path to the northern river boundary, she followed the path along the riverbank eastward to the Wylies' cottage.

Knowing that Malcolm, Peter, and Tibby would already be at the tower, seeing to their morning duties, she rapped firmly on the door.

When Annie opened it, Murie grinned, opened her arms wide, and stepped into Annie's welcoming embrace.

"Och, me lady, 'tis good tae see ye safe home again," Annie said.

She was half her husband's size and so skinny that many might have hesitated to hug her too tightly, lest she break. Murie had no such qualms, for she knew that Annie was as tough as an oak branch. Most of the men at Tùr Meiloach believed that if Malcolm displeased Annie—or if any of them did—she would hand him his head in his lap.

Despite graying red hair that was as curly and frizzy as Pluff's was, and her wrinkled nut-brown cheeks, she was spry and quick-witted. And Murie knew that Annie's own excellent memory had not faded one whit.

"Annie," she said as soon as the door was shut, "I may not have much time."

"I believe ye," Annie replied with a wry smile. "Malcolm told me ye'd somehow got yourself a husband whilst ye was at Arrochar."

"I did, aye. He is Master—Nay, he is Lord MacAulay of Ardincaple."

"So Malcolm did say," Annie said, eyeing her shrewdly. "Ye must ha' kent that he would, so ye didna come here tae give me the news. What is it, lass? I ha' me doots your man will approve o' ye whiskin' about in your bare feet now that ye're a lady wi' a grand laird for a husband."

Murie knew that Rob would disapprove, so she could not claim otherwise. She said bluntly, "Annie, do you ken aught of my father's missing charters?"

Annie's eyes widened and she said with credible astonishment, "Why would ye be asking me such a thing as that? D'ye think I'm a thief or worse?"

"You know I don't think anything of the sort," Murie said. "But I do know that my father came here to this cottage the night he escaped from Arrochar, with Pharlain's men hunting for him and my mother still on the other side of the river. Malcolm was a shepherd then, and you and he took Father in."

"Aye, and their sweet new bairn, as well," Annie said. "But if ye be a-thinking that your da carried them charters wi' him, ye dinna ken nowt."

"I know he did not," Murie said. "He told me as much.

He also said that they were already here at Tùr Meiloach. But he trusted you and Malcolm enough to take Andrena to you, so I'm thinking he must also have trusted you with other things. Did you know where he kept his charters? Might Malcolm have known?"

"That's all ye want tae ken, is it," Annie said grimly. "D'ye think I'd tell ye such things, even though ye were no mad enough tae put your questions tae Malcolm or tae *Himself*? D'ye think your da, as canny as he be, be daft enough tae tell anyone else where he'd put such valuable documents as his royal charters? Tùr Meiloach *will* protect them, Lady Muriella. That be all ye need tae ken."

"I know that when you call me Lady Muriella, you are angry with me," Murie said. "But this is gey important, Annie. I'm sure that Father does not know where his charters are, and he has to have them to show the King when we go to Inverness for the Parliament. If he cannot produce them there, Pharlain and his heirs will likely keep Arrochar forever. They may even win Tùr Meiloach, as well!"

"Nay, they will not," Annie said. "Did I no tell ye that this land protects its own? That doesna include Pharlain or his get, not since he betrayed his rightful chief. What it means is that when them charters *do* be needed, they'll show theirselves, another 'n another. That be all I can tell ye about *that*. Moreover, I hope ye didna defy your laird husband by a-comin' here, because I'm thinking—"

A heavy double-rap on the door interrupted her, and Murie had no doubt who stood on the other side of it.

Chapter 14 ————————————

The skinny little woman who opened the door to Rob made him a deep, respectful curtsy, which was the only thing that kept him from storming inside to confront his errant wife. As it was, he had all he could do to remain polite, because he could see Muriella standing a short distance behind Annie Wylie.

He said rather too curtly, "I bid you good morrow, Mistress Wylie. I have come for my wife."

"She's here, aye, m'lord," Annie said as she arose. "I'm that glad tae see her safe again, too. I thank ye, as all here do, for bringing her home tae us."

"I ken fine that you are also a storyteller, mistress," he said quietly, while keeping his eyes on Murie. "If you would show me gratitude, you will not make a song about her misadventure and will discourage her and others from doing so."

Since he expected the old woman to agree and was still staring sternly at his lady wife, it was with shock that he heard Annie say, "Someone *will* tell that tale, sir. It be too good not tae tell. 'Twould be better for the truth tae come from her ladyship or them who ken her best. But," Annie added, turning to address the last words to

Muriella, "it must be as your lord husband decrees, must it not, m'lady?"

Noting that Muriella's consternation was equal to his own, Rob kept silent until she said reluctantly, "It must be so, Annie, aye."

"Come along now, lass," Rob said. "I want to get underway as soon as we can. The men are already seeing to the galleys, so if you are not prepared to leave at once, you must make haste."

She gave him a measuring look, then nodded, gave Annie a hug, and bade her good-bye. When Rob opened the door, Muriella went ahead of him and walked briskly along the narrow path.

Pulling the door shut, Rob strode after her, catching up after just a few steps. "Do you know what you deserve for coming here without a word to me?"

"I know what you think I deserve," she said, glancing up at him. "You will doubtless add it to what the Brehon decreed for me. Meantime, I had to see Annie, and I did not want to fratch with you or risk your forbidding me to see her."

"All you had to say was that you wanted to bid her farewell."

"Mayhap that is true," she said. "But how was I to know that? I barely know you yet, and for the most part, you have just issued orders or told me that I cannot do what I want to do or be what I want to be. Therefore, when I awoke before you did this morning, I decided to see Annie whilst I knew I could."

"If it was only to say good-bye, why did you not tell Malcolm or Tibby last night that you wanted to see her? She would surely have visited you at the tower."

"Perhaps," she said, watching the path.

Rob gripped her arm, stopped, and turned her to face him. When she did not try to pull free but stared at his chest with her lips pressed tightly together, he said, "Look at me."

She continued to stare at his chest for another long moment. When he said nothing but continued to hold her arm, she drew a breath at last and looked up.

For once, he could not read her expression. His first thought was that she was being willful, but she seemed resigned, too, and wary.

He said sternly, "After we get underway, I am going to ask you again about your visit here, lass. I want you to think carefully about what you will say then. I suspect that you came to see Annie for a reason other than what you have told me, and you must know by now that I won't react well to lying or deceit."

Her expression did not change, nor did she speak.

When she started to turn away, he caught her chin gently and held it so that she had to look at him again.

"I mean what I say, Murie," he said quietly. "Think about that, too."

Her gaze met his, and she licked her lips.

His body stirred in response.

"Kiss me," she said. "Please, just kiss me."

With an uneasy sense that he was as wax in her hands but without a second thought, Rob complied. His hand still cupped her chin, so he bent just enough to touch his lips to hers. Then, releasing her arm, he pulled her into his embrace and kissed her more thoroughly, stroking her back as he did.

When she slipped her tongue past his into his mouth, he pulled away but held her by the shoulders.

"Would you bewitch me?" he asked.

"Aye, I would," she replied. But the wariness returned to her eyes.

"Likely, you can do it if anyone can," he admitted. "But do not forget that consequences follow every action. I do think that you've hitherto ignored such consequences, or dismissed them. That will change, especially if you ever put yourself in danger again as you did with Dougal. Do you understand me?"

She nodded, and he released her. They returned to the tower in silence, because she did not speak and he wanted to let her think, hoping that her fertile imagination would suggest penalties more undesirable than any he could devise.

❧

Murie decided that Rob was merely making a point, as men often did, and turned her thoughts to what Annie had said about the charters. It was true that Tùr Meiloach had protected the family for years, and true that it seemed to do so in mysterious ways. It was also true that Rob was determined to leave at once and Andrew just as determined to speed them on their way. Even if she tried to search for the charters first, she would likely have too little time to find them.

To her surprise and doubtless more to Rob's, she made good speed with her preparations and—with Tibby's help and Lina's willingness to supervise the lads who loaded Murie's spinning wheel—she was ready to leave within the hour.

The sun was up by then, and the sky was clear. Bidding her family and their guests farewell, she and Rob set forth for Ardincaple on the MacAulay galley.

The Colquhoun boat would escort them as far as Craggan Tower.

For a time, Rob and the captains of both galleys kept watch for other boats. The loch was calm and despite lingering patches of morning mist, it was clear enough to see that they were the only galleys on the water.

Sitting on a bench built into the stern bulkhead, Murie watched the passing shoreline and the water. With the rhythmic movement and sounds of the oars, her thoughts drifted idly until she saw Rob making his way along the gangway toward her.

His grim expression set her nerves tingling again.

Without thinking, she put a fingertip to her lips and nibbled the nail.

"Don't do that," he said brusquely when he reached her.

Cocking her head so that his body kept the sun from her eyes, she dropped the offending hand to her lap but said softly, "Or what?"

His eyes glinted but whether with humor or annoyance she could not be sure.

Sitting beside her, he said quietly, "You are my wife now, lass. Defying me is never a good idea."

"But what *might* you do?"

"I doubt you would heed aught I'd say about that now," he said. "But my father had his own laird's court planned to take place anon. If you want to understand my notion of penalties, you are welcome to attend."

Surprised, she said, "My father never let any of us attend his until he realized that Dree's ability to tell if men were lying or not could help him. Even then, neither Lina nor I attended them."

"Well, you may attend any that I convene," he said.

"You may also leave at any time if the proceedings discomfit you. Doubtless, my mother will attend them."

"You say that as if you wished she would not."

"She has a knack for putting me in the wrong," he said. "You will see that soon enough, though. I do not mean to encourage you to prejudge her."

"I would want to decide such things for myself, in any event," she said.

He nodded, and for a time they sat quietly side by side. Then, abruptly, he said, "Let me see your hands."

She almost shoved both of them behind her instead. At her hesitation, he reached out and took her left hand in his. Holding it firmly, palm down, he studied her nails, or what remained of them.

After an uncomfortable silence, he said, "Why do you bite them?"

She shrugged. "I don't know. I do it without thinking. Even Mam has given up scolding me for it. I hope you don't mean to start."

His gaze caught hers and seemed to pull her into its cool green depths. "I don't scold," he said, his deep voice as seductively vibrant as ever.

"Good," she said, a little dazed.

Gently stroking the back of her hand with his thumb, he added softly, "You have such beautifully shaped hands and such slim, elegant fingers. And you make such graceful, expressive gestures when you tell your tales. I just wondered..."

"Wondered what?" she murmured when he paused, her mind still echoing the intoxicating words *beautifully shaped, elegant, graceful,* and *express—*

"...why you succumb to such an ugly habit."

He said it in the same deep-voiced way that always seemed to pulsate through her skin to her very bones. So soothing was that tone that the words themselves took a moment to register.

When they did, it was as if he had slapped her.

"I'll admit," he went on before she could think of anything sensible to say, "I did not notice last year that you suffered from such a bad habit. I did notice your so graceful hands and fingers at a distance, though, when you told your tale describing the rescue of your sister and Lizzie Galbraith from Dumbarton Castle."

"You did? I thought you hated the whole thing, just as Mag and Ian did. Moreover, you have said that you won't let me become a seanachie."

"I did not say I would refuse to let you tell your stories. You are right, though, in saying I that dislike *that* tale and the fact of your having told it," he added bluntly. "It was a dangerous one to tell, and I'll wager that MacPharlain expressed his feelings about it to you, as well. Did he not?"

Grimacing, she said, "He hated it, aye. He said I could blame it *and* myself for my visit to Arrochar, but I don't care what his reason was. Nor did I expect him to enjoy hearing himself *called* a villain, although he seems bent on *being* one."

Rob looked as if he might say something but stopped himself. Then he said, "I meant only that since your hands are important to your storytelling and fascinating to watch, you should not torment them so. Just imagine what it is like for others to see them up close and realize how little you care about them."

She bit her lower lip. "You think my hands are beautiful?"

"I do."

"I did try to stop biting my nails at Arrochar. I thought of you then, whenever I realized what I was doing. It worked for a time, but..."

"Try harder then," he said when she shrugged. With a new glint in his eyes, he added, "I'll be happy to remind you, but you may not like the way I do it."

"Will you tell me now what you would do?"

"I'm imaginative, too, lass. Alhough I don't know exactly what the circumstances might be, I can easily imagine reminding you—no matter where we are or who else is present—that you must not indulge in such a childish habit."

The image he presented was staggering in its clarity.

"Even Mam would not humiliate me in front of others," she said.

"I am not your mam, Muriella. I'm your husband and therefore hope you will pay closer heed when I make a request. For example, I expect you to tell me the truth now about why you went to visit Annie Wylie."

She did not hesitate. "I knew she would be alone at that hour, and I wanted to find out if she knew aught about my father's missing charters."

"And?"

Looking down at her hands, she said quietly, "She said she did not know."

"I doubt that is all that she said."

"Well, *I* doubt that you will believe the rest of what she said might be true," she said, frustrated. "Hence, I would liefer not tell you."

"I want you to tell me."

Murie rolled her eyes but capitulated. "She said that when Father needs his charters, they will appear."

"I see," he said.

"I told you that you would not believe it."

"I do believe that those were her words," he said. "You would be wiser, lass, not to keep things from me, even if you doubt that I will believe them. And, prithee, do not forget that I mean what I say."

She nodded with a mental sigh. Clearly, Rob was not going to be as easy to charm out of his ill moods as Andrew Dubh usually was.

The rest of their journey passed without incident, albeit providing some fine and familiar scenery. With so much time to think and easily imagining certain difficulties ahead, Rob's impatience mounted as the hours passed.

He did talk more with his bride while they took their midday meal together from a basket that Andrew's kitchen had provided. Pointing out landmarks, they exchanged details of trips they had each taken on the loch. It was mostly small talk, and Rob was unaccustomed to sitting for long. He needed to move about.

Also, he had a feeling that the less they talked about more private matters on the boat, the less chance there was that any of what they said would reach his mother's ears. She would be disappointed enough in his marriage without giving her more cause.

He doubted that Muriella would repeat aught that he had told her about his mother, but he no longer knew all of his father's oarsmen. And voices traveled unexpected distances on the water.

He smiled at that thought, recalling that he did have the reputation of a man whose minions obeyed orders and were reluctant to defy him. Doubtless that word had spread to any new oarsmen or servitors at Ardincaple. They would be wary.

By the time they reached the MacAulays' wharf, the sun had neared the hills on the western horizon. The small clachan near the wharf provided stabling for the garrons they would ride to the castle, as well as for horses that Rob kept there.

The helmsman blew his horn to announce their arrival, although men were already hurrying to the wharf to greet them.

"Is that Ardincaple Castle yonder?" Muriella asked, pointing to the square, battlemented, four-story tower on a crest beyond the highest part of the coastline.

"Aye," he said quietly, feeling a renewed sense of belonging, along with the still unreal sense that he was master here now. From where they were, the one tower was all they could see, but it formed only the northwest angle of the stronghold.

"How do we get there?" Muriella asked.

"We ride up from the clachan," he said. "Would you prefer a garron, or are you accustomed to riding Lowland horses?"

"I can ride any well-mannered mount," she said. "My father taught all of us to ride well. I'd prefer to ride the same sort of horse you ride, though, so we'll be able to talk without one of us looming over the other."

"Then we'll take two of my horses," he said. "They are well trained and accustomed to caparisons and other draping, so your skirts won't trouble them."

After giving orders to MacKell for the galley and to lads on the wharf to fetch horses for him and his lady, and garrons for their baggage, Rob escorted Muriella ashore. There, he introduced her to people from the clachan, who all expressed their sympathy and dismay for the so unexpected death of his father.

Realizing that he was just delaying the ride home, Rob steeled himself and declared it time that he and his lady were on their way. Thanking his well-wishers again, he helped Murie mount the bay gelding they had chosen for her.

To his sudden sardonic amusement, he realized then that the villagers meant to escort them to the castle gates, if not farther. He devoutly hoped they did not expect to witness the meeting of his wife and his lady mother.

~

Murie easily interpreted the sparkle in Rob's eyes as amusement and wondered what had stirred it. Since she could not ask him in front of so many witnesses, she took comfort from her certainty about the emotion. His feelings were rarely as easy for her to read as her father's were, or Mag's or Ian's.

But either her skill was increasing or Rob was revealing more to her.

To be sure, her sisters had complained that they had initially had difficulty sensing their husbands' emotions, too. Lina had experienced less trouble with Ian than Dree had had with Mag, despite the fact that Dree had always possessed the strongest ability of the three to sense other people's feelings.

As Murie and Rob rode slowly up the steep track to the castle, the people from the clachan fell in behind them. The gillie leading the two garrons with her belongings followed, and Murie easily sensed the tense expectation they all shared.

Glancing at Rob to find him watching her speculatively, she wondered if he was judging her horsemanship or her reaction to their audience.

To converse over the thudding of the horses' hooves on the hard track that wound up the cliffside would require talking loudly. The people walking behind them would hear, so Murie kept quiet and enjoyed the view as they rode higher.

Southward, she saw part of the Firth of Clyde and land separating the Loch of the Long Boats from the Gare Loch. Before them loomed the square tower. In time, the path curved around a bend and a stone wall came into view on their right.

"Good sakes," she said. "Do you *need* a wall? I should think you could easily see trouble coming from your tower."

"Aye, sure, we can," he said. "But, as you can see, the castle perches on the edge of a steep plateau that overlooks the flat lands between here and the firth. The slope here is not nearly as steep, though, so an army could gather here on any dark night. The same is true Lomondside. Without the wall, we would be vulnerable. We also have a moat," he added with a smile. "You'll see it shortly."

"A moat? How?"

"You'll see."

The wall curved upward with the trail and continued to loom over them. Murie judged it to be fifteen or twenty feet high. The track they followed had flattened, though, and Rob's moat came into sight at the next bend. Murie realized that it guarded only the otherwise vulnerable, entrance side of the castle.

The drawbridge was down and the gates open, so Rob's people inside had seen and recognized the galley. She saw him nod to several men, but he did not speak until they had thudded across the plank bridge to the gateway.

A man-at-arms stepped toward him then, and Rob drew rein.

"Welcome home, laird," the man said. "Will I let all these folks inside or keep them out? Her ladyship did send word that she canna receive them the noo."

Rob said, "We won't deny them, Cully. You need only explain that, at present, the lady Euphemia is not receiving. They will understand."

"The lady Euphemia, sir?"

To Murie's surprise, Rob's eyes began to dance. He met the other man's gaze and said, "Cully, this lady riding beside me is Lady MacAulay now. Sithee, I suspect that my lady mother will forbid us to refer to her as the *dowager* Lady MacAulay. I may be wrong about that, and I will ask her, but—"

"Nay, nay, laird, I'll do as ye say," the man, Cully, said hastily. Turning to Muriella, he nodded politely and said earnestly, "'Tis grand tae meet ye, m'lady. It be time that our young master married. Welcome tae Ardincaple."

Grinning at him, delighting in her new title, Murie said, "I am pleased to meet you, Cully. Were you born here?"

"Aye, m'lady," the man said, smiling back at her.

"We must go in now, Cully," Rob said. "Come, my lady."

Still smiling, Murie nodded and urged her mount to follow his. They rode across the yard to a small stable where gillies waited to assist them and take charge of the horses. Dismounting unaided, eager to go inside, Murie saw that the castle extended well beyond the tall, battle-mented tower and included several outbuildings besides the stable inside its wall. Another was a low, thatch-roofed building from which aromas wafted that told her it must be the bakery.

Rob offered his arm and, without making further intro-ductions, escorted her up a set of railed wooden steps to the main entrance and thence to the great hall.

When they entered, a tall, rather plump woman, ele-gantly garbed and coifed, hurried toward them only to stop in her tracks and cast a baleful look at Murie.

"Who is this that ye've brought here to us, Robert?" she demanded. "I should think that at this dreadful time for all of us, ye might have refrained from inviting guests to Ardincaple. Where be the rest of them, and how many?"

Murie decided that she would never again call him "Robert."

"My lady wife is the only one I bring, madam," Rob said coolly. "I expect you will agree that she has every right to be here, even at such a time."

"Your *wife*?"

The woman's outrage was plain in both tone and expression, but Murie also sensed deep grief and pain. It was to those feelings that she reacted.

Lifting her hand from Rob's forearm, she snatched up her skirt and hurried to the woman, saying, "Pray, madam, do not blame him. This is all my fault!" Sinking to the deep curtsy that she had been practicing to make to the King or Queen if she chanced to meet them at Inverness, Murie looked up into leaf-green eyes exactly like Rob's. "I have looked forward to meeting you, madam," she said quietly.

"Rise, rise, for pity's sake," Lady Euphemia snapped. "Who are ye and from whence d'ye come?"

"I am Muriella, third daughter of Andrew MacFarlan of Tùr Meiloach and the lady Aubrey Comyn, his wife." Murie straightened as she spoke but sensed no softening in her ladyship's demeanor.

As she sought for something else to say, the older woman turned and said scathingly to Rob, "How dare ye, sir! A third daughter and likely impecunious? Ye be well aware that we had planned a much more eligible union for ye."

Murie's mouth opened, and as she fought to tamp down her temper, a firm hand gripped her arm. She pressed her lips together at once. So intently had her mind fixed on Lady Euphemia that she'd failed to sense Rob's approach.

Aware that he was holding Murie's arm too tightly, Rob eased his grip but kept his gaze on his mother. Knowing that to vent his temper with her would be unwise, he said evenly, "I know that you had hoped for such an alliance, madam. If my father had a similar expectation that your hope would result in a betrothal, he did not share it with me. In any event—"

"Never a bit, Robert," his mother interjected crossly, folding her arms across her plump bosom. "God kens fine that I'll no tolerate so daft a marriage. We will seek an annulment and set things aright. Furthermore—"

"That is enough," he interjected calmly but confidently. "Before you issue more orders, Mother, I would remind you—although I should not have to—that your status here has changed. You are my mother and will have due respect and a place here at Ardincaple for as long as you desire one. However, the final say here is now mine. You and I can continue this discussion later, if you wish. But we will do so privately and after I see my lady wife settled into our bedchamber."

Although Lady Euphemia had glowered at him throughout his rebuke, her mouth fell open at the last few words, and he had no trouble following her train of thought.

Gently, he said, "Since you had no warning, I do not expect you to remove your things from the laird's chambers straightaway. Nevertheless, I will expect those rooms to be ready to receive us within a sennight unless there is gey good reason that they are not. Meantime, you will oblige me by seeing that my current bedchamber is rearranged at once to accommodate Muriella."

He watched his mother try to digest his orders and saw that she was having difficulty. Deciding she might do better without Murie watching her, he said, "Come along now, lass. I'll show you where we will sleep and help you get settled."

As he spoke, he put a hand to her nearer shoulder and urged her rather quickly toward the stairs. To his surprise, as they neared the doorway, she abruptly stopped, her gaze again fixed on his mother.

"Muriella?"

"With respect, sir," she said, her tone carrying easily, "I ken fine that you have much to do and would be better pleased to be doing it. I would be happy to let her ladyship show me where I am to sleep, if she will be so kind."

Silence from Lady Euphemia being her only response, Rob bent his head close to Murie's and said, "You'd do better to follow my lead, lass, believe me."

"Prithee, sir," she murmured. "I think it would be wiser for me to talk with her. You'd liefer have the three of us live together in peace, would you not?"

He grimaced. "Art sure, lass? She practically eats wenches like you."

Giving him a secret, saucy smile and speaking close to his ear, she said, "You don't know yet *what* I'm like, Rob MacAulay. Mayhap I will surprise you."

As he turned away, suppressing his own smile, his mother said curtly, "Whilst ye're talking rude secrets, Robert, ye'll be glad to know I've put off the laird's court. Ye'll want time to find your way about as laird here afore that."

Rob turned back. "When did my father mean to hold it?"

"This Wednesday, midmorning," she said. "'Tis much too soon."

"I ken fine that you had no way to know how long it would take to find me," he said. "But since I am here now and we have three days to prepare, we have no reason to delay. I'll tell MacGurk to send out word, though. You need trouble your head no further about it."

She did not reply, and when her angry gaze shifted from him to Muriella, he decided that the latter might soon wish herself back at Tùr Meiloach.

She might even decide that she had been safer at Arrochar.

⁓

Realizing that Rob had made things worse for her by rejecting his mother's postponement of the laird's court, Murie knew that any anger Lady Euphemia felt would flow to her. Warning herself to stay calm, she thought about Lady Aubrey and Lina and imagined herself donning their habitual cloaks of dignity and calm.

"Prithee, madam, I hope you are not too vexed with me," Murie said, moving toward her again and allowing some of her own tension to enter her voice. Then, overruling her earlier decision never to call Rob "Robert," as Lady Euphemia did, Murie said, "Robert has told me gey little about Ardincaple or his family. But pray, madam, do not blame him for that, either," she added hastily. "See you, we have had little time to know each other, let alone to learn much *about* each other."

"D'ye mean to say ye've not yet consummated your union?" Lady Euphemia inquired with an irritating air of hopefulness.

Chapter 15 ——————

Seeking his steward, Adkin MacGurk, Rob found the slender, white-haired man in the buttery talking quietly with the housekeeper, a buxom middle-aged redhead known as Flora's Maggie. Maggie's mother had served as Ardincaple's housekeeper for many years before her.

MacGurk and Maggie turned as one and began in chorus to express their pleasure at seeing Rob and to offer their sympathy for the loss of his father.

Maggie said, "Such a shock it were, Master Rob—" Breaking off with a grimace, she said, "'Tis likely I'll do *that* more than once, m'lord. But it doesna seem possible, even after two days' time, that the auld laird be dead."

"'Tis hard for me, too, Maggie," Rob said. "But, prithee, call me 'laird' as you called him. It will please me more than 'm'lord.' Meantime," he added, "I must tell you something of importance."

"Ye've brung home a lady wife," Maggie said, exchanging a droll look with MacGurk. "We ken that fine, sir. Cully told us."

"I never could keep secrets from either of you," Rob said.

"The mistress…that is to say, her ladyship, Lady Euphemia—"

"I'll wager you both know how she reacted," Rob said. "But she is with my lady now at my lady's request. We must all wait and see what comes of that."

Neither Maggie nor MacGurk looked any more hopeful than Rob felt.

He said, "I mean to hold our laird's court on Wednesday morning, MacGurk, as my father intended. You will have to spread word again of this new change."

"Nae need, laird. I doubted ye'd go farther than Arrochar and would be back as soon as ye could tae report tae Himself. So I did nowt about his laird's court, 'cause I thought likely ye'd want tae get him underground then, too, so folks could be there tae see when ye did. See you, sir, wi' this chilly weather, I kent fine that we had time tae wait, if only until tomorrow."

Thanking him, Rob agreed with Maggie's suggestion that she might take a wee peek into his bedchamber to see if aught needed doing before he and his lady wife slept there. She took herself off at once, leaving the two men alone.

"Walk with me, MacGurk," Rob said then. "I want to hear all you can tell me about how Father died and what else you know of his plans for his laird's court. I've just sat through one with a Brehon justice setting the rules, so I ken more than I did about such things. But—" He spread his hands.

The older man chuckled. "I'd like tae hear more about that court, sir."

"In good time," Rob said. "Tell me how my father died."

The steward's version being the same as the galley captain's, Rob was no wiser afterward than before. Nor had MacGurk been privy to MacAulay's intentions toward anyone who would appear before him at his court.

Since Rob had been at Ardincaple for a sennight before going to Tùr Meiloach, the steward had little more to tell him. "I will say that them who serve the castle would be glad tae see more o' ye, sir," MacGurk added quietly.

Assuring him that he would stay at Ardincaple at least until the King summoned him for some task or other, Rob had turned away before he recalled that he would leave sooner than that.

"I did tell my good-father that I would try to attend the Inverness Parliament," he said. "Sithee, I must swear fealty to his grace as soon as I can, and Andrew Dubh expects to leave Tùr Meiloach in ten days."

"Will your lady accompany you, sir?"

"We'll see," Rob said. When that answer caused Mac-Gurk to raise his eyebrows, he realized that the older man feared he might be leaving Murie like a lamb for his mother's slaughter. Rob doubted that that would be the case, but he also hoped to take her with him. He just did not want to make that decision until he had a better idea of what he could expect of her.

After showing himself everywhere he thought necessary for the time being, he grew impatient to learn if his bride had survived her discussion with his mother.

Lady Euphemia's hopeful request to hear that Muriella and Rob had *not* consummated their marriage had shocked Murie, so she was glad that she could answer honestly. She was also grateful for the heat she felt in her cheeks. She said, "Mercy, madam, I did not mean to mislead you. We did that straightaway."

Well, almost straightaway after we reached Tùr Meiloach, she amended silently to herself. Lest her ladyship inquire more closely, she added hastily, "See you, madam, your brave Robert saved me from a dreadful villain and did so with great courage. I can tell you now, after seeing how *you* stood up to *him*…" Pausing, she added in a confiding tone, "I ken fine that you must be as aware as I am now that he can be a trifle domineering."

Dryly, Lady Euphemia said, "Robert can be willful, aye. I expect a young wife might think him rather intimidating."

"Aye, because he is forever telling me what to do," Murie said frankly. "But I meant only to say that he clearly inherited his courage from you, madam. My good-brothers told me that he is a gey courageous man, and then I saw as much for myself. But they told me little else. I hope to learn more about him *and* about Ardincaple from you. My mother has oft told me that the lady of a castle kens more about it and its people than her lord husband does."

"*That* is perfectly true," Euphemia said. "Why, I could tell you tales…"

When she paused, Murie clapped her hands together with sincere enthusiasm and exclaimed, "Oh, pray do, madam. I adore such stories and learning about how people think and act. You must know many, many tales that you can tell me. Robert talks so little about himself," she added. Then with a sigh that she hoped sounded sad rather than frustrated, she said, "There is one thing that he did tell me, although he mentioned only the barest facts and none of the reasons for it or names of people involved. He...he said he should tell me about it before anyone else did."

When her ladyship's eyebrows fluttered upward, then down into a frown, Murie realized she might be thinking of the scheming Euphemia was supposedly doing now with Duchess Isabella to marry Rob to the duchess's young daughter.

Hastily, but as casually as she could, she said, "He told me that a young girl...that he was nearly betrothed... and...oh, it was such an appalling tragedy!"

"You speak of poor Elizabeth Napier, I think," Lady Euphemia said. "Hers was a terrible fate, aye, and much Robert's fault, I fear. Sithee, he did not want to marry and rejected all that his father or I said about how little he need *feel* married until the girl was older. He offered her little wooing, so the poor child decided she would not have him. Her parents knew what an excellent marriage it would be, so they urged her to be patient with him. She cried out at them then, her mother said, and threatened to run away. So her father locked her in a tower and said he would keep her there until she came to her senses. The next time he entered, she threw herself out the tower window right in front of him, to die on the cobbles below."

"How horrid!" Murie exclaimed, too easily able to picture the lurid scene. Searching her memory as she watched Lady Euphemia, she added, "Robert never told me the poor girl's name. Did you say it was Elizabeth *Napier*?"

"I did, aye. Her father is a Clan Scott chieftain, so the connection would have been an excellent one for her and for Robert."

Thoughts awhirl, Murie fought to concentrate. "She was a Borderer, then."

"Aye, but her mother is kin to the powerful Earl of Sutherland, so the family has roots in the Highlands *and* the Borders. Why did you ask that?"

"I thought I had heard that tale before," Murie said. "I was gey young though. Robert said he was fourteen at the time. That would be ten years ago, aye?"

"I promise you, we did not spread the tale," Lady Euphemia said with a sniff of indignation. "Someone else must have done that if it is the tale you heard. People *will* gossip, and it does seem to fly about the country faster than real news does."

"I'm nearly certain that the name I heard wasn't Napier, though," Murie said.

"Well, it is sad but true that such tragedies are more common than we like to think they are," Lady Euphemia said. "Do you have a great deal to unpack, my dear? Come to that, did you bring your woman with you?"

Welcoming the endearment, Murie sensed that it was either sincere or a habit of speech for her ladyship. Either way, the rancor had disappeared from her voice and demeanor. That alone was acceptable progress, Murie decided, feeling more confident than she had when their conversation began.

In response to her ladyship's question regarding a personal servant, Murie said, "I brought no one, madam. Our Tibby would dislike leaving home, and Mam said she was sure that you would willingly provide someone to suit me."

Lady Euphemia nodded. "I know several maidservants who might do, but you will want to decide for yourself. I own, my dear, I was disappointed to learn that Robert had married without consulting his father or me. But I begin to think that you and I may deal together more comfortably than I thought we would."

"Then, mayhap, if you would not find it tiresome, you will show me something more of this wondrous castle," Murie said. "I have little to unpack, because Mam said she would send more of my things here after the Inverness Parliament. But I'd like to learn as much as you can teach me about Ardincaple."

"I don't tire as easily as that," Euphemia said. "Forbye, I know that Robert will not tell you many things that you *should* know about the place and its people. Sithee, I came here just as you have, so I ken fine how difficult it can be."

Murie felt as if she had achieved much but sensed that Lady Euphemia had reasons of her own for being kind to her and wondered what they might be.

⁓

Sunday and Monday, Rob and Muriella kept busy with duties at the castle, while Rob kept a wary eye on Murie and his mother. Long experience warned him that Lady Euphemia often had goals that did not mesh with his father's and were unlikely to appeal to Rob, either.

Evenings, when the sun neared the horizon, he and Murie took supper with Lady Euphemia. Afterward, they strolled about the castle yard together and talked before retiring early to bed, where they learned even more about each other.

Muriella having shown strong curiosity and eager willingness to explore the pleasures of the marriage bed, Rob was just as eager to teach her all he knew.

After supper Tuesday, they walked out onto the hillside beyond the castle, from the crest of which they had a view northwest as far as Loch Lomond. Realizing that a slight hollow just below them on the hillside there provided both privacy and shelter from the breeze, Rob spread his plaid on the ground there.

"Come here to me, lass," he said, still on one knee but looking up at her.

She stood where she was and cocked her head. "That sounded ominous," she said. "I hope you are not going to fulfill your promise to the Brehon out here, sir."

"You may hope," he said, but his eyes twinkled. "I doubt you will dislike what I mean to do."

"In that case, my lord, I am yours to command," she said with a smile.

"Then do as I bid you," he said, beckoning with a finger for her to approach. When she stood right in front of him, he said, "I think it is warm enough for you to take off your kirtle and shift."

"Here?" Her voice squeaked.

"Aye, sure," he said, grinning. "You said I had only to command."

"Very well, then, but you had better keep me warm, sir."

He kept her warmer than warm, stirring her senses until she cried out to him to stop, and then he stimulated her more, taking her to heights she had not known before, and clearly enjoying himself in the effort.

Afterward, as they walked back to the castle, Murie said casually, "I enjoyed that, and I would like to spend more time with you, doing things together."

"Then we will," Rob said amiably.

"Aye, but your mam said the laird's court will mean

having the castle full of clansmen, some of them strangers even to her. Must you hold it so soon? Your mam said that some people might think it disrespectful to your father not to wait until a more suitable length of time passes after his burial."

"Did she?"

"Aye, and I must agree with her," Murie said. "Sakes, your father is not in the ground yet, sir. You seem more concerned about your court than about him."

Easily keeping his temper, since he knew she was blameless, Rob said, "I must have forgotten to tell you, lass. We'll bury him Wednesday at dawn, so that as many clansmen as possible *can* be here. Because he was chief of our clan, it would be *un*wise to bury him with what some might deem to be unseemly haste."

Having sensed Rob's flash of anger, the one emotion of his that she could always sense, she wondered now at his calmness. Realizing that Lady Euphemia had neglected to mention Lord MacAulay's burial when she expressed her concerns about the laird's court, and strongly doubting that Rob had forgotten to tell *her* that both would take place on Wednesday, Murie deduced wryly that Lady Euphemia had not yet fully accepted her.

Although tempted to share these thoughts with Rob, she suspected that doing so would be like raising a din on one of her sisters at home. His flash of temper was over, so she knew he was not angry with her. However, if he was already angry with his mother, Murie doubted that he would thank *her* for telling him what he had likely deduced for himself. Even so, she had to say something.

At last she said quietly, "I hope I have not vexed you again, Rob. I am happier when we are having fun than when you are displeased with me."

Putting an arm around her shoulders, he drew her close, then stopped and turned her to face him. "I'm not angry with you, lass," he said, kissing the top of her head. Then with a little smile, he added, "In troth, I was thinking that I should tell you how much I appreciate the time you spend with my mother. I had feared that you would not get on with her, since I find it hard to do so myself at times."

Aware that she was blushing, and recalling that he seemed able to read her every expression, she said, "Then I should admit to you, sir, that I can easily tell when I have irked her and can tell as easily if what I say pleases her. I just talk more about topics that please her and avoid those that don't. People tend to like others who share an interest in things that interest them, do they not?"

"They do, aye," he agreed, albeit with an unnervingly thoughtful look. "I must say, though, that I have known her all my life and still cannot sense her feelings as easily as that."

"Well, I can," she said. "However, I will tell you that I also sense some…" She hesitated, seeking an acceptable word, then added, "Frankly, sir, 'mendacity' is the most suitable word. I ken fine that it is a dreadfully tactless thing to—"

"Never mind tact," he said. "If you thought she was being deceitful, why did you let her persuade you to urge me to put off my laird's court?"

"It wasn't like that," she said. "The sense of her that I just mentioned was something I felt the *first* time I talked with her, as if she were saying one thing but thinking another. Today, I believed she was telling me what she thinks is true."

"Then you have more faith than wisdom when it comes to your instincts, lass. I won't urge you to distrust all that she says, just to know her better before you make judgments about her truthfulness."

"Good sakes, sir, do you think your mother lies to you?"

Rob hesitated before he said, "I think she likes to get her own way. I know she sometimes refuses to hear what anyone else says, if it contradicts her belief about how things are. I respect her opinions in that I believe she has every right to express them. But I also know that she will go to great lengths in her efforts to control other people and make them dance to her piping."

Murie wished she could explain her ability to him, but he urged her ahead of him on the path. The sun was below the hill and the Loch Lomond area behind them already in deep shadow, so she walked silently until an echo of what he had said earlier returned to her. Then she looked back and said, "I know I do not always show wisdom, sir. You are not the first person to say that, as doubtless you know."

"You are young yet," he said.

"Aye, but young or not, I do trust what I sense about people. I don't pretend to be as gifted in that way as Dree is, though. Animals like me, but I cannot tell how one of them is feeling unless Lina's cat growls at me or a squirrel chatters angrily."

"Sakes, lass, no one can tell what animals feel or if they even *have* feelings, other than pain."

Stopping, she turned and stared at him. "How can

you think that?" she demanded. "One need only *look* at Scáthach to know if she is unhappy or excited. She watches you, sir. She knows your every move and mood. She can tell by your clothing if you are going outside or staying in and reacts with excitement to the one and resignation to the other. Your slightest gesture tells her what you want of her."

"Aye, because I have trained her well."

She shook her head at him but offered no further argument. She had seen an arrested look in his eyes while she described Scáthach's behavior, which told her that she had given him reason to think about all that she had said.

~

Rob could not decide whether he was more annoyed or intrigued by Murie's argument. She was right about Scáthach's ability to read his moods and intentions, though. Also, he could read Scáthach nearly as well, and in ways he had *not* taught her. Her demeanor when danger threatened differed from her demeanor when it did not.

The way she had growled to warn him of the ambush awaiting him in the pass the day he'd followed Dougal and Muriella there had told him that he needed his weapon ready even as he whirled to face the swordsmen.

But he did not want to dwell on that now or argue any more. Instead, he took his wife to bed and taught her a few more things about pleasuring him and obeying his commands. She was, to his increasing delight, an apt and inventive pupil.

When he awoke before dawn Wednesday, she was still asleep, so he got up, dressed quietly, and gave orders for his man to let her sleep until after the burial.

Finding Lady Euphemia downstairs breaking her fast, he bade her good morning and took his rightful place at the high table. It still felt strange, even disrespectful, to sit in the laird's chair, but he was sure the feeling would pass.

"It will be a fine day, I think," his mother said, daintily spooning a bite of her boiled egg from its shell. "Your Muriella told me when she arrived that she will need a maidservant. I have given the matter much thought, and I believe my Tressa's Mairi will suit her needs."

Knowing that Mairi would repeat to her mother anything that Muriella said and that Tressa would repeat it to Lady Euphemia, Rob said, "I think MacGurk's Fiona would suit her better, Mam. She is closer in age to Muriella."

"Oh, but my dear Robert, your Muriella is so young that she would surely do better to have someone older who can show her how to go on here."

"She can ask you or me if she needs help," Rob replied mildly, nodding to the gillie who approached with his customary breakfast on a tray. The lad set down a mug of ale, a large bowl of barley porridge, and a platter of cold sliced beef. Another lad brought a basket with oven-warm manchet loaves in it.

Waiting only until the two had turned away, her ladyship said, "Muriella does not seem at all shy. I will say that for her."

"I think she likes you, too, Mam."

"Are ye *sure* that Tressa's Mairi won't do. I do think—"

"I will talk to MacGurk," Rob said. "If he thinks his Fiona is not ready for such responsibility, he will say so. Forbye, it will be up to Muriella in the end." Lady Euphemia was still frowning, so he changed the subject. "Do you ken what sort of grievances Father expected to hear at this laird's court?"

She shrugged. "He told me naught, so I warrant there was naught of import. I do recall some sort of grievance over a death that he thought was odd."

"Odd?" Rob's eyebrows shot upward. "The grievance or the death itself?"

"He just said 'odd.' "

"Could it have aught to do with his own death? Might someone summoned to the court have thought that killing Father might somehow benefit him?"

"I don't know how," Lady Euphemia said. "The only thing that fretted him of late was that business of the fees that Campbell of Lorne and Pharlain of Arrochar were urging him to collect. Were ye at least able to set that to rest?"

"Greed is not something that one puts to rest," Rob said. He knew he would likely have to tell her all that had happened at Arrochar, but he did not want to discuss it over his breakfast or in the great hall where others might hear.

She said curtly, "Did ye even *see* Pharlain?"

Disliking her tone but knowing of old that he would gain nowt by saying so, he said, "I saw him. He made his feelings plain. But you need not fret, Mam. I will see that Ardincaple keeps safe and that the lochs hereabouts remain free to all vessels unless the King himself decides to set fees for passage."

"Ye sound gey sure of yourself," she replied. "Ye ken fine that your father did not approve of meeting force with force."

"And you ken fine that I am not my father," Rob said

in the same calm way, despite a stronger urge to snap at her. That urge was as familiar as it had been when he was thirteen, but the knowledge that his word was now law at Ardincaple and that Murie might suffer if he annoyed his mother, made it easier to be civil.

Evidently, Lady Euphemia was wise enough to know that she had gone her length, because she excused herself minutes later to prepare for her late husband's burial. Realizing that she meant to attend it and might take offense at Murie's absence, Rob went upstairs to wake her.

~

Lord MacAulay's burial took place efficiently and with dignity, after which, the gathered crowd being deemed too large for the great hall but small enough to accommodate in the courtyard, Rob convened his laird's court there.

As usual at such events, a wooden dais bearing a table and chairs for the laird and whoever would keep the record stood at the foot of the wooden steps leading to the main entrance. At Ardincaple, the accuser, the accused, and the witnesses would stand on the dais to declare their grievances, defend themselves, or give evidence.

Gillies carried a bench out and set it at the front of the gathering, near the table where Rob would sit. The lads kept the bench clear for Lady Euphemia and Murie, who soon took their places there. Other benches were available for those who wanted to sit. Most of the men remained standing, and everyone stood when Rob took his place at the table and declared the laird's court open.

Murie had never observed such a proceeding other than at Arrochar, although she had witnessed bits of one or two of her father's courts, unbeknownst to him, from a window overlooking the tower's yard. Such occasions there were always solemn, because men's hides or their lives often hung in the balance.

At first, she thought that the grievances Rob heard were petty, even boring. Each seemed to be a matter of someone taking a lamb, firewood, or another object that was not his—often by mistake. The accuser would state his view of what had happened. Then the other man would give his version or apologize and promise Rob that he would pay for or return the property. Rob would make his decision one way or the other, and that would be that. Rob seemed to be utterly fair and just.

Then a middle-aged woman stepped to the dais and declared that one Donnie's Ferg had murdered her husband. "He should hang for it, laird," she added grimly.

"If your accusation proves true, Mistress Cowen, he will," Rob said. "Step forward onto the dais, Fergus, and be heard."

A tall, gangly lad of some two score years, with corn-yellow hair and eyes so light blue they looked colorless, walked forward and stood warily at the edge of the dais on Murie's right. She could see his ashen, freckled face clearly. So terrified was he that she could sense his terror in other ways, too, as he warily eyed Rob.

"You may speak, lad," Rob said when silence fell.

"It...it were an accident," Fergus blurted. "I didna mean tae kill 'im!"

"But you did kill Gib Cowen, aye?"

"Aye, laird, but I couldna help it!"

Rob said, "Have you a witness to Gib's death, Mistress Cowen?"

"Aye, sure, laird, and Ferg kens it fine," the woman said. "Me son Jocky were there and saw the whole thing. He stands yonder. Ask him yourself."

Rob motioned for Jocky Cowen to step onto the dais. "Tell us how your father's death happened, Jock."

"Sakes, laird, Ferg there were a-climbing up one o' them cliffs yonder, seeking tae find eagles' eggs. Me da stood below 'im, 'cause Ferg told him to, so he could lower his basket tae him after he filled it with eggs. T' clumsy oaf fell on Da instead and squashed 'im flat! Had Ferg no been so clumsy, me da would still be alive. Ferg did kill him, though, so he should hang for murder."

Growls of agreement sounded from some of the men in the gathering, as well as mutterings of shocked protest.

Rob said evenly, "It does sound as if it might have been an acci—"

"Sakes, laird!" Jocky exclaimed. "Had Ferg no been up there at all, he'd no ha' fallen. He told Da tae stand there, so he kent fine that Da was there. Ferg could ha' kept from falling on 'im, had he tried, but he *didna* try. He just smashed intae him. It be murder, same as if he'd taken a club and beat Da tae death!"

More sounds of agreement and disagreement followed his words.

Murie watched Rob, but her thoughts had flitted elsewhere, to a tale she recalled that bore a slight resemblance to the incident described.

The resolution of that tale stirred a near smile. Knowing that Rob would not appreciate humor at such a grave time, she stifled the bubble of merriment and saw with relief that he had shifted his attention back to Donnie's Ferg.

Chapter 16 _____

What defense can you offer to Jocky's accusation, Fergus?" Rob asked.

"Sakes, laird, nae one could ha' done what he says I should ha'. I lost me footing and me handhold all at once and plunged tae the ground. It ain't as if I could spread wings and look doon first. Auld Gib were there and I fell on him, sure enow, and the blessed man were like a fat cushion. I bruised m'self summat fierce, but he saved me life. I'm that sorry I squashed him, but God kens I couldna help it!"

Moments before, Rob had noted a near grin on Murie's face. She had quickly suppressed it but there it was again, trying to break free.

Her gaze collided with his sterner one, and she looked hastily down, then looked up again and met his gaze more solemnly. Then she continued to stare intently at him, as if with a purpose. He glanced up at the sky, noted that the sun was almost directly overhead, and made a decision.

"I have heard your grievance, Mistress Cowen, and your defense, Fergus. But this is not an issue to decide in a trice." Summoning a nearby gillie, he said, "How long before our people will be ready to serve the midday meal?"

"We can begin straightaway, laird. Lady Euphemia and your own lady did see tae that. We ha' trestle tables set up inside, and if need be, we'll set more up out here. Folks can come in tae fetch their food and bring it outside if they want."

"Good." Rob stood and said, "We will adjourn and continue this court after our midday meal." Leaving his scribe and the gillie to explain where everyone should eat, he left the dais and went directly to his wife and his mother.

Lady Euphemia said, "We should go in and take our places before everyone else surges into the hall, my dear Robert."

"Here is your Tressa, Mam. You and she should go on in and see that all is in train there. I want a word with Muriella, so I will take her in with me."

For once, Lady Euphemia did not argue. She and her woman went inside.

Rob offered his forearm to Murie and led her toward the postern door. Everyone else was moving steadily toward the main entrance.

"We'll go in this way," he said. "From the way you were looking at me just then, I think you have something you want to say to me."

"I do, aye," she said. "You have told me that you are willing for anyone to offer an opinion or express a belief. Did you mean that, even for today?"

"I did, aye, or I would not have said it," he said. "Before you begin to speak on someone's behalf, though, you should know that I will not heed what you say unless you are willing to stand on the dais and say it before everyone."

"I don't want to do that," she said. "Nor do I want to speak on anyone's behalf. I just want to tell you a story."

"I could use some entertainment," he said with a smile.

⁓

When the laird's court reconvened in the courtyard after the midday meal, Murie and Lady Euphemia were in their places before Rob summoned Donnie's Fergus and his accuser, Mistress Cowen, to the dais.

"By my troth," Lady Euphemia murmured to Muriella, "I cannot imagine what my lord husband would have done with such a strange grievance. Forbye, this must have been the odd one he mentioned to me."

Murie did not have to reply, because Rob had gestured for silence and was about to speak. She held her breath.

"I have made my decision," he announced in a tone that carried throughout the courtyard. Looking at Mistress Cowen, he said, "I have listened carefully, mistress, and it is a fact that Fergus killed your husband, Gib." Turning to Fergus, he said, "Jocky Cowen's testimony does nowt to contradict yours, Ferg, so I will accept your version of events as the truth as you see it. Nevertheless, due to your own actions and for kindly aiding you at your request, Gib Cowen did die."

"Aye, laird, but—"

Waving him and a few mutterers to silence, Rob turned his attention to the witness. "Your version of events also appears to be correct, Jock. One does wonder why Auld Gib did not move out of the way, and simple logic suggests that he failed to pay attention as he should have and must bear at least some of the responsibility. We all want fairness, though," Rob added. "So I hereby order that when we finish here today, you, Fergus MacAulay, will stand under that same cliff exactly where Gib stood. Then you, Jock, will climb to the place from which Fergus fell, jump down, and thereby put Fergus to death in the same way that he killed your father."

Stunned silence greeted his ruling.

At last, Mistress Cowen said, "Nay! I never heerd o' such a thing."

"I ain't going tae do any such daft thing, laird," Jock declared. "Sakes, Ferg would likely move and then *I'd* be kilt. I'll kill 'im all right, but I'll do it in me own way and in me own good time."

Murie looked at the angry young man and then at Rob.

"If you do that, I will hang you for murder," Rob said without raising his voice. "I have given you a solution that is fair to all concerned. If you refuse to seek redress in the manner that I have ordered, I suggest that you and Ferg shake hands and agree to be friends again. As I recall, you and he were gey good friends before this happened. Forbye, I think all here will agree that Gib was careless to stand under Fergus whilst he climbed a perilous cliff, and more so not to keep an eye on him. You said it yourself, Jock. Gib could have moved before Ferg struck him, and Ferg would be dead now instead. Would you have expected Fergus's family to demand Gib's death in such an instance, just for moving *out* of danger?"

Jock shrugged unhappily, but Murie sensed that he had seen the logic in Rob's question. He looked at Fergus without expression and then turned away.

The laird's court proceeded then with dispatch. Rob dealt efficiently and, in Murie's view, fairly with one man after another, hearing more grievances than Andrew heard at any of his sittings. Murie wondered if Lord MacAulay had avoided holding his court. She had often heard it said that MacAulay disliked confrontation.

She was wondering about that when the word "flogged" diverted her again.

Realizing that she had let her attention drift for some time while she imagined various grievances and how a man who hated confrontation might have handled them, she saw that the two men in front of Rob both looked stunned.

He was looking from one to the other, and when his gaze fixed at last on one of the two, she assumed that that one was the accused. His demeanor and familiar face put that assumption to flight, though. The man was MacKell, the galley captain who had brought them from Tùr Meiloach to Ardincaple.

Rob said, "You ought to have expected the penalty, MacKell. Your man deserted his post. Suppose we'd had urgent need for a fully manned galley? Sakes, in that event, I would have *hanged* him."

"Aye, laird, and I'd have expected ye to. But the auld laird—" He stopped when Rob raised a hand.

"I do not want to hear what the auld laird might have done, since he can no longer speak for himself," Rob said in the same even tone he had used throughout the proceedings. "I want to hear what Sean Crombie has to say."

Murie looked at the oarsman then. He was nearer her age than Rob's, she thought. He looked wretched and frightened, as well he might, considering.

He stared silently at Rob.

"Well, Sean?"

"I dinna ken what ye want me tae say, laird."

"Just tell the truth. I don't want excuses, but if you

think you had good cause to leave your post, I'll hear what you have to say."

Sean Crombie licked his lips and glanced at MacKell. Murie could sense that he was nervous, uncertain, but feeling some sort of increased determination.

He straightened his shoulders. "I dinna ken if ye'll want tae hear it out here with all these ears a-hanging on me words, laird. But, by me troth, I left only 'cause I seen a boat pull in tae shore a wee distance doon the loch from me post. I were closer tae the shingle where it beached than I were tae anyone from Ardincaple, so I crept through the darkness tae see what I could see."

"Why did you not report this to MacKell?" Rob asked.

Again, Murie sensed tension and uncertainty in Sean Crombie.

When he did not answer, MacKell said sternly, "He may just be trying tae make himself important, laird. He's done it afore, and this time, he may be hoping tae escape punishment. Nobbut what he's a good man, sir, mostly."

Rob nodded, his gaze fixed on Crombie.

Murie wished she might speak, but she was sure she would be wasting her breath if she did. Not only would Rob dismiss what she burned to say, but the others gathered there might think she had not yet earned the right to speak.

～

Although Rob watched Sean Crombie, he was keenly aware of the audience. The lad seemed sincere, but one could rarely be sure if someone was lying or not, especially if his life or his hide were at risk. And Sean's hide surely was.

The lad had friends watching and others who were not so friendly. Under any such circumstances, Scots were quick to take sides.

Murie's visible uneasiness revealed her tender heart. She also had innate wisdom, though, as she had shown earlier when she had told him about a man who had fallen out of a high window onto another man. Rob knew she was clever enough at spinning tales to have made it up on the spot. But whether she had or not, she had given him an excellent way out of a ticklish situation.

As they waited for Sean to decide whether to speak in his own defense, he saw that she had fixed her gaze firmly on the lad.

She looked up, caught Rob's gaze, and gave him a small, winsome smile.

To Crombie, Rob said, "Speak up now, lad. Your chance is fleeting."

"'Twas the auld laird, sir. Not in the wee boat, but I did hear him speak. I didna ken any other voice. I think there must ha' been four or five o' them, but…"

Pausing, he glanced around, as if he'd rather be talking more privately. Then, drawing breath, he added, "I did hear the laird tell them others they had nae right tae be on Ardincaple land and should tell their greedy master he'd do better tae keep his ill-willie fingers off Ardincaple business. Then, one o' them whose voice I didna ken said Himself would be talking more civil after they took Ardincaple, which they would, he said. Then he said, ''Cause when the King's parliament fails, his grace will ha' nae control over any Highlander and we'll, none of us, ha' tae heed his daft laws.' Himself asked the chap what he meant by that, but I didna hear wha' he replied. Coom tae that, I didna hear nowt after that. I hied me back tae me post."

"Tell me again when this all happened, as near as you can say," Rob said.

"Last Wednesday after dark, laird, mayhap just one side o' midnight or t'other. The moon hadna come up yet, so what I saw, I saw only by starlight."

Rob looked at MacKell. "You said my father died Thursday morning, aye?"

"Aye, laird; this be the first I've heard aught o' Wednesday night, let alone Parliaments and ill-willed fingers." Giving Sean Crombie a look that boded further ill for the lad's future, he added, "One o' me other lads caught Sean a-coming back. When he asked where he'd been, Sean said he'd gone tae take a piss. Told me the same thing when I asked him. In troth, had I not known him afore for an honest lad, I might ha' suspected that he'd had summat tae do with the laird's death."

Crombie's shocked expression drew Rob's attention back to him. "Well, Sean-lad," he said. "What say you to that?"

"I didna!" Sean exclaimed. "I would never ha' harmed a hair on the auld laird's head. He were a good, good man. I didna say nowt, 'cause I thought he had his own men wi' him, and I...I didna want anyone thinking I'd been a-spyin' on Himself. Next day, when I learned he were dead, I were sore afeard, sir. Sakes, I didna ken which men I could trust or who would believe me."

"What made you think that his lordship was with his own men?"

"Nowt that I could put a name tae," Sean admitted. "I just thought he'd never go up tae four or five men arriving in a strange boat all by hisself. Sakes, I still think some o' them must ha' been our lot. Forbye, I heard more than one man heading back toward t' castle as the boat were leaving, but I'm thinking now that them from the boat may ha' put in farther south and gone for him."

Rob considered himself a good judge of men, and he was nearly sure that Sean was telling the truth. But MacKell was shaking his head, and so were many men in the audience. His gaze drifted back to Murie.

She looked solemnly thoughtful. When their eyes met, she gazed intently at him and gave a slight nod.

Recalling that she had said she could read his mother's moods with ease and her insistence that she could also tell when Lady Euphemia and other people were being truthful, he looked again at Sean Crombie. The lad's eyes welled with tears, and his face revealed only his sadness. Feeling a lump in his own throat at what could only be shared grief, Rob said quietly, "I believe you, Sean Crombie."

Wondering then if he had interpreted Murie's nod correctly, he looked at her long enough to see her nod again. Feeling unexpected but welcome relief, he said to Sean, "I do think you ought to have told someone, lad, and I expect MacKell agrees with me. However, I acquit you of ill intent and dereliction. You had duty and reason to look into the mystery of the strange boat, but you also had a responsibility to report it. Whether you were wise or not in keeping what you overheard to yourself must be for future events to reveal. I will therefore let MacKell decide your penalty for failing to report the boat. He is a fair man, and he is responsible for you. If you think he is in league with whoever killed my father—"

"Nay, laird," Crombie interjected hastily. "When I heard summat that I feared I were no supposed tae hear, I got that flummoxed that I didna think tae report just the boat. Forbye, folks would ha' asked me questions about it, and I'm none so good at lying. It were wicked enow deciding tae say I'd gone for a piss."

"Did you hear aught else about the Inverness Parliament?"

"Nay, sir, only about it failing and nae one having tae obey his grace's laws."

Rob nodded. "Aye, then, you may go. I expect that MacKell will explain exactly what things you must report so that the rules are clear to you."

"You may be sure that I will, my lord," MacKell said grimly.

Despite the grim tone, Crombie looked infinitely relieved.

The remaining grievances went quickly, and Rob dismissed the court at last with some time remaining before supper.

Many people departed at once, but those who had come longer distances would stay the night. As the assemblage dispersed, Rob politely disengaged himself from those who wanted to chat with him and went in search of his lady, finding her in the great hall with his mother.

"You managed your first court well, Robert," Lady Euphemia said graciously. "I will own that I expected you to have more difficulty, not only because you lack your father's experience but also because you had never done such a thing before. Not to my knowledge, at all events."

Since he had not seen Lady Euphemia since the midday meal and assumed that she had grown bored with the court, Rob was surprised to see her now. Her praise, however mild, was welcome, though, and she deserved candor in return.

"In troth, Mam, I surprised myself," he admitted. "But I did recall many of my father's comments regarding his courts, and I did not act entirely alone. For that, I must thank my lady." He smiled at Murie.

Lady Euphemia stiffened. "Mercy, what can *she* have done to aid you?"

"She told me a story about a man who leaned over so far that he fell out of a window," Rob said. "He, too, killed the person on whom he landed."

"Was the story true?" Lady Euphemia asked Muriella skeptically.

"I don't know, my lady," she answered with a smile. "One can never be sure of tales that begin with 'there once was a man' or 'long ago, in the days of Fingal.' Often, though, they are the stories with the best lessons in them."

"I see," Lady Euphemia said, still skeptical. She changed the subject by asking Rob if he had decided whether to attend the King's Parliament.

Murie was eager to hear the answer to that question. She believed that Rob meant to go, because he would have to swear fealty to Jamie. In truth, she was more interested in whether he would take her with him or leave her at Ardincaple.

He said, "I do mean to go, Mam. But I must also send a message to his grace, warning him that trouble is brewing. If you heard what Sean Crombie said—?"

"I did hear something about that, and Muriella was just telling me more."

"Aye, then," Rob said. "I think you will agree with

me that Sean is not likely to have made up a tale about someone wanting Jamie's Parliament to fail. I believe he repeated to me exactly the words that he heard."

"But if no trouble occurs and you warn the King to expect trouble, you risk lowering your own position in his esteem," his mother warned.

Murie opened her mouth only to shut it without speaking. If she had learned anything about her husband, it was that he could fight his own battles.

Rob said, "The King is one of Scotland's finest warriors, Mother. He knows that men may lay plans that go unfulfilled, but he would not thank me if, having heard what we all heard today, I did nowt to warn him of potential danger."

Summoning a gillie, Rob sent him to tell two persons named Alf and Eamon to meet him straightaway in the great hall.

Lady Euphemia excused herself to wash before supper, and Murie found herself alone with her husband.

"You did believe Sean Crombie then, sir," she said.

"I did, aye," he said, putting an arm around her shoulders. "I am sure you noticed that I looked at you and tried to guess whether *you* believed him or not."

She nodded, "Aye, and I'm sure he spoke the truth. His upset when he feared that you might not believe him was real, too. I do not know why you find it odd that I can see such things in others, sir. You have a gift that is much like mine. In troth, you seem to discern my thinking much more easily than I can sense yours."

Giving her a one-armed squeeze, he said, "You seek to flatter me, lass. But I do know what you've been thinking ever since Mam asked if I would go to Inverness."

Heat surged to her cheeks. She said warily, "You must know that I want to go with you. Mayhap you think that leaving me here might serve as part of the chastisement the Brehon ordered. But I hope you won't forbid me to go."

"Nay, lass, I won't," he said. "We'll go on Saturday. When we reached Ardincaple, I did think I'd leave you here, because it would be safer for you than the long journey to Inverness and into who knows what danger. But I fear not only that I would miss you and disappoint your parents, but also that I'd liefer enjoy your company. Also, I'd feel right cruel if I left you with my mother."

"Well, you need not feel so, sir," she said testily. "I like your mother. To be sure, I thought I would not when first we met. But I have seen that she cares deeply for you, and although her frank remarks can sometimes sting, they are as naught to Lady Margaret Galbraith's comments. In troth, your mam has been kind to me. But if you will not make me stay here as my punishment, what will you do?"

He shrugged. "I am still thinking about that, so you would be wise not to press me. Instead, you should think about what things you brought here that you'll want to take with you and what you need to collect from Tùr Meiloach."

Accordingly, Murie spent the next two days making lists but deciding in the end that she'd be wiser to bring things from the tower back to Ardincaple after their journey than to take things she had brought with her from Ardincaple to Tùr Meiloach and thence to Inverness only to carry them back again to Ardincaple.

Having made that decision, she turned her thoughts to Andrew's charters.

In the manner that had become customary when dealing with historical matters, she mentally sifted through the tales she knew about other charters, as well as those about Arrochar, Tùr Meiloach, and her own family.

The result was that she awoke rather abruptly Saturday morning to realize that remnants of a strange, rapidly fading dream had stirred a question in her mind that she was certain she had never thought to ask her father or anyone else.

"What's amiss, lass?" Rob murmured sleepily.

She wondered where it might lead if she told him and how much he'd believe.

⁓

Rob held Murie gently with her warm, naked back spooned against him and his right arm draped over her shoulder. His cock was reacting to her touch, but he had felt her stiffen before it did and wondered what had startled her.

When she did not answer immediately, he shook off lingering lassitude and said, "I ken fine that you're awake, Murie-lass. I would like you to answer me."

With a soft sigh, she turned in his arms to face him, her tantalizing lips and rosy-tipped breasts offering welcome diversion. Her lips pursed, inviting a kiss.

Knowing that she could feel his response, he said more curtly than he might have otherwise, "I asked you a question."

She nibbled her lower lip, then said, "Don't scowl at me like that. Am I not permitted to keep even my innermost thoughts private?"

"Not from me, and especially not when they distress

you," he said. "Something did, and I want to know what it was."

"I had a strange dream, that's all."

"Murie." He said only that, but he knew the warning was clear.

She rolled her eyes. "Very well, but I am not going to tell you all I think, sir, so you need not imagine that I will. I had a dream about something that Father mentions whenever he tells of his escape from Arrochar after Pharlain and his men murdered my brothers. You did say that you had heard that story."

"I've heard several versions of it, most of which are absurd," he said. "Andrew told me one himself but admitted leaving out details because he said he doubted that I'd believe them."

"What *did* he tell you about the escape?"

"Only that he and your mother fled Arrochar through a bolt hole and made their way to Tùr Meiloach."

"He usually adds that he had a bolt hole because any man of sense or wisdom *would* have one in such perilous times," Murie said.

Rob smiled, remembering. "He did say something like that, aye."

"Well, from some cause or other, it has never occurred to me to ask him if we have such a bolt hole at Tùr Meiloach. But does it not seem reasonable that since the one at Arrochar served him well, he would have one at Tùr Meiloach?"

"He might," he agreed. "He does keep things to himself. Sakes, he told me I'd have to ask you if I wanted to know how he and your mother managed to get over that pass with a newborn child before Pharlain and his men caught them."

She shrugged. "They did not use the pass, because Mam had said it would be too dangerous. Sithee, she had warned him of what Pharlain meant to do."

"How did *she* know Pharlain's intentions?"

As if she had not heard him, Murie added, "Nor did all three of them flee together that night." When he muttered her name again, she said, "Do you want to hear that tale now, or do you want to know why I reacted as I did to my dream?"

So it was something he would not believe. "Tell me about your dream."

"I dreamed that we were escaping through a bolt hole that brought us out near Tùr Meiloach's south pass."

"We? Do you mean you and me?"

"Nay, all of us were—you and I, Mag, Ian, Lina, my parents, and Dree. Oh, and Lizzie Galbraith was there, and I think Ian was, too. I did not see him, but I seemed to sense his presence."

"Who was hunting us?"

"I don't know, but someone must have been. We were in a hurry. In troth, I think the dream was of little import, except for making me think about bolt holes. I reacted as I did because I realized as I woke that I had never asked Father if we had one. He must have put the charters somewhere safe, aye? And, what could be safer than a place he trusts to protect us all from invaders? Also, what is more likely, after all these years, than that he's forgotten just where that hiding place lies?"

"Highly *un*likely, I should think," Rob said bluntly.

Murie drew a deep breath and fought to collect her thoughts. The last thing she wanted to do was to make him angry, especially over something she could not change. She had hoped she would not have to tell him the truth—at least, not all of it. He had already made it clear that he would not believe any such a tale.

She felt as if his sharp gaze were piercing right into her mind. "I wish you would not look at me like that," she said. "I cannot think when you do."

"One need not *think* to tell the truth, Muriella."

"The truth is that you won't believe me," she retorted. "You told me that you don't believe anything you cannot see, taste, feel, or know from your own experience. But you have heard stories about us, about the MacFarlan sisters."

"I have, aye."

"You have also made it plain that you disbelieve most of them."

He gave her a wry look. "I do not believe anyone can predict the future, control animals, or know their thoughts, let alone know other people's thoughts."

"I cannot blame you for that, even though you do so often seem to know mine," she said softly. "In troth, I do not believe in many such things, either. But odd events *have* happened at Tùr Meiloach."

"Do you believe you can see into the future? Is that why your dream upset you? Because you fear that we will have to flee from Tùr Meiloach?"

Murie shook her head. "I told you, our flight did not trouble me. It just reminded me of the bolt hole. Sithee, Lina did see odd things last year. She felt as if she were dreaming, even though she saw some of those things whilst she was awake. Once, she saw Mam taking scrolls from a chest and carrying them through a wood."

"Sakes, do you think your mother stole Andrew's charters?"

"Nay, nay! I ken fine that she did not, for she said so." She looked right into his eyes. "Mam does not lie, Rob, not *ever*. The thing is that every time Lina saw her, the scrolls were visible, too. Then someone grabbed Mam."

"But if the scrolls that Lina saw were not the charters—"

"I did not say that." Murie struggled to explain what she barely understood herself. "We think they most likely did represent the charters but not because Mam took them. Sithee, Dougal had threatened to harm us if Mam did not find the charters and give them to him. But she did not know where they were."

"She told you that," Rob said mildly.

"Aye, she did, and you need not look so all-knowing, sir. I told you. Mam does not tell lies. Nor do I...not real ones."

His lips twitched then, and she was relieved to see it.

"Truly," she said. "I may not always tell you the whole truth, or all that I am thinking. But I would not lie to you about anything important or lie on purpose about anything at all now, since it is important to you to hear the truth. I do value my skin, sir, and I believed you when you said you would not tolerate lying."

"I want to hear the exact truth *and* what you are thinking now," he said.

"Sakes, I'm trying to explain, but you must not interrupt or cross-question me, because I lose the thread of what I am trying to say." She paused, hoping he would promise not to interrupt her, but he merely motioned for her to continue.

Chapter 17 ———————————

Well, lass?" Rob said when Murie's hesitation outlasted his patience.

Reluctantly, she said, "What I said about our abilities is true. Mam says we do not possess strange powers but only strong instincts that women in our family have honed with each generation and passed on to their daughters."

"What does Andrew say?"

"That we do have reliable instincts but did not inherit them and won't pass them on. However, he trusts Dree and often looks to her to tell him if one of his men, or a visitor, is speaking the truth. He also trusted Mam when she told him she had 'seen' Pharlain seize Arrochar and kill all of us. Although," she added, "he did not believe her until Pharlain had killed my three brothers. The oldest was just six."

Uncertain whether the shock he felt was due to the matter-of-fact way she spoke of Lady Aubrey's prophecy or hearing her say that Andrew had needed such a tragedy to make him believe her, Rob was silent. Had he not come to know her, he would have thought she was exaggerating those long-ago events. He knew now that, in general, she repeated exactly what she had heard.

She frowned a little and said, "I ken fine that my words upset you. Even so, you're giving me that look again. It feels as if two green swords are piercing into my head to reveal what I am thinking."

"That's nowt save your imagination running amok," he replied, knowing that "upset" was not the word to describe his emotions. Nevertheless... "Do you truly believe that your mother and Lina can see the future?"

"I believe they can sense when danger lies ahead, whatever form it may take, and that Lina can soothe angry people and persuade them even when they resist her. She insists that I could do that, too, if I tried. I did try to calm Dougal's ire whilst he held me captive, but I saw no indication that my efforts had any effect. Dree says Lina can do it because she is so placid herself that her serenity calms others. Lina denies that. She says she feels as if she is imposing calmness *on* an angry person. She is sure that she sometimes succeeded in calming Dougal. But when she tried it on Ian, he reacted badly. So did Mag when Dree showed him what *she* can do."

An image leaped instantly to Rob's mind of Ian's volatile temper erupting, as it so often did if someone irked him or crossed his will. Stifling an incipient bubble of laughter, he said, "I expect it sent Ian into a fury." Then, more thoughtfully, he added, "Mag doesn't erupt like Ian does, but I would not want him angry with me."

"Nor I," Murie said with feeling. "Mag is more like you that way, I think."

"Then you had better not try such a thing with me, lass."

"I won't," she said, suppressing a shudder. "You are as strong of mind, I think, as you are of body. I doubt that even Lina's ability would have much effect on you. You do not fly into the boughs the way Ian does. You just…"

She paused and looked up at him from under her lashes.

"Go on," he said softly. "What do I do?"

"In troth, I think you do more with that swordlike look of yours than most men can do by shouting, scolding, or employing more physical ways of retribution."

"If you hope to make me believe I can terrify you with a look—"

"Not terrify, exactly," she interjected. "You can make me feel much worse than my father does with his shouts and scolding, though."

"I expect that is only because you know that his scolding is usually all you need fear from him," he said.

She shook her head. "It is not that, Rob. I love Father, but I worry more about what *you* think of me. Perhaps it is because I know he loves me as fiercely as I love him and that he would never really hurt me. I don't mean to say that I fear you though, so you needn't give me *that* look, either, sir."

He was not aware of any look in particular that he had given her. Even so, he realized that her apparently unintended implication that he might "really hurt" her had shocked him more than her words about Andrew and her mother had.

Snuggling closer, she said, "*Do* you think I fear you? I promise you I do not. I'll admit that I try to avoid making you angry, because I don't like it when you are. Sithee, I have come to care about you and your feelings in a way quite different from the way I care about the other people in my life."

"You have, have you?"

She licked her lips and raised a fingertip to them. Her expression dared him to object, then softened. Her pupils had become enormous, hiding nearly all of the light blue color in them. She put her wet fingertip to his lips, then between them. His tongue touched a short, smooth nail. She had been taking better care of them.

His cock stirred then. Smiling, he kissed her finger and moved his free hand to her nearest breast. "Ah, lassie," he murmured, stroking downward, then under the covers to test her heat. "You do bewitch me. Shall we find out how much?" His mouth covered hers, so he heard only a soft, sensuous moan in response.

Her increasing skills in what followed delighted him.

⁓

Sated, limp, and wholly pleased with her husband, herself, and her marriage, Murie would have liked to linger much longer in bed. However, having decided to get an early start, Rob was impatient to be away.

"I want to get underway right after we break our fast," he said.

"I need only to dress, comb my hair, and eat," she assured him. "Prithee send for Fiona, though. She does not like to disturb us when she knows you are here."

"Do you want her to go with you to Inverness?" he asked, the idea apparently having just occurred to him.

Never having had a maidservant all to herself, it had not occurred to Murie that she might take Fiona on such a journey. "I would not know what to do with her," she admitted with dismay. "I shared Tibby with my sisters and Mam, and Mam will take her with us to Inverness, because Annie hates to travel. Moreover, I'll need to sort the rest of my things into those I'll take with us and those I want ready for us to bring back here. It will be easier just to tell Tibby what I want and where than to explain everything to Fiona. Annie will help, too."

Rob agreed and sent for Fiona and his own man, Hamish. Dressing quickly, they left Hamish to look after Rob's baggage and Fiona to collect the few items that Murie would take with her from Ardincaple, and descended to the hall.

Lady Euphemia awaited them at the high table and chatted amiably through the hasty meal. Immediately afterward, Rob bade his mother farewell and stepped off the dais to speak to two lads who were waiting for him there.

As the three men talked, Lady Euphemia murmured for Murie's ears alone, "I will miss you both, my dear. I think you are going to make our Robert a good wife. I have not seen him as happy as he is now since he was a boy."

Surprised by the compliment, Murie thanked her with a smile. Then, seizing the opportunity to express a thought she had kept to herself, she said, "I doubt that any feardie such as Elizabeth Napier seems to have been would have suited him or you, my lady. Even so, at the time, I expect—"

"At the time, my dear, I cared only for making strong alliances," Lady Euphemia said. "That was a necessity for our own security, to which I thought my beloved husband paid too little heed. Faith, I even tried to ally Robert to Duchess Isabella's youngest daughter. But that..." She paused, glancing again at Rob.

Murie said quietly, "I know, *that* would have been a mistake, madam. The duchess may be a Lennox and thus part of what *used* to be the most powerful family hereabouts, but she is also second Duchess of Albany. The House of Albany now being wholly out of favor with his grace, allying with her would be—"

"Dreadful, I know," Lady Euphemia assured her. "Isabella did cozen Jamie into letting her live at home, though, so I thought she would win him over. In troth, I wanted so much to help Robert get on in life, to make him understand how much I care about his future, that I fear I've made an enemy of mine own son, instead."

"Blethers," Murie said with a smile. "I ken fine that I should not speak so to you, but it is blethers all the same. You love Rob as much as I do, my lady."

Hearing her own words echo in her mind, Murie nearly gasped.

Euphemia was nodding, though. "You do love him, don't you," she said. "I think I must have seen that from the start. I can also see how deeply he cares for you, my dear. In any event, I swear to you, I have wished for some time now that I had never sought the Napier betrothal."

"Perhaps I ought not to say this either, madam, but I did hear nearly that same tale long ago. It was not a Border tale then, though."

"I think you mentioned that you had heard it before, aye," Euphemia said. "Different seanachies do often tell the same tales, though."

"They do," Murie agreed, keeping an eye on Rob and the two younger men. "What I should tell you now is that the story I heard before was almost the same, word for word. Sithee, I remember things just as I've heard them. I nearly said as much to Rob—about the two tales. But he lacks faith yet in my abilities, likely because my memory is unusual. Also, I'm years younger—"

"We women always seem 'years younger' to our menfolk or just much less wise than they think *they* are," Lady Euphemia said dryly.

"I believe you," Murie said with a grin. "Even so, I want to gather more facts to support what I am thinking before I mention it to Rob. Tell me this, though, if you will. Did you or Lord MacAulay attend Elizabeth Napier's burial?"

"We were not invited to do so. Sithee, due to the scandal—she was a suicide, after all—they buried the poor lassie straightaway. They said nowt to us until we were preparing to visit them again. Then, of course, Lady Napier sent word to us."

"Were there other witnesses to Elizabeth's death?"

"She wrote only of their steward's shock when he saw the poor thing lying on the cobbles under the open tower window. Sakes, do you think someone killed her? It would have to have been Napier himself, since he says he saw her fling herself out."

"I did not mean to imply any such thing," Murie said. "I simply distrust an event so similar to one that I know took place in the northern Highlands. I am hopeful of learning more now that Rob is taking me with him to Inverness. At least one person who will be with her grace, the Queen, will likely know that other tale I heard. Also, I've heard that the King will have a few Border lords with him."

"Faith, I hope you don't mean to stir gossip, Muriella."

"I promise I won't," Murie said. "Sithee, many people—kinsmen and folks from other clans—know that

I collect stories. I may learn more about the Napier tale from a Douglas or a Scott. If I don't learn anything new, that will be that, but Rob does feel guilty about what happened. I'd like to lay his guilt to rest if I can."

"His guilt is my fault," Euphemia said. "Had I not—"

"Prithee, madam, forgive me," Murie interjected with relief when Rob gestured impatiently. "Rob is beckoning. Let me just see what I can learn."

"I'm glad you came to us, Muriella," Euphemia said, opening her arms.

Murie went right into them and gave her good-mother a warm hug.

⁓

Rob stared at the two women, stunned.

Murie turned then and hurried off the dais to his side. "Prithee, sir, do not be vexed with my dallying," she said with a smile. "Since you were talking with those two men, I decided to talk a bit longer with your mam."

"I saw that, lass. You seem to have bewitched her, too," he added, putting an arm around her to urge her toward the stairway. "I was talking to Alf and Eamon, the running gillies I'll send to warn Jamie of what we learned from Sean Crombie. It seemed more sensible to give the lads clear instructions here than to do it on the boat or after we reach Tùr Meiloach. I want them to understand the importance of warning his grace *before* he nears Inverness Castle."

"How ever will they find him?" she asked as they neared the stair landing.

"They don't need to find him, because I'm sending them to Jamie's cousin Alex Stewart, the Earl of

Mar, at Lochindorb Castle," he said. "If my lads run to Rothiemurchus—that's Mackintosh territory, friendly to Jamie—they can get directions and hospitality from the Mackintosh. Lochindorb lies less than a day north from there, and Alex has been Lord of the North longer than he's been an earl, so he'll know where Jamie is from the minute the royal party enters his domain and will send men to warn him. But come," he said, moving past her to go down the stairs ahead of her as courtesy required. "MacKell will have our galley ready by now, and I don't want to keep them waiting. I was surprised, though, to see how warmly my mother bade you farewell," he added, glancing back at her.

Murie's eyes danced. "I told you, I like her," she said. "She thinks I will make you a fine wife, although she did not think so when first we met."

"Don't set too much store by what she says now or ever, lass," he murmured. "She may like you for the time being, but she can change her mind in a trice if you disappoint her. When she does change, she does so swiftly and without warning."

Murie shook her head. "You do not listen to me, sir," she said. "I also told you that I can tell if aught that I say vexes her. Good sakes, I don't want to disappoint her any more than I want to upset you. I just wish you could have more faith in my abilities, although I ken fine that I have not yet proven them to you."

He gave her a quick hug but did not contradict her. He had seen for himself that her judgment was not always wise. Moreover, the likelihood that she could read his mother as easily as she claimed she could was slight at best.

His men had the galley loaded, and MacKell waited only until all passengers were aboard—including Rob's man, Hamish, and Scáthach—before giving his oarsmen orders to get underway. Minutes later, they were heading northward.

Their journey was uneventful, the weather sunny and warm, and they reached Tùr Meiloach's wharf shortly after midday. Andrew was again at the wharf to welcome them, and they found the rest of the family in the great hall, having delayed the midday meal until their arrival.

⁓

Lizzie ran to greet them and began at once to tell them how clever Wee Molly had been and how much Lizzie was enjoying her visit. To Murie's surprise, Lady Margaret was also still a guest at Tùr Meiloach. Being notoriously fond of her privacy, her ladyship rarely visited anyone for longer than two or three days before returning to her beloved Bannachra Tower in Glen Fruin.

"Liz, let us greet them, too," Lina said. Giving Murie a hug when Lizzie obligingly stepped aside, Lina added, "Ian will be here before you return from Inverness. His father and Alex Buchanan, bless them, will look after Dumbarton in his absence. I can scarcely wait to see him, although it has been wonderful to visit with everyone here."

"Has Father found his charters yet?" Murie asked her.

"If he has, he said naught to the rest of us," Lina said, watching as Andrena settled Wee Molly in a well-padded basket near enough the hearth for warmth, yet far enough away to protect the baby from flying sparks.

When Andrena moved to greet Murie, Molly began to whimper.

Scáthach, following at Rob's heels, turned at the sound and stepped with her usual grace toward the basket. Rob looked as if he might call her to heel, but Dree turned to him, smiled, and held up a hand, silencing him.

Scáthach looked into the basket, then lay down and curled herself around it so that she could see the baby's face and Wee Molly could see hers.

When the baby's whimpers stopped, Murie moved closer and saw that Molly's blue-eyed gaze had fixed in fascination on the dog.

Rob, evidently sensing Murie's presence, turned to her and said quietly, "She won't harm the bairn. But I'm gey surprised that your sister did not object."

"I can hear you, Rob MacAulay," Dree said with a laugh. "I ken fine that this beautiful animal of yours won't harm our Molly. Scáthach wants only to protect her, and since dogs move in and out of this hall as easily as people do, I can now relax my own vigil and know that none will get close enough to frighten my bairn."

"Mayhap it would be wiser to set Molly's basket on a table," Rob suggested.

Andrena shook her head. "Father warned me that you don't believe in our gifts, sir, but lest you have failed to notice, Molly shows no fear of Scáthach."

Surprised, Murie said, "Do you think Molly has inherited your gifts, Dree?"

Andrena shrugged. "It is too soon to know what she may or may not have inherited, but I can sense her even better than I sense you or Lina. I believe she senses things about me, too. We'll know more in time, of course. You need not look so skeptical, Master...but nay; it is 'my lord' now, is it not? Forgive me, sir."

"No need," he said, "for it must be 'Rob' to you now, Lady Andrena."

"Since we are all family now, Rob, Andrena is sufficient or just Dree."

Mag joined them then, putting an arm around his wife and looking fondly at their child. "Is our Molly not as beautiful as her mam?" he demanded of Rob.

"Certes, she is fortunate to have inherited Andrena's looks rather than yours," Rob retorted with a smile. "Do you go with us to Inverness?"

"Nay, I'm to stay and watch over Tùr Meiloach. Ian will be along in a sennight or so, though, and we'll be glad to see him again. Our visit to Dumbarton was gey short, because we thought we'd stay longer with Lina and Ian on our return from Ayrshire. Then Dree sensed Murie's distress, and we found Lina in the same state. So we all came home straightaway."

Rob stared at Mag as if he had not seen him before.

When a muscle twitched in Rob's cheek, Murie swiftly suppressed a smile.

"You seem surprised, Rob," Andrena said with false innocence.

Impatiently, Andrew said, "Are the lot o' ye planning tae eat, or no? This meat will soon be as cold as it were afore they roasted it an ye dinna sit down."

Rob collected his wits and turned to obey, but Mag stopped him with a hand on his shoulder. "Let the women go first," he said. "You looked a bit surprised just then, my lad. Did I say aught to distress you?"

Knowing his large friend well enough to be blunt, Rob

said, "Do you truly believe that Andrena and her sisters can each sense when another is in danger?"

Grinning, Mag slid an arm around Rob's shoulder and said, "I have experienced their ability more than once, so you may be sure that I believe in it. I won't try to explain how they do it or what they sense, but when one of them tells me she kens a thing, I listen. So should you. But my aunt Margaret is smiling now and beckoning to us. As I recall, she has a fondness for you, so be sure to talk with her before you vanish again. By staying just overnight last time, and barely saying a word to her, you made me fear you might have unseated yourself from her high esteem— a place, I would remind you, that gey few can claim."

"We must hope her ladyship recalls that that occasion was also my wedding night," Rob replied mildly. "I will take care not to offend her further, though."

The two took their places at the table, where Rob stood next to Andrew, who was impatiently waiting to say the grace before meat. Conversation afterward proceeded desultorily.

Rob told Andrew all he had learned from Sean Crombie and explained his plan to send two MacAulay running gillies ahead to warn the King.

"A good notion," Andrew said. "Since ye're sending them to Lochindorb, I'll send one of me own lads to show them the safest route. They should set off in the morning, I think. We'll travel much the same route ourselves, so your lads can ride on to Inverness with Mar or all three lads can await us at Rothiemurchus."

Agreeing, Rob considered asking if Andrew had found his charters but decided to wait. Something in the older man's demeanor—perhaps no more than a lingering impatience—warned him that the answer would be no.

Murie, too, was keeping an eye on her father. Lady Margaret had insisted that "Lady MacAulay" take her "rightful place" between her mother and Margaret, thus putting Murie much closer to Andrew. She asked him no questions, though. If he had found his charters, she was sure that Lina and Dree would know it.

Instead, she devoted her attention to the ladies on either side of her. Her mother had given her a searching look as Murie approached the dais but was now smiling as they chatted. Lady Margaret, having satisfied herself that Murie had met Lady Euphemia and come away unscathed, gave her attention to her food and an occasional brief but polite exchange with Andrena, at her left.

When Lady Aubrey suggested that the ladies adjourn to the solar, Murie stood at once with her sisters and Lizzie.

Lady Margaret, however, said that she would join them anon, adding bluntly, "I want a word with your husband, Muriella. Nay, do not stiffen so. To my great surprise and satisfaction, you chose exceedingly well. I like that young man."

Mouth agape at such an unexpected compliment, Murie recalled that Rob had met her ladyship the year before when he and Ian escorted Lina, their mother, Lizzie, Margaret, and herself to Tùr Meiloach from Inch Galbraith. Rob had even walked beside Lady Margaret's horse on the dangerously steep downhill side of their pass, when Lady Margaret had refused to dismount. Perhaps, Murie thought, that good deed had been enough to win him his high place in her ladyship's esteem.

Rob's approach just then diverted her attention to him, only to see him look past her when Lady Margaret said, "I heard the dreadful news of your father's death, my lord. I would extend my condolences to your lady mother. Pray, sit down with me here for a time and tell me how she goes on."

"I would be honored, my lady," he said. Then to Murie, he added, "Tell your mam I'll be along soon, lass, and don't wander off in the meantime."

With an impish look, Murie said demurely, "As you wish, my lord."

"We'll see about *that* later," he replied, briefly holding her gaze.

Before she could make herself believe that he had said such a thing right in front of Lady Margaret, he took a seat on the stool that Dree had vacated and assured Lady Margaret that his mother would be grateful to hear from her.

Following her mother and sisters, Murie saw Andrew watching her, while Mag poured wine into his own goblet from a jug on the table. Mag looked toward the fireplace just then, where Andrena was picking up Wee Molly in her basket.

Scáthach stood beside them, wagging her tail.

Andrew, Murie noted when she looked at him again, was still eyeing her speculatively. "Did you want to speak to me, sir?" she asked.

He smiled. "I just like looking at ye, lassie," he said. "Ye look fine and happy. Despite your trials, I'd say the marriage ye got yourself into agrees with ye."

"It does, aye," she said. "Rob is a good husband, sir. He even let me watch his laird's court. It was gey interesting."

"Sit down then and tell me about it," he said, patting Lady Aubrey's stool.

Murie complied and soon realized that Mag was listening to her with as much interest as Andrew did. Both of them laughed to hear how Rob had dealt with Donnie's Fergus and his "murder" of Gib Cowen by falling off a cliff on him. She nearly told them that she had suggested the penalty Rob had ordered but decided that that part of the story should be his to tell, if anyone did.

When she had told them all she could, she said quietly to Andrew, "I'm thinking you have not yet found your charters, sir. It did occur to me, though, that they might turn up in the bolt hole."

Andrew's eyes widened. Then he frowned. "What bolt hole would that be?"

"Why, you always told us that any man of sense would have one, sir, so one must assume that you provided one for us here." When he did not deny it, she added, "Annie did say that you will find them when you need them."

"I won't *need* them for three more days," he said.

"Does anyone else know where the bolt hole is?" she asked.

"Ye'd still be supposing there were such a thing, to ask *that* question."

Murie's gaze shifted to meet Mag's. His curiosity remained evident. Looking again at Andrew, aware of Rob's and Lady Margaret's low voices behind her, she murmured, "Prithee, sir, if you have *not* told anyone and aught should happen to you, what good would that route do us? No man as wise as I know you are would risk letting someone trap us here with no way out. Someone else *must* know. Moreover, if you did not move the charters and Mam did not…"

She stopped there to let his imagination fill in the rest.

Andrew looked at Mag, but Mag gazed back solemnly, and silently.

Andrew grimaced and said ruefully, "I should have shown ye long ago, lad. Ian, too, come to that. Sithee, I meant to. I thought of it when Pharlain attacked, then again last summer at Bannachra. In troth, though, trusting others comes gey hard to me. I once trusted me cousin, Parlan Farlan, as I would trust m'self, until he stole my lands, murdered my sons, and threatened to kill my lady and m'self. Then he declared himself Pharlain after our ancestor and claimed my chiefdom, as well."

Mag murmured, "*Does* anyone else know where it is, sir?"

"Aye," Andrew said. "But summat could happen to that person, too, so I'll no tell ye who it be. What I'll do instead is show ye the way." He looked at Murie. "Ye're a wise lass, daughter, but a gey curious one who tends to spill too much of what she kens to others. Yon tale about Dougal last year were a dangerous thing."

"I know it was, sir," Murie said. "I would promise never to tell such a tale again, but I do want to become a seanachie. And sometimes a seanachie *must* tell the truth, no matter how dangerous it may be. Even so," she added when he and Mag both frowned, "one is never bound to reveal family secrets or those that involve other people's safety. By my troth, sir, I would never tell. I will understand if you do not trust me to keep my word, but what I would ask is that you show Rob now, too. He has the same right as Ian and Mag, I think, and he is completely trustworthy. I think Mag will agree with me about that."

"I do, sir," Mag said. "Also, since Murie has given her word, I'd accept it."

Andrew nodded. "I agree. In the old days, she would have gone a-searching without mentioning the matter to me. Her curiosity being what it is, I'd rather trust her no to tell anyone than trust her no to search more on her own."

Solemnly, Muriella said, "I'll swear not to do that, either, sir, if you like."

In response, Andrew stood and said, "Rob, lad, when your conversation with her ladyship comes to its natural end, I'd have a word with ye in me chamber."

"Aye, sir," Rob said, glancing at him.

"Come along now, lass," Andrew said, extending a hand to Murie.

Surprised but delighted and hopeful that he meant to share his secret with her as well as with the men, she could not help but wonder if he might escort her as far as his chamber only to send her on upstairs to the other women in the solar.

*Chapter 18*_____

Watching Andrew and Murie leave the dais and seeing Mag finish off the goblet of wine he had just poured for himself before following them, Rob wondered if Murie had got herself into the suds again.

"You must not keep Andrew waiting," Lady Margaret said. "I have enjoyed our talk, sir. I will send my condolences to your lady mother straightaway."

Thanking her and suggesting that she precede him up the stairs as far as Andrew's chamber, he bade her goodnight on the landing there.

Waiting until she had vanished around the next curve in the stairway, Rob rapped once on the door and entered at Andrew's command. As he stepped in and shut the door, he saw Mag and Murie on two back-stools in front of Andrew's table. Andrew sat in the chair behind it. Two other stools stood empty just beyond Mag.

As Rob moved to take one, Andrew stood. "Never mind that stool, lad," he said. "I've summat to show ye."

Exchanging a look with Mag, who revealed nothing, Rob looked at Murie, who seemed to be having trouble sitting still.

Andrew moved to the corner where the cat, Ansuz, had

emerged on Rob's earlier visit to that room. The basket of maps or charts still stood there, so he suspected that Andrew wanted to discuss their route to Inverness.

However, the older man began instead to hand the scrolls to Mag, telling him to set them on the table for the nonce. When he handed over the large basket as well, Rob noted that the innocent-looking shutter fastened back against the wall, although apparently meant to cover the abutting, deeply set window in the event of extreme wind or rain, extended from just beneath the ceiling all the way to the floor.

Leaning down into the corner, Andrew clicked something unseen and then straightened. Reaching toward the top of the shutter, he flicked the hook there out of its eye and slid his fingers behind the wood. A similar click sounded, and he slid a bolt into sight, releasing the shutter. To Rob's astonishment, as Andrew "shut" it over the window, he revealed a dark, narrow doorway behind it.

"Throw the bolt on yonder door, will ye, lad?" Andrew said.

Rob did so at once and turned back only to have his gaze collide with that of his grinning wife, who might just as well have crowed, "I told you so!"

Shaking his head at her with a smile, he said, "Do we need a torch, sir?"

"Nay, lad, we'll do if Mag will light them candles yonder on the shelf."

⁓

Murie's delight threatened to overwhelm her, but she did as she had done when she had wanted to soothe Lady Euphemia's anger and imagined herself donning a cloak of dignity similar to her mother's or Lina's.

Feeling as if she were in control of herself then, she obeyed Rob's gesture and preceded him to follow Mag. All three men held candles, so she could see well enough, but the twisting stairway was perilously narrow, making her grateful for the rope banister bolted against the stone wall.

They came to a landing almost large enough to serve as a storeroom. Light came through a small hole in one wall there, and by standing on tiptoe, she saw through it to the hall dais. "Faith, it's another laird's peek," she muttered.

"Another?" Andrew growled from too close behind her.

She turned to him guiltily, but he only shook his head much as Rob had and murmured, "Doucely now, lass. Yonder be where I kept the charters." He pointed to the opposite wall, and she discerned a narrow stone bench built into it. Looking closer, while Rob held his candle so she could see, she saw that the top of the bench was a waxed wooden plank. Lifting it, she discovered only an empty space within.

"They dinna be needed yet," Andrew said.

The disappointment in his voice tore at Murie's heart. She wanted to reassure him, but a strange sensation stopped her. It was as if her mind had twitched and was tickling her memory in some odd way. Trying to make sense of it, she shut her eyes.

"What's amiss, lass?" Rob asked. His voice seemed far away, and fading.

Annie's voice in her head was stronger: "*When them charters do be needed, they'll show theirselves, another 'n another. That be all I can tell ye…*"

Collecting her wits, Murie said, "Father, are there *two* charters?"

Andrew shook his head. "I have charters for Arrochar from the days of King Alexander to the latest one from Robert III. I'd need only that latest one, though."

"You have two laird's peeks, sir," Murie said, persisting. "Might you also have two such benches in which to hide things?"

He frowned thoughtfully. Then he said, "Not to say 'benches.'" Pausing as he glanced from one to another of them, he added, "I did note long ago that there be a space farther downstairs where, if things went amiss, I thought I might…"

When he paused again, Rob said, "Where do these stairs end, sir?"

"At the cliff face," Andrew said. "Sithee, they be as ancient as the tower. Beyond the next landing, they straighten and emerge at the back of a wee cave near the high tide line. Boulders conceal its opening from the water, but it be big enough to hold a good-sized coracle and oars. Even so, the only time it would be safe to launch it is whilst the tide be on the turn." After another brief hesitation, he added, "There be a crevice nearby. When I first saw it, I thought it might serve as a hiding place if we had to wait long or if someone found us afore we could get away."

"Show us, sir," Murie said.

Mag produced another candle from his plaid, lit it, and handed it to her.

A short time later, the two younger men and Murie watched as Andrew reached an arm deep into a rough, narrow crevice in the stairway wall some yards before the archway opening to the cave. In the candlelight, Murie saw his eyes widen. Moments later, all four of them stood staring at an oilskin-wrapped bundle.

Unwrapping its contents with care, a smiling Andrew revealed his charters, their red wax seals gleaming in the candlelight.

"Murie-lass," he said, "I've told nae one else about that crevice, so I dinna ken how they got there, nor how ye knew to look further than their own hiding place. I'm thinking the Fates meant it to be, but if ye can explain yourself, I'd be grateful."

Searching her senses, and feeling naught to discourage her from telling all of them, she said, "As I told you, sir, Annie said they would appear when you needed them. Her exact words were 'When them charters *do* be needed, they'll show themselves, *another 'n another.*'"

Glancing at Rob, and seeing only encouragement in his expression, she added, "I might not have thought of that earlier had I not noticed the laird's peek and said aloud that it was *another* laird's peek. When I looked into the space in the stone bench, I heard the echo of my own words and yours, repeating them. The word 'another' just stood out, and I remembered that Annie had said it twice."

"Aye, well, the woman's as much a Seer as your mam is, but I can tell ye I'd no have thought as ye did, lass. I'm glad I brought ye along. Now that we've found them, though, we'll no linger at Tùr Meiloach. I heard today that Pharlain be setting out for Inverness on the morrow. I dinna ken why he's going. Mayhap he hopes to gain royal acceptance for himself as Chief of Clan Farlan. But whatever he's about, I'd liefer be there afore he can wrap his grace round his thumb. Your mam willna want to leave on a Sunday, but we won't wait 'til Wednesday, either."

When they returned to Andrew's chamber, Rob sent Murie up to the solar and went to find Alf and Eamon, to tell them that Andrew would send a man with them in the morning and to keep their mouths shut in the meantime.

"As I told you at Ardincaple," he reminded them, "we must not let word of your journey reach enemy ears. Nowt is more important than getting our message to Lochindorb, so the Lord of the North can convey it to his grace."

Since both men knew Rob well, he left it at that and went upstairs to find his lady and take her to bed. If the two events occurred rather farther apart than he had intended, the outcome was completely satisfactory to them both.

Waking early Sunday morning to find Murie more than willing to repeat much of their nocturnal exercise, he lingered in bed with her until Hamish rapped and said through the door, "The laird wants tae ken if ye're sleepin' all day, sir."

Grinning at Murie, Rob shouted back, "Tell him we'll be right along."

Since all he had left to do in preparation for the journey was see that someone loaded their baggage onto the garrons that would carry it, and Murie assured him that she and Tibby could have their own things ready in a trice, Rob made himself available to Andrew and Mag for the rest of the day.

That evening, Andrew announced that, unless anyone had an objection, they would depart the next day at dawn. So grim did he look that no one dared object.

"Aye, good," he said. "As it is, it will take us nigh a sennight to get there."

In fact, due to uncooperative weather and a circuitous

route—through Andrew's north pass (well-guarded against trouble), across the narrows of Loch Lomond and north along east Lomondside, through Glen Garry to Rothiemurchus and Loch Moigh, and on westward to Inverness—it took their party of nearly twenty-five men, three women, and a dozen sturdy garrons ten full days.

They reached Inverness Castle before midnight on Friday the tenth day of May and learned at the gate that Parliament had begun at midmorning that day. By the King's invitation, Andrew, his family, and their three servants were to stay inside the recently renovated castle. However, also by royal command, members of every nobleman's armed escort had to camp outside the castle walls.

To Rob's relief, no one objected to Scáthach's entering with him.

In the castle keep, they learned with shock from Sir William Fletcher, Jamie's boyhood friend, now steward and confidant, that due to widespread "failure of his most powerful noble guests to comply" with the law regarding the size of their retinues, his grace had put many of them "in ward" within the castle and warned them that, although they were free to move about as they chose, any who went outside the wall before Parliament ended would be punished for high treason.

"Does that restriction apply to me?" Andrew demanded indignantly.

"Nay, my lord," Will Fletcher said with a smile. "I'd advise ye to tread softly with his grace, though, for he's in a dour mood. See you," he added with a nod to Rob, "after hearing Lord MacAulay's warning of likely trouble, his grace decided tae keep the most quarrelsome chiefs under his eye and away from their armed men. Them chiefs gave him cause, too," he added. "Every one o' them came with an army, many more men-at-arms than his first Parliament's law allows for noblemen's tails. Sakes, Campbell o' Lorne alone brought four hundred men."

Rob said, "Did his grace meet any trouble on his way here?"

"Nay, but as ye ken fine, m'lord, that journey itself were a great risk tae him. Afore we left Aberdeen, he asked his principal nobles tae swear allegiance tae her grace, separate from hisself. He believes nae Highlander would slay our Queen."

"'Tis unlikely, aye," Rob said, hoping he was right.

Fletcher nodded. "But ye must all be weary now and longing for your beds." Summoning two gillies with a gesture, he added, "These lads will show ye tae your chambers. Come morning, we'll all meet in the great hall tae break our fast and begin the second day o' Parliament."

"Did the Lord of the Isles come?" Andrew asked.

"Aye, sure, and he be one o' them enjoying the King's ward, for he came wi' near regal ceremony and leading a fearsome great host."

"He does believe that he is equal to the King," Rob pointed out.

"Aye, but if we are tae have one law for all Scots, we canna have two kings," Fletcher said. "One will ha' tae bend a knee tae the other."

Noting that Andrew was on the brink of asking another question and doubtless another after that, Rob said, "If we are not to be late in the morning, Sir William, we should let your lads show us upstairs."

Fletcher grinned. "Aye, ye should. If today means aught, tomorrow will provide us much pompous posturing and fierce fratching. Sleep *well*."

Noting that Murie's eyes were alight with curiosity, Rob put a firm hand on her shoulder and nodded to Will Fletcher as he bade him goodnight. He was glad to see Lady Aubrey rest a gently insistent hand on her husband's arm and even happier when, obedient to that urging, Andrew and his lady followed the gillies.

As Rob offered an arm to Murie, she rose on tiptoe and tilted her face up to murmur, "I want to know more about what happened today. It sounds as if we missed much that our people at home and others will want to know, too."

"Not from you, though," Rob murmured back. "Certainly not tonight."

When she made a saucy face at him, he gave her a stern look. He did not want to argue about such things then, or at Inverness Castle, come to that.

~

Murie wished again that Rob would not look at her so, but she dared not protest lest he forbid her to attend the Parliament. He still had not kept his word to the Brehon, after all, and might easily seize on such an opportunity to make it good. To have come so far and miss seeing Parliament in action was unthinkable, but if she gave Rob cause, he might just order such a penance. And how many seanachies ever *had* an opportunity to be present when Parliament sat?

Biting her lower lip to insure that she would keep her tongue behind her teeth, she walked with Rob behind her mother and father and wondered how Lady Aubrey persuaded Andrew to heed her. The thought that her lady-ship's occasional ability to foresee events might be the key to her persuasiveness was daunting.

It was also unlikely, Murie decided. Although Lady Aubrey was widely rumored to be a Seer, and Lina had experienced similar incidents, both women maintained that other reasons likely existed for what they had seen.

Even if Lady Aubrey had passed their gift on to her, Murie had not come to Inverness to prove her gifts to Rob. She had come to see Parliament and hoped to learn enough about what had happened to Elizabeth Napier to ease the guilt that she knew Rob still harbored for the daft wench's death.

At the stairway, Rob motioned for Murie to go ahead of him and follow her parents. Tibby, Andrew's man Sor-ley, and Rob's Hamish trailed after Rob.

When her mother and father reached the second land-ing, their gillie opened a door there, saying to Andrew, "I hope this wee room will do for ye and your lady, m'lord. See you, we ha' more folks in the castle tonight than we'd expected tae have."

"Aye, we heard that," Andrew said. "Thank ye, lad. We'll be comfortable, but where be ye putting Lord MacAulay and his lady?"

"Just here across the landing, sir. 'Tis a gey wee cham-ber, m'lord," he added with a wary look at Rob.

Rob merely nodded, but Andrew said on a bark of laughter, "They need only a bed, lad. If ye've got one in there big enough for the two of them...Sithee," he added confidingly, "they be but newly wedded."

Murie's cheeks burned, and she avoided the gillies' eyes and hurried inside when the younger one opened the door. Tibby would help Lady Aubrey first, and Sorley and Hamish would doubtless see to the baggage.

Rob followed Murie into their room, and she heard the latch snap to.

Turning to face him, she wondered at first if she had irked him. Without thinking, she raised a fingertip and pressed its budding nail against her upper lip.

"Don't," he murmured.

"I wasn't," she said, hastily putting the offending hand behind her. "I just—"

He bolted the door. "If you want activity for your lips and tongue, *mo chridhe*, I can think of one that will entertain us both for a time. Come here."

Smiling, she moved into his arms and raised her lips to his.

~

The next morning, entering the great hall, they found it full of trestles and people, mostly men, breaking their fast amid a clamor of voices. Andrew and Lady Aubrey, however, had saved places for them to break their fast at their table.

As Rob took his seat, he heard Lady Aubrey say to Murie, "We women will all sit together in an area near Queen Joanna when the session begins, dearling. She will sit on the dais, so take care to stay near me as we make our way to and fro."

"Aye, Mam," Murie said.

Her reply came without hesitation or emphasis. Nevertheless, Rob could tell from her expression that she had something in mind other than the honor of sitting near Queen Joanna. Tempted though he was to warn her to behave herself, he kept silent. He had seen enough of his lady wife's skills with other people, primarily his mother, to know she could look after herself if only she did not somehow, at the same time, plunge herself into jeopardy.

The hall was crowded. Although the din was less than that of a hall full of warriors or more common folk, it was still noisy enough to make conversing difficult, so Rob focused on his food.

When increased activity at the high table drew his eye to the dais as Will Fletcher, evidently having left the seat beside his grace, returned to it, Rob saw that Murie was already watching. Fletcher leaned to speak into the King's ear, and as he spoke, Jamie looked increasingly vexed.

People on either side of them took evident, unseemly interest.

A gillie hurried to the dais, drew Fletcher's attention, and spoke into *his* ear. Then Will spoke to Jamie again, and Jamie gave what must have been an order, because Fletcher got up and strode toward the main stairway.

Deciding they would learn no more, Rob returned his attention to his food.

"What do you suppose that was about?" Murie asked, speaking just loudly enough for him to hear her.

"Whatever it was, we will either find out later or we will not," he replied.

"We will," she said confidently.

～

Delighted by her proximity to the King and Queen, Sir William Fletcher, and the nobles who sat with them on the dais—the King and Queen less than twenty feet from her and all of them facing the lower hall—Murie had been watching them for some time, with fascination and profound curiosity.

Neither her mother nor Rob, sitting on either side of her, tried to converse over the din in the hall, so she could indulge her curiosity as she liked.

Nothing happened after Sir William's departure, though, until the Queen arose from her seat and the ladies with her did, as well.

Lady Aubrey said quietly, "We will refresh ourselves now and meet her grace in a chamber behind the dais. Our gillie told me this morning that the inner chamber has a private entrance. He will show us the way."

Accordingly, they went upstairs, quickly washed and tidied themselves, and followed their gillie to what had evidently become her grace's sitting room.

Entering, they saw the Queen and several other ladies just as they all fell silent. "Must we stay here throughout the Parliament, Mam?" Murie whispered.

"I do not know," Lady Aubrey admitted. "The King did say that he wants ladies present during Parliament to keep his nobles' tempers in check, so I surmised that we would see and hear all. But we must make our curtsies now, love. 'Tis likely that her grace will tell us just what we must do."

Queen Joanna's beauty and tender heart were legendary. Her graceful figure; dainty, tip-tilted nose; and smooth, wide forehead were, Murie knew, especially admired. At present, her large, long-lashed eyes seemed to take in everyone around her, and her full, expressive lips smiled often and warmly.

As Joan Beaufort, daughter of England's powerful Earl of Somerset, her grace was undeniably English but now used the Scottish form of her name and had declared that her love for her adopted country matched what she felt for her beloved husband. Many had said that she was his grace's most valuable asset, because wherever she went, people fell in love with her just as Jamie had.

Curtsying deeply when her mother did, Murie looked up to see Joanna's gaze resting on Lady Aubrey. In a delightfully musical voice, the Queen bade her rise before saying how pleased she was to make her acquaintance.

Thanking her, Lady Aubrey added, "By your leave, your grace, I would present my youngest daughter, Muriella, now Lady MacAulay of Ardincaple."

Joanna smiled at Murie, who remained deep in her curtsy but had not taken her eyes from the Queen. "Ye may rise, too, Muriella," she said. "I have heard much about the MacFarlan sisters. I am gey pleased to meet one of ye at last."

"You are kind to say so, your grace, but the honor is mine," Murie said, rising as she returned the Queen's smile and feeling wholly at ease with her.

"We may talk more anon," Joanna said. "Since they must have finished rearranging the hall for his grace's Parliament, Lady Sutherland will soon show ye both where to go." She indicated a handsome woman of thirty-five or forty years, standing nearby. "Ye must remain standing until after James enters," Joanna added. "I will enter before he does, though, so just watch me and sit when I do."

"Does not the Lord Chancellor tell everyone what to do?" Murie asked. She faced Joanna, while obliquely eyeing Lady Sutherland and trying to decide if her ladyship might be too haughty to talk with one so much younger than she was.

"If we *had* a Lord Chancellor, he would," Joanna said on a note of dry amusement that returned Murie's full attention to her. "But as we do not yet have a replacement for dear Bishop Lauder, his grace will conduct Parliament himself."

Murie nearly asked if the reason they did not have a Lord Chancellor was—as she had heard—that the Pope had refused to accept the King's choice to succeed the bishop, and the King had refused to have anyone else, insisting that his Lord Chancellor would serve him, not the Pope. However, aware of Lady Aubrey's stern eye and the likelihood that Rob would hear of it if she did ask such a question, Murie recalled her fervent desire to speak with Lady Sutherland, if possible, and held her tongue.

She had her reward when an older woman approached Lady Aubrey and inquired politely about her health and family. Lady Aubrey had no sooner presented her to Murie as Lady Nisbet, a Border cousin, than Lady Nisbet said, "Ye must be wondering what we were discussing when ye came in, Cousin Aubrey. Sithee, six o' the great Highland chiefs did leave the castle overnight, thus breaking his grace's ward. He has ordered them captured and returned to face dire punishment."

"Which chiefs are they?" Murie asked.

"I dinna ken all six," the woman said. "But Lady Douglas sat nearer to his grace than I did. She heard him say Mackenzie o' Kintail and Campbell o' Lorne. I kent fine that your mam, being kin to the Campbell, would want to hear *that* news."

Lady Aubrey said politely, "'Twas kind of you, cousin. My kinship to Campbell of Lorne is distant, though. He is a second cousin to my grandsire. I doubt that I have ever met him, but I can tell you that Argyll is not amongst those who defied his grace. Nor is the Mackintosh, since his lady stands yonder."

"Aye, well, I dinna ken many o' the Highland chiefs," Lady Nisbet said. "We rode here from Aberdeen with the Douglas's party. Sithee, his grace did accept the Douglas's offer o' men tae escort him, so some Douglas chieftains and others also brought such o' their ladies as would ride wi' them."

Lady Nisbet continued chattering eagerly, about unrelated topics, so Murie received with relief Lady Sutherland's signal for them to return to the hall and wondered if she would be able to find Rob and her father there.

Following Lady Sutherland, they entered the hall near its dais end. Benches awaited them in a corner formed by the ladies' end of the dais and the side wall.

At the center of the dais, where the high table had been, an elaborately carved and gilded armchair awaited his grace. A table draped with cloth of gold over white linen stood nearby, and two less impressive chairs sat behind it. A second armchair bearing a red velvet cushion sat near the front of the dais on the ladies' side, apparently for Queen Joanna. Two plain back-stools stood behind it.

Delighted that she would be close enough to hear and see everything more easily than most of the men in the huge chamber, Murie took her place, standing between her mother and an unknown woman. The Border cousin, Lady Nisbet, claimed the place on Lady Aubrey's other side.

Turning so that she could see the rest of the crowded hall, Murie thought at first that she would never find anyone she knew in such a throng. To her shock, though, the first recognizable person to catch her gaze was Dougal MacPharlain.

The second was his father, sitting beside him.

She half-expected to see the Brehon justice on Pharlain's other side, but she did not know the man who sat there.

Glancing at her mother, wondering if she ought to direct her attention to them, she realized that Lady Nisbet was still talking to her.

A man in priest's robes mounted the dais and stood behind the cloth-draped table near the elegant armchair. Sir William Fletcher stood next to him.

Trumpets sounded, and everyone turned toward the hall's main entrance. When the echoes faded to expectant silence, the Queen entered with her two chief ladies behind her. They walked up the central aisle and took their places on the dais.

To longer, more tuneful trumpeting, the King entered, strode alone to the dais, and stood near the elegant chair. When silence reigned again, he nodded to the priest, who offered a prayer that was, to Murie's relief, blessedly short.

She had not come to hear prayers but to watch history take place.

Chapter 19 ————————

Sit," Jamie Stewart commanded as the echoes faded. "I will hear the Bishop of Argyll first on the subject of chiefly jurisdiction," he added, taking his seat.

What followed was, to Muriella, tedious business of barons, lairds, and the rights and powers that each possessed or wanted to possess.

Knowing that her father would ignore anyone who challenged his right to his powers of pit and gallows, and certain that Rob would, too, she decided to try again to find Rob in the gathering. A firm hand on the arm near her mother stopped her.

Resigned, Murie tried to recall what she heard but found it too hard to concentrate or care. Never had she imagined that such an important occasion could prove to be so dull. At last, the King said, "We'll suspend these proceedings now until after the midday meal, when we will discuss this subject further."

Murie sighed, hoping they would give everyone time to eat and walk about. Her bottom ached.

Rob, sitting next to Andrew, could see Murie and wondered if she realized the importance to the proud Highland chiefs of the subject under discussion.

He, too, had seen Dougal and Pharlain sitting on the other side of the central aisle from him and Andrew, and closer to the front of the hall. Dougal had looked back twice, and Pharlain did just then, and smirked. Glancing at Andrew to see him muttering to the man on his other side, Rob decided it was just as well that he hadn't seen the smirk and that he had his charters with him, safe from possible schemers.

Shifting his gaze to Murie, he noted that she was fairly twitching on her bench. When the King declared that they would take time to eat, Rob saw Lady Aubrey put a quieting hand on his wife's shoulder as if she feared the lass might spring to her feet.

When everyone began heading for the doors, Rob stuck close to Andrew.

In the inner chamber, Joanna told the ladies that they might do as they pleased until the servants were ready to serve the meal, whereupon Lady Nisbet said immediately, "Och, Aubrey, dearling, I must tell ye..."

Taking advantage of Lady Aubrey's distraction, Murie approached Lady Sutherland. Introducing herself and briefly explaining her love of folklore and clan histories, Murie said, "I heard a tale recently that I think came from the Sutherlands, my lady. I ken fine that that is your lord husband's family, but perhaps you might know the answer to a question I have."

"Prithee, which tale would it be, Lady MacAulay?

I dinna ken all of the Sutherland tales, but I have heard many. I will tell you what I can."

Explaining that the tale involved a girl who had jumped or fallen from a tower window, she got no further before Lady Sutherland said, "Faith, I ken that tale fine, my dear. 'Twas a Sutherland lass called Margaret, who fell in love years ago with someone quite unsuitable. Her father was furious and locked her in a tower room, but her maid-servant smuggled her rope enough to climb down to her lover. Unfortunately for the pair o' them, on the appointed night, Lord Sutherland had set his steward to watch, and the man caught the lad approaching the tower. Sutherland entered the tower chamber to see his daughter fling her-self out the window."

"How dreadful," Murie said. "Have you heard other, similar tales, my lady?"

"Not as horrid as that one," Lady Sutherland said with a grimace. "But I hear few others from outside our own clans. Tell me how you have learned so many."

Although Murie explained about Annie's teaching and the many *ceilidhs* that the three MacFarlan sisters had attended, thanks to their mother's many kinsmen, her mind was awhirl. Now that she knew *how* similar the two tales were, could she persuade Rob how unlikely it was that two fathers in two such distant parts of Scotland had locked their daughters in tower rooms and watched them leap out their windows?

By midafternoon, Rob had tired of the pompous decla-rations, bickering, and shouting over what sounded like fine points of law. But when a gillie mounted the dais and spoke to Will Fletcher, his interest reawakened. Evidently, everyone's did, because the din faded to silence so complete that Rob could hear Andrew breathing.

James said soberly, "Six men broke ward last night and fled the castle. I now hear that they have been arrested and are returning." Looking left and right, his stern gaze encompassing the hall, he added grimly, "I have striven for two years to institute one set of laws so that every Scot may understand them and know that *all* must obey them. I told every man under ward the penalty for defiance, did I not?"

"Aye, your grace," rumbled a chorus of male voices.

"If a King of Scots, as chief of chiefs, fails to keep his word," James went on, "the laws that our Parliament issues will mean nowt. Our nobles will continue to defy them, and common folk will know not which laws or whose they must obey. The penalty for high treason and thus for each man who broke the King's ward is death. They are Clanranald, Mackenzie of Kintail, Campbell of Lorne…"

Rob fixed on that last name and barely noted what followed until James said, "So be it then. I take nae pleasure in this, so we will move ahead. My lord of Sutherland, before the interruption you were about to make a suggestion."

Sutherland reminded everyone that they had agreed to further discussion of chiefly privilege. "Now might be a good time for it, your grace."

No sooner did Jamie nod than Pharlain stood. "Your grace," he said loudly, "I be Pharlain of Arrochar. A chief must be able to set fees for traveling on his waters, hunting his deer, or catching his salmon, aye?"

Rob's interest increased.

James said, "Do the chiefs pay such fees themselves when they travel?"

"Nay," Pharlain replied. "We collect them from others for profit, so if a laird passing through *our* waters collects fees on his as well, we excuse each other."

James shifted his gaze to Alexander, Lord of the Isles. "Cousin, do ye pay such fees when ye travel?"

"Nae, I tell them who I am," Alexander said with a snort. "So would ye."

Looking again at Pharlain, James said, "Where do you collect your fees?"

Pharlain shrugged. "We dinna collect passage fees yet, your grace. We expect to begin anon on the Loch of the Long Boats, though."

"You and who else?"

Pharlain hesitated, and Rob hid a smile. "Campbell," Pharlain said. Then he added hastily, as if he had just recalled that more than one Campbell chief was in the hall, including the all-powerful Argyll, "Campbell of... of Lorne, your grace."

Grimacing, James said, "If you mean to collect fees on the Loch of the Long Boats, you should know that I consider its entrance a royal property. After all, that loch opens on the Firth of Clyde, which the royal castle of Dumbarton protects for all Scots. Moreover, I did not hear you mention MacAulay, who, as I recall, does guard the entry to the Loch of the Long Boats. Lord MacAulay is here, is he not?"

"I am, your grace," Rob said, standing.

"What say you to this, my lord?"

"I say that the Gare Loch and the Loch of the Long

Boats shall remain open and free to all who would travel on them, your grace."

"That agrees with mine own expectation. So be it. The scribe will so note."

Looking chagrined, Pharlain sat down.

James looked over the hall as if he expected someone else to speak. When no one did, he said, "Now would be a good time for any man who has not presented the royal charters granting him rights to his lands to do so. Therefore, I do adjourn this body until tomorrow midmorning, when we will assemble in the courtyard."

Beside Rob, Andrew growled.

"What is it, sir?" Rob asked quietly. "You have your charters, aye?"

"Aye, sure. But this be the devil's own time to present them. His grace be in a foul mood after deciding to hang them scoundrels for breaking his ward."

"True," Rob admitted. "But the charters speak for themselves. Moreover, Pharlain irked him with his blethers about collecting fees."

"He did, withal," Andrew agreed more cheerfully. "The man were daft to do that, but ye're happy enough, I trow. Argyll himself wouldna try now to inflict fees on all of us who travel the loch. Nor would Argyll scheme to seize Ardincaple."

"'Tis unlikely," Rob agreed. While they stood awaiting his grace's departure into the inner chamber with Joanna on his arm, he saw Murie turn to her mother and could almost hear her asking if the ladies should follow them in there or not.

"Mam?" Murie asked when her query met silence.

"We go wherever her grace goes unless Lady Sutherland says we must not," Lady Aubrey said. "What were you and she discussing earlier?"

Murie smiled. "I asked her about a tale I'd heard at Ardincaple that was the same as one I'd heard long ago about the Sutherlands of Dunrobin," she said.

She had spoken quietly but apparently not quietly enough.

"Och, but I heard that ye ken many of our old tales, Lady MacAulay, and tell them at *ceilidhs* and such," Lady Nisbet said archly, moving closer. "Mayhap ye will tell us one tonight. What tale was it that ye got from Dunrobin?"

"A gey sad one," Murie said. "About a girl named Margaret who threw herself from a tower window to her death."

"Och, then I ken the other one ye must have heard," Lady Nisbet said. "It came from me own family, that. I dinna ken Ardincaple, but that tale be about me cousin's daughter, Eliza, who ran off wi' her lover. Her mam put it about that she had flung herself out o' her window tae her death, may God forgive her sin!"

"Put it about?" Murie said. "Do you mean that tale was untrue?"

"Nobbut foolishness. The lassock ran off tae Ireland wi' one o' their gillies when her mam and da tried tae make her marry the heir tae another noble house, one o' them dunamany Highland Macs. I dinna mean tae offend ye, Cousin Aubrey, but 'tis all I can do tae remember ye're a MacFarlan and no some other Mac."

"Such names can be confusing, aye," Lady Aubrey said mildly.

"'Twas the shame o' her beloved Elizabeth running off wi' a naebody as stirred me cousin tae spin her lies. Sithee, her own mam were cousin tae Sutherland, and we never hear the end o' *that*, so I'm thinking now that she may ha' taken her tale from theirs. Sithee, though, *we* never talk about Eliza or her tale," she added with a virtuous air. "So I'd ask ye tae keep a still tongue on it, too, *if* ye please."

Murie assured her that she would, ignoring the irony of such a request coming from such a bletherskate. Her thoughts had already flown to Rob.

If Lady Nisbet's version was true…

Without further comment, Murie followed her mother and Lady Nisbet to the inner chamber, where the King now stood near the great stone hearth. A fire burned gently in a fireplace big enough for two or three men to stand upright inside.

A number of people followed them into the chamber, including—not much to Murie's surprise—Pharlain and Dougal. Rob and Andrew entered last of all.

When they joined the three ladies, Murie impulsively turned to Rob only to have her eager gaze meet a beetling frown.

"Why do you look at me like that?" she demanded in an undertone.

His eyes twinkled in response, and his brow cleared. "Sorry, lass," he said, drawing her aside. "If I looked dour, it was because of Dougal and Pharlain. What can they be doing here?"

"Sakes, sir, they mean to mount an argument against my father's charters, of course. But, Rob, come away from Lady Nisbet. I must tell you—"

"Shhh," he said, nodding toward the fireplace. "His grace is about to speak."

The stocky James faced them all with his hands behind him and his legs apart. "I will see your charters, one man at a time," he said. Gesturing to the cleric at a nearby table, he added, "The scribe will note any details. Who would be first?"

Andrew hesitated while another man rushed forward. Murie thought her father seemed uncharacteristically reticent. He fixed his attention on the King.

Glancing at Pharlain and Dougal to catch Dougal smirking at her, she touched Rob's arm and murmured, "Something is amiss. Dougal looks too confident."

"What happens will happen," Rob murmured back. "Hush now, before you draw undesired notice."

She wanted to stamp a foot, but she knew he was right about drawing notice, so she kept quiet. Having all she could do to stand still, she watched Dougal.

Then she heard James say, "Ye're Andrew Dubh MacFarlan, aye?"

Murie's attention flew back to the hearth, where Andrew stood with James.

"Aye, your grace," Andrew replied with a polite nod.

"You have a charter to show me, I think."

"I do, aye," Andrew said, carefully spreading the first of his precious charters on the table for his grace and the scribe to see.

Murie glanced around the room but saw naught to disturb her other than the mere presence of Pharlain and Dougal.

"This is all in order," James said, as the scribe wrote swiftly on vellum.

The next one received similar attention and comment. Then, with a smile, James said, "That is more than sufficient, sir. Do you swear fealty to me?"

"I do, aye, and for all time, your grace," Andrew said, dropping to a knee.

Feeling a surge of pride in her father, Murie looked around again and saw Pharlain pushing forward as others made way. Prickles of warning stirred before he spoke, but she could do naught to stop whatever was about to happen.

Pharlain said dulcetly, "Forgive my intrusion, your grace, but if yon documents purport to bestow title to Arrochar, they are invalid, rendered so seven years ago. If you will permit..." Pausing expectantly, he hefted the scroll-like object he carried, wrapped in white cloth.

The sensations Murie experienced then made her feel faint. She was sure that only her awareness of Rob's strong, solid body close behind her kept her upright.

Frowning, James motioned Pharlain forward. Dougal was moving, too.

Pharlain removed the white cloth to reveal a vellum scroll with red wax seals attached to it, similar to the charters that Andrew had presented.

"What is this?" James asked as Pharlain handed it him.

"Why, what *would* it be, your grace, save the current charter?" Pharlain said smoothly. "It clearly entitles me and me alone to *all* the lands of Arrochar. As you can see by its date, it supersedes any charter in the possession of Andrew Dubh."

Murie's gasp brought a look of triumph to Pharlain's face and another smirk to his son's, making her wish that she could slap them both soundly.

Hoping to ease the shock he sensed in Murie, Rob put his hands on her shoulders. When he felt her press back against him, he hoped she was taking comfort from his presence but returned his attention to the King.

Jamie was still frowning.

Beside him, Andrew had turned white. Now, blood surged back into his face, and Rob knew that his good-father's temper was fighting his attempts to control it.

To his astonishment, Jamie put a gentling hand on Andrew's shoulder as he said to Pharlain, "Ye've admitted that ye were involved with Campbell of Lorne in this business of collecting fees, sir. I'm wondering now what other schemes ye've shared with him, or others. Sithee, we uncovered a plot to undermine the work of this Parliament, which appears to have included this recent business of hitherto powerful chiefs breaking the King's ward. My steward tells me that Lorne has fiercely cursed that plot's failure. D'ye ken aught of such scheming, sirrah?"

"I do not," Pharlain said flatly, but Rob saw Dougal blanch and step back.

"We will look further into that matter anon," Jamie said. "I am surprised, though, to see that this charter ye've presented bears my name. I do not recall signing it, however. In troth, what I see by its date is that I could *not* have signed it."

"Your honored uncle, the first Duke of Albany, as Governor of the Realm at the time and thus your regent, signed it on your behalf, sir," Dougal said smoothly.

"Since my uncle had much to do with my capture and nowt to do with my release, I do not agree that he had the right to sign my name to any document," James said. "I hereby declare your charter null, sir, and void. Since Andrew Dubh MacFarlan has shown me a royal charter properly signed by my father and has also shown me another signed by my grandfather, and has others, likely signed by their grandfathers before them, I declare Andrew Dubh MacFarlan to be the true Chief of Clan Farlan and entitled therefore to all the lands, estates, and so forth of Arrochar."

"By God, we should have finished you at Perth!" Pharlain exclaimed angrily.

"I thank ye," James said. "I expect I can infer from that outburst that ye were part and party to the assassination attempt in Perth and therefore also to the seizure afterward of the royal castle and burgh of Dumbarton. Will, arrest this man and clap him in irons until I decide if I'll hang him or relieve him of his traitorous head."

Pharlain, stupefied, stared at the King in disbelief.

Looking again for Dougal, Rob saw that he was whiter than ever, but he was still able to think, because he eased silently away amid the remaining onlookers.

Will Fletcher motioned for two men-at-arms, who stepped forward at once and efficiently hustled Pharlain away.

As they did, James handed Andrew's charter to the scribe. "Confirm this in my name as of this date and place," he said. "I'll sign it forthwith." Moments later, James added his signature, dusted it with silver sand, and handed the document to Andrew, saying, "Take this, sir, keep it safe, and look after our people at Arrochar."

Thanking him, Andrew accepted it with his left hand and extended his right. "I would shake your hand, your grace, if I may."

James, grinning now, grasped Andrew's right hand with his and clapped him on the shoulder with his left. "You may, aye, my lord, now and whenever we meet."

"Before we part, sir, I would ask leave to present my good-son, Lord MacAulay," Andrew said. "He has served your grace afore, I think."

"He has, withal," James agreed, turning as Rob stepped forward.

Sensing Muriella behind him, Rob put a hand back as he would to stop Scáthach. Murie did not as much as pause, though, and he could do nowt about it.

Murie stopped when Rob did and stayed behind him. She had seen him flash his palm at her and recognized the signal, but she wanted to keep close enough to see and hear him swear fealty to the King. She was aware that her mother followed her, but she sensed that Lady Aubrey simply felt as she did about staying together.

"'Tis good to see ye again, my lord," the King said to Rob. "I thank ye for your timely warning, but I was gey sorrowful to learn of your lord father's death."

"I thank your grace. I would swear my fealty and allegiance, if I may."

James nodded and extended his hands when Rob knelt before him.

Resting his palms on the King's, Rob said formally, "I, Robert MacAulay, Lord of Ardincaple, do swear fealty for that barony, which I hold and do claim to hold of your grace, High King of Scots, for myself and my heirs, heritably. Loyally will we serve you and your heirs, God helping, now and forevermore."

"I accept your vow in humble gratitude, my lord," James said. "Now rise and tell me how your lord father died. We will miss him sorely."

"We will, aye," Rob agreed as he stood. "I've no proof, but I suspect Lorne had a hand in it and mayhap Pharlain, too, due to that business of collecting fees. Father strongly opposed the notion. I believe Lorne has killed before, and whilst you may not know it, Pharlain killed Andrew's three small sons when he usurped his chiefdom and Arrochar soon after your grace fell captive to the English."

"If your father did fall to those villains, he can rest in peace, for neither man will kill again, I promise ye," Jamie said grimly. "Ye can see that for yourself if ye choose to be present in our courtyard at midmorning tomorrow."

Hearing Murie's indrawn breath behind him, Rob met Jamie's gaze.

"The lady behind you is your wife, my lord, aye?" James said.

"Aye, sir," Rob said, stepping aside, "and gey forward withal."

His tone was as calm as ever, but easily sensing his uncertain mood, Murie quickly made her curtsy to Jamie, and let Rob draw her up beside him.

"I have met your sisters, my lady," Jamie said with a smile as she placed her hand lightly on Rob's extended forearm. "'Tis a delight to meet ye, too."

"You are kind, your grace," she said. Then, before she could lose what little courage remained, she added, "May I have leave to ask you a question?"

"Aye, sure."

"When you make our laws the same throughout Scotland, will you keep just the sensible ones or must we still honor even the worst of the ancient Celtic ones?"

The dark royal eyebrows flew upward. "Ye sound as if ye have experience with Celtic law, my lady, or do I misunderstand ye?"

"I know of a daft one, your grace, because I was found guilty at Pharlain's court of abducting his grown son," she said. "'Twas not Pharlain who declared me guilty, though. *That* was a Brehon justice. He said that the person riding in front on the horse is, by Celtic law, the abductor—or, in my case, he said, the abductress."

She went on quickly to explain, aware the whole time of Rob simmering beside her, and thus doubly aware of her impudence in taking up the King's time with her personal concern. Recalling only then that the Brehon had condemned her as much for 'wasting his time and the court's' as for her so-called crime, she barely dared to breathe after watching James's expression change, as she spoke, from polite interest to surprise, frowning displeasure, and then... amusement?

"I see," he said, his dark eyes brimming with laughter. "Forgive me, my lady. I ken fine that your situation must have seemed dire, and my Joanna will scold me for making light of it. But picturing a wee lassock like ye abducting any adult male on his own horse..." He collected himself, adding, "Even so, there cannot be *any* good reason to keep such a daft law. I promise ye I'll do all in my power to see it and others like it abolished. Meantime, might a royal pardon ease your mind?"

"It would, your grace," Murie said firmly, not daring even a glance at Rob.

"Then so be it; I absolve ye of all guilt in yon

abduction and aught relating to it," James said. His expression hardened then. "Is Dougal MacPharlain still here? I'm thinking he should be joining that lot for the hangings and such."

A voice from the back called out, "He's left, your grace. He looked sick."

"As well he should," James said. "See if ye can find him for me."

Rob put his free hand over Murie's on his forearm, gave her hand a squeeze, and began to back away. She could still sense his displeasure with her, although none of it showed in his face. How she wished she could conceal her feelings so!

They had taken but a step or two when Andrew said, "By your grace's leave, we would retire to our chambers now. We must return to Arrochar as soon as we can, for I have much to do to secure my lands and reunite my people. I promise ye, though, they'll be gey willing to support their rightful King."

James gave his assent, wished them a safe journey, and turned away to summon the next man with a charter to present.

"We'll go right upstairs," Andrew said. "I want to tell Sorley we'll be leaving early, unless anyone here wants to watch the hangings."

Murie winced at the thought.

⁓

Rob watched Murie as they crossed the chamber with her mother in Andrew's wake. When Murie's brow furrowed, he suspected she was worried that he might be angry with her for speaking as frankly as she had to the King.

She glanced at him then, and although the lines in her

forehead smoothed, her expression became speculative. He wondered what she was thinking, and his cock stirred at what he hoped that subject might be. He loved the fact that her beautiful face was so expressive. As that thought occurred to him, he realized that its animation was a large part of her beauty.

Other men, less observant ones, might dismiss her as *nobbut a wee dab of a woman*, but Rob could as easily imagine her as she would look in years to come when her slender, curvaceous body grew a bit plumper after a child or six, and her flaxen hair grayed or turned white. He realized fondly that he looked forward to witnessing such changes and to growing old with her.

To be sure, she had habits that would sometimes irk him, although she had proven that she could change. Even so, she was accustomed to going her own road, and he was sure she remained determined to become a seanachie. However, he was accustomed to commanding obedience, so if he had to lay down a law or two, she would learn when she had to heed him.

In the end, he decided, although they would sometimes fratch, they would also talk, laugh, and enjoy each other's company, in bed and out. In truth, he was rapidly coming to believe that the best day in his memory was the day she had declared herself his wife.

She twitched his sleeve when a gillie held the door open for them and Lady Aubrey moved ahead to follow Andrew into the great hall. Looking into his wife's somber face, Rob remembered her wincing when Andrew mentioned the hangings.

Drawing her through the doorway and off the dais, he said, "Don't fret, lass. We won't linger here tomorrow."

"I know, but I must talk with you, sir, privately, *before* we go upstairs."

"Now?"

"Aye, straightway, because we will all go to supper soon, so Tibby will be waiting for me. And I shan't find another...Sithee, I've found out the truth about..." She paused, looking around as if to be sure that no one else could overhear her. Then, speaking so low that he barely heard her, she said, "...about your Elizabeth!"

Grabbing her by a shoulder, he took her out of the hall to a nearby anteroom that he had noticed earlier. Finding with relief that it was empty, he hustled her inside, shut the door, and said harshly, "What the devil did you mean by that? What business is it of yours to be discussing my private business with anyone else?"

"Don't be a noddy, Rob," she said, looking him in the eye. "I've done nowt o' the sort, as you would say. So, if you will just listen..."

~

Dougal's emotions were in turmoil as he urged his garron to a faster pace. Grief warred with his fury, frustration, and deep sense of loss. The two men riding garrons behind him kept their distance, doubtless wary of his temper.

He had gone from the disaster in the inner chamber straight out to the gate, so he had with him only his weapons and the plaid, tunic, cap, and boots he wore. Not, he reassured himself, that he needed more than that. What he *needed* was to reach Arrochar as fast as he could and prepare to keep Andrew at bay.

Wasn't it just like his father not to tell him about his

damnable charter and to damn him instead for trying everything *he* could to protect their claim to Arrochar? So smug had Pharlain been, too, and so critical of aught that his long-suffering son did. And where had it got *him* in the end? Hanged or beheaded, at the King's will.

Grief washed over Dougal at the thought, and he castigated himself for it. What had he expected? What had he wanted? For the man to live forever or only long enough to say, just once, "Ye've done well, lad"?

When he'd found their men and ordered them to depart at once, the captain of Pharlain's tail had refused. "No without the laird's say-so," he said.

When Dougal had favored him with the truth, that Pharlain would be dead before midday on the morrow, the man shook his head, making it clear that he did not believe it. So, Dougal took the two men in their tail who served him alone, and the three of them had set out together. After all, with Jamie so friendly to Andrew Dubh, Dougal knew that his own skin would be at risk if he lingered.

He was not beaten yet, though. They had held Arrochar by right of the sword for many years before Albany had signed the charter that Pharlain had shown to the King.

"And I'll hold it by that same right," he muttered. "If the Fates be willing."

Doubt surged in. The Fates had done nowt to help him so far, but by God, they would change their ways, or he would wreak havoc.

Chapter 20 _____

Elizabeth Napier is alive?" Rob said, staring at Murie.

She sensed shock and dismay in equal waves throughout his body.

"Aye, she is," Murie replied. "And living with her gillie in Ireland, poor dafty." She felt no sympathy for Elizabeth, only gratitude for the girl's stupidity in running away with an equally daft lover instead of marrying Rob.

He was shaking his head as if he might thereby make sense of it all.

She said, "How your parents could have thought that such a want-wit would suit you as a wife, I cannot imagine."

"Nor I," Rob said, resting his hands on her shoulders. "I prefer my own lady, outspoken though she is. By my troth, lass, I'm glad she ran off, though."

"So am I," Murie said with feeling. "Had she married you, I'd have had to marry Dougal. But what a dreadful tale for Lady Napier to have told your parents!"

"I'd wager she told only my mother," Rob said thoughtfully. "I cannot believe that Napier would be party to such a falsehood or that he knew aught of it, come to that. By begging Mam to keep the scandal of Elizabeth's 'suicide' to herself, Lady Napier effectively stopped that tale from spreading."

"Lady Nisbet recognized the tale but claimed she never talked of it until she heard me say I had heard it at Ardincaple. She seems to enjoy gossip, but mayhap she spoke the truth about that. Still, Lady Euphemia must have told your father."

"Aye, sure, but he never spread any gossip. The most he would have said to the Napiers or anyone else would have been to express his sorrow and sympathy at the loss of their daughter."

"Your mother told me that Elizabeth's father locked her in the tower as punishment and actually saw her leap out of its window," Murie added. "Would your father not have said something to Napier about *that*?"

"Nay," Rob said dryly. "He'd have said, 'A dreadful thing, Napier, dreadful!' That would have been the sum of it."

Murie smiled, thinking that Rob was like his father in many ways.

"We should go up now," he said. "They must be wondering where we are."

"Before we go," she said, "are you still angry with me for plaguing his grace about what happened to me?"

"Nay," he said. "If you had irked him…"

"But I didn't! He even granted me a royal pardon, which must include what the Brehon said, don't you agree?"

"Lass, if you think his grace would ever interfere with a husband's right to chastise a naughty wife or forbid a man to keep his word, you are much mistaken."

"But he said—!"

Rob's forefinger against her lips silenced her.

"Sweetheart, much as I may want to keep my word to the Brehon, I do *not* want to punish you. I just want to take you to bed and make love to you."

"I wish you could, but it will have to wait until after supper, because everyone will be waiting for us now."

"Aye, they will, so let us make haste," Rob said.

They reached their landing without incident, but no sooner did they open the door than Tibby said, "Och, I thought ye were lost in this great castle. Quickly, m'lady, ye must—"

"Be that ye, at last, Rob?" Andrew demanded, stepping into the open doorway. "I hope ye were giving our lass a scold for plaguing Jamie as she did."

As Murie turned toward her father, she caught Rob's gaze and saw a warning gleam in his eyes just as he said to Andrew, "I did, sir, but I am not finished yet. I fear that your daughter is going to go without her supper tonight."

"Aye, well, it doesna be the first time, nor will it be the last," Andrew said with a sigh and a twinkle. "Come along, Tibby. They won't be needing ye now."

⁓

The journey back to Loch Lomond was as tedious as the journey to Inverness had been, and it passed in much the same blur for Rob. They saw splendid scenery and had fine weather, but each day of riding and walking was much like another. They stayed in many of the same places, and in none of them was he able to sleep with his wife. Murie shared rooms as she had before, with Lady Aubrey and Tibby, while he slept in the same room as Andrew, Sorley,

Hamish, and others. Scáthach slept wherever Rob slept and ranged ahead of him when they traveled.

Rob missed having Murie curled against him at night and in other ways, as well. What little conversation they did enjoy lacked privacy, so the nearer they grew to Tùr Meiloach, the more cheerful he became.

When they reached the northernmost end of Loch Lomond, the women were riding, and Andrew insisted that they all keep to the MacFarlan side of the loch.

Murie said, "But Dougal may—"

"Dougal willna find enough men at Arrochar to challenge ours," Andrew said with more confidence than Rob felt where Dougal was concerned. "Between us," Andrew added, "counting Rob and m'self, we have more than a score of good men if we also count Sorley, Hamish, and the lads leading the baggage ponies."

Rob glanced at Murie, noted her calmness and Lady Aubrey's. Tibby looked resigned. When no one else reacted, Rob felt himself relax. He tensed only when he saw a watcher on the hillside above them and, now and again, saw others as they traveled. No one seemed more than curious, though, and when they reached the Tarbet, more people gathered to watch them but no one offered challenge.

Andrew waved, and two or three men waved back. Then, others did. Soon they were all waving and cheering, men and women, even children, although Rob could not imagine that the bairns understood why they cheered.

Andrew beamed, but just then Hamish said to Rob, "Laird, there be someone a-peltin' toward us yonder tae the south. Looks like that redheaded bairn."

"That's Pluff," Murie exclaimed. "Something must be wrong."

Her father had seen Pluff, too, and waited for him with his hands on his hips. "What the devil are ye doing here, where ye've nae business to be?" Andrew demanded when the boy dashed up to them.

The crowd around them had fallen silent.

"Lady Dree and Lady Lina sent me tae find ye, laird, 'cause I ken this road better nor most. Dougal's took Lady Lizzie again, and nae one kens where they be."

"How long ago?" Rob demanded.

"I dinna ken," Pluff said. "Nae one saw him come this time. They said Lady Lizzie went wrathful at summat that Lady Marg—"

"That's enough o' that," Andrew snapped. "D'ye *mean* to say that Lizzie went off on her own?"

"Aye, that be it," Pluff said. "God kens where...as Sir Mag said," the boy added hastily. "But one o' the gillies saw a man creeping through the woods, and he thought it were Dougal but didna let him see him. Said he thought it were wiser tae get help, and Lady Lina said he were right. She also said that Lizzie...*Lady* Lizzie, that is, will be safe 'til we find her, that Dougal willna hurt her. So he won't."

"Mercy," Murie said. "Can Dree not sense which way they went?"

"Nay, m'lady," Pluff replied, shaking his head so hard that his red curls bounced. "She says she still be none so aware o' Lizzie as she be o' ye and the lady Lina, and there be dunamany strangers moving about the noo."

Andrew said, "Strangers?"

"Aye, laird, 'cause Sir Ian brought his men, and the Laird o' Galbraith came wi' his, too, to see did we need them. He said he'd heard ye were off tae Inverness, and wi' Lizzie here, he came wi' Sir Ian tae be sure we'd all keep safe. They'd feared that Pharlain might get up tae mischief whiles ye were gone."

"He did," Murie said. "But he got up to it in Inverness, and the King hanged him for it. Dougal left the day before the hanging, though, and we left before it—"

She broke off when Andrew said sharply, "Never mind all that," and Rob touched her arm. Then Andrew shouted, "Does any man here ken how many Dougal has with him?"

A tall man stepped forward and said, "He's alone, laird. He tried tae roust us all tae go with him, but he'd already told us the King hanged Pharlain and signed your Arrochar charter, so we kent fine that we'd answer tae ye now, and glad we be tae do it. Few here be loyal tae Dougal. Sakes, we'd be fain tae help ye search."

"I thank ye, and if need be, I'll send the lad back to fetch ye. From the sound of it, we'll have enough men for that. I'll want to meet with everyone here, though, as soon as I get things sorted at Tùr Meiloach. Who's in charge here?"

The same man said, "Me, laird. I be Kai's Gavie. M' da were with Pharlain at Inverness. D'ye ken what became o' the rest of our men there?"

"Nay, but the King willna blame them for Pharlain's misdeeds," Andrew said. "Ye'll look after this lot for now, Gavie. I remember your da. He's a good man, and I'm thinking ye're another." To Rob, he said, "We'll go faster without the ponies." Calling to one of his men, he ordered him to choose two others and look after the garrons. "Just tie them in a string and lead them," he said.

Glancing at Lady Aubrey, who nodded, Murie dismounted at once.

She did not need the frown on Rob's face to tell her that he was about to order her to stay with the garrons, so she grinned at him and kilted up her skirts as she said, "I go where Mam goes."

—◯—

Rob looked to Andrew, hoping the older man would order both women to stay behind, but Andrew did not. Instead, he said quietly to Pluff, "We'll talk as we go, lad. What else d'ye ken?"

Half-running to keep up with their long strides, Pluff said, "Sir Ian and Sir Mag will likely ha' found 'em, laird. They sent men everywhere and tellt 'em tae report tae Sir Ian at the tower or Sir Mag near his cottage if they spied 'em."

"They are sure that Dougal hasn't left Tùr Meiloach, then," Rob said.

"Aye, sir; he couldna. Sir Mag and Sir Ian set guards on the passes and all round. They think Dougal must ha' swam over by hisself in the night and sneaked past the men a-watching the shore near where the wharf can lie down on the water. Sithee, Wee Molly were awake most o' the night wi' a new tooth, so Lady Dree didna ken nowt save her bairn's troubles, nor would she anyways wi' so many strangers about. See you, it were gey misty and black as pitch, and Sir Mag said Dougal must ha' come ashore after the moon set when the mist hid even the stars."

Making their way as fast as possible up the steep track to the top of the pass, they found some of Ian's men with

Andrew's there. Other men, one of them said, were scanning the landscape from the peaks above them.

"Nae one ha' come this way, laird," their leader assured Andrew.

Traveling faster downhill, they hurried through the forest to the tower, where they found Sir Ian Colquhoun with Murie's sisters in the great hall.

Lanky Ian jumped to his feet and shoved strands of blond hair off his face as he strode forward to shake Rob's hand and welcome the others.

"We knew you were coming," Lina said, smiling at Rob. "Dree sensed your approach late this morning, but none of us had any notion that Dougal was near."

"What happened?" Rob asked.

"We aren't sure. Lizzie broke her fast with us, as she has every morning, but she was restless. When Lady Margaret told her to go up to the solar and practice sitting quietly, Lizzie looked utterly mutinous. Even so, when she just got up and left, no one thought aught but that she knew whose side Galbraith would take."

Murie shook her head. "Did you ask her maidservant where she went?"

"Aye, sure," Lina said. "She *said* she knew naught. Dree and I could tell that she was being untruthful, but she seemed calm, not worried. We thought Lizzie might be up to mischief, but Galbraith had gone out early with Mag, so it never occurred to us that she might have dared to go outside the wall."

Rob said to Andrena, "She did, though, aye? You're sure of that?"

Rocking the sleeping Molly, cradled in her arms, Dree nodded. Quietly, she said, "Lina persuaded Lizzie's maidservant to admit that Liz was going to meet someone. She didn't know who it was. Then one of our men said he'd seen Dougal skulking in the woods. By the time others went to find him, he had vanished."

"And Liz *would* go to meet Dougal if she had somehow got a message from him, asking her to," Lina said. "She still believes we have all wronged him and he is not as wicked as we think. She has a gey soft heart, Lizzie does. But, to be fair, I doubt that Dougal will hurt her. The runes agree, and whilst we were captives at Dumbarton, he showed a softness toward Liz that I'd never expected of him."

"Nevertheless, he kept you both there," Rob said flatly. Whatever else he might believe, he did *not* believe that a few stones could predict the future.

Murie put a soothing hand on his arm just as Pluff dashed into the hall. "Some'un saw them on the cliffs!" he cried.

Andrew looked around the hall, and Rob knew he was counting the few men there, preparing to issue orders.

"Sir," he said, but Murie and Lina interrupted him in near unison, "Don't send an army after them, Father!"

The two women looked at each other, and Lina said to Andrew, "I believe strongly that he will not hurt her, sir. But, if your men anger or frighten him, he might do something daft. If they are on the cliffs, a mistake could kill them both."

Rob saw Murie nod in agreement. He had no idea how the sisters deduced the things they seemed to deduce. It wasn't by the runes, but he had learned enough about his wife and heard enough about the others to keep out of it now.

To Ian, he said, "I hope the men who saw them will have sense enough to await orders before confronting Dougal."

"Aye, we told them just to find the minx and report her location. I'll have a few words to say to her if Galbraith or Mag does not get hold of her first."

Andrew said, "We must find them, and speedily."

"We'll go, sir," Rob said. "You and I and Ian. We'll find them as fast and as quietly as we can and assess the situation then. We'll send Pluff at once to tell Mag where she is and assure him that Tùr Meiloach is not under siege or in imminent danger of invasion by Pharlain, as he may fear it is."

Andrew glanced at Ian, who nodded agreement, whereupon the three of them made for the stairway without a word to anyone else.

Murie looked at Dree and Lina and raised her eyebrows.

Andrena shook her head with a smile. "Men," she said. "As if we are of no account whatsoever. If Lizzie and Dougal are on the cliffs, then I can tell you they are some distance south of here. You should be able to walk along the clifftops until you see them. Ian posted no watchers on the cliffs, because no one save Mag has ever managed to climb or descend one. It is possible that no one searched there if they were sure that Dougal would try to take her away from here. Men are watching the rivers and the passes, and have spread throughout the woods. I'd wager that Dougal eluded them easily if Lizzie was compliant."

Lady Aubrey gestured toward the hearth, where

Scáthach lay quietly curled by the fire, and said, "If you are going, Murie, take Scáthach. You may need her."

Murie nodded, but she was watching Andrena, still rocking Wee Molly. "You aren't coming with us, Dree?"

"Nay, I must stay with Molly, and you don't need me. You and Lina know Lizzie better than I do…Dougal, too, come to that. But Murie…" She looked toward Lina, now talking near the hearth with Lady Aubrey. Drawing a deep breath, Dree said quietly, "Do *not* trust Dougal, Murie. I heard what Lina said, but what I'm sensing now tells me he may be gey distraught. If he is not, he will become so when they confront him."

"I know," Murie said. "The King hanged Pharlain for being party to the assassination plot at Perth and for murdering our brothers. Dougal got away."

"That explains what I've felt then. Sithee, I could not identify the source, but I did feel strong disquiet all morning and I sense it now from south of us."

Lina said, "Murie, if you are coming, we must leave now. Mam will stay with Dree and Molly."

"Aye, sure," Murie said, clicking her tongue to Scáthach as Rob did when he called her to heel. So certain was she that the dog would obey that she felt only increasing confidence when Scáthach followed her across the hall.

Hurrying down to the postern door, Murie and Lina slipped outside into the yard, through the gate and into the woods, where Scáthach ranged slightly ahead of them.

As they emerged from woodland onto the clifftop, Murie said, "Lina, are you *certain* Dougal won't hurt Lizzie? I confess I am not sure at all."

"If no one challenges him…" But Lina said no more,

and Murie knew that she was as worried about Lizzie's
safety as Dree was. She recalled then that Lina had proph-
esied dire consequences to Dougal if he dared to test the
nature of Tùr Meiloach's sacred ability to protect true
MacFarlans.

"Sakes, Lizzie is not a MacFarlan," Murie said. "Tùr
Meiloach will not—"

"Do you think I am unaware of that?" Lina asked. "We
must reach them quickly, before anything dire occurs.
Then, Murie, we must both do all we can to remain calm
and *impose* that calm on Lizzie and Dougal."

Muriella nearly disclaimed having any such power.
But, remembering what Lina had so often told her about
having confidence in herself, she nodded instead.

"No matter what Rob thinks, I can do anything that
Lina and Dree can do," she murmured to herself. Then
she repeated it silently, again and again, as they hurried
along the clifftops.

There was no path there because the granite was
strewn with boulders and scree, so they had to watch
every footstep. Keeping well away from the edges, they
made good time and soon saw Rob, Ian, and Andrew in
the distance ahead.

"They will be displeased to see us, you know," Lina
said. "Ian expected us to stay in the tower, but—"

"I know," Murie interjected. "Rob is beginning to grow
accustomed to my . . . my thinking for myself or acting on
impulse, as he would say. But . . ." She paused.

"Has he done as the Brehon ordered yet?"

Murie grimaced. "Sakes, you must have one ear inside
my head, for I just thought of that myself. He has not. He
said he doesn't want to. Moreover, his grace absolved me

of all guilt in the abduction and granted me a royal pardon, so that may have eased Rob's belief that he is *obliged* to keep his word to the Brehon. However, he might say that this, today, has nowt to do with the Brehon. Sithee, his principles do not succumb as easily to blandishment or even to logic as Father's might."

"Husbands are like that," Lina said. "Ian is as likely as Father is to fly into the boughs, *but*—" Cutting off her own words, she exclaimed, "Look yonder, Murie! They've stopped and are staring at something or someone between them and the loch. Hurry!"

"Don't come any closer if you want this lass to see another day!" Dougal shouted. He and Lizzie stood with their backs dangerously close to the cliff's edge.

Rob had seen them first, but having little experience with the sheer cliffs that guarded Tùr Meiloach against access from the loch, he had not realized until they were nearly upon Lizzie and Dougal how close to the edge the two were.

Seeing the loch behind them and knowing that the two stood a hundred feet above the water sent chills up and down Rob's spine. He had a healthy respect for such heights and had seen as he and the others hurried along the uneven granite that the tide was nearly at its ebb. Even if one of them could survive hitting the water, no one could survive hitting the rocky shallows.

The impulse to rush forward and grab Lizzie was nearly unbearable. Looking at Andrew and then Ian, Rob saw his feelings reflected in their faces.

Dougal did, too. "Don't try it, or I swear I'll step off and take her with me."

Aware of peripheral motion, Rob glanced to his right and saw Murie and Lina approaching quietly but swiftly. Wholly unexpected fury surged through him along with something less familiar. Realizing that the unusual emotion was pure terror, not for Lizzie but for Muriella, he strove to calm himself. What the devil were they doing here? Surely, Murie would not risk herself for—

The thought stopped in its tracks. Had he not *seen* her act in foolhardy ways more than once already? Had she not begun this journey of theirs with a foolish, impulsive act, albeit not nearly as terrifying as what he feared she might do now?

He tried to catch her eye, but she kept her gaze fixed on Dougal and Lizzie.

Standing beside Murie but looking intently at Dougal, Lina said gently, "It will not be as dreadful as you fear, Dougal, I promise. The anger you feel has mixed with your grief for your father and the disappointment of seeing your future hopes dashed. Some of it is selfish; some is honest grief. None of it is Lizzie's fault."

Seeing Dougal's head jerk up at those words, Rob thought Lina must be daft to risk speaking such a truth to him at such a time. Looking at Andrew and Ian, he saw, to his astonishment, that even Ian was calmly watching the tableau.

Murie listened to Lina but was trying to read Dougal and to project her own utterly unexpected sense of calmness to him. His emotions were in such turmoil that she could not interpret them. She knew only that what she sensed was dangerous, especially for Lizzie, so she had to do what she could to help Lina calm him.

As she did, she realized that it must be Lina's own calmness flowing through her and hoped that, together, they could ease the turmoil of Dougal's emotions.

Lizzie looked fearless. She was uncharacteristically quiet, though, and alert. Murie could sense no warmth in her now for Dougal and wrested her attention back to him, confident that she could remain calm and avoid the gimlet green stare from Rob that might otherwise prove her undoing.

She knew that look well enough to feel it aimed at her, but she reminded herself that he was beginning to trust her... in some ways.

At least, she knew that he would do nothing foolish. The very thought was alien. Rob was the steadiest, most even-tempered man she had ever known, except when she vexed him. Even then, his anger was more like the tide rolling to the shore, steady, unavoidable, and—in her case, at least—painfully effective.

She had done it again, drifted into her imagination.

Everyone else was standing still, scarcely daring to breathe.

Then a loud crack seemed to erupt through the very air.

Her gaze flew to Lizzie's widening eyes and gaping mouth, and she realized that the granite shelf on which Lizzie and Dougal stood had cracked.

Andrew shouted, "The cliff!"

Sakes, the crack was widening in front of Lizzie's toes.

What happened next happened in a breath but, to Murie, seemed slow and purposeful. Leaping forward, she reached toward Lizzie and was barely aware of Rob's shout or of Scáthach suddenly beside her.

Dougal shoved Lizzie into Murie's arms as Scáthach darted in and pushed them sideways, away from the edge and out of Rob's way as he passed them.

Stumbling, clutching Lizzie, Murie fought to keep them both upright and watched in horror as the rock under Dougal broke and Rob dove toward him.

Pushing Lizzie toward Lina, Murie dashed forward, but Ian grabbed her and swung her into Andrew's arms.

Rob lay flat on the ground, arms outstretched, sliding toward the edge.

~

By flinging himself down at the broken edge of the cliff, Rob managed to grab one of Dougal's upthrust arms, but the clifftop provided no traction. Despite Rob's great strength, Dougal nearly had him over at the outset, and although he slowed himself, he knew the other man's weight was too much for him to hold long.

Rob dug the toes of his rawhide boots into the rock as hard as he could, and now he felt Scáthach tugging at his breeks. The daft dog was more likely to pull the breeks off or go over the cliff with him than to pull both him and Dougal anywhere.

"I've got you," Ian shouted.

Rob felt him grab both ankles, but he was still sliding, and he knew that the only way Ian could save him was if *he* let go of Dougal.

Dougal, desperate now, evidently no longer willing to die, had managed to grip Rob's forearm with his free hand. In doing so, he pulled Rob's right shoulder and half of his chest over the brink. The heel of Rob's left hand caught and held a small, rough upthrust in the granite.

Ian, Scáthach, and one bit of granite were delaying the inevitable, but...

"I'm here, too, lad," Andrew said, grabbing a fistful of Rob's plaid. "I dinna think we can hold ye both if ye go over, so let go o' him afore that happens."

Rob gritted his teeth. He doubted that Dougal would let go of *him*.

"Hang on, lads!"

Rob let himself breathe again at the sound of Mag's voice. Friends though they were, it had never before sounded so welcome. Everything had happened so quickly that he had been aware only of holding Dougal. Now he could feel the painful strain, as if his arm were trying to separate itself from the rest of his body.

Seconds later, with Mag gripping one of his legs, Ian the other, and Andrew handfuls of his clothing, Rob managed to grip both of Dougal's wrists and haul him up. Scáthach barked and Rob heard Lina and Lizzie shouting encouragement.

⁓

Murie watched Ian and Andrew haul Dougal to his feet and vaguely heard Mag say that he would attend to Lizzie. Murie had eyes only for Rob, who still sat on the hard granite, too close to the broken edge to please her.

Scáthach poked him with her nose, and he patted her. Then, wearily, he got to his feet.

Dougal said bitterly, "I dinna ken whether to thank ye or curse ye, but—"

Rob's fist shot to Dougal's jaw in a swift, hard blow that nearly lifted the other man off his feet before sending him crashing to the ground.

It happened so fast that Rob had squatted and was rubbing his right fist in his left palm before Murie quite realized what he had done.

She was barely aware of moving toward him, let alone that she was running, until she reached him and shoved him hard to his backside, shouting, "What were you thinking, you dafty? First, to dive after him like that and scare us all half-witted, and then to strike him whilst you were still so near the edge! What if he'd hit you back? What if—?"

Her words ended in a shriek when Rob, moving faster than anyone would have thought possible, surged up and she felt herself being lifted into the air before he was on his feet. She caught a glimpse of Lina's shocked face, another of Lizzie clasped tight in her brother Mag's arms, and then Mag's delighted grin before she was facedown over Rob's shoulder like a sack of barley, and he was bearing her away from the cliff toward the woods.

"Put me down!" she shrieked, trying to kick him as she pounded both fists against his back. "Put me down, I say!"

Rob smacked her hard on the backside, drawing another outraged shriek and then a stillness of both fists and voice when he rested his hand there again.

Knowing that the others would look after Lizzie and Dougal, he strode into the woods with his burden. It was so quiet then that he wondered at the silence until he heard a squirrel chatter and realized that Mag would have spread word that the lost ones were found as soon as Pluff had told him. Likely, all the searchers had returned to their assigned duties or to the—

"Where are you taking me?" she muttered.

Where, indeed? he silently asked himself.

"Here," he decided, lifting her off his shoulder and setting her on the ground.

Her hair was tangled. Her face was red, and her eyes flashed. Her right hand flew up to strike but stopped where it was when her gaze collided with his.

"Go ahead, *mo chridhe*," he said softly. "I do recall warning you that defying me is never a good idea. Hitting me would usually be a worse one. Even so, I deserve a smack after what I just did, but when you said I'd scared you, I just—" He drew a breath. "You ran toward Lizzie as if to grab her, just as Dougal pushed her. I feared that the pair of you *and* Scáthach would go over."

She stared at him, tears welling in her eyes.

"Ah, lass, go ahead. Slap me as hard as you like. I swear I won't retaliate."

With a sob, she said, "I thought I was going to lose you, that Dougal would beat us, after all. And then, when you hit him—"

Rob opened his arms then, and she walked into them, sighing with deep contentment when they closed around her.

Epilogue ─────────────────

Loch Sloigh, Arrochar, three months later

Sakes, Muriella, are you daft? Why the *devil* did you not tell me this before now? What if—"

Murie put a fingertip to Rob's lips. It silenced him, but she eyed him nonetheless warily. They sat alone together on a wooded hillside above the long, oval loch that was Clan Farlan's ancient gathering place. She wore the new blue kirtle Lina had made for her, and Rob wore his plaid and his cap with eagle feathers in honor of Andrew Dubh's first clan gathering at his beloved loch in two decades.

Rob nibbled Murie's fingertip, and taking that as a sign that he would let her speak, she lowered the hand and said, "I would tell you that I just found out, love, but I promised always to answer you truthfully. In troth, though, I think you know why I waited. I was afraid you would not let me come and help celebrate this day."

"I would have brought you to Arrochar," he said. "I might have balked at letting you walk all the way up here."

She shook her head at him. "I am not ill, sir, or weak, or decrepit. And Father would be gey disappointed if we were not both here."

"He is having a grand day, is he not?"

She smiled. "He has earned it."

Below them, the water of the loch gleamed brightly in the summer sun. Its shoreline was alive with clansmen, women, and children. She and Rob were high enough on the steep hillside to hear only distant shrieks from children splashing in the water and someone singing. Above the trees, a hawk soared lazily on a breeze.

"Father is pleased that everyone came, because he feared that Ian might not get leave to return again in so short a time. Even Galbraith came, and Lizzie."

"Not Lady Margaret, though."

"Nay, but Liz told me that her ladyship means to move to Inch Galbraith. She says that Galbraith alone cannot keep Lizzie in hand. In troth, I think she has grown fond of Lizzie and that Liz will be pleased to have her there."

"Sakes, your father even let Dougal come."

"I know," Murie said. "I have not said so to anyone else, but I still don't understand why he did not just hang the villainous man."

Rob grinned at her. "Andrew said that hanging him would be letting him off too easily, that Dougal should have a finer understanding of his own behavior, and Pharlain's, toward their people and their 'guests.' These days, apparently, Dougal is an oarsman on one of Andrew's galleys."

Murie chuckled. "I'll wager Mag is pleased about that, but surely Father does not keep Dougal in chains as they did with Mag."

"Nay, Andrew insists that Dougal volunteered," Rob said. "I shudder to imagine what other choices Andrew offered him. He said he is merely letting Dougal work his way back into the clan's good graces."

Murie laughed.

~

Rob loved her laughter, and when she put a fingertip to her lips again and sucked on it, his body reacted as it always did, and his memory flew back to the day he had seen her on the ladder in Mag's cottage, looking so childlike and yet not like a child at all. She had so many sides to her that he found new ones every day, and he hoped that he would discover more and more of them long into their future.

He glanced around the small clearing. They could see people below them, but if he spread his plaid, the shrubbery ought to conceal them.

She chuckled, and he looked at her and grinned guiltily.

"They won't see us," she said. "And I won't break."

He caught her in his arms then, kissed her, and pulled off his cap. A moment more, his plaid was on the ground, and he was helping her out of her kirtle. She untied her shift and opened the gathered neckline enough to let it slide down her arms to the grass. Now that he knew, he could see the soft rounding of her belly.

Flinging his tunic to join her kirtle, he told himself he would teach his son that everyone had a right to his or her own thoughts and opinions but that there were mysteries in their world that defied understanding. Meeting his love's twinkling, too-knowing eyes, he also decided that he would advise that laddie that the best way to manage such things was to accept the mysteries that pleased him and let the others be what they would.

"You know that I mean to tell a tale at the *ceilidh* tonight," she said.

"Not about Elizabeth Napier."

"No, you dafty. Kiss me again."

He complied thoroughly, pulling her down beside him and into his arms. Within minutes, she was in full heat and ready for him.

As he eased his way cautiously in, Murie said softly, "What make you think our bairn will be a son?"

Dear Reader,

I hope you enjoyed *The Warrior's Bride*, as well as its predecessors in the Lairds of the Loch trilogy, *The Laird's Choice* and *The Knight's Temptress*.

Nine months after Jamie's Inverness Parliament, the North was in flames again and the town of Inverness, except for its renovated castle, reduced to smoking rubble by the Lord of the Isles. The King hurried north, where he was joined by Alexander, Earl of Mar, Lord of the North, who had summoned Clan Chattan to his banner under the Mackintosh (the clan captain), and Donald Dubh Cameron. Clans Cameron and Mackintosh were allies, and the Mackintosh had no love for the Lord of the Isles. Recall that these clans were supporters of the King in *Scottish Knights*.

Brehon law is the second-oldest codified law known, after Sanskrit law, and dates from the fifth century. A case and decision like Murie's supposedly occurred.

Now, a more personal note: Lest anyone out there wondered how a young woman who walks all the time in the woods could possibly be idiot enough to walk into a low-hanging branch, I should confess that two summers ago the author, who has many more years of such experience than Murie had, and who was thinking about the plot for this book, walked headfirst into a large, low-hanging branch that had not moved an inch since her previous passage, and many before that, on the same trail. Fortunately,

I was wearing a hat with a sturdy bill that hit the branch first, tilted down, and protected my face. To say that I felt like an idiot, however, is an understatement. An obliging friend nearby removed the hazard immediately with his chain saw. However, it was hardly the first time that my daydreaming nearly ended badly and it probably won't be the last. I often walk with my sister in a local wetlands area, and, twice, she has stopped me just short of a rattler.

I would again like to extend special thanks to Donald R. MacRae for his always extraordinary help and support, as well as to Matthew Miller, California Commissioner for The International Clan MacFarlane Society, Ltd; Michael MacFarlane of Celtic Jackalope, and everyone else who contributed to the website www.clanmacfarlane. org for their helpful commentary and excellent resources.

Also, as always, I thank my wonderful agents, Lucy Childs and Aaron Priest, my wonderful editor Selina McLemore, Senior Managing Editor Bob Castillo, master copyeditor Sean Devlin, my publicist Jennifer Reese, Art Director Diane Luger, Cover Artist Larry Rostant, Editorial Director Amy Pierpont, Vice President and Editor in Chief Beth de Guzman, and everyone else at Hachette Book Group's Grand Central Publishing/Forever who contributed to this book.

If you enjoyed *The Lairds of the Loch*, please look for Book 1 of my new Border Nights trilogy, *Moonlight Raider*, in September 2014. Meantime, Suas Alba!

Amanda Scott

www.amandascottauthor.com

Amanda Scott's exciting new
Border Nights series begins with

Moonlight Raider!

Please turn this page for a preview.

Chapter 1 —————————

Scottish Borders, 4 November 1426

What was she thinking? God help her, why had she run? When they caught her...But that dreadful likelihood didn't bear thought. They must *not* catch her.

Even so, she could not go any faster, or much farther. It felt as if she had been running forever, and she had no idea of exactly where she was.

Glancing up through the forest canopy, she could see the quarter-moon high above her, its pale light still occluded by the mist she had blessed when leaving Henderland. Although the moon had been rising then, she had hoped that the mist would conceal her moving figure until she reached the crest of the hills southeast of the castle. When she was safely on their southern slope, she had followed a narrow, little used track, one that she hoped they would never imagine she had taken.

Experience had warned her even then that the mist might presage rain ahead, but the mist had been a blessing all the same. In any event, with luck, she would find shelter before the rain arrived, or the light of day, come to that.

Long before then she had to decide what to do. But how? What *could* she do? Who would dare to help her? Certainly, no one living anywhere near St. Mary's Loch. Her father was too powerful, her brothers too mean, too greedy, and Tuedy...But she could not bear the thought of Ringan Tuedy at any—

A low, canine woof abruptly curtailed her stream of thought, and she froze until a deep male voice somewhere in the darkness beyond the trees just ahead of her said quietly, "Whisst, Ramper, whisst."

Impulsively, knowing she could neither outrun them nor risk time to think, eighteen-year-old Molly Cockburn dove into the shrubbery and desperately eased her way in as far, as quietly, and as deeply as she could, giving no thought to the brambles and branches that scratched and tore at her face and bare skin as she did.

A susurrous sound came then of some beast—nay, a dog—sniffing. Then she heard scrabbling and a rattle of dry shrubbery nearby. Was the dog coming for her?

Hearing the man call it to heel, then a sharper, slightly more distant bark, and realizing that he and his dogs were closer than she had thought, she curled tightly to make herself as small as possible and went utterly still, scarcely daring to breathe.

She was trembling, though, and whether it was from the cold or sheer terror didn't matter. She was shaking so hard that she would likely make herself heard if the nosy dog did not drag her from the shrubbery or alert its master to do so.

Above the sounds of the animal that had sensed her presence came others then that were even more ominous. Recognizing the distant yet much too near baying of dogs, Molly stifled a groan. The dogs were doubtless Will's sleuthhounds, trained to track people, even—or especially—rebellious sisters.

Twenty-four-year-old Walter Scott, Laird of Kirkurd since childhood and a scant twenty-four hours of being the sixth Lord of Rankilburn, Murthockston, and Buccleuch, had just taken a long, deep breath and was savoring the energizing, chilly air that filled his lungs, and trying not to think of the vast responsibilities that had just descended upon him, when his younger dog gave its low, curious woof.

"Whisst, Ramper, whisst," he said. When the shaggy pup ignored him, its attention fixed on whatever wee beast it had sensed in the always-so-intriguing shrubbery, Wat added firmly, "Come to heel now, lad, and mind your manners as Arch does. I'd liefer you waken no badgers or other wildlife tonight."

Hearing its name, the older dog perked its ears, and Ramp turned obediently, if reluctantly, toward Wat. Then, pausing, Ramp lifted his head, nose atwitch.

Arch emitted a sharp warning bark at almost the same time, and Wat heard the distant baying himself.

"Easy, lads," he said as he strode toward the sound.

Both dogs ranged protectively ahead of him, but seeing torchlight in the near distance and now hearing hoofbeats over the hounds' baying, he halted a few yards past the area where young Ramper had sought whatever wildlife had gone to earth there. Calling both of his dogs to heel, he looked swiftly around.

The moon's position told him the time was near

midnight, so whoever was coming with hounds, was coming for reasons other than to offer condolences to the new Lord of Rankilburn and hereditary Ranger of Ettrick Forest. That they might be raiders occurred to him, but he dismissed that thought. A second thought, then a third that brought a wry smile to his face, led him to shout, "Tam, Sym, to me!"

Doffing his warm cloak, he watched the torches draw nearer and waited.

Except for the ever-closer riders and dogs, silence ensued. It was possible that neither man, or perhaps only one, had followed him from Rankilburn. As the riders drew nearer, he drew his sword, draped his cloak over a shrub, and eased his dirk forward, hoping that he would need neither weapon.

The dogs were quiet now and kept close, awaiting commands. Hearing a slight rustle behind him, Wat said, "Are you alone, Tam, or is Sym with you?"

"We both be here, sir," Jock's Wee Tammy said quietly. "Three of us should be enough, though, laird. It be just four or five riders, I'm thinking."

Even more quietly, Sym Elliot said, "Herself did send us, laird."

That term, at Rankilburn, referred to only one person, his grandmother.

"Are you saying that, had she not, you would not have followed me?"

Sym cleared his throat.

"Aye, well, I'm glad you did, both of you," Wat said, looking right at the two as he did. Jock's Wee Tammy, despite his name, was nearly sixty and thus the older as well as much the larger of the two. A much-proven warrior and still fierce with a sword, he was captain of the guard at Scotts Hall. Both he and Sym had served Wat's father and grandfather before Wat was born. "I was wool-gathering," he added. "But Arch and Ramper warned me of our visitors."

Lanky Sym said, "Herself sent me to tell ye that her lady-ship were a-frettin' earlier and restless. She said to remind ye that if she wakens...her ladyship, I mean...she'd be gey worried tae hear that ye was out roaming in the forest, so..."

"My mother and grandmother are both stronger women than most," Wat said. "I do know that my lady mother is grieving, Sym. We all are."

"It were too sudden," Tam said.

"It was, aye," Wat agreed, stifling the new wave of grief that struck him. "We will sorely miss my lord father, but death does come to us all in the end."

"Not from this lot we be a-seein' now, though," Sym said confidently, drawing his sword. Tam's was out, too, Wat noted.

"Don't start anything," he said. "Take your cues from me."

"Aye, sir, we know," Tam said.

He knew that they did, but the riders were close, their baying dogs closer, and he hoped that their dogs were well trained. Arch and Ramper would fight to the death to protect him, but he didn't want to lose either one, so he kept them close.

Moments later, a pack of four hounds, dashed amid the trees toward them.

"Halt and away now!" Wat bellowed, shouting the command that the Scotts had long used to keep their own dogs from tearing into their quarry.

Either his roar or his words were enough, because the

four stopped in their tracks and two of them dropped submissively to the ground. The other two stared at him, poised, teeth bared.

He stayed where he was and watched the riders approach, four men, in pairs, the two on his right bearing torches. In their golden glow, he recognized the two leaders, decided the third was their younger brother, and although he did not immediately recognize the fourth man, Wat thought he looked familiar.

When the four drew rein, Wat said to their leader, "Will Cockburn, what urgency brings you and these others to Rankilburn at this time of night?"

Cockburn was a wiry man some years older than Wat with a reputation for leading raids across the border or on his own side of it, a not uncommon reputation in a territory rife with reivers. He glowered at Wat, exchanged a look with his younger brother Thomas, beside him, and then looked back at Wat.

The look was speculative, as if he hoped Wat would say more.

Wat waited stolidly for the answer to his question.

At last, Will Cockburn said, "One of our maidservants seems to have lost her way home. The dogs picked up her scent near St. Mary's Loch and led us here."

⁓

Molly nearly gasped. So she was a maidservant, was she? It was not far off the mark, but did they really think that Walter Scott of Kirkurd would care about a maidservant missing from Henderland? And, surely, it must be Walter Scott of Kirkurd if Will called him "Wat" and they were on Scott land near Rankilburn.

"A maidservant who has wandered all the way here from Henderland?" he said, his tone heavy with skepticism. "Sakes, the distance is eight miles or more."

"I ken fine how far we've come," Will snapped.

She could easily imagine the sour look on his face as he said it, too, so heaven help her if he got his hands on her after chasing her such a distance. He'd get his own back. Then he'd turn her over to Ringan Tuedy, and Tuedy had already told her what he meant to do to her. A shiver shot through her at the memory.

"You won't find your girl here," Kirkurd said, his deep voice reassuringly calm. "My dogs would have alerted me to any stranger within a mile of here, just as they did when they sensed your approach."

A snarling voice that Molly identified with renewed dread as Tuedy's snapped, "So ye say, but since ye've no said what ye're doing out and about at such an hour, how do we ken that ye didna come out tae meet some girl yourself, and *kept* them dogs quiet?"

She had never met Walter Scott of Kirkurd, but her father had told her that he was just six years older than she was. Tuedy, on the other hand, was older by nearly ten years, powerfully built, an experienced warrior, and one accustomed to getting his own way. Would Kirkurd therefore defer to Tuedy?

She hoped not. Recalling then that Kirkurd's authoritative tone had stopped Will's dogs before they could surround her and let Will know they had found her, she told herself she should be thankful for that blessing and not be praying for more.

At last, in a surprisingly mild tone that revealed only slight curiosity, Kirkurd said, "Ring Tuedy, is that you?

I thought you looked familiar, but it must be five or six years since last we met. Do you often help search for lost maidservants?"

Molly's lips twitched grimly, but her terror eased to more familiar dread.

"I was visiting Piers Cockburn," Tuedy said, as if his had been an ordinary visit. "But ye've not answered me question, Wat. What be ye doing out here?"

"It is unnecessary for any Scott to produce reasons for a moonlight stroll on Scott land," Kirkurd said. "However, you may not yet have heard that my lord father died last night. We buried him today, so it has been a grievous time for us here. I came into the forest to seek some fresh air and solitude."

Rankilburn was dead? Sadness surged through her at that news. She had met him only a handful of times, but unlike her brothers and even her father, Rankilburn had always treated her with the respect due to a lady. He was younger than her father, and she had thought him a kinder and gentler man, too. She wished she could see the men as they talked, but she was facing away from them and dared not move.

Tuedy said mockingly, "Ye come seeking peace, yet ye come fully armed and wi' Jock's Tam and Lady Meg's Sym at your side, likewise full-armed."

"Most Borderers carry weapons at all times," Scott said.

She realized then that she ought no longer to think of him as Kirkurd, because Walter Scott was Lord Rankilburn now and Chief of Clan Scott, as well.

He added then, "I won't ask why you four come armed to seek a missing maidservant at midnight, but you do seem over-familiar with my people, Tuedy."

"Sakes, everyone hereabouts kens that Sym Elliot is your Granddame, Lady Meg's, man and that Jock's Wee Tammy is captain of Rankilburn's guard."

"Enough of this talk," Will said curtly. "Ye won't object if we have a look through the forest hereabouts for our lass, will ye, Wat?"

Molly held her breath again.

"But I do object to such an unnecessary intrusion, especially now whilst we here are grieving our loss," Scott replied, his voice still even but with an edge to it, as if he disliked Will but had resolved not to show it. "Tammy and Sym were nearby, because a few men always are. If I whistle, two score more will come."

A brief silence fell before he added amiably, "Methinks you should train your sleuthhounds better, Will, because they must have followed a false trail. Moreover, you ken fine that you have no business hunting man or beast in Ettrick Forest without my permission, so you would all be wise to turn around now and go peacefully back to Henderland."

"And if we don't?" Tuedy demanded provocatively.

"You are on my land, Ringan Tuedy. Recall that I now wield the power of the pit and gallows. Do you think I will hesitate to use that power if you make trouble here whilst my mother, sisters, and grandmother are in deep mourning?"

When another silence greeted those words, Molly bit her lip in frustration. Then, to her deep relief, she heard Will mutter something to the others, followed by the shuffling sounds of horses turning. Calling the dogs to heel, Will shouted, "Ye'd best not be lying to me, Wat. If ye've given shelter to the maid, ye'll answer to me."

"I am not in the habit of sheltering lost maidservants, Will. Rest assured that if one turns up here, I'll get word to Henderland at once."

Although she was sure Will must have heard him, he did not deign to reply.

She listened intently until she could no longer hear any sound of horses, dogs, or men. She had been vaguely aware at first that the new Lord Rankilburn was issuing orders to the two men who had come when he'd shouted. But silence had descended on the forest by the time she decided that Will and the others had truly gone and she had begun to feel the icy chill again. Had everyone gone?

After a few more moments, she decided that they had and carefully wiggled the toes of one bare, chilly foot to make sure that they had not gone numb.

"You can come out now," Walter Scott said quietly. "They've gone."

Ramp whined then but stayed obediently at Wat's side. The shrubbery was still, but he was sure she was there. The sleuthhounds, although as obedient as Ramp, had quivered in such a way that if Will Cockburn had been paying more heed to them and less to getting his own way, he would surely have noticed.

"Come on out now, lass," he said again. "No one here will harm you. I've sent my lads on ahead, as you must have heard, so I'm the only one here now. I have small interest in runaway maidservants, but I don't have infinite patience."

"I can't," she said, her voice little more than a hoarse squeak.

"Are you stuck in the shrubbery?"

"In a manner of speaking, I expect I am."

Her actual manner of speaking stunned him briefly to silence. She spoke much as the women in his family did, so she was no ordinary maidservant.

"You will have to explain your situation more clearly, I'm afraid," he said. "I do not know what you meant by that."

"I meant that my appearance is not such that I can show myself."

Was it his imagination or had she sounded just on the verge of laughter?

"There is little moonlight here in the forest, as you can see," he said. "I doubt that I would see whatever it is that you'd liefer not show me."

"There is gey little to show, my lord."

He could not mistake it this time, definitely a near gurgle of laughter. His patience fled. More sharply, he said, "I can see nowt in this situation for humor."

"Nor do I, sir, I promise you. 'Tis not humor but hysteria, I fear."

"Whatever it is, I have had a surfeit for one night. Come out at once."

"I'm nearly naked," she said flatly.

He pressed his lips tightly together, suppressing the sudden strong urge he had to see her. Something in the way she'd said those three words challenged him to *make* her come out. Ruthlessly reminding himself that he was a gentleman and that it was likely that the spirit of his father, a gentleman in every sense of the word, was still watching over him, Wat said, "I have my cloak, lass. If I hold it up between us and give my word as a Borderer not to peek, will you trust me and come out?"

Silence.

"'Tis a gey warm, fur-lined cloak," he murmured. "It even boasts a hood."

"I'll trust you, sir. I have heard that your word is good. 'Tis just that I feel so…so…" The words floated softly, even wistfully, to him, and although she did not finish her last sentence, he heard rustling in the shrubbery and knew that she was trying, awkwardly or otherwise, to wriggle her way back out.

"Can you manage by yourself?" he asked as he doffed his cloak and held it up high enough to block his view of the relevant shrubs. "Or should I try to help?"

"I'll manage alone if it kills me," she muttered grimly.

His lips curved, and he realized he was smiling. Until Cockburn's arrival, he had felt utterly grief-stricken, miserable, even lost. He'd worried about whether he was ready yet to step into his father's and grandfather's shoes and assume all the burdens of his immediate family, Rankilburn, all of Clan Scott, Ettrick Forest, and the other Scott holdings; but her fortitude had somehow banished his despair.

Whoever and whatever she was, she was damned intriguing.

A low cry from the shrubbery almost made him shift the cloak to see what had gone amiss.

"What is it?" he demanded.

"Just another scratch," she replied. "I'm nearly there."

He steeled himself to be patient, expecting her to remind him of his promise, as his sisters nearly always did when he promised them something. But she did not.

Silence at last from the shrubbery told him she had extricated herself, and he sensed when she stood.

"I'm here, sir," she said quietly then, and he felt her move against the cloak. "My shoulders are a bit lower down than that, though."

Gently, he draped the cloak around her shoulders, noting that she was more than a head shorter than he was, and after she had pulled it close around her, he saw that she was slenderly curvaceous. He could also see that her long, dark hair was tangled and full of dry leaves. When she turned, he gasped at the scratches he could see, even by moonlight, on what was otherwise a pretty but exceedingly dirty face.

"Are you going to tell me your name?" he asked, resisting an impulse to use his thumb to wipe away a bubble of blood from the deepest scratch.

"I'm Molly, sir."

"Molly what?"

"Molly is sufficient for now, I think," she said. "It is kind of you to let me borrow your cloak," she added quickly before he could object. "Mayhap you know of a tenant or one of your servants who might lend me a cot or pallet for the night."

"We won't trouble anyone else," he said. "I collect that you are not the maidservant that Will Cockburn and those others were seeking."

"What I am is cold and hungry, my lord. Those men and dogs frightened me, but I am as naught to them."

"Nevertheless, you are running from something, lass. No self-respecting female would be running about half naked in this forest without good cause. And prithee, do not spin me any farradiddle about being something other than self-respecting. I won't believe you."

"The truth is that I am not feeling at all self-sufficient.

I simply acted when the possibility arose, without due thought. Consequently, the great and fearful likelihood is that my actions will prove futile."

"Sakes, lass, then why did you run away?"

Giving him a direct, even challenging look, she said with careful calm, "I have asked myself that question more than once tonight, my lord, and the answer is that I ran for no reason that you are likely to think sufficient."

"Tell me anyway."

"Very well, I ran because it is…or, more precisely, *was* my wedding night."

Prologue ─────────────

Arrochar, Scotland, early August 1406

They're coming, my love! I must go."

The woman lying on the ground—nearly hidden by darkness, shrubbery, the thick bedding of pine boughs on which he had laid her, and the fur-lined cloak that he'd spread over her—opened her eyes and smiled wearily.

"Keep . . . safe."

Had his hearing been less acute, he would not have heard his beloved wife's soft murmur. As it was, he feared that he might never see her again.

"I'll come back for ye, *mo chridhe*," he said. The certainty in his voice was as much for himself as for her.

"Aye, sure," she said. "I wish I could keep the bairn with me, though."

"Ye ken fine that it wouldna be safe. If she cried, they'd find ye both, and I'll take her straight to Annie. She has a wee one of her own and milk aplenty for two."

"I know," she whispered. "But guard our wee lassie well."

"I will, aye."

With that, he drew more shrubbery over her, but he

could linger no longer. Sounds of pursuit from the north were louder, too loud. In the distance to the south, he could hear the raging river that might be their salvation. Reluctant though he was to leave her, he dared not let them catch him or all would be lost.

Turning toward the last stretch of hillside he had to climb before descending to the river, he shifted the strap of his baldric and felt the reassuring weight of the sword and spear across his back. In the cloth sling he carried across his chest, his wee daughter nestled, sound asleep, one tiny ear near his beating heart.

Cradling her in one large palm, he moved through the woods with the silence gained only by a hunter-warrior's lifetime practice in such an environment. Pale rays of a slender summer moon slipped through the canopy to light his way.

He allowed his pursuers to see him only once, as he hurried across a clearing in the moonlight. He knew they would easily spot his movements there from below.

In the trees near the crest of the hill, he heard the river's roar, still distant but louder. However, sounds of pursuit were louder, too. His enemies numbered a dozen or more, all warriors like himself. Doubtless, others hunted him all across his lands.

His mind raced. Thanks to a late thaw, snow still capped nearby mountain peaks. But the days had been warmer for a fortnight.

Although he had not seen the river for weeks, experience told him it would be running high, still in snow spate. The glen that it had cut was steep-sided and narrow, but below where he stood, the river's course flattened for a short way.

With luck, he could cross it there in a manner that his pursuers would be unlikely to emulate. His primary concern was the babe he carried.

She was silent, still sleeping. But if she cried, they would hear her. Also, the river would be too deep and too turbulent—in its long, plunging course—to cross without swimming. That fact was the very one that might save them, though. He tried to imagine how, carrying her, he could get them both safely across.

The answer was plain. He could not. But safety lay only on the other side, on the sacred ground of Tùr Meiloach.

He carried his dirk, his sword, and his spear. He had also brought his bow from the castle but had left it with his lady wife. She had kept her dirk, too.

Although she had assured him she would keep safe until his return, he held no illusions. In such matters, he had never doubted her, nor had she ever proven wrong. But as weak and exhausted as she was now, she could not defend herself against so many had she every weapon in Scotland at her disposal.

Her only hope, and thus his own, was that he succeed in getting their bairn to safety. Then he could return for her.

Reaching the swiftly flowing river at last, unable to hear his pursuers over its roar, he wasted no time in deliberation but untied the sling. Then he pulled his spear from its loop on his baldric, uncoiled the narrow rope he'd wound around his waist against any such need, and fashioned a knotted cap with it for the blunt end of the spear. Working swiftly, he found two suitably curved lengths of bark, bound the swaddled babe inside a bark shell and then securely to the center of his spear. Then, hefting the result, he gauged the distance, hesitated only long enough to hear male voices above the din of the river, and let fly with the spear.

He knew he had chucked it far enough, that his arc was high enough, and that his aim would be true despite the added weight of the babe. But if the high end of the spear struck a tree branch, or if he had misjudged the position of the babe on the spear, she might land too hard. The spear might also hit a boulder. He knew that the thicket where he had aimed it boasted little such danger. But the Fates would have to be in a gey gracious mood for such a daring act to succeed.

If it did, the spear's point would bury itself in pine duff and soft dirt, the knotted rope cap at its top end would prevent the babe in her swaddling and sling from hitting the ground, and the bark shell would prevent any other damage.

Then, if he made it across the river to her, all would be well. Muttering prayers to God and the Fates, he hurried to the upper end of the river's flat section, arriving just as the sudden, unmistakable baying of a wolf struck terror into his soul.

His pursuers' shouts were loud enough to tell him they were topping the rise, so he knew they had not seen him throw the spear. Also, he could at least be hopeful that the river's noise would prevent their hearing the babe's cries when she squalled. And she surely would, if not now then later, unless...

That thought refused to declare itself. He had to focus on his own actions now and draw his pursuers as far from his lady as he could. If they thought he was dead, so much the better. But they would have to see him in the river first.

Accordingly, he waited until he saw movement on the steep hillside above him. Then he leaped onto a moonlit boulder that jutted into the roiling flow.

Hearing a shout above, knowing that they had seen him, he flung himself into the torrent. Although the shock of the icy water nearly undid him, he ignored it and swam hard. Letting the current carry him, he also fought it to swim at an angle that would, he prayed, carry him to the opposite bank before it plunged him over the hundred-foot waterfall into the Loch of the Long Boats and out to sea.

When the river swept him around a curve, he swam much harder for the distant shore. His pursuers could not move as fast as the water did. And, if anyone was daft enough to jump in after him, he would see the fool coming. He also knew, though, that if he mistimed his own efforts, the sea gods would claim him.

Minutes later, nearing the shore and battered by unseen rocks beneath the surface, he dragged himself out and lay gasping in unfriendly shrubbery to catch his breath. Then, creeping through the shrubs, he prayed that the hilt of the sword still strapped across his back would look like a branch if anyone saw it moving. As fast as he dared, he made his way to the shelter of the trees and back up the river glen.

He heard only the water's roar. Then, as that thought ended, he heard the wolf bay again, a she-wolf by its cry. Finding a path of sorts, he increased his pace.

The usual fisherman's trail lay underwater. So this was a deer trail or a new one to the river from Malcolm the sheepherder's cottage. In any event, the warrior's finely honed sense of direction told him that the cottage stood not far away.

He soon reached the clearing, where he saw a pack of wolves gathered close around the spear. The weapon with its precious burden had landed perfectly.

The wolves' heads turned as one at his approach, their teeth viciously bared.

He halted, terror for his child again clutching his throat. When the leader lowered to a crouch and crept slowly toward him, he could almost hear its growl. The others watched, their narrowed eyes gleaming reddish in the pale moonlight.

The warrior stood still. Hearing a faint sound above the river's rushing roar, he recognized it for his daughter's wail of hunger...or pain.

It stopped as suddenly as it had begun.

The lead wolf stopped, too, still in its threatening crouch, ready to spring.

The warrior drew his sword and took a step forward, mentally daring the beast to charge him. He had counted a half-dozen in the pack. But now he saw other dark, beastly shadows moving through the trees behind them, too many to count and far too many to kill before the pack would take him down.

The lead wolf, unmoving, bared its teeth again.

The man stood watching it, sword ready, long enough for the icy chill of his wet clothing to make him shiver.

Then, abruptly, the wolf rose, turned away, and vanished into the forest.

The others followed.

The baby remained silent.

Chapter 1 ———————

Dree, what's amiss?" fifteen-year-old Muriella Mac-Farlan demanded as she stopped her spinning wheel and pushed an errant strand of flaxen hair off her face.

Tawny-haired Andrena, now six months into her nineteenth year, had stiffened on her stool near the fireplace in the ladies' solar. Dark blue eyes narrowed, head atilt, listening but with every sense alert, Andrena remained silent as she set aside the mending she loathed.

"Dree?"

Standing, holding a finger up to command silence, Andrena moved with her usual athletic grace to the south-facing window, its shutters open to let in fresh, sun-warmed afternoon air that was especially welcome after the previous night's fierce storm. She could see over the barmkin wall to the steep, forested hillside below and others rolling beyond it to the declivity through which the river marking their south boundary plunged into the Loch of the Long Boats and on out to the sea.

When Muriella drew breath to speak again, the third person in the room, their seventeen-year-old sister,

Lachina, said quietly, "Murie, dearling, possess your curiosity in silence for once. When Dree knows what is amiss, she will tell us."

After the briefest of pauses, and not much to Andrena's surprise, Lachina added, "*Is* someone approaching the tower, Dree?"

"I don't know, Lina. But the birds seem distressed. I think someone has entered our south woods—a stranger—nay, more than one."

"Can you see who they are?" Muriella demanded. Resting her spindle in its cradle, she moved to stand beside Andrena at the window.

"I cannot see such a distance or through trees," Andrena said. "But it must be more than one person and likely fewer than four. You see how the hawks soar in a tight circle yonder. Such behavior is odd even for goshawks. Forbye, if you look higher, you'll see an osprey above them. I'm going out to have a look."

In the same quiet way that she had spoken to Muriella, Lachina said, "The woods will be damp after such a furious storm, Dree. Mayhap you should tell our lord father what you suspect, or Malcolm Wylie."

"What would you have me tell them?" Andrena asked with a wry smile. "Would either of them send men out to search for intruders merely because I say the birds are unsettled?"

Lina grimaced. They had had such discussions before, and both of them knew the answer to the question. Andrew Dubh MacFarlan would trust his men to stop intruders. And his steward, Malcolm Wylie, would look long-suffering and declare that no one could possibly be there. By the time either decided, for the sake of peace, to send men out to look, there would *be* no one. Andrena had suggested once that their men had made more noise than the intruders did. But her father had replied only that if that was so, her intruders had fled, which was the best outcome.

"I'm going out," Andrena said again.

"Surely, men on the wall will see anyone coming," Muriella said, peering into the distance. "Both of our boundary rivers are in full spate now, Dree. No one can cross them. And if anyone were approaching elsewhere, watchers would blow the alarm. In troth, I think those birds are soaring just as they always do."

"They are perturbed," Andrena said. "I shan't be long."

Her sisters exchanged a look. But although she noted the exchange, she did not comment. She knew that neither one would insist on going with her.

Instinct that she rarely ignored urged her to make what speed she could without drawing undue attention to herself. Therefore, she hurried down the service stairs, deciding not to change from her green tunic and skirt into the deerskin breeks and jack that she favored for her solitary rambles. It occurred to her that she would have no excuse, having announced that strangers had entered the woods, to say that she had not thought anyone outside the family would see her in the boyish garb.

Andrew did not care what his daughters wore. But he did care when one of them distressed their mother, who had declared breeks on females to be shameful. Moreover, the mossy green dress would blend well with woodland shrubbery.

From a rack by the postern door, Andrena took her favorite cream-colored wool cap and twisted her tawny plaits up inside it. Then she donned the gray wool shawl hanging beside it and took down the dirk that hung by its belt under the shawl.

Fastening the belt so that the weapon lay concealed beneath the shawl, and leaving her untanned-hide boots where they lay on the floor, she went outside barefoot and crossed the yard to the narrow postern gate.

Four of the dogs, anticipating a walk, sprang up and ran to meet her.

Catching two by their collars, she said to the wiry red-headed lad eyeing her as he raked wood chips near the gate, "You must keep them in for now, Pluff. If anyone should ask for me, I'm going for a walk. But I don't want to take the dogs."

"Aye, m'lady," the boy said with a gap-toothed grin. Setting aside the rake, he ordered the dogs back to their naps and unbolted the gate for her, adding, "Just gie a shout when ye come back and I'll let ye in."

Smiling her thanks, she went through the gateway and heard the heavy gate thud shut behind her and Pluff shooting the bolts. Looking skyward as she crossed the clearing between the barmkin and the woods, she saw that the circling birds had moved nearer. Whoever it was, was still two hills away but was definitely moving toward the tower.

Looking over her shoulder, she saw one of their men on the wall and waved.

He waved back.

Satisfied that her sisters and at least two of their people knew she was outside the wall, she hurried into the woods. She had her dirk and the wee pipe she always carried in the pocket that Lina had cunningly woven for it in the shawl.

Thanks to Andrew's teaching, Andrena was skillful with the dirk and, if necessary, could use the wee pipe to summon aid. Since she did not expect anyone in the woods to see her, she doubted that she'd need any help.

～

He was out of breath from running. But he knew that in dashing away from his pursuers earlier, he had left evidence of his flight for a regrettable distance before he was far enough ahead of them to take precautions.

As it was, he needed to find cover and catch his breath. That his pursuers lacked dogs to track him was a rare boon from the ever fickle Fates.

He had been both careless and foolhardy, and it irked him. He had sensibly managed to keep his wool plaid with him, even as he swam, knowing he would need its warmth. Scaling the cliff from the stormy loch had been necessary, since he could not stay on the shore and in the rainy darkness he'd seen no safer way to go.

After reaching the top of the hurtling waterfall, sleeping for a time, and waking in foggy dawn twilight, it had come as a shock to find that he could not travel farther south without fording the damned river.

To be sure, he *had* seen this area from the water, including the distant sharp ridge of peaks beyond its cliffs and forested hills. The two great waterfalls had been full even then, but he had assumed he'd be able to cross the river somewhere.

However, it raged furiously down through its bed, tumbling over and around boulders and rocks in its path—too deep to ford, too wide and dangerous to swim.

He had followed it inland until he had seen and recognized the three men.

Now the fog had cleared, and the sun shone in a cloudy sky. He was well away from the river, deep in ancient woods—a magnificent mixture of tall beeches, oaks, thickly growing conifers, and where it was dampest, spindly birches and willows. The woodsy scents filled him with a heady sense of freedom. But his pursuers were not far enough behind yet for safety.

Although he had not entered such dense woodland for nineteen long months, he had hunted from the time he could keep up with his lord father and knew that he retained his skills, had even heightened most of them. Quietly drawing deep breaths and releasing them, he forced himself to relax and bond with the forest while he listened and waited for its creatures to speak to him.

Thinking of those creatures and the fact that he had come ashore north of the waterfall, he was nearly sure that he must be in Tùr Meiloach woods. He had heard men warn that the place was rife with danger, either haunted or bewitched. Some swore that it was a sanctuary for true MacFarlans, others that it was a taste of hell for unwary strangers. Wondering which it was would do him no good now, though.

It occurred to him that although he had moved carefully and in near silence for the past quarter-hour, the denizens of the forest remained remarkably still. He had not listened for them earlier, knowing that the din of the river would cover any sound they made and being more concerned about eluding his pursuers.

As if it had intercepted his thoughts, a hawk shrieked above. Then an osprey replied with its shrill whistle, declaring the woods its territory. It would, he thought, have better luck taking fish from the nearby Loch of the Long Boats and should leave the woods to the hawks, which were better suited for hunting in dense foliage.

All thought ceased then, because he sensed someone in the woods north of him moving as silently as he did. Had one of the devils got round him? Was one north of him now and the other two south? He had seen only three men earlier on the far side of the devilish river. They had swung across it on a rope tied to a high branch of an ancient beech rooted in what looked from a distance like solid rock.

The three carried swords and dirks. When he'd recognized them as Pharlain's men, he knew they were seeking him.

A soughing of leaves above drew his glance to a female goshawk on a high branch. The canopy above her was thick. But he knew that hawks, even big ones like the gos, with two-foot wingspans, were perfectly at home in the Highland woods. He had occasionally delighted in watching one take prey by flying at speed between trees that left insufficient room for it. To fit through, the bird seemed to fold itself, wings and body, into a thinly compressed, arrowlike shape and to do it without missing a single sweeping beat.

The hawk above him fixed a fierce yellow eye on him. Then, as if that glance were all it required, it opened its wings and swooped down and away.

He eyed the gos's erstwhile perch. It was high, but in the dense canopy above it a man might rest unseen for hours. A rustle of disturbed shrubbery south of him, accompanied by a man's muttered curse, made the decision easy. He paused only to conceal his plaid in the shrubbery.

~

Andrena heard the curse, too, and froze in place to listen. She had sensed the trespassers' approach more easily with each step, because the woods were her home, their every sound familiar. She had noted the eerie silence, had seen the goshawk as it shot through the trees in front of her without making a sound.

The hawk's presence might have frightened nearby small creatures to silence. But it would not account for the unusual quiet of the forest at large. It seemed to hold its communal breath, to be waiting as she was for the intruders to reveal their nature.

So still was it that in the distance to her right and far below, she could hear waves of the loch, unsettled from the storm, hushing against the rockbound shore.

The strangers were much closer.

Sound traveled farther through woodland than most people realized, and her ears were deer-sharp. The intruders were a score of yards away, perhaps more, but an effortless bowshot in the open. She would soon see them.

Noting movement in shrubbery near the ground, she saw that at least one creature had managed to follow her from the tower. Lina's orange cat eyed her curiously through slender branches sprouting new leaves.

Without a sound, the cat glided off ahead, doubtless prowling for its supper.

Andrena moved on, too. She heard no noises specific enough to identify but she knew now that there were at least two or three men. Careful to stay hidden but watchful, she also knew that her sweeping gaze would detect any movement.

A large shadow passed between two large-trunked beeches ahead to her left.

Going still, she watched as a stranger stepped between the two trees. Two others followed. All three wore saffron tunics, kilted plaids of dull red and green, swords slung across their backs, and dirks at their belts.

So much, Andrena thought, for Murie's certainty—and their father's—that no one could ford the wild river south of their tower without plunging into the loch and out with the tide. Either the three men had forded it or they'd found other means of trespassing onto Andrew's land without his or his men's knowledge.

⁓

The man in the tree suppressed a curse when he saw the lass. Who the devil, he wondered, would be daft enough to let a girl wander out alone in such dangerous times? His eyes narrowed as she carefully shifted her shawl and he saw the long dirk in its sheath suspended from her narrow leather girdle.

If she had an ounce of wit she would at least try to keep it hidden, because if the louts searching for him saw it, and they would, they might kill her just to teach her a lesson.

Knowing that they might sense *his* presence as easily as he had sensed hers, he decided that he ought to do what he could to prevent that. Fixing his gaze on a leaf midway between the three men, now only five or six yards away, and the girl moving toward them—ten paces from his tree—he let his mind go blank.

The last thing he wanted was for anyone to sense him watching them.

⟍⟋

The men had moved much faster than Andrena had expected, stirring irritation with herself as well as with them. Having expected to get her first look at them from the next rise, she realized now that she had taken longer than she had intended. In truth, she had paid more heed to the forest creatures' silence than to its most likely cause, that the men were nearer than she had judged them to be.

Lina would say, and rightly, that having formed an image in her mind of what would happen, Dree had let her thoughts wander and, thus, had failed to think through all the possibilities of what *might* happen before coming out to investigate.

Hoping that Lina would not learn what had happened, Andrena considered what to do next. She was close enough to the tower for people on its ramparts and wall to hear her pipe if she blew it, so she slipped it out of its pocket into her hand.

The hawks still lingered nearby, as well.

It occurred to her that she would offer help without hesitation had the men simply been storm-tossed onto the shore and missed their way. Perhaps if she . . .

⟍⟋

What the devil was she doing now?

He tensed as he watched her step out into the path of his three pursuers. At least now he knew he need worry no longer about their sensing *his* presence. The louts had seen her, and the Fates knew that she was stunning enough, even with that ridiculous boy's cap covering her hair, to stop most healthy men in their tracks.

She walked with unusual grace on the uneven forest floor and did so without glancing at her feet. Her posture was regal, and the soft-looking gray shawl did little to hide a curvaceous, womanly body.

Hearing a scrabbling on the bark below, he glanced down and saw her absurd cat clawing its way up the tree toward him. He could even hear it purring when by rights it should be flying, claws out, at the villains approaching its mistress.

"Forgive me, good sirs," the lass said in a clear, confident tone, her voice as warm and smooth as honey. "Doubtless, you have lost your way and entered our woods unaware of whose they are. I fear that my father, the laird, requires that men present themselves at Tùr Meiloach before trespassing hereabouts."

"Does he now, lassie?" the tallest of the louts said, leering at her. "And how might we reach yon tower without stepping on your father, the *laird's*, land?"

"We be searching for an escaped prisoner, mistress," the second man, dark-haired and midsized, said sternly. "Ye shouldna be out here alone like this."

"I'll see her tae safety," the tall one said. "Come along, lass. I dinna think ye belong tae the laird at all. A laird's daughter wouldna wander about all by herself. Doubtless, when we tell him ye've been pretending tae be his daughter, ye'll find yourself in the suds. But I'll no tell him if ye plead kindly wi' me."

"I would willingly direct you to the tower," she said. "It lies—" Breaking off when he grabbed her right arm, she stiffened and said icily, "Let go of me."

"Nay, then, I'll ha'—"

Putting two fingers of her other hand to her lips, she whistled loudly.

"Here now, what the—"

A sparrow hawk flew from a nearby tree right at his face, flapping its wings wildly and shrieking an angry *kek-kek-kek* as it did.

With a cry, the man flung up an arm in defense. Shearing away at the last second, the bird swooped around and struck again. Flinging up both arms this time, the lout released the young woman, who stepped away from him.

The cat had reached the branch on which the hunted man lay stretched. It walked up his body to peer over his right shoulder into his face, still purring.

Short of grabbing it and dropping it on one of the men below, he could do nothing useful. So he ignored it.

Had he had his sword with him or even the lass's dirk, he might have dropped in on the conversation. As it was, he hoped they would realize from her demeanor that she was as noble as she claimed to be and were wondering, as he did, why men were not already rushing noisily to her aid, summoned by her whistling.

He had barely finished the thought when three goshawks arrived silently, all much larger than the sparrow hawk. The lout already intimidated by the small hawk took off running, back the way he had come. The other two tried to shoo the birds away. But the birds screamed then as if they were new parents and the men had disturbed their young.

"Our hawks are exceedingly territorial, I fear," the lass said matter-of-factly.

"Call them off, ye devilish witch!" the tall man yelled at Andrena while flapping his arms as wildly as the birds flapped their wings. Since he was also trying to protect his eyes with his hands, his flailing elbows had little effect.

"They are scarcely *my* birds, sir," she replied, elevating him with that single word far above his deserved station in life. "They just know that I belong here and you do not. Had I brought my dogs, they would act in a similar way, as I am sure your dogs do when someone threatens you. I cannot call them off. But if you two follow your friend back to where you came from, they *may* stop attacking you."

The hawks, acting more helpfully than hawks usually did, continued flying at the two despite their waving and shouts. One of the men reached for his sword.

"Don't touch that weapon if you value your life," she said, raising the wee pipe, still in her right hand, to her lips. "If I blow this pipe, our men-at-arms will come. So I should warn you that my father wields the power of the pit and gallows. Our hanging tree stands right outside our gate, and he will not hesitate..."

The man was staring beyond her, his mouth agape.

Glancing over a shoulder, she saw that with the racket the hawks had made, she had failed to hear the osprey arrive. The huge bird perched nearby, looking even more immense when it tensed, puffed its feathers, and glowered at the intruders.

Andrena said, "She has much worse manners than the others. So do *not* challenge her."

"We're a-going," the dark-haired one said. "But tell

your father that if he finds our prisoner, he must send him back tae the laird in irons."

"I shall give him your message. But you must tell me who your laird is. I cannot pluck such information from your mind."

"Aye, well, I thought ye'd ken who we be. The missing chap be one o' Pharlain's galley slaves, taken in fair capture whilst raiding."

"Then doubtless my father will do as you wish," Andrena said mendaciously. Andrew would more likely help the man on his way.

The osprey, balefully eyeing the intruders, spread its wings and twitched its talons menacingly.

Abruptly, the men turned and followed their erstwhile companion.

The goshawks, one of the few hawk species that will hunt together and now a veritable flock, swooped after them.

Andrena stood for a time, listening, to be sure they were well on their way. Then, hearing a loud purr at her feet, she looked down and saw the orange cat. It walked across her bare feet, rubbing against her shins.

"Where did you spring from this time?" she asked.

The cat blinked, then continued around her and back toward the tower.

Turning to follow it, Andrena found herself face-to-muscular-chest with a huge, broad-shouldered, shaggy-bearded, half-naked stranger. He wore a ragged, thigh-length, saffron-colored sark, the ripped left shoulder of which revealed a bad abrasion and bruising that extended along his upper arm.

Startled nearly out of her wits, she snapped, "Where did you...? That is, I never even knew that you were—"

"Hush, lass, they may still be near enough to hear you." His voice was deeper than her father's, and mellow, unlike any she might imagine coming from a villain.

"They are halfway across yon hills to the river by now," she said.

"They may be, aye. But I want to be sure."

"Then follow them. But how did you get so close to me, especially as big as you are? Faith, you're a giant, and I can always—" Breaking off, aware that she was talking too much, she said, "You must be their missing prisoner, aye?"

His twinkling gaze met her frowning one. "They would identify me as such, aye. But I disapprove of slavery. So I don't see the matter as they do."

"I suppose not. But—" Breaking off when she saw how steadily he gazed at her, she eyed him askance. "Are you *not* going to follow them, then?"

"Nay, for I cannot leave a wee lassock like yourself out here alone. I'll see you safely to your gate first."

"Thank you, but I don't want or need your escort," she said firmly.

"Aye, well, you need not look so displeased by the notion," he said. A wistful smile peeked through his unkempt beard as through a shaggy hedge. "Unless you fear that your da will hang me for escaping," he added.

"He will not do that. He feels no love for Parlan Pharlain."

"Then why do you hesitate to go home? Art afraid he'll punish you for coming out alone and learning how dangerous that can be?"

"He won't do that, either. By my troth, although he

will not hang you, you are the one who should be leery of him."

"Why should I?"

"Because, since you managed to escape from Cousin Parlan and must therefore be Parlan's enemy, I fear that Father will insist that you marry me."

THE DISH

Where Authors Give You the Inside Scoop

♥ ♥ ♥ ♥ ♥ ♥ ♥ ♥ ♥ ♥ ♥ ♥ ♥ ♥ ♥ ♥

From the desk of Marilyn Pappano

Dear Reader,

One of the pluses of writing the Tallgrass series was one I didn't anticipate until I was neck-deep in the process, but it's been a great one: unearthing old memories. Our Navy career was filled with laugh-out-loud moments, but there were also plenty of the laugh-or-you'll-cry moments, too. We did a lot of laughing. Most of our tears were reserved for later.

Like our very first move to South Carolina, when the movers lost our furniture for weeks, and the day after it was finally delivered, my husband got orders to Alabama. On our second move, the delivery guys perfected their truck-unloading routine: three boxes into the apartment, one box into the front of their truck. (Fortunately, Bob had perfected his watch-the-unloaders routine and recovered it all.)

For our first apartment move-out inspection, we had scrubbed ourselves to nubbins all through the night. The manager did the walk-through, commented on how impeccably clean everything was, and offered me the paperwork to sign. I signed it, turned around to hand it to her, and walked into the low-hanging chandelier where the dining table used to sit, breaking a bulb with my head. Silently she took back the papers, thumbed through to the deduction sheet, and charged us sixty cents for a new bulb.

There's something about being told my Oklahoma accent is funny by multi-generation Americans with accents so heavy that I just guessed at the context of our conversations. Or hearing our two-year-old Oklahoma-born son, home for Christmas, proudly singing, "Jaaan-gle baaaa-ulllz! Jaaan-gle baaaa-ulllz! Jaaan-gle *alllll* the waaay-uh!"

Bob and I still trade stories. *Remember when we did that self-move to San Diego and the brakes went out on the rental truck in 5:00 traffic in Memphis at the start of a holiday weekend? Remember that pumpkin pie on the first Thanksgiving we couldn't go home—the one I forgot to put the spices in? Remember dropping the kiddo off at the base day care while we got groceries and having to pay the grand sum of fifty cents two hours later? How about when you had to report to the commanding general for joint-service duty at Fort Gordon and we couldn't find your Dixie cup anywhere in the truck crammed with boxes—and at an Army post, no less, that didn't stock Navy uniforms?*

Sea life was great. We watched ships leaving and, months later, come home again. On one homecoming, the kiddo and I watched Daddy's ship run aground. We learned that all sailors look alike when they're dressed in the same uniform and seen from a distance. We spied submarines stealthing out of their bases and toured warships—American, British, French, Canadian—and even got to board one of our own nuclear subs for a private look around.

The Navy gave us a lot to remember and a lot to learn. (Example: all those birthdays and anniversaries

Bob missed didn't mean a thing. It was the fact that he came home that mattered.) I still have a few dried petals from the flowers given to me by the command each time Bob reenlisted, as well the ones I got when he retired. We have a flag, like the one each of the widows in Tallgrass received, and a display box of medals and ribbons, but filled with much happier memories.

I can't wait to see which old *remember when* the next book in this series brings us! I hope you love reading A MAN TO ON HOLD TO as much as I loved writing it.

Sincerely,

Marilyn Pappano

MarilynPappano.com
Twitter @MarilynPappano
Facebook.com/MarilynPappanoFanPage

♥ ♥ ♥ ♥ ♥ ♥ ♥ ♥ ♥ ♥ ♥ ♥ ♥ ♥ ♥

From the desk of Jaime Rush

Dear Reader,

Much has been written about angels. When I realized that angels would be part of my mythology and hidden world, I knew I needed to make mine different. I didn't want to use the religious mythos or pair them with demons. Many authors have done a fantastic job of this already.

In fact, I felt this way about my world in general. I started with the concept that a confluence of nature and the energy in the Bermuda Triangle had allowed gods and angels to take human form. They procreated with the humans living on the island and were eventually sent back to their plane of existence. But I didn't want to draw on Greek, Roman, or Atlantean mythology, so I made up my own pantheon of gods. I narrowed them down to three different types: Dragons, sorcerers, and angels. Their progeny continue to live in the area of the Triangle, tethered there by their need to be near their energy source.

My angels come from this pantheon, without the constraints of traditional religious roles. They were sent down to the island to police the wayward gods, but succumbed to human temptation. And their progeny pay the price. I'm afraid my angels' descendents, called Caidos, suffer terribly for their fathers' sins. This was not something I contrived; these concepts often just come to me as the truths of my stories.

Caidos are preternaturally beautiful, drawing the desire of those who see them. But desire, their own and others', causes them physical pain. As do the emotions of all but their own kind. They guard their secret, for their lives depend on it. To keep pain at bay, they isolate themselves from the world and shut down their sexuality. Which, of course, makes it all the more fun when they are thrown together with women they find attractive. Pleasure and pain is a fine line, and Kasabian treads it in a different way than other Caidos. Then again, he is different, harboring a dark secret that compounds his sense of isolation.

Perhaps it was slightly sadistic to pair him with a woman who holds the essence of the goddess of sensuality.

Kye is his greatest temptation, but she may also be his salvation. He needs to form a bond with the woman who can release his dark shadow. I don't make it easy on Kye, either. She must lose everything to find her soul. I love to dig deep into my characters' psyches and mine their darkest shadows. Only then can they come into the light.

And isn't that something we all can learn? To face our shadows so that we can walk in the light? That's what I love most about writing: that readers, too, can take the journey of self discovery, self love, right along with my characters. They face their demons and come out on the other end having survived.

We all have magic in our imaginations. Mine has always contained murder, mayhem, and romance. Feel free to wander through the madness of my mind any time. A good place to start is my website, www.jaimerush .com, or that of my romantic suspense alter ego, www .tinawainscott.com.

Jaime Rush

♥ ♥ ♥ ♥ ♥ ♥ ♥ ♥ ♥ ♥ ♥ ♥ ♥ ♥ ♥ ♥

From the desk of Kate Brady

Dear Reader,

People ask me all the time, "What do you like about writing romantic suspense?" It's a great question, and it always seems like sort of a copout to say, "Everything!" But it's true. Writing novels is the greatest job in the world. And romantic suspense, in particular, allows my favorite elements to exist in a single story: adventure, danger, thrills, chills, romance, and the gratifying knowledge that good will triumph over evil and love will win the day.

Weaving all those elements together is, for me, a labor of love. I love being able to work with something straight from my own mind, without having to footnote and document sources all the time. (In my other career—academia—they frown upon letting the voices in my head do the writing!) I love the flexibility of where and when I can indulge myself in a story—the deck, the kitchen island, the car, the beach, and any number of recliners are my favorite "offices." I love seeing the stories unfold, being surprised by the twists and turns they take, and ultimately coming across them in their finished forms on the bookstore shelves. I love hearing from readers and being privy to their take on the story line or a character. I love meeting other writers and hobnobbing with the huge network of readers and writers out there who still love romantic suspense.

And I *love* getting to know new characters. I don't create these people; they already exist when a story begins and it becomes my job to reveal them. I just go along for the ride as they play out their roles, and I'm repeatedly surprised and delighted by what they prove to be. And it never fails: I always fall in love.

Luke Mann, the hero in WHERE EVIL WAITS, was one of the most intriguing characters I have met and he turned out to be one of my all-time favorites. He first appeared in his brother's book, *Where Angels Rest*, so I knew his hometown, his upbringing, his parents, and his siblings. But Luke himself came to me shrouded in shadows. I couldn't wait to write his story; he was dark and fascinating and intense (not to mention gorgeous) and I knew from the start that his adventure would be a whirlwind ride. When I put him in an alley with his soon-to-be heroine, Kara Chandler—who shocked both Luke and me with a boldness I hadn't expected—I fell in love with both of them. From that point on, WHERE EVIL WAITS was off and running, as Luke and Kara tried to elude and capture a killer as twisted and dangerous as the barbed wire that was his trademark.

The time Luke and Kara spend together is brief, but jam-packed with action, heat, and, ultimately, affection. I hope you enjoy reading their story as much as I enjoyed writing it!

Happy Reading!

Kate Brady

♥ ♥ ♥ ♥ ♥ ♥ ♥ ♥ ♥ ♥ ♥ ♥ ♥ ♥ ♥

From the desk of Amanda Scott

Dear Reader,

The plot of THE WARRIOR'S BRIDE, set in the fourteenth-century Scottish Highlands near Loch Lomond, grew from a law pertaining to abduction that must have seemed logical to its ancient Celtic lawmakers.

I have little doubt that they intended that law to protect women.

However, I grew up in a family descended from a long line of lawyers, including my father, my grandfather, and two of the latter's great-grandfathers, one of whom was the first Supreme Court justice for the state of Arkansas (an arrangement made by his brother, the first senator from Missouri, who also named Arkansas—so just a little nepotism there). My brother is a judge. His son and one of our cousins are defense attorneys. So, as you might imagine, laws and the history of law have stirred many a dinner-table conversation throughout my life.

When I was young, I spent countless summer hours traveling with my paternal grandmother and grandfather in their car, listening to him tell stories as he drove. Once, when I pointed out brown cows on a hillside, he said, "Well, they're brown on this side, anyhow."

That was my first lesson in looking at both sides of any argument, and it has served me well in my profession. This is by no means the first time I've met a law that sowed the seeds for an entire book.

Women, as we all know, are unpredictable creatures who have often taken matters into their own hands in ways of which men—especially in olden times—have disapproved. Thanks to our unpredictability, many laws that men have made to "protect" us have had the opposite effect.

The heroine of THE WARRIOR'S BRIDE is the lady Muriella MacFarlan, whose father, Andrew, is the rightful chief of Clan Farlan. A traitorous cousin has usurped Andrew's chiefdom and murdered his sons, so Andrew means to win his chiefdom back by marrying his daughters to warriors from powerful clans, who will help him.

Muriella, however, intends *never* to marry. I based her character on Clotho, youngest of the three Fates and the one who is responsible for spinning the thread of life. So Murie is a spinner of threads, yarns...and stories.

Blessed with a flawless memory, Muriella aspires to be a *seanachie*, responsible for passing the tales of Highland folklore and history on to future generations. She has already developed a reputation for her storytelling and takes that responsibility seriously.

She seeks truth in her tales of historical events. However, in her personal life, Murie enjoys a more flexible notion of truth. She doesn't lie, exactly. She spins.

Enter blunt-spoken warrior Robert MacAulay, a man of honor with a clear sense of honor, duty, and truth. Rob also has a vision that, at least for the near future, does not include marriage. Nor does he approve of truth-spinning.

Consequently, sparks fly between the two of them even *before* Murie runs afoul of the crazy law. I think you will enjoy THE WARRIOR'S BRIDE.

Meantime, *Suas Alba!*

Sincerely,

Amanda Scott

www.amandascottauthor.com

♥ ♥ ♥ ♥ ♥ ♥ ♥ ♥ ♥ ♥ ♥ ♥ ♥ ♥ ♥ ♥ ♥

From the desk of Mimi Jean Pamfiloff

Dear People Pets—Oops, sorry—I meant, Dear Readers,

Ever wonder what's like to be God of the Sun, Ruler of the House of Gods, and the only deity against procreation with humans (an act against nature)?

Nah. Me neither. I want to know what it's like to be his girlfriend. After all, how many guys house the power of the sun inside their seven-foot frames? And that hair. Long thick ribbons of sun-streaked caramel. And those muscles. Not an ounce of fat to be found on that insanely ripped body. As for the…eh-hem, the *performance* part, well, I'd like to know all about that, too.

Actually, so would Penelope. Especially after spending the evening with him, sipping champagne in his hotel room, and then waking up buck naked. Yes. In his bed. And yes, he's naked, too. Yeah, she'd love to remember what happened. He wouldn't mind, either.

But it seems that the only one who might know anything is Cimil, Goddess of the Underworld, instigator of all things naughty, and she's nowhere to be found. I guess Kinich and Penelope will have to figure this out for themselves. So what will be the consequence of breaking these "rules" of nature Kinich fears so much? Perhaps the price will be Penelope's life. But perhaps, just maybe, the price will be his…

Happy Reading!

Mimi

♥ ♥ ♥ ♥ ♥ ♥ ♥ ♥ ♥ ♥ ♥ ♥ ♥ ♥

From the desk of Shannon Richard

Dear Reader,

I knew how Brendan and Paige were going to meet from the very start. It was the first scene that played out in my mind. Paige was going to be having a very bad day on top of a very bad couple of months. Her Jeep breaks down in the middle of nowhere Florida, during a sweltering day, and she was to call someone for help. It's when she's at her lowest that she meets the love of her life; she just doesn't know it at the time. As for Brendan, he isn't expecting anyone like Paige to come along. Not now, not ever. But he knows pretty quickly that he has feelings for her, and that they're serious feelings.

Paige can be a little sassy, and Brendan can be a little cocky, so during their first encounter sparks are flying all over the place. Things start to get hot quickly, and it has very little to do with summer in the South (which is hot and miserable, I can tell you from over twenty years of experience). But at the end of the day, and no matter the confrontation, Brendan is Paige's white knight. He comes to her rescue in more ways than one.

The inspiration behind Brendan is a very laid-back Southern guy. He's easygoing (for the most part) and charming. He hasn't been one for long-term serious relationships, but when it comes to Paige he jumps right on in. There's just something about a guy who knows exactly what he wants, who meets the girl and doesn't hesitate. Yeah, it makes me swoon more than just a little. I hoped that readers would appreciate that aspect of him. The diving in headfirst and not looking back, and Brendan doesn't look back.

As for Paige, she's dealing with a lot and is more than a little scared about getting involved with another guy. Her wounds are too fresh and deep from her recent heartbreak. Brendan knows all about pain and suffering. Instead of turning his back on her, he steps up to the plate. He helps Paige heal, helps her get a job and friends, helps her find a place in the little town of Mirabelle. It just so happens that her place is right next to his.

So yes, Brendan is this big, tough, alpha man who comes to the rescue of the damsel in distress. But Paige isn't exactly a weak little thing. No, she's pretty strong herself. It's part of that strength that Brendan is so drawn to. He loves her passion and how fierce she is. But really, he just loves her.

I'm a fan of the happily ever after. Always have been, always will be. I love my characters; they're part of me. They might exist in black and white on the page, but to me they're real. At the end of the day, I just want them to be happy.

Cheers,

ShannonRichard.net
Twitter @Shan_Richard
Facebook.com/ShannonNRichard